A MATCH MADE IN SPAIN

ROCHELLE MERRILL

Published By: Celie Bay Publications, LLC

Cover design by: 100 Covers

Edited by: Edit Me This – Kelli Collins

Cultural Read by: Laura Bailo

Proofread: Allison Behrens

Formatting by: R.L. Merrill – Vellum

❦ Created with Vellum

DEDICATION

To the Spain Crew 2018
Zoya, Sarah, Will, Anthony, Kolja, Travis, Walter, and of course Kevin,
Mairin, and Lucas. I'm so glad we had this adventure together!

CHAPTER ONE

 :45 a.m. PDT
San Francisco International Airport

There actually is such a thing as too early for coffee. Even if Cecilia Galván wanted coffee, not even Starbucks was awake at this ungodly hour.

If only she were back in her home sleeping soundly...not that she had a home any longer. Her ex-husband had seen to that. She was now a thirty-five-year-old woman living with her mother once again—not exactly the fairytale ending she'd imagined in her life. She'd gotten married, but the happily ever after eluded her.

She was ready for a fresh start. Though that fresh start was going to have to wait while she took a group of teenagers on an international school tour. If she survived unscathed.

Cecilia's high school students looked stunned to be vertical at this hour, as though they were in some dystopian film where their Xboxes and smartphones no longer functioned, and they were seeing the world for the first time. Her group was comprised of kids who were pretty innocent and square, which made her feel a little better about taking them to Europe. None of them had likely ever even seen this time of day unless they'd been up studying all night for an AP exam or playing video games. They wandered around the terminal in some sort of fugue. Cecilia hoped it would keep them manageable, a hope that was quickly dashed when the questions started.

"Mrs. Galván? How long 'til we get on the plane? I want to go back to sleep."

"How long is the flight?"

"Is there going to be food on the plane?"

"What's the weather going to be like when we land?"

"Will they have Starbucks there?"

Ugh. More stomach acrobatics.

The bottom line? Cecilia was anxious about taking a group of kids abroad and she hated flying with a burning passion, even more than she hated the fact that she was awake at this time. It took all of her adulting power to keep it together in front of these kids who trusted her. But she'd agreed because her loyalty to her best friend and her administrator was stronger than her anxiety over traveling.

"No questions," she whispered, their voices louder than she was ready to handle. "Please. No questions."

Two of the boys, Joseph and Eduardo, giggled and moved toward the rest of the group. They could see right through her lack of adulting prowess this morning.

"Everyone, we're going to count off by threes." The teacher in charge, Gabrielle Reyes, effortlessly gathered their group while Cecilia struggled to remain upright. Thank goodness one of them was functional. Besides the two of them, there were four additional adults on the trip who could help out in a pinch, but she and Gabrielle were the school's representatives.

The groggy travelers stood in a circle, likely trying to remember their numbers. When the counting got to Cecilia, she almost said "four."

"Uh, one."

"Muy bien," Gabrielle said, shooting her a questioning look. "Find the others with your number."

It took the kids much longer to separate into groups than, say, in

Cecilia's third period American Sign Language class, but then third period didn't take place before the sun rose.

Cecilia found herself with Tui, one of her favorite students, and Tony, a former GVHS student who apparently had been on these trips with Gabrielle and her older sister Zoey before. He and his boyfriend were in their early twenties and had no current connection to the school other than their friendship with the Reyes sisters. Bill and Tony, and the parents of one of the students would be traveling with the group as chaperones. Tony, Tui and Cecilia mumbled "good morning" and then turned to face the rest of the group.

"These people will be your amigos for the entire trip. Wherever we go, you must know where these people are at all times," Gabrielle announced. "Now, vamos, amigos. It's time to start our journey."

"How does she have so much energy?" Cecilia asked rhetorically.

"It's kind of creepy. She's like this all the time, even when she hasn't slept," Tony answered. "But then you get used to it and it's almost, like, contagious. Her sister is exactly the same," he said. He seemed to be pretty chipper himself.

"I'm glad I'm with you, Mrs. Galván," Tui said. "This is my first time traveling without my family."

Cecilia gazed way up at Grass Valley High School's star center. "Are you nervous?" she asked.

He gave her the sign for "so-so" and she smiled. He'd remembered one of the signs she taught all of her students, whether they were in ASL or Life Skills with her. He was just that kind of kid, always eager to learn and very conscientious. She hoped he kept that spirit about him when he eventually reached the NFL.

Cecilia tried to pay attention to Gabrielle's instructions, which were probably important, but the music playing in the terminal made it difficult to focus on conversation, considering her hearing loss. Her stomach had her on high alert. She didn't even see a bathroom in case she needed to make a break for it, and that wasn't helping her anxiety at all.

Her group shuffled over to the Air Canada ticket counter, Cecilia, Tui, and Tony, with Bill, Tony's boyfriend, bringing up the rear. While the guys chatted excitedly, Cecilia leaned heavily on the handle of her twenty-two-inch rolling suitcase. They'd been forbidden to bring anything larger. It had certainly made packing for twelve days a challenge, but she'd managed.

A sharp pain in her foot alerted her to the fact that someone was having spatial awareness issues while on their cellphone this morning. *Awesome.* Cecilia turned around to find a man speaking rapidly in a language she'd never heard before, standing danger-close to the thin strip barrier that separated the line of plebes like her from the upper crust-travelers like him. His suitcase rammed her ankle bone again as he used the handle to add emphasis to what he was saying on the phone. As if the other person could see him.

Cecilia moved her foot out of his path and the line inched forward. When they stopped, he nailed her again. He hadn't noticed her yet as he was staring off into that phone-conversation dimension like people do. One more hit and she was going to—

"Ow?" She turned on the talker and gestured toward her foot.

Her irritation lessened as she took a long look at her abuser.

Dark-haired, olive-skinned perfection stood there staring back at her, dressed in strategically distressed jeans that hugged slim hips. He wore a pair of casually expensive-looking shoes and a sporty leather jacket over some sort of athletic shirt. His conversation sounded important, or at least it did when he was talking. At this moment, he happened to be staring at Cecilia.

"Are you all right?" he asked in heavily accented English.

"It's too early to tell," she muttered.

"I'm sorry?" He frowned as though her response perplexed him.

"Thank you." Cecilia turned around in time to move forward with the line and tried to disappear. Having intelligent conversations with attractive men was never her strong suit, but the early hour and lack of caffeine had her feeling even more awkward than usual. She heard the man end his conversation and hoped that meant no more collisions with her foot. He moved farther away from her as their lines split, but she noticed him watching her with a puzzled expression.

Then he smiled at her and nodded before turning away. He had a really nice smile.

Whatever.

She had no time to ogle gorgeous foreign men, not this morning.

She and Tui made their way up to the ticket counter when it was their turn and she had a helluva time understanding the woman's thick French accent.

"Pardon me?"

"She asked if you were my mom," Tui said in a loud whisper.

Cecilia frowned. "Only from eight to three, honey. Then you're someone else's responsibility."

Tui laughed, but Cecilia's comments did not amuse the woman at the ticket counter. She proceeded to check them in and take their suitcases. Tui's had seen better days, and Cecilia predicted they might need to purchase a new one for him along the way. She hoped for his sake it would make it intact to Madrid.

The ankle-banger strolled up to the premier counter as they were finishing. He caught Cecilia's eye again before cheerfully greeting the woman working the counter, resting his elbows on the kiosk and treating her to that nice smile.

He probably does this a lot. Traveling businessmen. Ew.

Cecilia's ex-traveling-businessman had let her know he wanted to sell their house sooner rather than later, forcing her to pack and move in the forty-eight hours between the end of school and leaving for this trip.

Don't even go there.

"I was just going to line up with the others in security," Tui said, and she realized she'd spoken out loud.

"Of course. Sorry. Don't mind me, I'm still half asleep," she said, attempting a joke.

Tui gave her a concerned look, hoisted his backpack onto one shoulder—he was too broad to wear it over both—and walked ahead.

She sighed. This move and trip and shaken her a bit, but she was a strong woman, despite how her ex-husband sometimes made her feel.

Their divorce had been final for seven months, and they'd been separated longer than that.

Cecilia often wished she could move to that mythical island where Wonder Woman was from so she could get in battle-ready shape, become a badass warrior and never have to talk to another man again. Well, maybe not *never*.

She was pretty badass already and she needed to remember that. Being a teacher required Wonder Woman-esque levels of skill. She didn't even need the golden lasso to get people to tell her the truth. Just her trusty teacher face. This regular self-examination helped give her the confidence necessary to keep moving forward, which is what she wanted more than anything; to be done with all connections to her ex-philanderer and to start a new life where she was a carefree hottie with a good job and no need to depend on anyone.

She was done with fairy tales.

Definitely ready for some distraction.

Okay, she'd had to move back in with her mom. That wasn't too terrible. It would likely put a cramp in any sort of social life she might have, but she'd make do. Maybe it was time she got into some trouble. Just a little, though. Cecilia liked her quiet life. A hot bath and a good book were all she needed for a good time. But then she hadn't really ever gotten out there, had she?

Cecilia gave the ankle banger one last appraisal as she walked away. Too bad he appeared to be a traveling businessman. He looked like the kind of trouble that had already gotten her into trouble.

CHAPTER TWO

5:15 a.m. San Francisco International Airport
       TSA Checkpoint

Security was crazy this morning. There were well over a hundred people in lines that wound back and forth like intestines until they reached the angry-looking TSA agents hunched over their podiums. Felip really needed to sign up for the pre-approval to avoid this mess in the future, but then he hadn't planned on so much travel back and forth from Barcelona to California.

The fierce-looking agent who took Felip's ticket was built like he'd burst out of his uniform any minute. The agent scribbled something illegible on his boarding pass and carefully examined Felip's passport photo at least seven times before handing his items back to him. He gestured for Felip to follow the group of people in brightly colored shirts. He'd noticed them at check-in while he'd been deep in conversation with his father about the family business.

It was *always* about the family business, which weighed on Felip like concrete shoes these days. It was getting harder to keep a smile on his face and his head in the game with all the pressure.

The line came to a grinding halt as the teenagers in the group struggled to send their bags through the scanners. There were signs posted, warning what they needed to take out of their bags, but it seemed several of them had questions. Thankfully there were some adults helping them along, but there were unhappy travelers behind Felip who weren't amused.

"Dude, you have to take your shoes off," a large boy said to his much smaller friend.

"Do you know how hard it is to get these Jordans off?" the smaller one asked.

"Do you want them to take 'em off for you? My brother almost got banned from the airport for life when we flew to Tonga last year for our grandmother's funeral. He didn't want his Jordans leaving his feet, and the big-ass TSA dudes like mean-mugged him until he finally cooperated. That, and Mama pinched him hella hard and warned him that if he got banned for life, he'd be back sharing a room with our baby twin brothers."

"Damn," the smaller one said. "I ain't about to miss this flight, yo. Moms will lose her shit if I get in trouble on this trip."

Felip grabbed two extra bins. "You look as though you can use these." He handed them to the boys and they thanked him. Felip chuckled and prepared his bags for the scanner. Just a few more steps and he'd be through and one step closer to a long flight, where he could finally get some peace and quiet.

His phone buzzed. It was his right hand, June Fontaine.

"I can't talk right now," he answered.

"Felip! We need to discuss the hotel contracts! We've put it off long enough and—"

"And I'm going through security. You want me to be arrested by airport security and detained here?"

He couldn't help but laugh when she growled at him. He and June had been friends since his university years in Berkeley, and when his father semi-retired and appointed him CEO eight years ago, he'd asked her to come onboard.

His youngest brother Mateu recently took over the California operation, leaving the Chief Operations Officer position vacant. As soon as he returned, he planned to sit down with June and work out the details for her promotion, but for now, he'd let her blow off some steam.

"Fine. Call me when you are through."

She hung up on him and he stuck his tongue out at his phone. June brought out that kind of immature behavior in him. At least she paid attention to him, almost too much, to be perfectly honest. Having June in his life was the closest thing he'd had to a relationship since his divorce four years ago, and that was sad.

Which may have been why he was back to staring at the blonde woman who was apparently traveling with the group of teenagers. Felip hadn't noticed her until she'd turned on him at the ticket counter with a glare. Her expression had been almost comical. It reminded him of when he'd tease June, actually. Like a match to a fuse. Didn't take much to make her blow up. Would this lady be the same?

It was her turn to place her things on the conveyor belt. She opened the back zipper of her backpack and slid her laptop and a smaller tablet out, placing them gently into a bin. The SpongeBob stickers on her laptop case suggested she had a sense of humor.

She grabbed another bin for her backpack and bent to slip off a pair of Vans with Charlie Brown characters on them. Felip tried not to be too obvious as he ogled her backside, in case any of the kids were watching. The more he stared, the more he found her attractive. Her beauty wasn't in-your-face like that of many women he knew. There were subtle aspects of her appearance that intrigued him. For example, her deep-set eyes were a lovely shade of blue and lined with long lashes, although she wore no makeup to accentuate them. Her chin jutted out as though she was packing quite a bit of attitude for her small frame and medium height. She wore her short hair in a no-nonsense style that framed her face dramatically.

But it was her droll way of talking to the kids that had Felip's full attention. He liked watching people, figuring out what made them tick. But with this woman, his thoughts began to wander to such crazy things as what made her happy, turned on, excited...

It had been a long time since he'd spent quality time with a woman, and he began to fantasize about having a playful conversation with her over a glass of sangría.

"What the...?" The blonde straightened and looked around, confused, with her shoes in her hands.

He hadn't been paying attention and he'd pushed their bins ahead, meaning her bin was entering the scanner.

"I'm sorry." *What an idiot.* "Here, take this one." He handed her an empty bin, and she took it with a frown.

She hurriedly placed her shoes in the bin and slid it onto the rollers in front of his bins. She raised an eyebrow at him as she turned to enter the body scanner.

He really shouldn't find her reaction amusing.

"Breathe," he heard her mutter under her breath. She stepped inside the machine and placed her hands over her head.

"Ma'am? Your belt?"

Felip knew how frustrating it was to hold up a queue, and he felt awful for her. Her group waited for her on the other side, and Felip could see the tension building in her shoulders as she slid off her belt. The annoyed TSA guy monitoring the scanner held up an empty bin for her to place her belt in.

"Thank you," she said.

There was something different about the way she spoke, almost like an accent, but not quite.

"Ma'am?"

The agent pointed at her bottom, and Felip heard her groan. She'd left her phone in her back pocket.

Felip felt a twinge of guilt that he'd made a potentially stressful situation more difficult for her. He knew how hard it was to get going this early in the morning, and being part of such a large group, she'd likely been paying more attention to the kids than herself. Being the oldest of four boys with busy parents, he'd been the one to get them dressed and out of the house in the mornings, so he had an idea of her struggle.

The annoyed TSA guy held up the bin again and she placed her phone in it.

"So sorry," she said, hurrying back into the scanner.

"Ma'am?"

"Now what? Oh, I'm sorry."

Her exasperation was clearly evident, and the TSA agents were obviously frustrated with her. Felip wanted to step in and help, but that probably wouldn't go over well.

"Are you wearing a device?"

Device? Felip watched as she tucked her hair behind her ears. The agent nodded and waved her through.

She placed her arms up and Felip saw her hands shaking.

The female TSA gestured for her to go through, but then stopped her. *Oh no.* She'd been randomly chosen to receive the full security treatment. They pulled her aside and swiped her hands with a cloth and patted her down. Another agent waved to catch her attention and pointed to where they'd put her things. She thanked him and picked up her three bins, balancing them precariously in her arms as she made her way over to the benches.

Felip was allowed through with no hassle at all. He carried his bins to a bench a few paces away from her, debating whether it would be appropriate for him to approach her and apologize. He started to speak when two girls wearing the bright shirts sat on either side of her.

"Are you okay, Mrs. Galván?"

Felip's heart swelled as he saw her put on a brave smile. She shook off any tension she'd had going through security. For someone like him, it was a routine process, but he knew that for people who didn't travel often, it could be stressful.

"I'm fine. I'm glad it was me and not one of you guys," she said to them.

Felip fumbled with his own shoes as he watched her slide her dainty feet into her slip-ons. She smiled at her companions as though she hadn't just been through a stressful ordeal.

Felip realized he was still sitting there with only one shoe on while he watched her gather up the rest of her belongings. She took a deep breath and strolled out of security with her chin held high. He gazed after her until she was out of sight.

Mrs. Galván. So she was married. That was the end of that social observation.

Or it should have been, but he couldn't stop thinking of her. Why wasn't her husband with her? He hadn't noticed a ring. She looked like she could certainly handle herself, but he had this strong sense that he should have done something, well…something *helpful* for the woman, rather than stand there and gawk.

His phone buzzed again. June.

Are you done yet? We need to talk about this.

Felip sighed. He was tempted to put his phone in airplane mode.

I promise you I will call during my layover in Toronto. Give me some peace, woman.

That probably wouldn't go over well. His answer came thirty seconds later.

If it's peace you want, you better call me from Toronto. This can't wait much longer or we're liable to lose the contract, Boss.

. . .

Her calling him boss was like his mother calling his father the head of the family. Ernesto Segura might be the owner of Cava Segura, Barcelona's largest and most successful maker of sparkling wine, but Felip's father had always answered to his wife, as had the rest of the Segura boys. Felip was the eldest son, heir to the cava dynasty, but June held nearly as much power as him in Cava Segura.

His phone buzzed again. *Mateu.*

"Hermanito, how are you?" he asked.

"Felip?" Mateu sounded like he'd recently rolled out of bed. "Did you make it to the airport on time? I'm sorry, I tried to wake up to see you off—"

"Totally fine. Everything okay?"

Felip was worried about Mateu. Things had been chaotic when Felip arrived at their California facility two weeks ago, and it had taken some work to straighten everything out. There were issues with the employees, a problem with a major distributor, and Mateu's accountant had been stealing from them. But what had worried Felip the most was the fact that his youngest brother, who was more than capable of running the operation, seemed off. His usual level of energy wasn't there, and he'd been quiet. Reserved.

Felip had pried—it was an older brother's job to do so—but Mateu hadn't confessed to anything. Felip had left with the feeling he might be back soon.

"I'm fine. Thanks for your help with everything. I'm sorry about Mona. I never thought—"

"Sí, horrible situation. When someone you trust is stealing from you, it's awful. That violation..."

"Mm-hmm. I appreciate you coming out."

"Anytime. Happy to help."

They hung up and Felip sighed. He hated leaving his brother right now, as his gut told him something wasn't right, but he was needed back home.

It would really be nice to *not* be needed quite so much right now.

CHAPTER THREE

6:00 a.m. PDT
San Francisco International Airport
Gate C38

As soon as Cecilia's butt hit the funky airport seat near Gate 13, a barrage of duffel bags, backpacks, and tote bags were dropped at her feet.

"Thank you, Mrs. Galván," repeated about fifty times, or so it seemed. Everything sort of echoed in her head. She watched all the kids scamper off, talking excitedly, and once again she felt the weight of her responsibility as heavy as the backpack now resting against her shin.

She was taking these kids to a foreign country, one in which the native population spoke a language she barely knew, and it would be up to her and Gabrielle to bring them home safely. It was a monumental task. She loved these kids—each and every one had been in her classes at some point—and she worried something might happen. But hey, at least worrying kept her mind off of the flight for about a minute. *Ugh.*

Cecilia hadn't been particularly superstitious until thirteen days before the end of school, when her principal, Perla Guerrero, came to her at lunch with a huge favor to ask—the kind of favor you only ask family or someone who owes you.

"Zoey was in a car accident this morning and she's got a broken pelvis. She's supposed to take the Language Club on the annual trip two days after school finishes. I need another representative from the staff to go with Gabrielle, and you're the only person in the language department who hasn't led a school tour."

"Well, yeah, because there's not exactly another country to visit for American Sign Language," she'd replied. "We're kind of *in* it." It probably hadn't been the best time for sarcasm, but Cecilia lacked a filter most of the time.

But now, looking at her excited charges all lined up in their matching neon-green shirts that said, "Grass Valley Travel Club – ¡Vamos!" with a map of their tour on the back, she couldn't help but smile. She'd summon all of her badassery to make this trip awesome for each and every one of them.

Her phone buzzed. Mom.

Are you awake and ready?

"No, comma, Mom, period. I'm still in bed having a nightmare that I'm at the airport before dawn with a bunch of teenagers, period. How are you? Question mark." She didn't even have the energy to type. Voice text was excellent, even when it went horribly wrong. Especially when it went horribly wrong.

They're lucky you were able to go. Did you at least get some coffee?

. . .

"Nope. Period. Afraid it will make me spew. Period."

Told you to take some of my Valium.

Cecilia smiled at the phone. Her mom had offered her not only her choice of prescription drugs, but also her medical marijuana edibles to ease the jitters. She'd had to remind her mother that she was a) a teacher, b) responsible for students, and c) the TSA would likely frown upon her having a controlled substance that wasn't even prescribed for her.

"I earned that pot, Cece," her mom had said. Fair enough. Mom suffered from painful arthritis, it went with the artist-for-a-living territory, and her edibles kept the pain away better than any of the other drugs the doctors had tried.

Well, get some sangria when you land. You'll feel better.

"Chaperone here. Period. Remember? Question mark."

Fine. But if you get busted for anything, I'll come bail you out. Spanish cops are supposed to be really hot.

Cecilia shook her head and typed **I love you. Psycho.**

When her phone buzzed again, she couldn't imagine what else her mom could come back with, but it was WhatsApp, the app they'd all downloaded for ease of communication since many of them wouldn't have cellular data on this trip and WhatsApp uses WiFi.

. . .

It's Joseph. Eduardo took his contact out because it was in wrong and he needs his cleaner from his backpack.

Fabulous. Gabrielle had wandered over to the makeup vending machine and was out of earshot. The Santiagos, parents who were traveling with one of her students, had gone to grab breakfast, and that left Cecilia alone with approximately thirteen carry-ons and no help in sight.

I can't leave our stuff. He's going to have to wait until Ms. Reyes comes back.

Cecilia stood, hoping that frantically waving her arms would get Gabrielle's attention away from the lip liners and brow pencils, but no dice.

If you don't hurry, he's going to use his spit. I've watched him do it before and it's not pretty. He's going to end up with pink eye and then we're all going to get it. Please, Mrs. Galván?

Shit. Pink eye in Europe would be no joke. *Ew.* Thankfully Gabrielle appeared to be making her purchase and, as she turned, she spotted Cecilia's insistent gesturing.

"What's wrong?" she asked as she jogged over in her cute little stretch pants with Converse the same neon-green color as their tour shirts.

"I gotta take Eduardo his backpack. He's having issues with his contacts."

"Oh, okay. Do you know which one is his?"

. . .

Which bag is his?

Pokémon. This is Eduardo we're talking about.

Cecilia chuckled. Eduardo was a tad bit obsessed with Pokémon, both the cards and the mobile game. He'd organized a Pokémon Go club at school, and he'd already mentioned how excited he was to be going to another country to play. Something about legendary creatures. Whatever. As long as they fit in his carry-on.

She spotted his bag and reached for it as she stood up, knocking a heavier one onto her other foot.

"Son of a beehive, that hurts!" She hopped around in a tight circle and then snatched up Eduardo's backpack, nearly tearing her rotator cuff as she hauled it up to her shoulder. What on earth had he brought?

She limped over to the nearest men's room and messaged the boys she was outside. No response. She called out, "Hello? Boys?"

Nothing.

"Joseph? Eduardo?"

Nothing.

"Dammit." She hated to march right in there. Not that she hadn't been in a men's room before, but after all she'd been through at security, she wasn't anxious to cause a ruckus. She'd send the next man who came out right back in there to look for the boys.

A minute later, a man appeared.

"Not you," she said, exasperated. The ankle-banger from the ticket line was busy on his phone and walked right into her.

"Oh," he said, glancing up from his phone. "I didn't see you there."

"Right." *Why does he have to be so freaking hot?* This would be much easier if she could actually speak to a good-looking man without sounding like an idiot. "My boys are in there, I think."

"Oh, vale," he said, smiled at her. He looked as though he wanted to say more, but then his phone buzzed again and he started to walk past her.

She grabbed his arm out of frustration. "Can you please go back in there and let them know I have their bag?"

"Of course," he said, sliding his still-buzzing phone into his back pocket as he turned.

"Thank you," she called to his back. *And what a nice back.* She waited a moment or two but he came out empty-handed.

"What do they look like?" he asked.

Cecilia looked down at herself and pointed to the neon, can't-miss-me shirt.

"Ah. Vale." He turned to go back in, and she thought he must not be a terrible person if he was willing to help a grumpy woman outside a bathroom find her kids to avoid a pink-eye epidemic.

Now that she was up and moving, she had to pee, and, she feared, other things. She shifted her weight back and forth as it took an extraordinarily long amount of time for him to return.

"Are you sure they are in here?"

She growled. "Yes! They just texted me—"

Her phone buzzed and she looked down.

We're lining up to board now.

Sure enough, the neon squad was attempting to line up by their seat numbers. Joseph and Eduardo motioned to her to hurry up.

She growled again, and this time the guy laughed.

"Is everything alright?" he asked.

"Do you have kids?" she asked, swinging the giant bag over her shoulder, which caused her to stumble very unladylike. Not that it should matter, but the fact that he was smiling at her made her feel like more of a clod. It was way too early for this.

"No. No, I—"

"Well, it's an adventure. Excuse me." She took two steps and then turned around. "Thanks for your help."

She hurried over to the group before he had a chance to respond and shoved the bag at Eduardo.

"Hey, thanks Mrs.—"

"Where were you guys?"

"Oh, this dude in the bathroom offered us some of his contact solution, and guess what? It was the same brand Eduardo uses and everything! He said we could keep the bottle."

Deep. Cleansing. Breaths.

"Fantastic. Remember that little device you have in your hand?"

The boys looked down at their phones and then back at her in confusion.

"You could have messaged me and told me you were all set! I hassled some poor man outside the bathroom trying to get you help!"

"Oh. We came out the other side. My bad." The boys did their best to be serious despite the fact she was doing the pee-pee dance.

"Cecilia, here's your bag," Gabrielle said cheerfully, handing it over. "Is everything—"

"I'll be back."

She ran as if her life depended on it and barely made it into the stall, cursing her belt once again for getting between her and the promised land. She had her pants down before the flow erupted. She prayed the gurgling in her stomach would hold off and resisted the urge to sigh in relief. When she thought she'd emptied as much as possible on such short notice, she jumped up and dressed herself, did a quick wash job and darted out the door.

The kids hadn't moved. She chanced a quick trip into the shop for something to settle her stomach. Once she'd grabbed a water and hastily snatched a pack of mint gum, she headed over to the snack rack—and there was Ankle Banger, blocking her view. She tried to look around him, but he was everywhere she needed to be. He wasn't freakishly tall, or heavyset or anything, he just *was*.

She tried to lean around his left side and he shifted his weight, thwarting her attempt. She was ready to bang *his* ankle to get him out of the way. Time was ticking!

Cecilia took one last chance and somehow managed to weave around his right side, plant a foot, and grab for the saltine crackers. Of course, she could have said excuse me, but there was no time for words. She placed her purchases on the counter and thrust her money at the cashier, who looked at her like the crazy person she was sure she appeared to be.

She made it to the gate as the rest of her group was starting to have their boarding passes scanned, and she slid into line behind Gabrielle. She wanted to get into her seat, pull out her Kindle, and escape into a book. Or sleep. Either of those would be excellent.

She couldn't help glancing over her shoulder, though, to see if perhaps Ankle Banger was on her flight. She spotted him standing outside the shop, on his phone once again, gesturing this time with an open bottle of water. A woman brushed by him and he sloshed water on her.

"That guy is a mess," she said with a smile as she turned and had her boarding pass scanned.

"Enjoy your flight," the woman said.

Flight. *Shit.* Cecilia felt a sudden urge to flee and had to remind herself that she was the adult in this situation. That usually wasn't a struggle for her, but flying?

The walk down the jetway was tough. Her knees wobbled and for a couple steps, she thought she was going down, but before she knew it, she was entering the cabin of the plane. And then she heard the boys being rowdy up ahead and it gave her back some of her badassery.

"Dang, it's hella small in here," Tui muttered.

Cecilia was seated in row 13, with Tui, Joseph and Eduardo in row 14. She slid her backpack under the seat in front of her and sat back against the rest, closing her eyes. If she was one to pray, this would be a good time, but nothing came to mind.

"How much food did you actually bring on this flight?" Tui asked Joseph.

"I got them tasty snacks. Moms made us lumpia and pinaypay and I got hot Cheetos and Oreos. Get on my level!"

The seat jerked forward as Eduardo, who was directly behind Cecilia, kneed it in his hopeless quest to get comfortable.

"Dude," Eduardo said. "Your size sixteens are taking up the whole aisle. My feet can't even breathe."

"I'm sorry," Tui said. "I can't help the way God made me, bruh."

"Bro, man, I hope you brought enough deodorant," Joseph said. "If I'm smashed against you on the plane *and* sharing a hotel room for the next twelve days, I better not smell you."

"Relax. I smell delicious. And for those moments I don't, I've got essential oils my grandmother sent with me."

"Great. You'll smell like stinky old lady flowers."

Ahhhhh, teenagers. It was a good thing she found them entertaining.

Her gut clenched when the engines cranked up. She knew she should be happy to have a free trip to Spain, and she would be once they landed. She wished she didn't feel like she might hurl at any moment.

"Mrs. Galván? How long is our flight to Toronto?"

"About six and a half hours, Eduardo. Just like the last time you asked."

"My feet are already asleep," Tui said.

"Joseph, can you guys make sure Tui has room for his feet."

"Mrs. Galván, it's not my fault he's gigantic. He needs, like, another row or something, and I need access to my snacks."

Cecilia turned around to see that, yes, Tui was squashed into the middle seat and doing his very best to make his 6'2", 220 pounds fit into a space for someone half his size.

"Maybe you could let Tui have the aisle?" Cecilia asked. "Or at least switch off?"

"It's okay, Mrs. Galván. I don't mind." Tui always made the best of situations. She loved his positivity.

Eduardo and Joseph grumbled, but they settled down.

"It's fine," Joseph said, turning his body sideways and resting his head on Tui's massive shoulder. "He makes a good pillow."

The two boys snuggled up to Tui and he shook his head with a smile, used to being teased about his size. He carried himself with pride, wearing his long hair natural at school in a massive puff of curls. Students and staff recognized him for his intelligence, great sense of humor, and generosity, above his football prowess.

His seatmates were also great kids. Joseph was a string bean who she finally gave up scolding for eating in class when she realized he was really that hungry all the time. And Eduardo had been on the student council and started an anti-bullying campaign after coming to the aide of Jorge, who was bullied incessantly their first year due to his long-winded explanations of various topics. The four boys made an odd group, but they were great friends, and she hoped they would have the time of their lives in Spain.

Cecilia laughed at the picture they made. "You'll forget all about the discomfort when we get to Madrid." At least that's what she kept telling herself, anyway.

Joseph and Eduardo both sighed in acceptance of their fate and pulled out their phones. They were laughing within minutes, while Cecilia's anxiety ramped up. Her hands were clammy and pools of sweat gathered under her arms.

Please, God, don't let my deodorant fail.

"I hope *everyone* brought enough deodorant," Gabrielle whispered from next to her, as if she'd read Cecilia's thoughts. "We've had a few smelly ones on these trips and *gahhh*, the bus rides." She shuddered. "It's supposed to be in the mid-nineties the first week. Too bad we're not going to hit the beach until the second week. I can't wait to work on my tan."

Gabrielle had just finished her third year of teaching. Cecilia had twelve years under her belt, and Gabrielle's sister Zoey, who was Cecilia's best friend, was a fifteen-year veteran. Cecilia had known Gabrielle since she was a teenager. She'd wondered if there had been much growth in that time, but then she'd observed Gabrielle in the classroom, and the younger woman had the right combination of passion, knowledge and flair to be a strong teacher. Gabrielle had always been one of those lucky women who seemed to have everything going for them—beauty, opportunity and popularity. Nothing Cecilia possessed.

Cecilia's luck had manifested in the fact that she retained some of her hearing and technology provided the means for her to have a nearly normal life. Well, that, and the fact she'd escaped from her divorce mostly unscathed. She hoped she could say the same for this trip.

If only the plane would move! She leaned out into the aisle to see the flight attendants laughing with each other, all relaxed and happy like in a commercial.

Cecilia sighed as she sat back in her center seat. She'd given Gabrielle the window so the younger woman could nap and be refreshed once they got to Spain and could take over the lead.

A family sat in the row in front of her, and their little girl glared at Cecilia from between the seats. Cecilia tried to smile at her, but the girl gave stank eye like nobody's business. She fussed to her mother about having to wait, and Cecilia thought maybe they had a little something in common, but then the girl stuck out her tongue.

Fine. Let it be war then. Cecilia stuck hers out, and the girl wrinkled her nose and bared her teeth.

"You need anything before I plug in and zonk out?" Gabrielle asked.

A Xanax? A couple shots of whisky? Mom's weed? "I'm good," Cecilia said, patting her arm. "I hopefully won't be far behind you."

"Fantastic," the younger woman said. "If any hot guys get on, elbow me. I'm on the prowl this trip."

Zoey had warned Cecilia that her younger sister, while perfectly responsible and great in an emergency, was having a bit of biological clock-itis.

Cecilia had gone to see Zoey several times before the trip to learn all she could and to bring her ailing friend magazines, romance novels, and meals. While Cecilia was nervous about taking on the excursion, she felt awful for her friend and wanted to do right by her.

"I promise I won't let her run off with any Spanish royalty."

"If she finds royalty, or someone with any money at all, you let her go! You and I both know it's hard to get by on a teacher's salary, and I'd like for her to *not* live with me forever."

Within minutes of putting on an eye mask and headphones, Gabrielle was out like a light. Cecilia envied her. She always had a helluva time sleeping on planes and in cars.

Cecilia anxiously watched as people continued to file onto the plane and prayed by some miracle the seat next to her would be unoccupied. It could happen. The rush began to slow to a trickle and her hopes continued to climb. It would be nice to be able to stretch out, or she could be all responsible and let one of the boys behind her come up so Tui would have more room. She'd make the sacrifice for them, most likely.

She took out her Kindle, made sure her water and snacks were within reach, and pulled out her sweater in case she got cold.

When she looked up, Ankle Banger stood right next to the empty aisle seat.

"Lucky thirteen, eh?"

Cecilia tried to ease her resting bitch face and smile, but whatever she'd managed to do, it only seemed to amuse him. He pushed his wavy dark brown hair—which she now noticed was subtly streaked with silver strands—out of his face and his bright smile showed off a crooked tooth in the front. For some reason, that crooked tooth made Cecilia not hate him, despite his ankle-abusing ways. His handsome features and obvious charm were made a little more human by the fact that his teeth were a tad off.

"I'm not superstitious," she lied.

He smiled wider as he slid one arm out of his jacket, revealing his athletic shirt. It looked like a soccer jersey, with navy blue and red stripes, and said FC Barcelona. He'd placed his duffel bag under the seat in front of him and was attempting to make room for his messenger bag in the overhead bin. With each shove, his shirt rose up from his well-worn jeans to display his smooth, tan skin and a small patch of dark hair just below his navel. She became sort of mesmerized by the movements of his muscles.

"I can't get it in," he said. "It's too big."

She heard snickers from the row behind her.

"Pardon me?" she asked, shocked.

"Yours is big enough. Can I slide it in there for a bit?"

"That's what he said," one of the boys whispered.

Cecilia turned around and glared at the boys and then balked at this guy. What the—

Then she realized he was still holding his bag and gesturing to the compartment under the seat in front of her.

"Yeah," she finally said. "Whatever." *How embarrassing!*

She needed him to sit down and stop hypnotizing her with his navel.

The flight attendant came over to see if Mr. Magic Abs Ankle Banger needed any assistance.

"Thank you, this lovely lady has invited me to use her space."

That wasn't exactly what she'd said, but she just wanted to get on with it. The flight. Not the...never mind.

"Felip," he said, sticking out his hand covered with more tanned skin and a light dusting of dark hair. Cecilia stared at it for a moment as if it might bite. Or she might bite *it*. She took it and gave a quick shake before letting go as if she'd been burned. Why couldn't she act like a normal human woman with a good-looking guy?

"Cecilia," she finally said, averting her gaze before things got any more awkward. She was stuck next to him for the next six-plus hours. Better to not act like a complete head case.

"You're breaking my heart," he said as he slid into the seat next to her. He was immediately all over the armrest and manspreading so much, his long leg pressed against hers. Was he hitting on her?

"Cecilia, like the song," he said, gesturing with his hand. "'You're shaking my confidence daily.' You know, Simon and Garfunkel?"

"Oh," she said, horrified she'd misunderstood his intent. "Right."

One of the boys whispered "Fail!" loud enough for her to hear. She mustered up her ugliest teacher look and turned to nail them with it. They suddenly got really busy with their phones.

"Mrs. Galván? I'm sorry but Aaliyah needs you."

Kristin stood in the aisle, her eyes wide.

"Excuse me." Cecilia stood and hunched under the console above her head.

"Of course." He lifted himself off the seat enough for her to squeeze past his long legs.

Cecilia stumbled over his feet and felt only a slight ounce of guilt when he grunted softly. She followed Kristin back about four rows to find that Aaliyah's minor panic attack that had started before they'd left this morning had reared its ugly head.

"Hey sweetie," she said, crouching down next to her. "You need some water? Some crackers?"

Aaliyah shook her head, her big brown eyes filled with tears. "I don't think I can do this," she whispered. She'd clenched her hands so tightly, her knuckles were white.

Cecilia leaned in close and whispered, "Do you need me to do some breathing with you?"

"No. I just don't know if I can..."

"I know you can. *You* know you can, remember? We talked about it at the meeting before school was out. Let's make it happen."

Aaliyah's upper lip shone with perspiration, but her breathing seemed to slow down.

"Didn't you say you chose an audiobook that was exactly as long as the flight? Maybe you could start that now?"

She nodded and searched for her phone. Her seatmate Janelle handed it to her.

Once her earbuds were in she relaxed a bit more. Her mom had assured Cecilia the audiobook would give her plenty to focus on, and if that didn't work, she'd taught Cecilia some breathing exercises that would hopefully do the trick.

After a few moments, Aaliyah smiled. "Thank you, Mrs. Galván."

"Anytime, sweetie. You need me on this trip, you just holler."

Aaliyah nodded and Cecilia turned to scan the rest of the plane to check on her students. All of them seemed to be talking quietly in their seats. Mr. and Mrs. Santiago sat on either side of their son Jorge, as he explained the safety features on the plane. Cecilia smiled. She was used to the brilliant kid asking a million questions and reciting sophisticated facts about topics they'd been discussing in class. He was on the spectrum and extremely high functioning. He probably could have made this trip on his own, but they didn't seem quite ready to let him go, and honestly, Cecilia was grateful to have a set of parents with her that she knew fairly well. They would be wonderful to have if anything went wrong or if she needed a break.

When Cecilia returned to her seat, Felip stood in the aisle, staring at her and blocking their row.

"That was very good what you did for that girl. Are you a counselor?"

His heavily accented voice sounded interested rather than mocking. Without looking at him, she said, "Just a teacher." *And you are incredibly distractive. Make that attracting. Grrr!*

"Ah, you are on a school tour, yes?"

"Yes."

The flight attendants indicated it was time to buckle up. Cecilia tried to pass by Felip without getting too cozy, but there was really no way to avoid contact. She cringed when her breasts brushed against his arm and she stepped on his foot again. His cheery disposition wasn't affected and he continued to smile at her as she sat down.

CHAPTER FOUR

7:45 a.m. PDT
Departing San Francisco International Airport

Felip grinned as the lovely woman avoided eye contact and slid back into her seat. She made herself busy pulling a tablet out of the pouch on the seat in front of her, arranging the cord of her earbuds, and folding and refolding her sweater.

For whatever reason, Felip was in a mischievous mood and not even a little bit put off by the American woman's attitude. Besides, she couldn't be an awful person. The patient and caring way she'd dealt with the young lady, as well as how she'd been with the kids in the terminal, said otherwise. Perhaps he could get her talking more and loosen her up. He had a gift when it came to making people feel comfortable. She was too interesting to not chat with. It would make the long flight pass by quickly. He'd keep it harmless. They'd called her Mrs., and he hadn't forgotten that detail. There was just something about her that made him curious.

"Where are you taking your group?" he asked her.

She pointed to her shirt that said "Spain 2018" on the front without looking at him. *Ah.* She intended to resist his attentions. He wished her luck. He was not easy to resist, a characteristic that served him well in his business.

"Oh! Bon. What part of España will you see?"

"Madrid to Barcelona. Up through some of the northern cities."

She was being vague on purpose. Fair enough. She didn't know him, and she had children to protect. But she presented a challenge, and Felip loved a good challenge.

The flight attendants came through the cabin while one of them gave the safety talk. Cecilia watched their demonstration attentively. Felip traveled often enough he had it memorized, so he took his time to get comfortable. He'd been in a hurry to get home and took the next flight available, which had been sold out of first class. He'd mentally prepared himself to be a bit squished in the tiny seats. No matter. Luck was on his side, as he'd ended up next to this intriguing woman.

So she was a teacher. He thought he might enjoy being in her class, although he'd most likely be sent out for bad behavior. He couldn't help it. He was incredibly successful in his business, but he also enjoyed playtime. It had been a long while since he'd had fun.

The plane pushed back from the gate and headed toward the runway. Cecilia stiffened in her seat and blew a breath out slowly. She tried to grasp the ends of the armrests, but when her forearm brushed his, she jerked it away.

"Here, you can have it," he said, crossing his arms over his chest. He'd been all arms and legs since puberty, although instead of being gawky now, he merely took up more than his share of space. It couldn't be totally helped in this situation, but he didn't want to be rude.

"Thank you," she said through gritted teeth. The plane was now in the queue for departure and the captain's voice came over the intercom, telling the flight attendants to secure for takeoff. The engines' roar became louder and Cecilia sucked in a sharp breath, her knuckles white around the grips on the armrests.

"Excuse me, Cecilia, but are you a nervous flyer?"

"I just don't like it."

Without thinking, he placed a hand on her knee. "You are in good hands. It is much safer to be in a plane than a car, yes?"

She glanced down at his hand and then glared. "Your hand would be much safer in your lap than on my knee, yes?" she asked, mimicking him.

He barked out a laugh and removed his hand. "I stand corrected, señora. It was a reflex," he said.

"I'm not scared," she said, staring straight ahead once more with her chin stuck out. "I don't like—"

She stopped speaking as the plane rushed forward. Her eyes widened and she began panting.

"It's a shame your husband isn't here to hold your hand."

"My husband? You mean my *ex*-husband. I don't like him much, either."

Felip grinned. "Ah, but you still use his name?"

She shook her head and rolled her eyes. "Do you know how hard it is to get a school full of people to start calling you by a different name? In the middle of the school year? Not to mention all the questions high school kids will ask about your life."

The plane began rising in the air and her hands grasped at the grips once more.

"You married a Spaniard?" he asked.

"No. Portuguese. His father was, anyway. I don't know about his mother. She passed before I married him. And why are you asking me so many questions?"

He listened for a second and then...

"We are about to reach our cruising altitude of thirty-four thousand feet, on our way to Toronto. If you need anything, don't hesitate to ring for your flight attendants. Other than that, sit back, relax, and enjoy your flight."

"Just trying to take your mind off of the ascent. A lot of people get nervous."

She smiled, genuinely this time, not like that awful fake smile she'd given him when he'd first approached her row. He'd been worried about being stuck next to a pretentious priss who was too good to speak to him, but instead, he'd discovered she was merely preoccupied with her thoughts. He could only imagine the responsibility it must be, taking students to Europe. Felip was no stranger to responsibility, but children were another matter entirely.

"Thank you," she said. Her cheeks warmed to the gentlest pink of a blush, and something in him wanted to roar in triumph. Putting a smile on this lady's face felt like winning an Olympic medal. "I've only flown to Europe once and it wasn't fun then, either."

"Maybe you're doing it wrong," he joked. "Perhaps you need some wine to take the edge off."

She scrunched up her nose. "I don't like wine."

His heart dropped. She'd committed blasphemy. "Perhaps you have not found the right one."

She turned her body to face him and raised an eyebrow. "Like no one has ever said that to me before. Honestly, it's not a crime to not like wine."

Oh, but it is, Felip thought to himself. *Good thing I love a challenge and I have six more hours in which to teach the teacher.*

As soon as the fasten seat belt sign was turned off, his seat was bumped from the row behind him. Several times.

"I gotta go, bruh. Let me out!"

The boy on the aisle pulled back on the headrest of Felip's seat as he moved to let a big kid out of the middle. That one shoved against the seat, pushing Felip forward a bit, then the third boy climbed out and elbowed Felip in the back of the head.

"Boys, be careful," Cecilia admonished from beside him. "I'm sorry," she said to Felip as she glanced at their shared armrest that he'd taken over. "They're not very spatially aware." Somehow, he thought her comment wasn't meant only for the boys.

"We're sorry, Mrs. Galván. I thought we were going to have more room on an international flight. Aren't these planes bigger or something?"

"This *is* more room," Felip said with a laugh. "Coach on a domestic flight is even smaller. However, with new aviation technology, they can fly smaller jets to long-distance destinations. I imagine soon we will all be packed like sardines so they can make more money."

The big kid's eyes went round in horror. "I'd never be able to fit in a smaller seat."

"That's okay," the one from the aisle seat said. "You'll be making that grain playing football and will only fly first class, bruh."

They did some sort of handshake that led to a victory dance. The smaller one nearly fell against an older woman on the opposite side of the aisle.

"Oh, excuse me," he said, hurrying back to his seat when she shot him a fearful look.

Felip laughed at their antics and turned to say something to Cecilia, but he paused. She had the strangest expression on her face. Her lips were pulled back from her teeth and she made chomping motions with her jaw while crossing her eyes. Felip started to ask if she was all right, thinking maybe she was having a fit or something, when movement from the row in front of them caught his eye.

A little girl, maybe five years old, faced them and, through the gap in the seats, he saw her stick her tongue out and put her thumbs in her ears, waving her hands back and forth.

"I see you've made a friend," he whispered to Cecilia.

She switched it up, using her index fingers to pull down her lower eye lids and her pinkies to push her nose up. "I'm going to win at this game. I can go the whole flight."

The little girl reached over the top of her head and pulled her eyelids up. She made a grimace, showing her baby teeth, a couple of which were missing.

"I don't know," he said, "she's pretty scary." He flipped his lower lip down and curled his tongue up over his top lip then crossed his eyes. "How's this?"

"Good, but flick your tongue a little. That makes it even better."

They spent several minutes alternating goofy faces until the little girl's father caught her.

"Brianna, stop that," he said, peeking between the seats. He caught Felip wagging his tongue from side to side with his eyes rolled back.

Cecilia elbowed him, and he stopped in time to see the little girl spin around and sit facing forward.

"Caught," he said with a shrug.

Cecilia raised an eyebrow at him. "You're pretty good at this. One might think you were a clown or circus performer for a living."

"Sadly, nothing quite so glamorous. Just the eldest of four boys. I had to keep my little brothers out of trouble. Sometimes you do whatever it takes to entertain them."

She smiled, and again Felip felt the desire to pound on his chest in victory, or maybe try that little dance move the boys were doing.

Speaking of the boys, they returned to their seats and another round of bumps and bashes from behind him ensued. Cecilia wisely leaned forward while Felip's hair got pulled.

"Oh, my bad, man," the big kid said.

Felip reassured him. "No harm done."

He sensed Cecilia was trying to busy herself with her tablet. She kept flipping pages but wasn't really reading anything.

"¿Enseñas español?" he asked.

"Excuse me?"

"Spanish. You are the Spanish teacher? I assumed—"

"Oh! Your accent is different than I'm used to. No, I'm just chaperoning. I only know the bare minimum of Spanish. I teach ASL and Life Skills."

"ASL?"

She signed to him the letters. "American Sign Language. You probably call it something else." She brushed her hair away from her cheek for a moment and he got a look at her hearing aide. All that was visible was a tiny tube running into her ear.

"That's wonderful. We do have sign language in Spain, but it is different in Catalonia where I am from than in the rest of España. I didn't know they taught that in regular schools."

"It's becoming more popular. I learned at home. My mother is hard of hearing as well."

Fascinating. "And Life Skills? This is a required class?"

"It is. They learn basic survival skills like first aid, personal finances, communication, and sex ed."

He gulped. "You teach them about sex?"

Her expression was blank. "It's required for all freshmen."

"But that's..." He peered behind him to find the boys all with earbuds in. The little girl in front of them had headphones on as well. "That must be uncomfortable at times."

"Not at all. It's human anatomy and biological function. The students need to know how to protect themselves and make good decisions. I give them the information they need and the means to stay safe." She cocked her head. "Does talking about sex make you uncomfortable?"

"No. Well. It would have at their age. But I guess Americans are more open about such things."

She shrugged. "Yes and no. It depends. We live in a very small town. Sometimes there are parents who excuse their children from that unit, but most don't. Where did you learn about sex then, if not in school?"

"I learned from my older cousins, I guess."

"And the problem with that is, kids get wrong information and make decisions based on that wrong information, and that gets them into trouble."

"I had no trouble with sex," Felip said, feeling his skin heat up around his collar. Maybe he'd underestimated this woman. She was far more assertive than he'd given her credit for. If he'd had to stare at her beauty while learning about the act of...

No. No way. He'd never make it.

She smirked at him and went back to flipping pages. "I bet you didn't."

He couldn't help the smile on his face.

CHAPTER FIVE

Time Unknown – Somewhere over the northern United States

Cecilia didn't like how much this man entertained her. Not one bit. Part of her wanted to put in her headphones and fake sleep. She wouldn't have to interact with him anymore. But the curious part of her was enjoying this last respite of adult conversation before she had to be totally on for the kids.

And what a lovely conversation companion to have. He was the quintessential Spaniard. Eyes so vibrant, the whites visible completely surrounding the irises that were like golden amber. When he wasn't smiling, his brows were dramatic and serious, Cecilia could only compare him to the portraits she'd seen of European nobility, or a supermodel perhaps. His nose was perfect, his cheekbones high, his expression serious one minute, then laughing, and the next looking as though he were plotting some sort of mischief.

And just as she was thinking that, he cleared his throat.

"You have never been to Spain?" he asked.

She loved the way he said "esSpain." His English was excellent.

His accent was thick but understandable and sounded sophisticated. Lots of rolled r's. But then he almost had a lisp the way he spoke. Zoey had warned her that in some areas, the Spanish in Spain—Castillian or Castellano— was different, and that instead of the s sound in, say, España, it sounded like Ethpaña.

And he was waiting for an answer.

"No. I've only left the country once." *And I'm not going into that story with you.*

"No? But there is a whole other world besides United States. You should get out more."

She started to prickle at his statement, but that grin of his let her know he was teasing again.

"It's hard to be a jet-setter on a teacher's salary," she replied with snark. "Besides, if you lived where I do, you wouldn't want to leave, either."

"In California?" he asked. Cecilia loved the way he pronounced every syllable the way it was meant to be spoken. "True. It is a beautiful place. You will appreciate it more when you have seen other places. My home in Barcelona is perfect. The city, the people, the food, the countryside in Catalonia. It is the most beautiful place in all of España."

"I guess I'll see soon enough."

"And you must try the wine, sangría y cava és molt... Sorry. It is hard for me to speak of my home in English. It doesn't do the description justice, eh? But you must try the wine. We have the best in all of the world in Barcelona."

"That's great," she said, fighting the urge to roll her eyes. "I don't drink wine, and I certainly won't be drinking it while I'm leading a group of teenagers on a tour."

He sat back. "You are probably right. Well, the food will be wonderful for you. Jamón y queso, cochinillo y las frutas, y tapas..."

He looked overrun with his desire for food, and Cecilia laughed at the look of pure happiness on his face.

"Just how long have you been gone? Do you need a napkin? I think you have some drool..."

She pointed at his chin and he wiped at it, his eyes wide.

"Oh, you joke. Bien. I see how it is. As a matter of fact, I have been gone for the past month on business. I spent the last two weeks in California and I have missed my home very much. When you live in a place such as I do, you would miss it, too."

"What do you do for business?" she asked, trying to be polite. She wasn't really sure she cared.

He paused before he spoke. "I am in charge of a large company in Barcelona." He was obviously holding something back.

Fine. She didn't want to know that badly. "And you travel frequently?" *Because we all know what guys like you do while you're on business trips.*

"Some. Mostly in the country, but sometimes to the United States and other parts of Europe. I try to stay home, eh? I'm a bit like your Dorothy."

"Dorothy?" Cecilia asked, confused.

"Toto? Eh, the dog? She's from Kansas?"

"Oh! *Wizard of Oz.* There's no place like home. Ah. I get it."

He beamed as though he'd just won a valuable hand at cards. "Then you agree with me."

He'd said that as if it was inevitable that she would see things his way, and that type of man could really get her hackles up. She'd resisted her husband for many years, refusing to accept whatever he said as law, but this guy... He didn't seem like he was being arrogant, more like...enthusiastic.

She supposed everyone was partial to their country, to a point. Perhaps he was right and Spain was amazing.

When she was quiet for some time, he leaned back in his seat and sighed. It was almost a disappointed sound. "I will let you get back to your book," he said. He smiled but it held much less wattage this time.

Well, shit. She hadn't meant to be rude. Maybe she should—

Felip put in earbuds and started watching something on his phone.

Probably just as well. She needed the rest.

Cecilia turned on the Bluetooth setting for her earbuds and put on her comfort playlist. The Romantics, Elvis Costello, Pat Benatar, The

Knack…all the old hits. Made her feel like she was right back in her grandfather's living room, where she'd beg him to play the jukebox every time she came over. He'd put it on long-play for her and she'd dance around for hours. Her grandmother had been completely deaf, so Grandpa would play it as loud as he liked and she'd never complain. He used to say it was one of her best qualities.

Grandpa repaired jukeboxes for a living before he passed away five years prior, a year after Grandma had lost her battle with cancer. He kept some of his restorations for himself. Cecilia and her mother still had a couple of his favorite machines, ones that played 45 records rather than the later ones that played CDs.

As Foreigner sang "Cold As Ice," Cecilia let her head fall to the right and sighed. Some sleep would be good. She felt Felip shift in his seat and his leg brushed against hers. He left it there. She smiled and shook her head as she felt sleep pull her under.

CHAPTER SIX

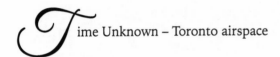ime Unknown – Toronto airspace

Felip must have nodded off at some point during the movie he'd been watching. He had downloaded *The Transporter* series, thinking he'd escape into some action flicks, but instead he found himself pulling up one of his comedy favorites. *Addicted to Love* with Meg Ryan. He loved her attitude in the film. He admired how Matthew Broderick was intent on fighting for the love of his life, until he realized that this love wasn't meant for him. For whatever reason, Felip found their journey something that gave him hope. He needed that hope.

Getting divorced was never in his plan, and it hadn't been his idea. His family supported him of course, and they never gave him a hard time, but he'd been angry. He felt like a failure. When Francesca first said she didn't want to remain married, he'd taken it as a challenge to be a better husband. He'd leapt over buildings and gone to the ends of the earth for her, and she still wasn't satisfied. He was still bitter about their breakup from time to time, and watching a film like

Addicted to Love gave him hope that perhaps he had simply been barking up the wrong tree.

Such a ridiculous romantic.

But instead of dreaming of Meg Ryan on the motorcycle, he saw a different blonde. And it made him smile.

"We are beginning our descent into Toronto and it's time for you to stow your laptops and larger electronic devices for landing. Please put your seats in their upright positions and place your tray tables in their locked positions. Thank you for flying Air Canada."

Felip's senses came online slowly. He attempted to stretch, but he felt an added heaviness on his right shoulder.

Cecilia. She'd fallen asleep before him, and sometime during the flight, she'd shifted and her head was now resting on his shoulder. There was a little puddle of drool on his shirt. It would have bothered him if it were anyone other than her.

He grinned and had to force himself to keep his hands in his lap when all he wanted to do was push her hair out of her face and watch her sleeping peacefully.

"Mrs. Gal— Oh."

The boy sitting behind him, who'd been eating the whole flight, leaned over their seat and was now chuckling.

"She's asleep," he whispered loudly to his friends, and Felip heard more chuckling.

"I am not," she said. Her words were slurred as if she were waking from a deep slumber. She stirred and shifted, placing her hand on the armrest, which currently held Felip's arm. He didn't dare move. He was stunned to be so close to her, and surprised he had no desire to move away.

"Oh, God," she said, sitting up slowly. Her eyes were wide with horror. "Oh, God, I'm sorry. I drooled on you."

Felip laughed, thinking all kinds of inappropriate thoughts. But he remembered they had an audience and he didn't want to embarrass her.

"It is fine. No harm done."

"No harm done?! *I drooled on you.*" She rooted around in her bag and found a napkin. "I'm so sorry. Here," she handed it to him. "I'm absolutely mortified right now."

There was more laughter behind them, and she turned what Felip could only describe as a death glare on the boys. Their chuckling stopped and Felip couldn't help but look back at their expressions.

The boys all sat up tall and did their best to not laugh, but the results were even more comical.

"Is something funny? Joseph? Do you have something to say?"

"No ma'am, Mrs. Galván, ma'am."

"That's what I thought. Nobody in your row would like to laugh at their teacher now, would they? Because why, Tui? Why would you *not* want to laugh at Mrs. Galván?"

"Uh, because you'll get us back?"

Felip bit his lip to keep from laughing as well, but he was not as successful as the boys. When a tiny little guffaw slipped out, her eyes of steel blue turned on him and the fire was back, only hotter than before.

"Do you have something to add?" she asked, her voice completely calm.

He shook his head. "No, ma'am, señora." His heart beat hard against his ribs. It was as if he were a student again, and that annoyed him and amused him at the same time. What power did this woman have that she could make a grown man like himself, the CEO of Cava Segura, quake in fear of her wrath? Or maybe it was more like a smitten man who desired to keep his woman happy.

Now he was getting way ahead of himself.

Her lip twitched, and he realized that she, too, was fighting back a laugh.

"Now, none of us will speak of this moment, will we?"

"No, Mrs. Galván," the boys recited in unison.

She nodded at them and then turned to look at Felip, her eyebrow raised.

He held up his hand in surrender. "Never. I swear."

She turned around to face forward and her lips turn up at the corners, which allowed him to breathe a sigh of relief.

This woman was intriguing. He wished their flight wasn't about to land.

The woman sitting in the window seat stirred and removed her eye mask. "Are we here already?" she asked sleepily. "Oh! Helloooo," she said to Felip, sticking her hand across Cecilia's lap. "I'm Gabrielle Reyes, and you are?"

Felip glanced at Cecilia as he reached across her and she looked...disappointed?

"Felip Segura. Mucho gusto."

"Sí. ¿Eres español?"

"Sí. Jo soc de Barcelona."

"Ah," Gabrielle purred, batting her eyelashes. "Catalán. Molt bé."

The woman was younger than Cecilia and much friendlier, but her attention meant very little compared to the enchanting woman beside him. Felip had had his share of women after him for his money, including American tourists out for a good time, but at thirty-nine, he was getting a bit old for that. He was always polite, but never encouraging.

The plane hit some turbulence and the cabin bounced, eliciting frightened sounds from many of the passengers. Cecilia grabbed for the armrest, and Felip let her have it.

"It's turbulence," he whispered to her, now aware how important it was to her that she seem in control in front of the kids.

"Say something," she whispered to him.

"Excuse me?"

"I don't know! Tell me something about Spain. Just move your mouth and make sounds. I need something to—"

"Ah! Vale. You are going to which city first?"

"Madrid."

"Excellent. Eh, you will most likely see the Prado, yes? The museum?"

"I guess," she said, her jaw muscles tense. The plane dipped low and she sucked in a breath.

"There are many important paintings there, but you must see el

Bosco, or the Bosch. It is breathtaking. You know Hieronymus Bosch? The Flemish painter?"

She shook her head and closed her eyes.

Felip was worried for her. He glanced at her traveling companion, who was speaking to the young men behind them, ignorant of Cecilia's plight.

"And you will see the Palacio Real, the king's palace? It is very beautiful. But one thing you might want to do, if you have time, is be sure to take the boys to the armory. It's not on the main part of the tour, but they will get to see suits of armor and weapons used by the Spanish kings. It is exciting for young men."

"Boys and their toys," she muttered.

"Sí," he said with a laugh. Even when she was terrified, she made jokes.

"What else?"

"Hmm? Oh, eh, how many days?"

"I don't know. Uh, three. I think. I think we go to Toledo one of the days. What's in Toledo?"

"Ah, the great painting of El Greco is there, the cathedral, and also the sword factory where they use the Damascus steel—"

"More toys. Got it."

"Cecilia, are you alright?" Gabrielle asked.

"I'm fine," she said through clenched teeth. "Felip was telling me about Madrid, weren't you?"

She gave him the fire eyes again.

"Sí. Claro. Eh, you should try to eat bocadillos, y calamari... Oh, churros con chocolate. Los madrileños love their churros. Of course, they are better in Barcelona, but Madrid is fine."

Cecilia turned to him, still not smiling but her jaw had loosened. "I'm going to make a guess that you're a little biased. You probably think everything is better in Barcelona."

"És clar. Por supuesto." He gave her his most winning smile and waited a few beats.

She raised her eyebrow at him, but this time her mouth was softer, almost a smile.

The plane hit the landing strip hard and they were thrown forward a bit. As a reflex, Felip threw out his arm to keep her from hitting her head on the seat in front of her, and she grasped his arm. They looked at each other in shock, and it was a moment before they moved back to their own spaces.

"Ah, shit. Mrs. Galván? Eduardo has a bloody nose."

Cecilia immediately shrugged off her fear and sprang into action.

"Excuse me," she said as she turned around in her seat. She shoved a wad of napkins at the boys. "Here. Put this under your nose and pinch the bridge if you can. Are you alright?"

"Uh-huh. I hit my face on the seat," he said through the napkins.

"Yeah, because you forgot to put your seat belt back on," Tui said.

"Shut up, I know," Eduardo said.

"He gets nosebleeds, like, all the time, though," Joseph said.

"Right," Gabrielle said. "I remember seeing that on your form. Let me see if I can get some ice." She pushed the button for the flight attendant, but since the plane was still taxiing to the terminal, the flight attendants remained strapped in.

"Do you have another shirt in your bag?" Cecilia asked him. The poor kid had blood all over his clothes and was bleeding through the napkins.

"Here," Felip said. He retrieved a handkerchief from his pocket and handed it over the seat to the kid, Tui. "Let me see if I can get the attention of the flight attendant."

Felip leaned out into the aisle and waved. One of the flight attendants hurried over to them as the other one got on the microphone.

"We're pulling into the gate, but I need to ask all of you to please remain in your seats while we see to one of our passengers."

The flight attendant approached with a concerned look.

"Can you please get this young man some ice and some more towels?"

"Of course," she said. "One moment."

She rushed off, and Felip turned to find Cecilia up on her knees, leaning over the back of the seat.

"Is it stopping, honey?"

"I don't know. I'm sorry, Mrs. Galván."

"It's not your fault, sweetie," Gabrielle said. "That was a tough landing."

"And hey," Cecilia said with a smirk. "You can say you've shed blood on Canadian soil."

Eduardo and Tui laughed…while Joseph tried really hard not to look at his injured friend.

Felip recognized that look. "You feeling all right?"

Joseph shook his head, his lips pressed together.

The flight attendant returned with the kind of ice pack you break open and handed it to Tui to give to Eduardo, in the window seat.

"The captain sends his apologies," she said. "Shall we get you and your group off the plane and then we can let the other passengers disembark?"

"That would be lovely," Gabrielle said.

Felip stood to let the ladies out, then stepped back to let the boys out. When Joseph pushed past him, Felip grabbed his arm and handed him the bag from the seat pocket.

"Just in case. I understand," he said quietly. "My younger brother can't stand the sight of blood, either."

Joseph's eyes grew wide and he gulped. "I almost lost it," he whispered.

Felip patted him on the shoulder. Tui grabbed his bag, as well as his fallen compañero's, and Cecilia led them off the plane. Felip watched her go in admiration and with a twinge of sorrow. That was the problem with meeting people on a plane, especially one as enticing as Cecilia. Their time was limited.

Once the flight attendants ushered Cecilia's group off the plane, people began to get up and get their things. Felip stood in the aisle waiting for his turn to leave when he looked down and noticed Cecilia had left her bag. He picked it up and slung it over his shoulder, slid his messenger bag strap over his other shoulder, grabbed his bag from under the seat in front of where Cecilia had been. He'd try to find her in the terminal, or else he'd leave it with the flight attendants at the counter.

He made his way off of the plane, and looked around for Cecilia. He spotted her and the three boys near the closest men's room and strolled in their direction.

"No, it doesn't hurt, Mrs. Galván. I'm fine. The doctor said I have a weak blood vessel in there. I try to be careful, but…"

"Face-planting into the back of a seat didn't help," she said as she wiped at his face with a wet napkin. "What you're saying is we're going to have to pick up some wet wipes and keep gobs of tissue handy just in case, huh?"

Eduardo laughed and then spotted Felip coming towards them. He elbowed Tui, who stood by his side, and they both smiled knowingly.

"¿Señora? I brought you—"

She turned on him as though she were irritated to be interrupted, but then she actually blushed. The slight pink hue to her cheeks had him puffing out his chest ever so slightly. He wished he could do more for her than bring her a bag…cook her dinner, massage her feet, run her a hot bath…

"Thank you," she said. She ducked her eyes, an indication of shyness he wouldn't have expected. She took the bag from him and slipped it over her shoulder. "For… Just thanks." She turned away quickly, and her dismissal stung.

The boys looked between them, then at each other, as if they realized a fellow man had been rebuked and were silently expressing their sympathy.

"Did you have another shirt in your bag?" he asked Eduardo.

"Nah. My mom told me I should in case my suitcase got lost, but I forgot."

Felip knelt down and unzipped his duffel bag. He'd placed his clean clothes in this bag and left his soiled ones in his suitcase. He found another FC Barcelona shirt and handed it to the kid. "Can't have you walking around covered in blood."

"Thank you, Mr.—"

"Segura. Best of luck." He gave one last smile to Cecilia before turning away.

Felip wasn't usually one to mope, but he was disappointed. He'd had a nice conversation with a pretty lady on a plane and that would have to be enough. It was time he moved on. It was a shame, though, that they hadn't exchanged any information.

No matter. Nothing he could do now but hit the food court. Eating would make him feel better. But he wasn't about to forget this lady anytime soon.

CHAPTER SEVEN

4:45 p.m. EDT Toronto, Canada – The Food Court

Cecilia had managed to avoid getting any of Eduardo's blood on her, but she was unhappy with the way she'd left things with Felip. She'd had a pleasant conversation with a very nice and incredibly handsome man, but she'd managed to be less than polite to him. He'd left before she could really thank him for returning her bag and helping with the kids. It wasn't entirely her fault. She'd been distracted by Gabrielle's flirtatious interruption and the nosebleed.

It wasn't like a man would pay attention to Cecilia when Gabrielle was around. The younger woman was gorgeous with her long, flowing, mahogany-colored hair, model good looks, and curves that would make Shakira feel inadequate. And she spoke Spanish, and apparently Catalán, as well...

"Check for amigos, everyone," Gabrielle called out to their group. They'd gone their separate ways to grab food, and it was time to board their flight to Madrid.

Cecilia made sure she saw Tui and Tony in line before reaching Gabrielle.

"Do you think your seatmate will be joining us?"

Cecilia had actually looked around for Felip at the food court but hadn't seen him since she'd had her awkward moment.

"I don't know. He didn't say which flight he was taking. We didn't talk that much." No, but she'd thought about asking him and decided she'd sound desperate.

"It could be ours, right? I mean, he is from Spain."

Cecilia shrugged. "Sure, I guess."

Gabrielle's eyes flared. "Aren't you even curious? The man is the definition of gorgeous."

"He's alright, I suppose," Cecilia said, and what a liar she was.

"Yeah, well, next time you should let me sit next to him," Gabrielle said, flipping her hair over her shoulder.

Cecilia had never been the man-eater type and didn't care for the competition aspect of dipping her toe into the dating pool. If Gabrielle wanted to dip whatever in that pool, it was fine by her.

"I'll be sure to do that," she said with a wink.

Okay, maybe she could take a gander and see if he was near their gate. She spotted him over near the restroom charging his phone, which he was talking on once more. Seemed the guy was either really popular or was never left alone. Was he talking to a wife? Girlfriend? Did he bang her ankles? Or anything el—

Jesus, Cecilia. You sound like a teenaged boy right now.

She'd always been a people watcher, fascinated by other people's lives, even when she was married to Greg. She'd try to make up stories about the person and the life they lived. Only now that she was single again, instead of it being innocent—"he probably gets three shots of espresso in his Starbucks," or, "she probably watched the Macy's ads for weeks waiting for that coat to go on sale"—it was almost lecherous—"I wonder when was the last time that guy pushed his girlfriend up against the wall and talked dirty to her while he ripped her panties off and..."

Yeah, she was definitely channeling her inner teenaged boy these days. Occupational hazard, or the result of too many years married to a mostly absentee husband whose idea of mixing it up involved leaving the lights on? The jury was out on that one.

They boarded the plane for the last leg of their journey and Cecilia prayed for sleep. Instead of her prayers being answered, she ended up sitting next to Jorge, who talked her ear off about all the things he'd learned about Spain in preparation. After three hours, his attention wandered to the screen on the seat-back in front of him, and he put in headphones to watch a movie.

Cecilia took the opportunity to get some rest and curled up to sleep. She was on the aisle this time and had watched to see if Felip was on their flight, but between the boys fighting over who would sit next to Tui and what movie they were going to watch on Eduardo's iPad, she'd been too distracted.

Gabrielle sat with Tony and Bill, and Mr. Santiago sat on the aisle across from her, with Mrs. Santiago on the other side of Jorge in the window seat. She'd offered to switch so the three of them could sit together, but he'd declined. She figured Mr. Santiago could probably use the break, since Jorge had talked to his father the entire flight to Toronto. Plus, Jorge was concerned that if they didn't remain in their assigned seats, there would be trouble identifying their bodies if there was a crash. Comforting.

She hadn't even been bothered by takeoff and landing this time, because she'd been thinking of how sweet Felip had been to try to distract her. That led to other wonderings about him, and by the time they'd landed in Madrid, she was really kicking herself that she hadn't asked for his number. There wasn't time to think any more about it, however, once they stepped off the plane. It was time for the show to start.

Once they'd passed through customs and retrieved their bags, they were greeted by their tour guide, Rosana. She was a petite blonde with large brown eyes and long hair expertly curled into long ringlets. She was dressed stylishly in an adorable gauzy skirt and blouse outfit with wedge heels that made Cecilia feel even more of a mess. Rosana was entirely put together and chipper early in the morning, something

Cecilia struggled with even on her regular schedule with a full eight hours of sleep. Gabrielle made the introductions and then they stood around Rosana in a circle, getting strange looks in their bright green shirts.

"Buenos dias, amigos. I am Rosana, and I probably slept more than you did last night."

They all chuckled, though many of them looked as though they were nearly sleeping on their feet.

Cecilia felt funky, and not in a good way at all. Airplane funk, public restroom funk, greasy food funk—she'd eaten the airplane food, and while it was decent, there had been a layer of grease on top of her pasta and cheese. What was up with Canadian cheese products?

"I have good news, eh? We go to the hotel first. You can take your bags up to your rooms and have five minutes to clean up before we go to see Puerta del Sol en Madrid, ¿vale? And later we go to el Prado."

Jorge raised his hand.

"¿Sí, señor?" Rosana asked, and they all looked concerned, wondering what he might ask.

"Why did you say 'bally'?" Jorge asked her. "What does that mean? I speak Spanish and that doesn't sound anything like any words I've ever learned."

Rosana smiled and glanced at Gabrielle. "Muy bien. We say vale like you would say okay. V-a-l-e is how it is spelled, eh? Vale? Are you ready to go to your hotel?"

"Ohmygawd, yes," Bill said from behind Cecilia. "I'm going to take the fastest shower humanly possible and get out of these disgusting clothes."

"That actually sounds like a great idea," Cecilia said as they walked out the doors...and into some majorly thick humidity.

"Oh, gross," Janelle said. "It's so sweaty, already. It's only eight in the morning!"

"It is warm, eh?" Rosana asked as she led the group across the lot to the bus. "Here it has been raining for weeks until last week. We finally have summer now. It will be around thirty degrees during your stay, but don't worry. Our bus has air conditioning and you will be cool inside your hotel. It is important to stay hydrated, eh? You will want to drink a lot of bottled water, which you can buy for around one euro at most places. Vale? Vale. We go now."

Cecilia hung back and let the others go before her. As she stood next to the bus, she took a look around. Madrid looked much different from an American city, but not like she'd expected, either. They were surrounded by large, blocky, beige and gray buildings with tons of wires and antenna visible. The airport seemed small from this perspective as well.

And then she spotted Felip as he climbed into a taxi.

"He's here in Madrid," Gabrielle said as she put her arm around Cecilia's neck. "Maybe we'll get lucky and run into him."

That reminded her of what Felip said when he'd sat next to her on the flight. Perhaps 13 *was* a lucky number.

CHAPTER EIGHT

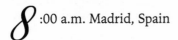:00 a.m. Madrid, Spain

"It is good to see you, hermano," said Tomás in Catalán when he answered the door to his flat. "I'm sorry I couldn't get you from the airport. I had a tour starting this morning and there was a problem with the bus driver. I had to call in Luís to drive for them."

Luís was their cousin, and together with Tomás, they'd formed a tour company that contracted with one of the larger international organizations to provide Spanish tour guides locally for their tours. Tomás was the only Segura son who'd opted not to work for the family wine business, which had been a point of contention with their father for many years. Felip had understood his need to get out from under Papa's shadow and had never begrudged him.

Felip was the eldest, followed by Alonso, then Tomás, and Mateu was the baby. Alonso remained in the military reserves and ran the security operation for the vineyard. The three eldest Segura brothers had been required to serve in the military, but Mateu had been fortunate to benefit from the change in Spanish law that stated after 2002, there would be no more compulsory service unless there was a national emergency. They'd all given him a difficult time about it and claimed it made him even more of a baby, a point he'd tried hard to overcome by being accepted to university in America, as Felip had, including earning a post-graduate degree at UC Berkeley.

"No problem. I should let you pay for my taxi though, eh?"

"Probably I should offer, but I won't. You can afford it."

The brothers hugged and Felip took a deep breath and let it out, glad to have a short visit with his favorite brother in one of his favorite cities before heading home.

"I can afford it, but you absolutely need to feed me. I'm famished. It has been too long since I've had decent food."

"Vale. I'll make sure Rosana has picked up her group and we go."

Tomás's thumbs tapped away on his phone for several moments while Felip stretched his back and looked around. Tomás had procured a nice place near the center of town, Puerta del Sol, and he had a fantastic view of the square. Today there seemed to be some sort of protest going on at one end. The Guardia Civil had trucks blocking off one of the streets.

"What happened?" he asked his brother.

"Eh, pensions, I believe. At least they aren't camping out like they did before."

Not too long ago, Felip had been visiting and the whole of the square was filled with protestors. They camped out with tarps and kitchens and vowed to stay until there was real democracy. It had been overwhelming, to say the least. Tomás had even lost business when some of his tours had been canceled due to the crowds.

"Everything is settled with Luís and the bus. He took the tour group to Hostal Persal and then he's going to be driving them around some today and tomorrow. He wasn't happy, as I'd given him these days off, but he's a good partner."

"That's good, though. Better than you driving a bus around Madrid. Those poor tourists."

Tomás joined him at the window and socked him in the arm.

"So, what do you want to do while you're here? You go back when, Thursday?"

"Sí. We're hosting an event at the vineyard this weekend. June will kill me if I'm not back. She's already mad I flew here instead of straight home."

"Why don't you sleep with her and get it over with? You two will likely end up together eventually anyway. She runs your life. It only makes sense."

Felip chuckled. "No way, hermano. I drive her crazy, and not in any way that involves chemistry unless it has to do with wine. She's married to the business. Besides, I've already been with a woman who doesn't know how to have fun and enjoy life. I won't make that mistake again."

Tomás patted his back. "Claro. Francesca leaving you was the best thing that ever happened to you."

Even Tomás knew what Felip hadn't recognized himself. He'd been so involved with growing the winery business, he'd neglected his marriage without realizing it. Then he'd done everything to be the perfect husband—until she asked for the divorce. He'd never failed at anything before. He hoped a second chance at love was in his future.

"It sure didn't feel that way at the time, but now? Maybe?"

Tomás laughed. "California was that good, eh? You meet someone?"

Now, why did that teacher with the fire in her eyes suddenly pop into his mind? Not that it mattered. "Not really. Hey, where was that tour group from that you had coming in today?"

Tomás frowned and pulled out his phone. He flipped through some pages until he found the itinerary. "Some place called Grass Valley, California," he said. "High school trip. Why?"

Felip rubbed at the stubble on his jaw and smiled. "They were on my flight."

"And?" Something in Felip's tone must have piqued Tomás's interest. "See something you like?"

Felip certainly had. But what did it matter? He was here, she was with a bunch of teenagers on a tour, and then she'd be back in California. It wasn't likely he'd have to go back there anytime soon. He'd set up Mateu with a smooth fix to his problems. But maybe...

There was always the chance that one of the boys would give her his card.

Oh yeah, he'd handed over his business card to the kids at the café in the airport. One of them had said he was a huge futból fan but had said he liked Real Madrid. Felip couldn't help himself; he'd told the kid, "You want to see real futból, come to Camp Nou and watch Barcelona play. If your teacher will allow, I could set up a visit."

The kid's eyes bugged out. "No way! Think Mrs. Galván would let us?"

Yes, bring your lovely teacher.

"I'll take that as a yes, since you're practically drooling over there."

Felip frowned at his brother. "It's because I'm hungry. Take me out and feed me. What are you good for, anyway?"

"I know, I know, vale, vale. I filled my kitchen with food for you, your highness, but I'll take you out. Don't worry."

"Let me clean up and then we go."

Felip carried his bags into the spare room, which doubled as Tomás's office for his business, and set them down on the bed Tomás had readied for him. The room was spotless and perfectly organized, with maps and schedule boards covering the walls. A big change from the younger brother who couldn't get his underwear into the hamper to save his life.

To be sure, Tomás was a great host. It was what made his tour company successful. Felip was proud of his brother's accomplishments. After years of traveling around the world with various tour groups, Tomás had started his own company and was completely self-sufficient within two years of business. At thirty-two years old, he was on top of the world. He was even dodging questions about marriage and grandkids from their mother better than Felip, who'd been given a bit of a reprieve after his divorce, but he knew time was running out.

"Four sons and no grandkids," she'd say often, shaking her head and muttering curses in Catalán. They were all on her list. Felip had certainly tried to give her what she wanted.

He changed into a clean set of clothes, washed up in Tomás's bathroom, and met him in the living room, where he was hanging up from a phone call.

"Rosana said they are all checked into their hotel. They'll tour the town center and el Prado this afternoon, then tomorrow they go to the Palacio Real and the Parque Retiro for a picnic and then dinner. Then the next day they go to Toledo…and you leave for Barcelona."

Felip let that information sink in. He could certainly find a way to happen upon them, couldn't he? That wouldn't be too creepy?

Tomás read him well. "Let's go get you some lunch, Casanova."

The heat radiated from the concrete and warmed Felip's skin like a lover's embrace. He was thrilled to be back in Spain. California was certainly beautiful, but he'd had no time to do anything but clean up messes while there. Someday he'd like to travel the entire United States… someday. He had a lot of somedays, unfortunately, because now was for work. For keeping Cava Segura on top of the Spanish wine industry and for keeping Segura's California operation in the black. He had his dear papa to answer to, and he didn't want to let him down, but sometimes he wondered what he was missing, devoting so much of his life to his work. Francesca hadn't seemed to care as long as she had his money to spend, but perhaps that had been in part a way for her to cover up any dissatisfaction.

"You look like you ate a sour grape." Tomás elbowed him as they walked down the narrow streets toward Plaza Mayor, where they could feast and toast Felip's success in California.

"No, tired of living in the past, eh? Do you ever think about all you sacrificed to get your business going? Maybe wonder if life could have been different for you?"

"Sí, claro. I could have continued traveling, seen the world, maybe found an island princess and lived in a hut by the sea. Then again, I could have ended up robbed and beaten on the streets, left for dead. Who knows what would have happened to me? I did what I needed to do, and now I do what I love."

Felip was happy to hear him say that. He wanted his brothers to be happy. As the eldest, it was his job, right?

They sat on the patio outside Gustos Madrid and ordered sangría. The server brought a pitcher and two glasses, and Felip licked his lips as he poured for both of them. They toasted and Felip downed the sweet and tangy mixture with a satisfied moan.

"This is exactly what I needed," Felip said as he finished his first glass of sangría and his second piece of bread. The server brought them two plates of tapas and some agua con gas, and they thanked him. "Good food, good company." He toasted Tomás again, and his brother shook his head.

"I'm glad you're here. It's not often that my big brother comes to visit me."

"It should not be this long between visits," Felip said with a frown. "I wish you could run your business from Barcelona, but I understand—"

"Barcelona is your town, hermano. Let me have something of my own." Tomás chuckled, but Felip understood there was something to his statement. It was difficult for Tomás to be in Felip's shadow, and some distance from their parents made his vocational decision easier to bear.

Shouts and laughter drew their attention to a group entering the plaza from the archway across from them. They made their way to the statue of Felipe III in the center and their guide called them together. Felip couldn't miss the bright green shirts.

"Ah, that's Rosana. Ohhhh. You mean the one with the long dark hair? She is beautiful—"

"The blonde. Señora Galván."

Tomás frowned at him. "A married woman? That's not like you."

"Divorced. Didn't change her name, you know; it is hard during the school year, eh? The kids are used to calling her by that name... What? Why are you looking at me like that?"

Tomás coughed a bit, as though his sangría had gone down wrong. "You got her whole life story on that flight, eh?"

Felip's cheeks hurt from grinning. He'd smiled more in the last twenty-four hours than he had in a very long time. His face was out of practice.

Across the plaza, he watched as she walked around the back side of the group, peeking over their shoulders as though she couldn't see or hear their guide.

Hear. He wondered more about her hearing impairment. Did it interfere with her quality of life? He had so many questions.

Just then, she tapped the big boy, Tui, on the shoulder. He turned and looked over her head before glancing down with a smile. She smacked his shoulder and gestured for him to move aside so she could push past him, and he laughed. From the little Felip had watched her with the kids, he imagined she had been teasing him about being in the way. She seemed to know all of them so well. It was fascinating, watching her interact with the students.

"So, I sold a kidney on the black market last week to pay my rent."

"What did you say?" Felip asked in shock.

Tomás gave a belly laugh and even slapped his thigh. "You are so preoccupied you did not even hear what I said to you. She's that interesting, eh?"

"More," Felip said. "I apologize." He folded his hands on the table and broke his gaze from the little teacher who was now standing off to the side of the group with her arm around one of the girls.

"And I'm going to be giving birth in about three months…"

"What?"

"Felip! If you want her so badly, why don't you go talk to her?"

"She is busy with the kids. They mean a lot to her. Besides, it will look like I'm stalking her. That's not very romantic."

Tomás shrugged. "It's not stalking if it's business, eh? I could simply go over and say I'm doing a review of Rosana's performance."

From a distance, he watched Cecilia walk the young girl away from the group toward a man with a cart selling bottles of water. She bought two and gave one to the girl to drink. The other she placed on her forehead. The poor young girl was very red in the face.

"I wonder if that girl is sick?" he asked, concern filling him with the need to act.

"It's very possible. It's much warmer than she's probably used to."

"Well, it was this hot when we left California. At least in St. Helena it was."

Cecilia paid the man for the water and led the girl over to a seat in a patio area, where the girl took a sip as Cecilia placed the cold bottle on the back of her neck.

"We should—"

"Sí, we should go." Tomás walked even faster than Felip over to the teacher and her student. Rosana was on her way over as well.

"Hola, Tomás. Felip. What are you doing here?"

Cecilia looked up as the two groups converged on her position, confusion evident on her face.

"Hola, Señora. I am the president of Viaje España, Tomás Segura." Tomás held out his hand to Cecilia, and Felip wanted to hip check him out of the way to be the one to help this enchanting lady and her señorita.

Cecilia shook his hand, her eyes wide, and when they landed on Felip, they went from surprised to suspicious. "This is Aaliyah. I'm afraid she's having a bit of heat stroke."

Rosana eyed them curiously. It wasn't like Tomás to hover over his guides. "I was about to send these two back to the hotel—"

"We can take them," Felip said without thinking. Tomás placed a hand on his shoulder and squeezed hard enough to remind him that he was trying to *not* be a stalker.

"Felip got into town this morning and we were having a drink over there," Tomás said, pointing at their table, perhaps to give credibility to their story. "It is no problem for us to take them back to the hotel. Does she need to see a doctor?"

The girl shook her head and looked up with tears in her eyes at Cecilia.

"No. I think I need to get her some water and perhaps out of this heat for a bit."

"Vale," Tomás said. "Rosana, I will lead them back to the hotel. You are going to lunch soon?"

"Sí. We were going to break for lunch when we get back to Plaza de la Provincia and then we're going to walk to the Prado."

"Bon. Vale. We will take them back to the hotel, and if the young lady is feeling better, we can send them to the Prado in a taxi. Vale?"

Rosana nodded and spoke to Cecilia. "You are in good hands. Tomás taught me everything I know about this city, and Felip, he—"

"We go, eh? Can you walk?" Felip said, holding out his hand to help Aaliyah up from her seat. He'd interrupted Rosana, unsure what she might say about him in front of Cecilia. Might she say Felip had taught her the best places to drink? Or maybe that they'd gone out on a disastrous date once? He hoped she might be more professional than that, but he couldn't take the chance.

Aaliyah took his hand and stood up shakily. "I think I can. If we go slow."

"Vale. We go slow. It is very, very hot here, also we are at a higher altitude than what you may be used to. It will take some time to adjust, eh?"

Aaliyah's eyes darted to Cecilia's and then she looked down at the ground as they walked away.

Something told Felip there was more than the heat going on here, and he was determined to see them back to the hotel, where hopefully the young lady would begin to feel better.

CHAPTER NINE

1:00 p.m. Madrid Local Time – Plaza Mayor

Cecilia didn't know how to feel about Felip showing up in Plaza Mayor. He hadn't said anything about his brother when she'd mentioned being on a tour, but then, she hadn't volunteered much personal information either.

She snuck looks in his direction as they walked back to the hotel. He and his brother were nearly identical, although Tomás had shorter hair, minus the silver, and didn't have the crooked tooth. Tomás walked alongside Aaliyah, talking to her about their surroundings and reassuring her that she would adjust after a little bit of rest. As the street narrowed, Cecilia dropped behind Aaliyah to let others past, which put her right beside Felip.

"I swear I was not following you," he said quietly.

Cecilia decided to have a bit of fun with him. "Maybe you were. How should I know? Do they have such things as restraining orders for stalkers in Spain?"

He halted and his eyes went wide. "I am sorry. I meant no harm, I will go—"

She laughed and pointed at him. "Gotcha."

His frightened expression faded, and his eyes narrowed. "You have a good poker face."

Cecilia shrugged. "It comes in handy in my profession." She figured since they'd been thrown back together, it couldn't hurt to ask him a few more questions about himself. "Do you work for your brother?"

He frowned and laughed like that was a ridiculous proposition. "Me? Work for my little brother? No, no. I work for the family business. My brother decided to go on his own to start his tour company. He is quite successful. But no, I do not work for him."

Cecilia raised her eyebrows. "Oooo, touchy subject."

"Not touchy, no. Just accurate. My brother is a free spirit. He has always wanted to travel the world. He did for many years, and then he wanted to share that experience with others, share what he loves about his country with them. I am very proud of him."

"That's really cool, actually." But she couldn't let him off the hook. "So, the family business. Like, the *family* family business? Like the Corleones?" *Oh God. What if he does? And I just asked him if he was in the mafia?*

"Ah. *The Godfather*. Well, we do have our fingers in a lot of areas, and sometimes I have to make someone an offer they can't refuse." He said the last with the sides of his mouth turned down like Brando, and Cecilia snorted in a very unladylike manner.

"What? You think that's funny?"

She tried to control her giggles.

"As a matter of fact, señora Galván, we run a very reputable business in the Catalonian wine industry."

It took all of Cecilia's willpower not to roll her eyes. *Great.*

"I guess that's reputable."

They turned the corner and she could see their hotel up ahead. Part of her wanted to run into the air conditioning and flop onto a bed for a couple of days, but she fought the urge as she was insanely curious to know more about this man. Even if he sold wine for a living.

"It is entirely reputable, I promise you. My family has been making wine for five generations. The vineyard survived the phylloxera plague of the 19th century, which killed off most of the grapes in Spain, and my great-grandparents replanted when their children were born in an area outside of Barcelona called Penedés. The company, Cava Segura, withstood the civil war. Today our winery thrives and we have the top-selling cava in all of Spain."

"Cava?" she asked, unsure what that was. Well, to be honest, she didn't know a whole lot about wine period. Grass Valley was close to California's wine country, and there were vineyards around the area, but she always thought the whole wine scene was pretentious. Probably would have been a good idea to have learned a little bit so she wouldn't seem like an idiot talking to him.

"Cava, sí, it is sparkling wine made here. It was invented after the plague and is one of the best-selling wines in the world. My family makes one of the finest."

He was so proud, but it wasn't like arrogance. He believed in his family and all they'd accomplished. She supposed there was something sort of endearing about that. Plus, she could truly listen to him talk all day and never get enough of his voice.

"Here you are, ladies," Tomás said. "You must pick up your room keys from the front desk each time you return. You may go to your rooms and get some rest. Felip, will you run next door and get them some bottles of water?"

Felip nodded. "Señora, is there anything else I can get for you?"

She shook her head. "No, thank you. I want to get Aaliyah some rest and then I think she'll be fine."

He gave her that smile that strangely made her feel like one of her high schoolers and left them in the lobby with Tomás.

Cecilia turned to thank Tomás, and his knowing smile gave her pause. She began to wonder about the coincidence of their meeting in the plaza. Perhaps it had been arranged after all. She raised her eyebrow and he chuckled.

Felip trotted up with bottles of water, a loaf of bread, and a bag of fruit in his arms.

"I thought she might be hungry as well."

Handsome and generous. She needed to focus on Aaliyah, not on how well his jeans hugged his—

"Thank you," she said, handing the water bottles to Aaliyah and taking the bread and fruit.

"Here is my card, señora Galván," Tomás said. "Please call or text me if you and Miss Aaliyah feel up to joining the group at the Prado museum, or we can come and collect you when it is time for dinner."

"Thank you, Mr. Segura. I will touch base after I let her rest for a while. Thank you again for your quick intervention."

Felip looked as if he wanted to say something. And she didn't move. They were caught in a tractor beam, staring at each other.

"Señora—"

"Thank you," she said, and dammit, but her face lit up in a goofy smile. Only thirty something hours with teenagers and she had turned into one. Hopeless. But then, he was so friggin' handsome. "Will I be seeing you again? Here in Madrid? Do you plan on following us again?"

His cheeks reddened ever so slightly. "Would that result in a call to la policía?"

"Depends on where you pop up." *Oh, gawd, Cecilia!* Before she got any more inappropriate in front of her student, she placed an arm around the girl's shoulders and led her away. "See you around," she said as they reached the stairs.

He was still smiling when she glanced back.

Aaliyah crashed as soon as they reached Cecilia's room. She had two beds in case one of the kids needed to be separated due to teenaged hormone-induced drama. While the girl slept, Cecilia took the time to text her mom.

I made it. I didn't die. And I might have met someone.

. . .

Cecilia looked at the clock. It was one in the afternoon, which meant it was four in the morning in California. Even though her mom was a ridiculously enthusiastic morning person, it was still a bit early for her to be up, she figured.

The bed looked so amazing. It was soft and neatly made with perfectly turned down sheets. She could lie down, just for a few minutes, and she might wake up human.

Gabrielle's voice came back to her. *"We stay awake until bedtime locally. That's how we defeat the evil that is jet lag."*

"Not even for a little cat nap?" she asked out loud, feeling the waves of exhaustion that rendered her incapable of rational thought. She was seriously having aural hallucinations.

"Trust me, you'll feel phenomenal after that first night of sleep, like it will be the best sleep you've ever had in your life and you'll wake up refreshed and ready to conquer Spain!"

"But what if I take a quickie rest and wake up feeling sort of okay and ready to at least..."

Buzzing against her cheek woke her from what felt like a coma. She flopped an arm over like a fish at Pike's Place Market, or at least what she'd seen on TV. She'd never actually been there.

Felip's image came back to her like some sort of dream sequence from a movie, all cheesy and wavy-like, as she let her face fall back on the bed. And his voice.

"I think she's asleep...I just woke up... Yes, I feel better, thank you... Let me see if she's awake. Mrs. Galván?"

Cecilia rolled over onto her back and her phone came with, still stuck to her cheek.

"Oh God, I'm dead. RIP me."

Aaliyah giggled. "I think she's going to need a minute... Okay... We'll meet you downstairs in ten—"

"Twenty!"

"Uh, twenty minutes. Thank you, Mr. Segura." Aaliyah hung up the room phone and moved over to Cecilia's bed. "Are you alright, Mrs. Galván?"

"That is yet to be determined. What time is it?"

"It's six o'clock. I guess we both took more than a nap."

Shit. She gave Aaliyah a worried glance. "We're going to be so busted. Ms. Reyes is going to be all 'you have to push through or you'll be a complete wreck.' Well, look at me! I'm a complete wreck!"

Aaliyah laughed again. "Well, we can't let her see you like this or she'll use you as the example. Come on. I'll help."

She checked her phone. Mom.

Well, hallelujah, single lady. Give me the deets.

Oh, God. She couldn't feel her fingers. Her hand had fallen asleep along with the rest of her. She gave it a shot and prayed it came out

I think I was coma. Sleep during day bad. Jet lag. He is handsome and his tooth is crooked.

Aaliyah helped her use a straightening iron to fix the creases in her hair and she held a warm washcloth against Cecilia's face to try to loosen up the outline of the phone on her cheek.

"It's no use," Cecilia finally said. "I'll have to slap some makeup on and pray."

Aaliyah seemed much better after water and rest. She'd been awake for a while before the phone call, apparently, as she'd also changed clothes and had freshened up. She looked adorable and happy, no longer frightened or worried. Cecilia hoped she'd remain like this throughout the trip.

Twenty minutes later they went down to the lobby and found

Tomás and Felip waiting for them. He'd changed into a short-sleeved button-up shirt and dress shoes with his phenomenal jeans.

"The rest of the group went ahead to the restaurant. We said we would wait for you," Tomás said.

Cecilia was mortified. She'd changed into a sundress, which was definitely cooler than her t-shirt and pants, but she was sure she still looked like she'd been in a coma. The bags under her eyes were giant suitcases. No, more like steamer trunks.

And damn, but Felip looked just as good, just as fresh as he had at oh-dark-o'clock. It wasn't right! Maybe he was a Spanish vampire, like Antonio Banderas in—

"Are you all right, señora?" Felip asked as they approached.

"Sure. Why? Do I not look all right?"

Tomás burst out laughing, and Felip's eyes went wide.

"I was worried when you did not answer the phone the first two times we called. I was going to have the manager let us in."

Cecilia worked desperately to keep her teacher face void of any alarm. If he would have found her in her previous state, she would have been mortified. She shuddered involuntarily.

"There was no need. We were, um…"

She looked to Aaliyah for help and the girl shook her head as if she had no clue.

"We were, um…" she tried again. Her brain was still too frazzled to come up with an excuse.

"Oh! We were in the bathroom trying out my straightening iron on Mrs. Galván's hair. Doesn't it look nice?"

Great. Now they had even more reason to look closely at her. Both men turned their attentions on her and she buckled under the pressure. She ducked her head and walked toward the door.

"So, we're meeting the others? Is it walking distance?"

The men chuckled, and Aaliyah scrambled to catch up with her. Cecilia was already out the door and looking in both directions before turning her body toward the right.

"Sí, pero, we're not walking that way," Tomás said. He gestured to the left. "Ladies first," he said.

Cecilia fought to regain her composure. It wasn't his fault she'd been unable to resist smashing her face into a pillow for several hours, which was forbidden.

"I think the rules about jet lag are kind of bullshit," Felip said quietly as he walked beside her. He leaned in closer and whispered, "I myself took a siesta back at Tomás's flat."

Cecilia's cheeks warmed. This man was too cute for his own good. But then she thought about how he didn't seem to have bedhead, nor a giant crease, and she grew irritated again. Perhaps she needed food? She didn't normally consider herself evil or to have bad intentions toward her fellow human beings. If only his wavy supermodel hair was a little more out of place, she might feel less of a mess.

Right. He had the kind of hair that looked even better messed up. *Hopeless.*

They walked about three or four blocks. Cecilia lost count as she was too busy looking around at all of the classic architecture and the number of international boutiques and eateries. She'd heard from Zoey that when she'd first started leading trips to Spain many years earlier, there hadn't been nearly as many options for shopping or food. Cecilia was happy to be there taking it all in. She loved the way the people moved about with a purpose but not in a hurry, how couples and friends carried on conversations in rapid-fire Spanish that sounded almost musical, and how everything seemed so easy. That was the vacation mind speaking. Of course, people here had struggles like anyone else, but at this hour of day, locals could be seen sitting at tables outside bars and restaurants, drinking cervezas or wine while talking animatedly or even singing together.

"Ah, here we are," Tomás said as they reached the restaurant. It was empty with the exception of their group.

"You made it," Gabrielle said. She stood up and walked over to them with a concerned expression. To Aaliyah, she whispered, "Are you feeling better?" When Aaliyah nodded shyly and took her leave to sit with her friends, Gabrielle's expression changed to one of suspicion.

"You slept, didn't you?"

Cecilia's eyes bugged out. "Well, not really. I mean, I wouldn't call it sleep, I—"

"I told you that was the worst possible thing you could do!"

"I didn't mean to—"

"She'll be fine," Felip said, coming to her rescue. "A little siesta is good for the soul, eh? She'll feel fantastic tomorrow. Jet lag can never interfere with a good time en España."

Felip winked at Cecilia and immediately her hackles relaxed. She didn't need a man to stand up for her, but if it meant getting her off the hook with Gabrielle...

"They should be bringing out the food any minute," Rosana said as she joined them. "Here, señora. You can sit here so you and Ms. Reyes and I can discuss the plans for tomorrow." She gave Tomás and Felip an appraising look, as if to determine whether they were evaluating her performance or just in her way.

"We'll let you ladies work," Tomás said. He grabbed Felip by the arm and led him over to the bar.

Gabrielle ogled them both unapologetically, but her eyes lingered on Felip. He smiled at them and then turned to hear whatever Tomás was saying close to his ear.

"They sure make them beautiful in this part of the world," Gabrielle said with a sigh.

"Who? Those two?" Rosana asked. "I suppose you could do worse than a Segura."

That seems rather cryptic. Cecilia wondered what she meant, but it appeared Gabrielle was sold.

"I certainly have done worse. I'd like to try one of them on for size."

Bleck. Wow. Okay, so it seemed Gabrielle had laid claim like some sort of conquistador. Like she'd planted her flag and said, "I claim this man on behalf of my vagina." That thought had Cecilia chuckling to herself.

"What's so funny?" Gabrielle asked innocently.

"Oh, nothing. Just wondering if they're one-size-fits-all? Or do you have to be—never mind. Oh, look! It's dinner. I'm starving." She sat at the table Rosana had gestured to and thanked the server for the plate he'd placed in front of her.

A huge slab of grilled pork took up half of the plate and the other half was French-fried potatoes. That was it. No veggies, no fruit. Oh. And bread for everyone. Cecilia looked around and watched the kids poke at it, look at each other's plates, and hesitantly take bites. Most of the kids shrugged and dug in after that, but there were a few who ate the French fries and tried to make the meat look a little smaller on their plate. Regardless, the kids were energized by the infusion of food and they chatted excitedly about the afternoon.

"How did everything go?" she asked Gabrielle.

"Oh, fine. The kids were great. They were a bit too exhausted to really enjoy the Prado, however. I found several of them sleeping in the café with their heads on the tables."

Rosana chuckled. "It is tough for the first day, but I think most of them at least got to see the Bosch and *Las Meninas*."

"Oh, that painting was amazing. I remember the first time I came here and saw it," Gabrielle replied.

"You will see *Las Meninas*-inspired statues all over the city as well as in other places en España, as the exhibit is moving around the country. The students will enjoy it."

Cecilia only half listened as her attention was drawn toward Felip and Tomás at the bar, where they were talking to Tony and Bill. Felip stared back at her. He held up his drink in a toast and smiled, while Tomás and the other men spoke to each other in Spanish in what seemed like a heated debate.

"What are they arguing about?" Cecilia asked.

Rosana listened for a moment and then rolled her eyes. "Futból. Claro. It appears your friends are rooting for Selección España for the World Cup, eh? Pero, the coach of the team was fired a few days ago for taking the job with Real Madrid. As my illustrious boss and his brother are both from Catalonia, they are not big fans of Real Madrid, nor the national team right now. In Catalonia, the people are not happy with the Spanish government. We will talk more about that when we go to Barcelona. But tomorrow we see the Palacio Real."

"The palace sounds cool," Cecilia said, feeling very out of her element. What could she even talk to these women about?

"It is beautiful, you will enjoy learning all about the history of our royal family."

"Felip mentioned something about the armory when we were on the plane. Will we be seeing that?"

Rosana's eyes flared. "You sat with him on the plane?"

Gabrielle pushed her long, lustrous hair over her shoulder. "Only because I fell asleep before he boarded, or else I would have insisted on having the center seat. He's delicious."

Rosana wrinkled her nose. "If you say so," she said. "I got him out of my system years ago. He and Tomás are more like brothers to me, eh? I don't see them like that." She glanced over at them at the bar, now speaking even louder. "Felip *would* know all about the royal palace. He dated one of the docents there. Anna."

Cecilia sighed. Of course he did. He'd probably dated all of the eligible women in Spain, or all of the women on the continent while traveling for business, and with that gorgeous smile and his charming ways...

Rosana thankfully moved her commentary from the brothers Segura to their itinerary for tomorrow.

"We go on a bus tour in the morning with Luís, and he will drop us off at the palace. We will have our tour, eh? And then then we go to lunch. We stop at a market and let the students experience shopping for food. We go to el Retiro for our picnic, and there we can rent the boats and the students can have turns with the paddles. We have dinner at a tapas restaurant and then we go to see flamenco."

"Wow, sounds like a full day," Cecilia said, praying the shoes she brought would stand the test of walking.

As if she read her mind, Rosana said, "Sí. I hope you brought your good walking shoes. You wouldn't want to hurt yourself so soon into the tour."

Cecilia looked down at Rosana's tall wedge sandals and wondered about the practicality of them while leading a tour.

"We'll be fine," Gabrielle said, waving off Rosana's concern. "We've been walking together for...how long, Cece?"

"Um, for at least two years, since we did the breast cancer walk. Thirty-six miles."

Perla, their principal, had battled breast cancer valiantly two years prior, barely missing any work, and the staff had all pitched together to raise money and awareness in their community. They'd trained for months to do the walk around the San Francisco Bay Area, and they kept up the habit, taking their half-hour lunch out on the track to gab and catch up. Sometimes they even walked after school for longer conversations, like when Cecilia was going through her divorce, or when Zoey and Gabrielle had been taking care of their grandparents in order to keep them from assisted living as long as possible.

Cecilia and Zoey, plus Perla, and their assistant principal Kate, had been friends for years. When Gabrielle was hired three years ago, she joined them. Walking, in addition to her yoga and spin classes at the local gym, kept her in fantastic shape.

Cecilia really did like her, but it was hard not to be a bit envious of younger women who hadn't been tarnished by divorce and still enjoyed the thrill of the chase, especially a woman such as Gabrielle, who possessed attributes that made the chase a sure thing.

"Vale. You have no problem then."

The kids finished their meals and seemed to be fading fast. Cecilia figured they should start walking back and let the kids all crash. Sadly, she was wide awake, and now that she'd had a meal, the last thing she wanted to do was lay down. Perhaps she'd take some melatonin and that would do the trick.

On the walk back to the hotel, Cecilia hung back, thinking she should take up the rear so as not to lose any students. Dusk had darkened the sky outside and the city streets were bathed in a soft orange and gold light as the sun went down. She took the opportunity to really look around, and she found herself wondering how many people had walked this path? How many women like her, at a crossroads in their lives, had walked down this very street at dusk and wondered about this beautiful place? She felt as if she could breathe in the history. The air was thick and heavy, as if the weight of experiences shared within the city still lingered. Tears shed by mothers over the loss of their children, laughter shared between lovers, violence enacted on unsuspecting tourists—

"You don't want to fall too far behind," Felip said next to her ear, and she nearly jumped out of her skin.

"Where did you come from? Jesus Christ! Here I was imagining Madrid may have its own Jack the Ripper! You're a menace!" She pushed him away playfully, now laughing at herself.

Felip chuckled and rubbed at his arm where she'd pushed him, as though it might have actually hurt. "I wouldn't want you to get lost," he said. "I apologize if I startled you."

She raised an eyebrow at him. "I'm going to have to keep an eye on you," she said in her best teacher voice.

"Maybe you should," he said with a wink and then gestured for her to continue walking.

Something about the tone of his voice sent a thrill through her. If some guy back home had dropped a line on her like that, she would have gagged on it, but something about Felip was so earnest and sincere, it didn't bother her. She could still see the kids up ahead, but they were out of earshot. She might be able to actually have an adult conversation with this man. That thought almost had her panicking.

"I get the impression that you aren't sure whether or not I am to be trusted. Is this true?"

Cecilia shrugged and strolled along slowly, glancing at him every so often. She peered into a window that had delectably decorated bins full of gelato. In fact, every block or so there were sweet treats. How did these damned Spaniards stay so thin with all of this goodness at every turn?

"I haven't decided. You haven't convinced me you're not in the *family* business, you committed assault in the airport, you're way too cheery in the morning…"

Cecilia looked ahead and counted to be sure no students had

gotten separated. Tui and Aaliyah walked at the back of the rest of the rowdy group, who shouted and hopped around more than actually walking. Cecilia loved their energy. Perhaps some of it was rubbing off on her because she was being downright flirtatious with a virtual stranger.

"I see," he said, his smile wide. God, she couldn't stop looking at that tooth. It was so endearing! His smile alone lit her up like a concert stage. "I do happen to like mornings. I like beginnings."

"Fair enough," she said. Their shoulders brushed, and she sucked in a breath. He was everywhere; his leg touching hers on the plane, his hand on her knee, and now... She stepped to the side to give him more room even though she was beginning to like his presence, perhaps too much.

"I'm sorry. I realize Americans like their personal space." He shoved his hands in his pockets, but the grin on his face was anything but apologetic.

"I'm not used to the, um, proximity," she said, and boy did she mean more than brushing shoulders with a man.

"Give it some time. You may find many things about España rub off on you."

She snorted and then pressed her lips together to keep from laughing out loud.

"What is funny?" He frowned and looked as though he might be questioning what he was doing with her.

It was her turn to apologize. "I'm sorry, it's...you spend enough time around teenaged boys and you find even innocent statements naughty."

His smile and blush were way too much. No way this guy was really this sweet and fun.

"My English is pretty good, but I admit sometimes I put it in my mouth."

Cecilia lost it at that. She stumbled on a cobblestone and fell against a wall, laughing heartily. Felip stopped walking and looked confused. It was obvious when he realized what he'd said.

"My foot! My foot, I put my *foot* in my mouth!"

"Yes, you do," Cecilia said, gasping for air at that point. "I couldn't...that was...wow."

"Fine. Have a laugh at my expense. I don't mind."

He was such a good sport, she felt bad laughing. "I'm sure if I tried to speak Spanish, I would make a complete fool out of myself. I shouldn't laugh at you."

"You were laughing *at* me? I thought you'd say you were laughing *with* me. That seems very un-teacher like, señora." He leaned against the wall next to her and elbowed her gently. Oh, this was too fun.

"Technically, I'm off duty, and you're not my student, señor." She cringed at her pronunciation. It always sounded funny to her because r's were always tough. Most of the time she managed to make it work, or at least enough for her ears.

"If you are off duty, we should have a drink. I must insist you at least try some sangría while you are here."

Damn. He had to bring up the wine again. She sighed. "I might be off duty, but I don't think I should drink if I'm going to be around the kids, and I think they'd notice if I didn't show up at the hotel. Sorry, you cannot tempt me with your wine."

He chuckled and placed an arm around her shoulder. "It was worth a shot. Vale. We should catch up to the others."

She didn't move away from him. Instead, she chanced a smile.

CHAPTER TEN

8:45 p.m. Madrid Local Time – Calle de Carretas

He held his breath. He'd invaded her space once more and this time she didn't protest. *She feels like heaven against me.* He let his hand slide down to the small of her back as they walked, and she continued to smile, but he thought if he got any more proprietary with her, she'd likely kick him in the shin.

He was cheeky enough to try it, so he removed temptation by removing his hand.

They walked a bit more down the block, laughing at nothing. She gazed appreciatively at everything around them and he loved seeing the joy on her face. He'd wished for this when they first spoke on the plane, that he could be a part of her happiness. He imagined the cheers of the Olympic crowds as he took the stand with his bronze medal. It was merely a half-embrace, after all. He wouldn't be at gold medal status until she—

Shouts up ahead shook him from his dreams, and he pulled Cecilia out of harm's way as a group of moped drivers dashed by them on the narrow street. She crashed against his chest, her blue eyes wide.

"Holy shit! That was close."

"Are you alright?" he asked. And then realized her body was flush with his. For a moment, they stood frozen, staring at each other as though they were the only two people left in the world. He couldn't help but admire the cleft in her chin below her dainty pink lips. He loved that she wore no makeup, her natural beauty was so strong, so proud. Her jaw, often stuck out in defiance or in demand of respect, made his insides molten.

"Mrs. Galván!"

Cecilia stepped away as Tui came trotting up to them.

"Are you okay? I saw that guy almost hit you."

"I'm fine. I didn't hear it coming." She tucked her hair behind her ear, and Felip nearly groaned at her blush. "Is everyone okay up there?"

Tui looked between the two of them as if he could read Felip's mind and knew how close he'd been to kissing the teacher.

"Actually, no. Mr. Segura? Your brother asked for you. I think Rosana is hurt."

Díos mío. Without thinking, he grabbed for Cecilia's hand and she went willingly. The three of them jogged up the street to where the group was crowded in a circle.

"¿Qúe ha pasado?"

Tomás crouched next to Rosana, who sat with her leg out in front of her.

"Can you take them to the hotel?" Tomás asked. "Necesita que la vea un médico."

Felip knelt beside her. "Are you hurt?" he asked.

Her face was streaked with tears, but she was putting on a brave façade for the kids. "Sí. Uno de los chicos se chocó conmigo esquivando al maldito ciclomotor. I think I bruised my tailbone."

"The driver barely missed us as well." Felip and Tomás helped her to stand, and she grimaced.

"I'll be fine. I need to, well…I'm not sure. Lie down?"

"I insist on taking you to see a doctor, Rosana." Tomás kept his arm around her for support, his concern evident.

"I'll escort the group back to the hotel and remain there until I hear from you," Felip said to his brother. They shook hands and Felip took a deep breath. He'd tagged along on Tomás's tours enough times to know what to do. He'd get the kids back to the hotel and stay there until Tomás sent word.

"Ladies and gentlemen, thank you for your patience," Tomás addressed the group. "I will be taking Rosana to a clinic to make sure she is not seriously injured, and my brother, Felip Segura, will be leading you back to the hotel and will get you settled in for the night. Don't worry," he said with a smirk. "He may be old, but I've taught him everything about being a guide he needs to know. You are in good hands. Vale? Buenas noches, estudiantes."

The kids waved goodbye to Tomás and Rosana as they climbed into a waiting taxi and sped away. Felip looked around to make sure they had everyone and noticed Cecilia attempting to soothe a distraught Tui. He was coming to see that her concern for her students was one of the things he admired most about her.

"Check for amigos?" Gabrielle asked.

The kids all looked around for their friends.

"We have everyone?" All of the groups checked in and Gabrielle nodded to him. They walked to the end of the block, where they'd turn left and walk a short distance to their hotel. The kids chattered excitedly about all they'd seen so far, including how crazy the drivers were to fly down the narrow streets so fast. If they thought this was crazy, wait until they got to Toledo, or even Segovia. The streets were far narrower in both places.

Once they reached the hotel, he counted to make sure they all made it inside. Cecilia and Tui brought up the rear.

"Go get some sleep. Everything's okay," she said before giving his arm a squeeze.

"Thank you, Mrs. Galván. Good night." Tui trudged up the steps, his head hung low.

"What happened to him?" Felip said to Cecilia.

She sighed. "Oh, he feels terrible. He'd pulled Aaliyah out of the way of the mopeds, but in the process, he managed to knock poor Rosana to the ground. He feels awful she got hurt."

Felip shook his head. "He should not worry. She's had much worse than a fall on her rear," he said, chuckling. "She once slipped on the stairs at the royal palace and barely missed taking out a group of tourists from Singapore. Thankfully, she only twisted her ankle that time and she was fine the next day. Those damn shoes she wears."

Cecilia didn't smile, she only raised her eyebrow at him. Oh no. he was coming to recognize that teacher look. He was in trouble now.

"What is that look for?" he asked, more curious than worried.

"She mentioned you dated a docent at the palace."

He thought about that for a moment. "Who? Anna?" He scratched his head. "Or was it Claire? Or maybe it was Babette?"

He couldn't resist teasing her. With every name, her eyes grew wider.

"No wonder you knew to tell me about the armory. You probably know that place top to bottom, ahem, so to speak, if you've dated all the docents."

Felip let out a boisterous laugh. "Maybe I'm secretly dating a member of the royal family, too."

"Do you know the royal family?" she asked, her curiosity overriding any jealousy.

"King Felipe? Sure," he said, feigning seriousness. "We Felips need to stick together, even if he is Castellano."

She rolled her eyes.

"Vale. I tell you the truth. My father met King Juan Carlos, the father of the current monarch, many years ago. Juan Carlos was a fan of my family's wine and even visited our winery once when I was a child."

"No kidding?" she asked. "That's pretty cool."

He laughed. "Sí. Meeting the royals is pretty cool. I met King Felipe shortly after his coronation as part of a business delegation from Catalonia."

"Really? What was he like?" she asked.

All the kids had gone upstairs, then a few had come back down to buy water from the vending machine before trotting noisily back up the stairs. He figured he'd be here for a while. Might as well get comfortable.

"Would you like to sit, señora? Or do you need to go upstairs?"

She shook her head and smiled guiltily. "I'm not tired," she whispered. "I probably did mess up by taking that 'nap'," she said, using finger quotes to insinuate she took more than a short siesta.

Gabrielle came down the steps then and her face lit up when she saw them. "Hey you two. I was going to sneak a quick glass of wine in the bar before going to sleep. Care to join me?"

A slight crease appeared on Cecilia's forehead, letting Felip know she did not approve. "I'm okay," she said.

"Felip? Can I tempt you?"

There was more behind her words than just a glass of wine, Felip thought. He smiled and shook his head, uninterested in both the wine and the offer.

"No, gracias. Señora Galván and I will keep watch."

She shrugged. "Suit yourselves." She sashayed into the bar at the back of the lobby and approached the bartender with a flirtatious smile.

Felip turned to continue his conversation with Cecilia and noticed her making a face at the younger woman. She froze when she realized he was watching.

"Oh my God, I'm sorry. I love Gabrielle, don't get me wrong. We've been friends since she was a teenager. She's…"

"A little overzealous?" Felip offered.

"Yeah, sure. Let's go with that. Her older sister is my best friend. She was supposed to be on this trip, but she was in an accident." Cecilia said.

"That's terrible," he replied. "I hope she is all right?"

"She will be. So, you were telling me about the king."

Felip chuckled at her interest. He gestured for her to take a seat in the oversized easy chairs of the hotel lobby. He really liked the Persal. Bold colors adorned the walls, broken up only by prints of modern

Spanish art and old photographs of Madrid from pre-Franco days. Low tables made of marble with industrial-looking metal legs held antique books, and worn leather armchairs with metal rivets around the armrests invited guests to stop and chat about their experiences in the city. Felip appreciated that they had the lobby to themselves at this hour and intended to enjoy this time with the teacher.

"What can I tell you about King Felipe. He's tall? Quite dashing? Married a television personality? He is not a huge fan of Catalonia right now, nor are we of the government's current political leanings, but for a king, he's 'pretty cool,' as you say."

Cecilia laughed and tucked her hair behind her ears. She slid off her shoes and tucked her feet up underneath herself. When she'd come down to the lobby after she and the young girl had rested, she'd changed into a loose-fitting sundress in a lovely pale blue that brought out the color in her eyes. It ended right at her knees and revealed shapely calves. Her skin looked luminous, as if it hadn't seen much sun. She'd need to be careful here in Spain. The sun sought out lovely skin such as hers and would burn her painfully if she did not take precautions. He'd have to warn her. Perhaps he'd keep her close and offer to rub sunscreen onto her shoulders and...

Felip had likely been staring while he'd let his mind drift, but Cecilia brought it back.

"So, Anna, and Babette, and Claire. And Rosana?"

He flinched. Just how much had Rosana talked about him?

"It's not like it sounds. Whenever I am in town, Tomás and I often meet up with people he knows from the tourist industry. I may have had a few drinks with them, but that's about it. Rosana...we attempted to go on a date once, not too long after my divorce, and it was a disaster." He barked out a laugh remembering the evening.

"You're divorced?" she asked.

"Sí. Going on four years now."

She nodded, but he couldn't discern her feelings about his statement. "Tell me about the date."

"You really want to know?"

She laughed. "Sure. I love disaster stories. *Godzilla* is one of my favorite movies."

He laughed. She said such things…

"Alright. I arranged for us to have dinner and go to a club that Tomás swore was a great place here in Madrid. She hated the dinner, complained about the food, the wine was shit—"

"No! It wasn't your wine?"

"No. I let her order. She wanted something French and it was awful."

"And you being a gentleman, you went along with her wishes. Okay. Then what?"

Felip couldn't believe he was telling her this. "So, we got to the club, and I had been a little unsure. I'm not a great dancer, I much prefer to watch the people, but she insisted. Tomás is the dancer in our family, not me. After the third or fourth time I stepped on her feet, she groaned in frustration and took us back to the bar, where she proceeded to keep drinking that awful wine. I suggested we try something else. We decided on a Segway tour. I hadn't realized how affected she was by the wine until we arrived at the meeting point for the tour and she got sick all over me. We agreed after that night that we weren't compatible for dating, but have remained good friends."

Cecilia regarded him with some expression he couldn't quite interpret. Had she been horrified? Would she think he was not someone she would want to have fun with? Felip hadn't realized how much he'd laid himself open with that story, or how much he desperately hoped she wouldn't be turned off. The moments it took for her to speak were torture.

"Segways sound more fun than dancing," Cecilia said.

And he could breathe again.

"Mrs. Galván?"

One of the girls stood at the foot of the stairs.

"Yes, honey?"

"I'm sorry. I went by your room… Do you have any Band-Aids? Janelle got a blister on the back of her heel today. She didn't even know and now it's bleeding."

"Sure. I'll be right there. What room are you in?"

The girl told her room 7 and then turned to go back upstairs. Cecilia pushed herself out of the chair and smiled apologetically. "I'm sorry. Duty calls." She pushed her hair behind her ears and looked at Felip from under those bangs. He'd already decided that was what she did when she was unsure.

"Will I see you again? I mean, are you going to continue stalking me?"

Felip stood and approached her. "Would you like to see me again?"

Cecilia tried to seem unaffected. "I guess. Madrid is a huge place, Spain is a giant country. We're bound to run into each other again, right?"

He took her hand in his and rubbed his thumb across her knuckles. *Dios*, how he wanted to pull her into his arms and taste those sweet pink lips... "I have a feeling I'll see you again, señora. Go tend to your flock and try to get some sleep. I'm sure tomorrow will be a challenging day."

Ever so lightly, she squeezed his hand before letting her fingers slip through his as she pulled away. "Thank you, Felip. Goodnight."

He watched her climb the steps, his chest puffing out once more when she turned back and smiled before turning the corner and moving out of his line of sight.

"Qué bonita," he murmured.

"She *is* cute," Gabrielle said. "A bit standoffish at times, and she can be impatient with others, but she and my sister have been friends for a long time. I could have handled this trip on my own, of course, but our principal insisted two of us go." She rolled her eyes.

"You are lucky to have her," Felip said. "She's wonderful with the children." His phone buzzed. Tomás. "Perdón," he said as he stepped outside the lobby doors to take the call.

"Hermano," Tomás said. "Necesito un favor."

When he hung up the phone, he knew three things:

He would not be returning to Barcelona on schedule.

June was going to kill him.

And señora Galván might very well think he was stalking her, but he was going to take advantage of this extra time to woo her.

CHAPTER ELEVEN

8:00 a.m. Madrid Local Time – Hostal Persal

Cecilia was late getting downstairs the next morning. She'd helped Janelle put moleskin on her shoe to avoid further damage to her heel and applied fresh Band-Aids to provide a barrier. Then Eduardo was having contacts issues again so she went over to the Santiagos' room and was able to get a fresh bottle of solution from Mrs. Santiago, with the promise she'd replace it as soon as they could get to a pharmacy. Then Tui needed to borrow a portable charger for his phone, as the adapter he'd brought didn't work in the plug and he hadn't noticed until this morning. Thankfully Cecilia had brought two, just in case.

When she got downstairs, she was greeted with a surprise. The group was gathered in the lobby listening to a man speak. When she was able to push through the tall kids in the back to get to the front, she found Felip.

"It appears Rosana will need to be on bedrest for the next couple of days at the very least, as she's bruised her tailbone. Quite painful, unfortunately. Until she is able to rejoin us, or my brother fires me, I'll be your guide."

His eyes found Cecilia's and he smiled weakly.

She backed away from the group and tried to compose herself by gathering up a small, portable breakfast from the room at the back of the lobby. Food. Right. Necessary for the day. The layout looked delicious. Fresh yogurt, cereal varieties, organic fruit juices in tiny bottles. There were hard-boiled eggs, some kinds of meat and cheeses, and several different types of toast. The kids had definitely been through, as there wasn't much left, but she grabbed a couple of pieces of fruit, two chocolate chip muffins, because they looked delicious, and—

"Cecilia," Felip said.

Just the way he said her name made her swoon. She wasn't one to be turned on just by an accent, but there was something about the earnestness, the sincerity, the admiration he showed her that made her feel respected. Who knew respect could be sexy? Aretha did, of course, but Cecilia was seeing it and feeling it in action now, and it thrilled her.

She turned around with her hands full and a guilty smile on her face. "Hi." At least she didn't have food in her mouth, but this was equally embarrassing.

Felip grinned at her haul. "Good to see you grabbed provisions. It will be a long day."

"Yeah, well, I always eat breakfast." *Wow, that was a clever comeback.*

"Check for amigos, everyone," Gabrielle called out from the other room.

Cecilia set down her food on the table and started wrapping it in napkins to shove in her bag.

"Cecilia, I hope this isn't…I didn't mean for this to happen. My brother didn't have anyone else to step in last minute, so he asked me."

She slung her bag over her shoulder. "Did you hire that crazy moped gang last night to rundown Rosana?"

He balked. "Of course not."

"Then it's not your fault. You stepped in to help your brother, right?"

"Right, but I don't want... I just—"

"What?" she said, confused.

"Felip! Venga aquí, por favor. ¡Nos vamos ahora!"

Cecilia wanted to roll her eyes. Gabrielle obviously wanted to impress her new partner guide. She glanced at Felip as they walked over and noticed he looked a little green.

"Um, I guess it's time?"

"Are you nervous?" she asked, surprised. "Mr. Wine Peddler? Mr. World Traveler?"

"No!"

But he was, she could tell. His eyes were wide and he pulled on his collar.

"No?"

"No. I have led tours before," he said, sounding rather indignant.

"Really," Cecilia said. "Where?"

He rested his hands on his hips and glanced nervously at where Gabrielle had gathered the kids and was lecturing them about what they would be seeing today.

"At the winery," he mumbled.

"Excuse me?" she teased.

"At my winery. But I've been on plenty of tours with Tomás, and besides, we're picking up a madrileño for the bus tour, and then we will have a guide at the palace."

Cecilia tapped a finger against her lips. "Would that be Anna? Or Claire? Or maybe Babette?"

Felip paled noticeably and he started to speak, but Cecilia decided to give him a break.

"Vamos, señor Segura," she said, pushing him playfully toward the kids. "Your estudiantes await your expert tour guide skills."

She laughed and sauntered off toward the group. Felip caught up to her, placed a hand at her lower back as he had last night, and spoke close to her ear.

"Enjoy your breakfast, profesora."

He enunciated the four syllables of that word so clearly, she got chills from his breath against her sensitive ear.

Oh, today was going to be fun. This was a safe way to get in some trouble, right? Felip could be a nice man, a safe man, for her to flirt with, have a good time with, and she wouldn't have to worry as she was leaving in a week or so. This was exactly what a woman like Cecilia, recently divorced but separated long enough to know her feelings, should be doing with her life.

They walked about four or five long blocks to catch the bus. Felip explained that due to construction, the bus couldn't get any closer to their hotel. Cecilia was glad the driver hadn't even tried. Once again, she brought up the rear so she could keep an eye on the group. Gabrielle walked up front with Felip, talking his ear off from the looks of it.

"Do you think we'll get to see the king?" she heard Kristin asking Janelle.

Jorge overheard as he was only a few steps behind them.

"He doesn't live at the palace. The royal family keep apartments outside of town. The palace has three thousand, four hundred and eighteen rooms and is over a million square feet. If he's even there right now, we likely wouldn't see him as they only have part of the palace open for tour groups."

The girls looked at each other in surprise. "How do you know so much?" Janelle asked him.

He blinked a few times before he answered. "I read about it before we came. I wanted to know what questions to ask."

Kristin giggled. "Sounds to me like you don't have any questions. Maybe you'll teach the tour guide a lesson or two."

Jorge shrugged and kept walking. Cecilia loved that he'd been well-accepted and respected by his peers. The other boys ribbed him, naturally, but they took care of him, also. Eduardo was one of his fiercest protectors.

They reached the bus and piled on. Cecilia climbed on last and fought the urge to roll her eyes. Gabrielle sat next to Felip in the front row and had her hand on his arm while she laughed at something he said.

So that was how it was going to be.

But Felip caught her eye as she moved past their row, and he gave her a smile that took her back to the previous night.

Whoa.

When they'd nearly been run down by the moped gang, Cecilia had been embarrassed to be clutching the poor man. Until she'd looked in his eyes.

Lust. She hadn't been looked at like that in...maybe not since before Greg. Maybe not ever. No, it had been years since a man looked at her like he wanted to consume her, and though it was fleeting, she could have sworn he wanted to kiss her. She wouldn't have minded one bit, which was unsettling. Just as she hadn't been lusted after by her ex-husband, she hadn't felt this out of control around a man.

Greg had been like an old standby. He'd been comfortable, like a broken-in recliner. He'd been safe, like the boy next door he literally was. Growing up in Grass Valley meant everyone knew each other, and when his family moved in before they'd started high school, they'd immediately hit it off. They separated for college, her to Sacramento State and him to UC Berkeley, but they'd remained close. When they graduated, they had a long conversation and he compromised when they married, agreeing to move back home for a few years while he and his friends gave their startup a shot.

He'd had ambitions. His start-up company he and his college buddies formed grew astronomically until they expanded, opening an office in Oakland and another in Boston. He'd never wanted to move back to Grass Valley, but in the beginning, he was fine with it because he could work remotely. It wasn't until they had product to sell that he had to start traveling. He'd been so excited, Cecilia couldn't exactly tell him no. And it was fine for the first couple of years, she actually didn't mind the time alone. And then she'd become suspicious.

"If everyone could please take your seats. I am Antoinette, your local tour guide, and I would like to welcome Grass Valley High School, and joining us today we have Rio Grande High School. You are both from California, eh? Bien. Today, you make friends."

Cecilia introduced herself to the chaperones that were sitting in the row behind her and glanced back to see that their group was much larger. There must have been thirty of them. That made Cecilia grateful for her little group. She watched as her students, who'd chosen to sit at the front of the bus all together, looked around curiously at their fellow travelers. From what Cecilia knew about Rio Grande, they were in a much different socioeconomic level than her students. She hoped that they all played nicely together. She turned around when she heard Antoinette addressing the group again.

"We go to see the city of Madrid, eh? The capital of España. We will explore some of the neighborhoods and then we tour Palacio Real. After that, we go to Parque del Retiro, where we will have a picnic and you will have the choice to see the botanical gardens or rent the boats on the water. ¿Vale? Any questions before we leave? Muy bien. Everyone say hello to our bus driver, Luís Segura."

The bus occupants all said a loud "Buenos días" and Luís waved enthusiastically before pulling away from the curb and into the busy Madrid traffic. Antoinette kept up a steady commentary about the areas of Madrid they were exploring this morning, and Cecilia was glad she'd grabbed a coffee to go. She didn't want to miss a moment. She'd been so grumpy about taking this trip in the days leading up to their departure, so resistant to trying something new, but now her mind was opening to the beauty of exploring an unfamiliar place.

Every stretch of street brought new sights that planted ideas and questions in her mind. What were the people really like? Did they go to jobs like back home? Did they drive themselves into the ground with their desperation to succeed? She'd heard that in Europe, people had different philosophies on life and work and the measure of success. And what about education? What were the schools like here? What were teachers like? Students?

She surprised herself with how much she wanted to know. Virtually overnight, she'd gone from hoping to survive this cross-country trek to a true traveler. Could she actually relax into the role of observer? Would she be able to venture out of her comfort zone and try new experiences?

The more titillating venture...would she allow herself to get to know Felip?

What could be the harm? It wasn't like anything could happen romantically between them. They were surrounded by teenagers, ones she was responsible for, but they also lived an ocean apart. He was attractive, sweet, and ridiculously fun to be with. They could play, but when she left a week from Friday, they would say goodbye. It would behoove her to remember that. The attention was fun, and the thought that he might be attracted to her was thrilling, but anything more than that could hurt. Really hurt. Cecilia knew herself well enough to know that she needed to be careful.

"And here we are approaching the Plaza del Toros de Las Ventas, Madrid's premiere bull fighting venue, the third largest in the world. Built with Moorish architectural influences, which we call Mudéjar, Las Ventas can seat twenty-five thousand spectators and was inaugurated in 1931. Madrileños just finished the San Isidro festival, which is the height of bullfighting in Madrid. We will be leaving the bus here for a short visit. You can walk around and take pictures. Please be back at the bus in fifteen minutes. Vale?"

The bus came to a halt a bit abruptly, pulling Cecilia out of her daydreams. She'd only been half-listening to Antoinette as it was noisy in the bus. The other group was not quietly and respectfully listening to their guide. Thankfully her kids were, but Antoinette was not where Cecilia could see her, so lipreading had been out of the question. She stood and stretched her back and waited her turn to exit the bus. When she stepped down onto the curb, her breath caught.

The arena was massive, much more majestic outside of the bus than from behind the tinted glass of the windows. Her eyes couldn't take in the totality of the arena from this perspective. She listened to the kids gasping and murmuring their "whoas," which tickled her. She loved that the kids were excited about this, too.

"Mr. Segura? Have you ever been to a bullfight?"

Joseph and Eduardo descended the long concrete staircase with Felip, one on each side, peppering him with questions. Cecilia remained behind them, listening attentively.

"I have been to a bullfight, yes. Although, in my native Catalonia, bullfighting has been banished. In fact, the major bullfighting arena in Barcelona is now a shopping mall. You will likely see it on your trip there."

"A mall? Get out!" Joseph said.

"Sí. All of the popular stores are there, some you may recognize, like Lush, Sephora, Desigual and United Colors of Benetton, all stores I believe I've seen in America. It's actually quite impressive. I was happy to see the building repurposed rather than left to rot or torn down as in other countries."

"Is it really, like, bloody? Bullfighting?" Eduardo asked.

"It's, eh, mmm, I'm not sure how to describe it. There is blood. The matador makes several strikes before the bull is killed, so yes, there is blood. As a boy, it was very exciting but disturbing at the same time. You put yourself in the bull's place and you think it is not very exciting. My brothers and I were pleased when it was banned in Catalonia. The last bullfight there was in two thousand eleven."

"Dude," Joseph said to Eduardo. "I kinda want to see it, you know, to like, experience it, you know?"

"Yeah, but I don't know," Eduardo said. "Like, I've already thought about going vegetarian because I can't stand the cruelty in how we get our food, feel me? Like, watching a bull get taunted and killed just seems like glorifying the cruelty."

"True story," Joseph said, then he shuddered. "I can't even watch those SPCA commercials, for real. I hate to see animals suffer."

Cecilia was proud hearing her boys talk. She'd encountered so many students in her time who had strong moral compasses and were thoughtful about the things that really mattered. Whenever people complained to her about "kids these days," she'd barrage them with tales of all the good things her students said and did on a regular basis. Good kids were generally the rule, not the exception.

"Mrs. Galván? Would you ever watch a bullfight?"

All three turned expectant gazes on her. "Um, I'm not sure. I think it would be interesting to observe and try to understand why it's important to them, but at the same time, I don't think I could watch an animal be tortured."

The boys nodded. Felip offered a guarded smile, as though he'd been uncertain what kind of response she might have had.

"When we went to Mexico to visit my family two years ago, my uncles took me to a cock fight. It was awful, bruh. I couldn't get out of there fast enough."

The boys walked on, talking about what Eduardo had experienced in more detail, and Cecilia chose not to follow and hear any more about it.

"The boys are quite astute when it comes to discussing morality."

Felip strolled alongside her as she took in the massive stone structure.

"They really are. With kids like that, teaching is really more facilitating. You set them loose and they run with whatever topic you're trying to teach them."

"I'm sure in many ways, your guidance has helped them reach that level of maturity."

"Yeah, well, they've all come a long way from Life Skills."

Felip chuckled. "Right. Sex education. I can only imagine."

Oh, Cecilia could imagine. *He smells so good. How is that possible?*

The air outside was already stifling and her perspiration was reaching unsafe levels. She felt moisture on her upper lip and wondered if she needed to wipe it away. Would he notice if she started sweating like a pig? And oh, what if she had a catastrophic deodorant failure? As close as he was to her right now...

"It's warm already," she said, stepping away from him a bit out of sheer terror.

"It will be much hotter by the time we reach the park. Luckily there is shade there next to the water. The boats are fun to paddle. What do you think? Would you like to be in my boat?"

"Felip? Felip!"

Gabrielle strolled over, looking perfectly coiffed and made up, as though the temperature didn't affect her at all.

"Antoinette wanted to ask a question, can you come with me?"

Felip gave an apologetic smile and walked off with Gabrielle. Antoinette was probably about the same age as Cecilia and dressed conservatively in slacks and a blouse. Cecilia had opted for a knit sporty dress that had advertised it wicked away sweat. Lord, she hoped the ad was correct.

Cecilia caught up to the girls and together they gazed in wonder at the large sculpture of a matador suspended above the ground, while a bull was taunted by his cape. As they circled the statue, taking it in on all sides, they noticed that from the rear, it appeared the matador was headless. Then they noticed on the backside of the statue, a chair with a matador's suit hung on the back and a weeping angel kneeling beside it, all made of bronze. It was meticulously detailed and the girls took several pictures.

"Look! Mrs. Galván! What is this?"

The girls hurried over to a statue of a woman in a wide-bottom dress. It was painted red and gold and seemed somewhat out of place in front of a bullring.

"Ah, recall the painting you saw yesterday in el Prado? *Las Meninas?* De Velázquez?" Felip asked as he joined them. "These statues are all over the city and beyond. The artist, Antonio Azzato, created them and spread them around the city for artists to decorate in ways that evoke all that is Madrid. They are very creative."

Cecilia turned to look at him and he smiled, standing close to her once again.

"Are you sure you aren't needed for some important guide meeting?"

He chuckled and rubbed at his jaw. He leaned in and spoke close to her ear.

"Your partner, señorita Reyes? She is quite persistent."

Cecilia snorted. "Well, you are an eligible bachelor, aren't you? Heir to the *family* business? You're just the sort she's been looking for." Cecilia winked at him.

"I wouldn't say I'm that sort." He put his hands on his hips and frowned, looking in Gabrielle's direction.

Cecilia glanced at Gabrielle in time to see her wave at Felip.

He waved back and said through gritted teeth, "Help me."

"Mrs. Galván? Can you take our picture?" Kristin asked. She handed her phone over and the girls posed.

Cecilia snapped several different pictures of the girls. "And how do you suppose I do that?" she asked Felip as though they weren't discussing such a sensitive topic.

"Mr. Segura? Will you take a picture of Mrs. Galván with us?"

"I would be happy to," he said, taking Kristin's phone from Cecilia. She smiled innocently at him, and he mumbled something under his breath in another language. Cecilia wasn't sure if it was Spanish or Catalán. She didn't know enough of either to be able to tell, but they both sounded sexy as hell coming from him.

Cecilia walked around the back of the statue, which was nearly as tall as her, and posed with her arm around Janelle's shoulder. She smiled at Felip and held up the peace sign like the girls were, trying to imitate their swag and probably failing spectacularly.

Thundering footsteps echoed behind them as Felip steadied the phone, then the weight of Tui's giant arm came down on her shoulder, nearly knocking her over. The boys had evidently decided to join their picture. Felip grinned and took a few more shots, which grew progressively sillier.

As Felip handed the phone back to Kristin, she thanked him, and the girls meandered off. Aaliyah glanced back at Tui and smiled invitingly. Oh, Cecilia was going to have to watch those two. It appeared love was in the air.

"Mrs. Galván, those kids from the other school are—"

"Bruh," Joseph said to Eduardo in warning.

"What? They were all bragging and shit that they get to drink here. We signed papers saying we wouldn't, but they get to?"

Cecilia had wondered about that rule. Gabrielle had said that while the drinking age is 16, Zoey had always decided to not let the students drink as it made it much easier to monitor them, and she didn't want to be held accountable if the kids had issues related to drinking. Made sense to Cecilia, but she knew it would be a temptation, especially if the other kids they were traveling with were drinking.

"You signed a contract," Tui said, saving Cecilia from having to answer. "That's your word, bruh. Who cares if they get to drink? I don't need to drink to have a good time here."

Cecilia knew that Tui's family were very conservative and very involved in their local LDS organization, therefore alcohol of any kind was not permitted. Most of the Mormon kids she knew were outspoken about their abstinence from drinking and drugs, and the fact that many of them were popular helped out a lot.

"Drinking is much different here than in America," Felip said.

Cecilia wondered what he might say about it, since he made his living off of alcohol sales, but then Antoinette called them back to the bus. *Saved by the bell.*

CHAPTER TWELVE

*1*0:20 a.m. Madrid Local Time – Palacio Real

By the time the bus arrived in the underground parking, Felip was ready to bolt.

If Gabrielle touches my arm one more time and throws her head back in laughter...

He needed to make it clear that he was not interested without being rude. He'd promised Tomás he'd stay with the tour at least through the weekend, when he might be able to relieve one of his other guides to take over or Rosana might feel better. That meant he'd be working with Gabrielle and he couldn't take the constant flirting, especially not when he hoped to be closer to Cecilia.

June, as he'd predicted, had thrown a complete tantrum.

"So help me, Felip, if you are not here Sunday for the event, I will make you suffer! Don't think I won't!"

He wisely kept his comments to himself. He already knew she'd make him miserable for taking a vacation. Perhaps he'd send *her* on one, make it mandatory for her, when he returned. None of this could be helped. As Tomás's silent partner in the tour company, he had a vested interest in this tour going off without any more problems. Though he'd only planned on a couple of days with his brother before returning home, he knew he had a mountain of issues waiting for him. His mind knew it would be best for him to return to Barcelona as soon as humanly possible.

His heart, however, was thoroughly committed to spending this time with Cecilia. He was having more fun than he'd had with a woman in a long time. She gave as good as she got, and she was bright and inquisitive. He felt relaxed around her and was thoroughly enjoying sharing his country with her.

Relaxed probably wasn't the right word. He'd certainly let down his guard. He'd allowed himself to have a few laughs and smiles. And he'd touched her. Dios, he'd held her close, and now all he could think of was doing it again. Yet at the same time, he wanted to talk to her, to know her, to keep watching her with her students.

Her students. They were a welcome source of hope for humanity, entertaining to interact with, but an unavoidable obstacle as well. He would never get to spend any time alone with Cecilia on this trip. He'd have to settle for loaded glances, split-second opportunities to pull her aside or brush against her. He imagined her resting her head on his shoulder during a long ride, her hair inches away for him to touch, to smell....

That thought had him chuckling out loud.

"Something funny?" Gabrielle asked. She stood to direct the students off the bus.

"Just remembering something one of the kids said. Excuse me." He moved out of her way and stepped across the aisle to stand behind the driver so he could check in with his cousin.

"Nice driving, cousin," he said to Luís in Catalán and they shook hands.

"See?" Luís replied, answering in their native tongue. "You had nothing to worry about. Tomás told me you were nervous about riding with me."

"I've seen what you can do to an automobile," Felip said, recalling the time he'd gone to Bilbao with his brother Alonso and Luís. His cousin had offered to drive and managed to go off the road and into a ditch, because he was apparently trying to pass a car on the shoulder to catch up with a beautiful woman. "You'll forgive me for being concerned."

"Just because you are an old man and you drive like one. Tell me, have you ever taken that Audi of yours out on the open road and let her loose?"

Felip sighed. Just one more thing he hadn't had time to do. "Sadly, no, but hanging around with you slackers has me thinking about an extended vacation."

Luís frowned. "You? I thought you were trying to conquer the international wine markets. All of them. No? You ready to come enjoy life with us slackers?"

The idea was tempting.

"See you after the tour," he said to his cousin and exited the bus.

His father had made their family business a success for many years, but when Felip came on, he'd had ambitions, delusions of grandeur some might say. He wanted to take their respectably successful winery and go international. He'd brought June in, they'd increased production, and then began distributing all over Europe and the United States. Segura International had such a nice ring to it. But staying on top meant long hours, countless business trips, and in the end, it had cost him his marriage...what little of a marriage it actually was. The divorce made him stop and think a bit, as much as he could in between trips. He realized that his business plan hadn't accounted for personal happiness, and at thirty-nine and single for four years now, he was lonely.

The last conversation he'd had with his mother, she'd reached across the table and brushed the strands of gray back from his face with a frown.

"Your father worked himself into the ground, and now I see you doing the same thing, only worse because you have no wife to care for you."

He'd teased her about having ulterior motives. "You're just anxious to hear the pitter-patter of tiny feet in the house," he'd said. "You'll have your precious grandchildren someday."

But his parents were growing older as well. At sixty, his mother was still quite healthy despite a difficult childhood during the Franco regime, and the hard work she and her husband had put into his family's wine business. They'd inherited a winery that had limped along throughout the fascist government's reign, and only after Spain joined the European Union had they really become successful. Felip watched his parents' happiness grow as their sons and their profits grew. Felip wanted to continue that for them, to make them proud, and he'd done that.

Now? What came after success in business?

"So, who do you think is going to be our guide here? Hmm? My vote is Babette. Sounds so exotic."

Felip looked down to see Cecilia's smug smile as she climbed the steps to the plaza next to him.

"It is a rather exotic name, isn't it?" He could play her game just as well.

She raised her eyebrows at him in surprise and he cracked up.

"It doesn't matter. I have a new favorite name that is much more enticing."

"Oh! Let me guess. Does it start with a G?"

"Hurry everyone. Check for amigos!"

They'd reached the top of the stairs and were now in front of the arches leading into the palace plaza. The stark white stone was nearly blinding after being in the bus with the tinted windows.

Cecilia moved away to find her amigos, Tui and Tony. Tony and his boyfriend were taking selfies in front of the arch with a selfie stick. Cecilia walked behind them and poked her face between theirs as Bill clicked the button. They cracked up and she backed away, giving an exaggerated bow. Then she ran into Tui and bounced off of him.

"Are you okay, Mrs. Galván?"

"Peachy, Tui. Just peachy."

Felip laughed as he watched her collect herself. She had to step aside and fix her shoe, as she'd managed to step out of it during her performance. He caught up to her as she started to fall to the side.

"Allow me," he said, grasping her arm for support.

"Thanks," she said. "Tui knocked me right out of my shoe."

"Or it might have been while you were making such a graceful exit from your photo intrusion."

She shook her head to dismiss that. "Not possible. My middle name is Grace, you know. I've got moves."

He nearly lost *his* footing laughing. "Grace? Well, then shall I refer to you as Your Grace?"

Felip managed to pull off a perfectly executed bow—and when he stood, he froze. The kids were all watching.

"Do you, like, have to learn how to do that? Like when you're growing up?" Joseph asked.

Cecilia pressed her lips together to keep from laughing, but the pink hue to her cheeks said he'd had an effect on her. Good. She should remain on her toes around him.

"Amigos, gather round."

Felip forgot he was supposed to be getting their entrance squared away and meeting up with their scheduled docent. He really hoped it wasn't Babette. Or Anna. Or Claire, for that matter. *And please, Lord, don't let it be Amalia.*

He told Gabrielle to wait there with the group and he hurried over to the admission gate. He let the guard know who they were, showed his credentials, and was told they would be meeting Claudia for their tour. Felip nearly groaned in relief.

When he returned, the group was listening to Jorge tell them about the current King of Spain.

"He's actually in Washington, D.C., at the White House right now meeting with our president. He's on a tour of America to celebrate former Spanish colonial anniversaries in New Orleans and San Antonio, both of which are having tricentennial events. The king, Felipe VI, and his wife Leticia are actually friends with the Obamas."

There were murmurs of excitement from the kids.

"Man, I wish he was still president. I don't like—"

"Eduardo," Gabrielle interrupted and shook her head. "Thank you. I believe Felip has instructions for us?"

All eyes turned on him and his mouth went dry.

"Ehm, eh, we are to meet our palace guide Claudia inside the building to my right," he said, pointing toward the entrance for tourists. "If you look across the plaza, you will see a row of arches, and beyond that are some of the most beautiful vistas in all of Madrid. After our tour, if you would like, you can go there to take your pictures. At the very end on the left, there is another smaller museum, but one I think will interest the young men of the group. In this museum, you will find—"

"Is it the armory?" Jorge asked.

"Sí, it is. The armory—"

"Isn't that where the suits of armor and the weapons of previous kings are kept?"

"Sí, there is quite a collection—"

"I saw pictures. They even had armor for their horses and their dogs, right? Will we see those?"

"Sí, you will see—"

"And will we be able to take pictures? I couldn't find on the website if you could take pictures in there. I know you can't take pictures inside the palace, only in a few places, but can we take pictures inside the museum?"

Felip waited to see if he was truly taking a breath this time. Jorge's mother leaned in and put her arm around him and that seemed to distract him from his interrogation.

"We will find out when we get to that portion of the tour," he said. "Now come, we have a time slot and we mustn't be late. And please, keep your phones in your pockets when we go inside. The Guardia Real can get very aggressive if they think you are taking pictures."

The boys all looked at each other, wide-eyed.

"I joke with you. The Guardia Real won't likely be around. But you can't take pictures. And be sure you don't step over any lines or they will kick you out, and you'll have to wait for us out front by yourself."

There were frowns and looks of worry from the kids.

"I joke once more. Please, be respectful and enjoy a little bit of Spain's political history. Claudia is an excellent guide and will tell you all the juicy palace gossip, won't you, Claudia?"

He'd led the group over to a stout older woman who gave the best hugs. She held out her tiny hands to embrace him and he bent to kiss her cheeks.

"Por supuesto, Felip. ¿Cómo estás?"

"Bien, señora. Muy bien."

She gave his arm a squeeze before turning to address the group in Spanish.

Felip had known Claudia since Tomás had first started giving tours in Madrid. She'd been an excellent resource and had given Tomás many connections to get started and eventually grow his company to what it was today. At sixty-seven years old, she was a live wire.

After giving a lengthy introduction to the students, during which she approached several of them speaking in rapid-fire Spanish, she approached Cecilia and said to her, "¿Por qué los estudiantes no entienden castellano?"

Cecilia's eyes went wide and almost without skipping a beat, she began to make signs with her hands back at the woman.

"Oh, I'm so sorry," Claudia said, clutching her chest. "Do you need an interpreter?"

"Not if you speak English, I don't," Cecilia said with a wink. "I'm sorry, I'm the Sign Language teacher." She pointed at Gabrielle. "She's the Spanish speaker."

Felip exhaled, then laughed at her quick thinking. Claudia gave a grandmotherly squeeze to Cecilia's arm and said, "I'm going to have to watch this one," to Felip in Spanish before turning her attention on Gabrielle. They discussed the rules, in English this time, and the students lined up to enter. Felip knew he should stay with Claudia, but he desperately wanted to see Cecilia's response to visiting the palace. It truly was a sight to behold.

All throughout the palace, Felip found himself scanning the rooms for Cecilia, trying to see her reactions. She stayed close to the front the first few stops, and Felip watched as she'd strain to hear, her eyes on Claudia's mouth the whole time. Why had he not noticed before? She always seemed so present in their conversations... But then he remembered their very strange conversation back at the airport, when he'd first interacted with her. It could have been that she was half asleep, as she'd claimed, or perhaps she hadn't heard him? How hard she must have to work to keep up. How did she manage in a class-room where not every student spoke loudly?

After a few rooms, she wandered around looking at the different items by herself. She seemed very engrossed in the king's clock collec-tion, so much so that the rest of the group left the room and she was still staring at it. Felip took this as an opportunity.

"Señora, you mustn't get separated. There are over three thousand—"

"I know, I know," she said with a laugh. "Three thousand, eight hundred and blah blah, I heard Jorge. Sorry."

She started to move past him, and he stepped close to her. "Are you enjoying the tour? Would you prefer to have a head set? I didn't even think to get one for you."

She shrugged. "Why would you?"

"To be sure you could hear the guide."

The few moments it took her to respond had Felip hanging on a cliff. Had he totally fouled up this situation? Would she be offended that he'd even brought up her hearing loss? It seemed like such a nonissue most of the time, but how could he be sure?

"That's very thoughtful of you," she said, her tone guarded. "Sometimes I like to read the plaques and make up my own mind, my own stories."

Her answer was not at all what he'd feared, and yet it was very odd. "You just...make it up. The history of the Spanish royal family."

She laughed and swatted at his arm. "No, don't be ridiculous! But take this clock right here," she said, pointing to one of the many clocks the former king had collected. "I keep thinking to myself, 'who in their right mind would have spent this much money on such a weird clock?' And 'why did he need all the clocks? It's not like he couldn't take three steps and see another one?' You know? Don't you ever wonder why rich people do— Wait. You probably *are* rich, so maybe you don't think like that. Forget it, I'm sorry."

He chuckled, trotting to catch up with her as she left the room. "Wait! Hold on. You're exactly right. And yes, my family is quite comfortable now, but for a long time we were not. My childhood was a struggle. But I too look at this stuff and wonder why the king wanted to have so much of it around, and I know it was expected of them to be eccentric. Wealth meant power, and power called for respect, and the more he could show off his wealth to others in power, the more they would respect him. Does that make sense?"

She quirked her head to the side. "It does, but then...what? The king of France collects his random shit, and the king of England collects his random shit, and they just go around admiring each other's random shit?"

Felip closed his eyes and let the laughter spill out of him, his shoulders relaxing even more, thanks to her and her sense of humor.

"You're right. It's all about who has the most random shit. Of course. Why didn't I think of it that way? Why don't we teach our Spanish children about the power of random shit?"

Cecilia clasped a hand over her mouth to muffle her laughter, which had grown in volume to unacceptable levels here in the palace.

"Shhh, señora. You will get us kicked out."

She turned to him suddenly and placed a hand on his arm. "Felip? Can I ask you a favor?"

He stopped and she moved closer, almost chest to chest with him. His breath caught and things stirred in him. Not only because he found himself incredibly aroused in her presence, but because whatever it was she was about to say, whatever she wanted, he wanted to do for her. He was again that Olympic athlete, this time awaiting the scores of his latest performance.

"Can you not call me señora?" She blinked up at him and then shook her head when he frowned. "I'm sorry, I'd just rather *you* not call me that."

"I did not mean to offend you," he said, feeling as though he'd committed a dreadful sin. Instinctively he stepped back to give her space, but she reached for his arm.

"No! You didn't offend me," she said, tucking a lock of hair behind her ear. "I'd rather you call me Cecilia. I like the way you say my name."

The second half of her statement came out in a breathy voice that sent a jolt of desire straight to places Felip shouldn't be thinking with while in this position...with her, in front of the kids, at the royal palace. That was enough to cool his ardor.

"I *do* prefer Cecilia. I don't want to call you by another man's name. But in front of the students..."

She frowned. "Yeah. I've been debating going with my maiden name next year when school starts, but it's suuuuuch a pain. There are so many questions, and it's, like, every period for the first day, and then they're still slipping and calling you the old name...I know this from when I got married. It was a good year before I stopped hearing 'Miss Simon, Miss Simon.'"

"Wait," he said and grinned widely. "Your maiden name is Simon? Cecilia Simon? Like Simon and—"

"Yeah, yeah. My mom was a hippie, okay?" she said, laughing. "My grandfather collected jukeboxes and there were several Simon and Garfunkel songs on them, as well as other famous name songs, like 'Lay Down Sally' and 'You picked a fine time to leave me Lucille' and 'Sweet Melissa.' I guess I'm lucky they picked Cecilia and not Lucille."

"Oh, I don't know. It is a nice name, although 'four hungry children' would be a terrible foreshadowing of a future together if they'd named you Lucille."

She bumped him with her shoulder as they walked along, following the group but staying back far enough that they could talk quietly and not disrupt anyone.

"How is it you know your American rock 'n' roll songs so well?"

"My uncle. Luís's father. He lived in America for many years. He left to escape the poverty and terrible conditions under Franco, and he only came home after Franco died so he could run the wine business with my father. He's retired now, and he and his American wife moved back to

California. He's part of the reason why we expanded our business there. He saw wine becoming so popular, he thought we should try to build our international name. It turned out to be a very lucrative project."

"So your uncle brought you American music?"

"Sí. He brought a large record collection with him when he came. He and his wife even went to Woodstock."

"Ha! They probably ran into my grandparents—oh. Wait. Not trying to say you're old or anything."

Felip feigned horror. "Old? Me?"

"I'm sorry!" she said, grabbing his arm again. "I didn't mean that!"

He laughed and placed his hand on her hand, and suddenly they were walking arm in arm through the royal palace. There he was back on that pedestal, silver medal this time, the Spanish—no, wait—the Catalonia anthem. He'd bow his head as they lowered the medal around his neck...

"Felip!"

He groaned. He knew better, but he actually groaned.

Cecilia laughed. "You better go. Her excellency awaits, señor Segura."

He touched his forehead to hers. "Eres de la piel del diablo, profesora."

She gaped at him. "What did you just call me?"

He trotted away, glancing back at her as he laughed triumphantly. He loved her attitude as she stood there with her hands on her hips, her chin stuck out defiantly, that eyebrow... Little devil teacher.

"Felip! I need to know how much time we have until Luís picks us up."

Gabrielle was a beautiful woman who was intelligent and spoke perfect Spanish. She was confident, and graceful...and Felip felt no attraction to her. In many ways, she was like Francesca, bold with her attentions and self-assured in her presentation. Perhaps that was why Felip could appreciate her, but not feel anything other than admiration.

"Let me text him and be sure we have some time. It would be

wonderful for the students to be able to tour the armory." He texted his cousin and received an answer right away.

"We have about twenty-five minutes until he picks us up and we go to the market to pick up lunch and then on to el Retiro."

"Very well," she said, tossing her hair. "Claudia said we are almost finished here."

They were indeed nearing the end of the tour. Claudia had the whole group laughing up ahead. She was such a funny old woman. The very first time he'd gone on a tour with Tomás after he'd started the business, Claudia had chosen him as the butt of all her jokes. She'd always pick on someone in the group, making comments about them at every stop. As he approached, it seemed she'd chosen Tui as her victim this time.

"I swear! I didn't touch anything," Tui said, laughing.

"Methinks he doth protest too much," she said. "Always trying to fool an old lady." Then she winked at him and he shook his head, shrugging to his friends. Felip knew it was all in fun, but he should have warned the kids.

"Mrs. Galván," Tui said as Cecilia joined them. "Tell her I'm not a troublemaker."

She raised her eyebrows as if to argue, but then said, "Of course you aren't." She lifted her chin in Joseph's direction. "It's him you gotta watch out for."

Claudia's eyes widened. "It was you all along, heckling me, setting off alarms, I should have known." She shook her head, and Joseph giggled.

"Okay, check for amigos," Gabrielle said, and all of the kids and adults looked around at each other, smiling when they found their partners. "Now, you have twenty minutes to go and take pictures from the plaza, or if you'd like, you can head to the armory—"

No sooner had she said that than the boys began pulling each other excitedly toward the door.

"Wait! Make sure you're back at the steps in twenty minutes! Not a moment later!" Gabrielle shouted after them.

They took off at a run, and Felip prayed they didn't run over any of the older guests.

Cecilia brushed past him. "You're really going to let a bunch of teenaged boys in a room with priceless antique weapons unsupervised? Are you crazy?"

She jogged after them to catch up and Felip was momentarily mesmerized by her movements.

"You see something you like?" Gabrielle asked, standing next to him all of a sudden.

"She is..."

"She's one of my very good friends. She's taught me a great deal about being an excellent teacher, and if you harm one hair on her head, I will have your balls."

She smiled at him and sashayed away.

Felip chuckled to himself. *At least now perhaps she will keep her hands to herself.*

However, the comment about his balls had him subtly shifting his weight.

CHAPTER THIRTEEN

1 2:40 p.m. Madrid Local Time – Palacio Real

Cecilia nearly panicked when the boys took off running for the armory. She'd been nervous throughout the palace tour that they might knock over some priceless antique and they'd all be evicted from Spain, but in the armory? Weapons? There could be actual bloodshed!

She caught up to them before they entered. "You three, you better swear on your mothers' lives that you will not touch a single thing in this room, do you hear me?"

Tui, Joseph and Eduardo all turned around and eyed her warily.

"Yes, Mrs. Galván," they said slowly and in unison.

"Good. Now let's go see some cool stuff!"

She pushed past them and entered first as they chuckled behind her—but she stopped inside the entrance to the gallery.

In the center of the room, there were model horses covered in armor. She would have been shaking in her boots had some knight come bearing down on her on the battlefield dressed like that. As she walked closer, she stared in awe at the detail on each piece of metal formed to shape the bodies of the horses, and even the dogs! She wondered what life was like for the men who made weapons like these.

"Damn, that's *heeeeeeella* small," she heard shouted from across the hall. She glanced over and saw her boys and Felip standing in front of a row of suits of armor.

"I mean, look at them! Are you sure these weren't for little kids?" Tui asked, elbowing Joseph when Felip frowned.

"It is true that men, most men, were much smaller in the earlier centuries. But size doesn't matter when you are a skilled warrior, eh?"

"Size always matters," Eduardo said, and he and Joseph slapped their hands together and shook.

Cecilia cleared her throat, and the boys immediately put their hands in their pockets.

"We were just saying that—"

"Uh-huh." She gave her boys her teacher face and they all looked admonished. Felip had an amused grin on his face, and that meant Cecilia had to mess with him too.

"Maybe these suits are so small because there were secretly women who did battle and that's why the Spaniards were so success-ful." She made the sign of an explosion and mouthed the word *boom*. Her boys laughed—they were used to her throwing down the male/fe-male gauntlet—but Felip frowned again.

"Revisionist history." He shook his head but didn't elaborate.

"Oh, right. Women were home taking care of the children and couldn't possibly have gone to battle. Although, your Queen Isabella was quite the mastermind, wasn't she?"

He smirked and then looked down at his watch. "We'd better get back to the bus," he said.

"Uh-huh." Cecilia smiled at him knowingly. She appreciated that he didn't launch into that debate in front of her kids, but she had a feeling the two of them might have some words eventually over the roles of men and women. She found herself looking forward to it. He would be a nice sparring partner. He was intelligent, seemed to be genuinely honest, and his sense of humor was refreshing. It would be easy to get sucked into his vortex, and she needed to remember that before she started wondering any more about him.

Once they returned to the bus, she sat quietly reflecting on the beauty of the palace, but her thoughts kept going back to their discussion about names. She had no idea where she'd gotten the nerve to say that to him.

I like the way you say my name.

Cecilia had never been so bold before, but perhaps it was being in a foreign country, where she was somewhat anonymous. Or even the fact that she'd moved out of the home she'd shared with her ex-husband the day before leaving on this trip, and with every box she'd carried out, she'd felt lighter and lighter. He'd been gone for over a year, and he'd certainly moved on. Now she was free. Free from the shackles of a marriage that had left her feeling less-than on many occasions. Free from continuing to pretend she and Greg still loved each other because of vows they'd taken when they were too young to know better.

When the heart and mind are free, they tend to wander, and hers were taking a nice stroll right about now, following a very attractive and charming man.

The bus pulled to a stop and Felip stood.

"This afternoon, we are going to have a nice picnic in Madrid's most popular and beautiful park, el Parque del Retiro. But first, let's have an adventure in a Spanish market. Here in this building, you will find many different types of food the madrileños love to feast on for their afternoon meal. We'll cross over to the park, have our lunch, and then, for those of you who would like, we can rent small boats. ¿Vale? ¿Tenéis preguntas? ¿No? ¡Vámonos!"

The kids all murmured to each other as they exited the bus. Cecilia counted them and all of her kids were there. The other group milled about, and Cecilia wondered if her kids would venture out of their comfort zones to socialize with them. At first glance, she'd thought they looked like any other teenagers, but then she noticed the subtle nuances. The girls wore clothes that probably cost more than anything she owned, and they'd certainly put more effort into their appearance than she ever did. And the boys? Well, they were interesting in that they didn't seem to be *interested*. They were in a beautiful, magical place, and they were much more engaged with their phones than anything going on around them.

She followed the kids into the market and they all stopped short. They looked around the store with varying degrees of excitement. Some kids saw what they wanted and took off, trusting their fledgling Spanish skills to navigate the confusing place. Everything was in Spanish from the labels to the signs marking the departments, and none of the packaging looked familiar. Besides the fruit and vegetables, everything else was a mystery. Cecilia and Aaliyah hung back while Kristin and Janelle followed along with Jorge and his parents to find sustenance.

"Is there something you fancy, profesora?"

Felip rubbed his belly absently as he gazed around the store.

"I'm not even sure where to begin," she said. "That fruit over there looks delicious, but other than that…"

Felip picked up a shopping basket. "Do you trust me to shop for you?"

Cecilia looked at Aaliyah and they both shrugged. "I suppose?"

He frowned. "That doesn't sound very confident. Tell me, is there anything you don't like?"

Aaliyah glanced around. "I can't have anything spicy. My stomach can't tolerate it."

Cecilia imagined her anxiety probably had something to do with that. "Yeah, I'm not a big fan of spicy either."

"No spicy. Bien. How about you ladies choose which fruit you would like and I will collect the rest of our rations?"

"Thank you," Cecilia said, choosing a basket for their selections. "Let's go, Aaliyah. You're going to have to do the talking, though. I'm just along for the ride."

"It's okay, Mrs. Galván. I gotchoo."

Cecilia had noticed Aaliyah smiling a lot more today. She was about to ask about it when Aaliyah cleared her throat.

"Mrs. Galván? Can I ask you a weird question?"

"Sure, honey. What's up?"

Aaliyah looked around to be sure they weren't heard. She had the biggest brown eyes, deep-set above round cheeks, and her smile lit up her features. She wore her dark brown hair straightened today, framing her heart-shaped face. She leaned in, blinking her meticulously mascaraed eyelashes.

"How do you know if a guy is just being nice or if he, like, *likes* you? I mean, like, how can you tell for sure?"

Cecilia looked around herself and leaned in. "I'm not sure I'm the best one to ask about this, but can I venture a guess that it's about a certain football player?"

Aaliyah blushed and smiled, too nervous to say anything else. "He's so nice to me. Most guys aren't nice like him."

Cecilia sighed loudly and put her arm around Aaliyah, guiding her over to the produce section. "My dear, boys in high school are kind of like those mangoes over there. Not quite ripe. They're colorful and nice to look at, but when you take a bite, you either get a bitter taste or something so tangy it literally hurts you to eat it. Okay, that sounds wrong," she laughed. "Basically, they're underripe. They need time to come into their full flavor. But sometimes, if you care for them just right, they'll turn out with the right amount of sweetness."

"I don't know," Aaliyah said. "I think they're all like those bananas. They're either green or they're all covered in bruises and smushy and gross. There's not really an in-between."

"True. They get knocked around a lot, but if you sit them in the right light on the counter... Okay, I can't do this," she laughed, shaking her head. "They're not all rotten. Tui is a genuinely nice guy. My only caution for you would be that you guys are kind of under a lot of scrutiny here in this group and anything that happens will be fodder for gossip with your fellow travelers."

"Kind of like you and Mr. Segura?"

Cecilia gave her a look. "What do you mean? There's no me and Mr. anyone."

Aaliyah started giggling, and Cecilia couldn't help but join in.

"Don't even say you can't tell he likes you, Mrs. Galván. He's totally into you."

Cecilia rolled her eyes and reached for a bag of grapes. "See, a man his age is more like this bag of grapes. They might look perfect, but they're better at hiding their imperfections. Underneath the plump, juicy, crispy ones you often find mold. Or a sour one. And you can't tell because they look good on the outside, so you—"

"¿Estáis listas? Are you both ready?"

Cecilia nearly jumped out of her skin at his proximity. "Stalker! Geez. You have to stop doing that!" Her hand rested on her heaving chest. Had he heard their conversation? It was like he was everywhere, lying in wait to catch her off guard.

"Come on, profesora. I thought no one could sneak up on you." He laughed, taking the bag of grapes from her. He looked over the bunch and tested the firmness with his index finger and thumb. "These look perfect. You have a good eye for grapes." He smiled as though he were proud of her accomplishment.

She was still freaking out, wondering if he'd heard her.

"What would you like to drink?"

"Diet Coke. Please. I need."

Aaliyah giggled as he turned to her. "Just water, please. Thank you."

He nodded and strolled away, stopping at a small refrigeration unit next to the check stand. Cecilia stood there dumbfounded as he bent over to retrieve the drinks they'd asked for, his shirt riding up and exposing the skin of his lower back. He stood, looked back at them with a sly smile, and set their purchases on the conveyor belt.

"Close your mouth, Mrs. Galván," Aaliyah said. She pushed Cecilia towards the line, and she woke from the trance he'd put her in with his—

"Hey! Hey, you stop right there." She rushed over to him, pulling her wallet out of her bag. "Don't you dare pay for that."

Felip stepped back with his hands raised. "Lo siento, profesora."

She pushed past him with a grunt and he broke out in peals of laughter. She stood facing the checkout girl with euros in hand, waiting for instructions.

And then the girl spoke in such rapid Spanish, Cecilia was momentarily dazed. She looked between the girl, who continued to ask questions, to the register's display and back to the girl.

"It's thirteen euros fifty. Do you have change?"

Cecilia looked at Felip, confused, and then finally it clicked what he was saying.

"I'm so sorry," she muttered as she pulled out the right amount of money. "Gracias," she remembered to say.

The girl slid their purchases to the bagging section with a nod before moving on to the next customer. She wasn't rude at all, merely efficient in her work.

Felip bagged up their groceries as Cecilia watched the young girl. She glanced at Cecilia as though she felt herself being watched and offered the slightest hint of a smile. Cecilia had noticed that a lot of the people they met carried austere expressions. They weren't rude or angry looking, just serious. Felip could be like that at times, too. There was something different about it. People back home either looked happy, angry, stressed or some variation or combination of the three. She'd have to do some more observational research, but now she had to hustle if she wanted to catch up to the group. Once again, she'd fallen behind.

She caught up to Aaliyah, who was walking with the girls. "See? Grapes. All of them. Sometimes they jump out and scare you and then act all sweet like *you're* the problem."

The girls looked at her like she'd lost her mind, which she probably had.

The group crossed a busy street and entered the Parque del Retiro, which they'd driven past that morning on the bus. She hadn't gotten a good look at it as trees lined the entire area. But once they walked through the entrance, she was truly dazzled. It didn't seem possible that this park, a veritable urban forest, was steps away from the busy lives of the madrileños. She felt as though she'd fallen through time. It seemed so grand it should be attached to a royal palace. There were arches and statues as they got closer to the water surrounded by lush green trees and shrubbery. If it weren't so hot, Cecilia could see herself taking leisurely strolls, maybe even jogging through the park. She imagined at twilight the place would be truly magical. It seemed to go on forever in all directions.

Felip led them to a densely shaded area under some trees and the group began to spread out their purchases. Kristin and Janelle had gone to the shop next door and picked up some sort of empanadas, which looked delicious. They waited for Aaliyah to grab some food from the spread Felip displayed on a torn-open paper bag on the ground. He'd placed two loafs of crusty French bread and the grapes Cecilia had picked out next to some cheese and two small packages of meat.

"I picked out some jamón y pavo…eh, ham and turkey. I hope that meets with your approval."

Cecilia smiled, still a little embarrassed at how she'd acted in the store. Just when she felt comfortable around him, like maybe she wouldn't make a total ass out of herself, she made an ass out of herself.

"Gracias," Aaliyah said. She knelt down next to the food and broke off some of the bread, some of the cheese he'd unwrapped and a small portion of meat. She placed them on a napkin she'd opened and then she reached for the grapes. She glanced at Cecilia and giggled as she took a small branch. Cecilia's face turned red as she inspected the bunch and nodded in approval.

"No bad ones hiding." Aaliyah wrapped them up with the rest of her food, and the girls went to go sit with the boys.

"Bad ones? Did I miss something?" Felip asked.

Cecilia felt her embarrassment fade with relief. *He didn't hear me. Thank God.*

"I'm just glad you didn't grab the bananas." He shook his head. "All bruised up and gross."

Cecilia closed her eyes and sank to the ground, wishing it would eat her up. "How much exactly—"

"Why? Did I miss something important? Your description of the grapes was excellent, I must say."

She opened one eye to find him serving himself from the food with his lips pressed together. She recognized that look.

"You're enjoying this, aren't you?"

"What? All I said was that you have a way with fruit, profesora." He took a bite of the makeshift sandwich he'd thrown together and chewed with a thoughtful expression on his face. He swallowed and wiped his mouth a napkin. "I thought your explanation of how men are like grapes to be quite fitting. It *is* more difficult to spot the rotten ones."

"You can say that again," she muttered.

"How was yours rotten?" he asked in a low voice.

Cecilia glanced around and somehow, they were apart enough from the rest of the group that they could actually have a conversation. Gabrielle sat with Bill and Tony, the Santiagos sat together with their backs to Cecilia, and the kids all sat in a big group, laughing and talking excitedly about their experiences in the market.

"He wandered," she said, her voice strong despite the vulnerability she still felt whenever discussing the demise of her marriage. "It happens, I guess." She busied her hands with preparing a sandwich from the meat and cheese Felip had bought. She took a bite and the strong flavors combined in her mouth in a most pleasant way. "Mmmm, oh, this is good. What is this cheese?"

"It is Manchego. What do you mean, he wandered?"

Cecilia was still chewing and that gave her time to think of the appropriate response. She'd put it out there, and that would be that. Maybe he'd stop flirting with her and they could go about their business. It would certainly make everything easier. Less fun, a little sad, but easier in the end.

"He traveled for business, frequently." She paused to take another small bite. "And then he moved away. His company grew, and he needed to be at the office in Oakland permanently instead of working remotely from our home three and a half hours away. After a year, he asked me to move with him, but school had just started so I said no, he'd have to wait until summer. I guess he didn't want to wait that long."

She chanced a glance at Felip to find him holding his food suspended on the way to his mouth, staring at her as though she'd said the pope wasn't Catholic. When he remained silent, she went back to eating her sandwich. And grew more uncomfortable by the second. *What is he thinking?*

"He moved away? Just picked up and left you?"

Cecilia nodded. "It was only supposed to be until June. I told him we could talk about me taking a leave at that point, but I really didn't want to give up my job."

He frowned. "You did not want him to support you?"

"I did," she said, her hackles vibrating. When she spoke again, her voice was tight. "I wanted him to support me in my *job*, not expect me to pick up and move after school started."

Greg could have commuted, kept a place in the city and come home on the weekends. He claimed he needed to be available seven days a week because they were at a crucial time in their development, and didn't she understand?

"What happened then?" He'd moved on to the grapes and Cecilia found it quite distracting, watching him eat the fruit. His fingers were long and graceful. She hadn't noticed that before.

"Carol happened, I guess. He took me to London in September for a long weekend and tried to convince me to move. I told him I wouldn't quit my job and leave the students in a lurch. It's not that easy to find an ASL teacher. I told him that we could talk about it in June. He called me in October and said he'd met someone and he wanted a divorce. It all happened very quickly. I didn't find out until later that Carol had been happening for the past year...along with Pam in Boston. And Tracy in Chicago. Those are just the ones I knew about."

"He's a fool."

"No, I was the fool. I should have known better."

He shook his head and took a drink of water. "You *deserved* better."

"Amigos," Gabrielle called out. "Gather round! Felip! Ayúdame, por favor."

Felip frowned and finished the last bite of his sandwich. "Perdón, Cecilia." He stood and walked over to Gabrielle.

What the hell was she thinking, telling him all of that?

"¡Amigos! It's time to decide whether you want to go out on the lake on a paddle boat or have a nice leisurely stroll through the botanical gardens. If you'd like to do the boats, please stand with señor Segura. If you want to see the gardens, you can line up with me."

CHAPTER FOURTEEN

2:38 p.m. Madrid Local Time – Parque del Retiro

Felip was grateful for the activity as he didn't trust himself to speak to Cecilia yet.

What kind of stupid moron would dare treat her in such a way? When he thought about the story she'd reluctantly told him, he nearly became violent. And the questions he'd wanted to ask...he could tell she was uncomfortable talking about her situation, but she was so brave. The way she stuck that chin out...

They stood in line to pay for the boats and then a worker took them down to the dock to load them in groups of three. There were many kids from the other school who had chosen to row, but his group requested to stay together. Felip decided that despite the value of putting them with other kids to work on their Spanish or cooperation skills, he wanted them to have a good time. Their chaperone seemed like a nice enough guy, but he wasn't a lot of help getting his group organized. Before long, his kids were spread out all over and not paying attention to the instructions.

"Señor, which of the children will go together?"

Felip looked around and it appeared the kids had already separated themselves.

"See, Tui needs to go with the girls because—"

"Joseph—" Cecilia warned as she approached.

"What? I'm saying, he needs to row for them because—"

"I highly advise you do not continue that line of thinking."

Joseph snapped his mouth shut and heeded Cecilia's advice.

Kristin and Janelle grabbed Jorge. "Come help us row. You're bound to know more than these guys."

"Hey, I resent that deduction," Eduardo said. "Just because he knows more about everything than we do... Oh. Yeah, probably a good choice."

"Mrs. Galván, I want to go with you." Tui moved to stand next to her, and Felip found himself relieved. He wasn't ready to be alone with her. He hadn't calmed down enough, and it would be worse with a student between them, trying to act like everything was okay.

"Why do you want to be in my boat, Tui?"

Cecilia gazed up at the boy with her eyebrow raised, and he suddenly seemed uncomfortable being on her radar.

"Because, um, I figure, you know, your boat is the least likely to capsize?"

She burst out laughing. "Why would you think that?"

Tui breathed a sigh of relief. "Look at those two! Would you trust them in your boat? And the girls...no offense—"

"No offense?" they protested.

"Well, Aaliyah's not going to knock the boat over, and I think Mrs. Galván has a higher level of competence than any of us here, that's all."

Felip smirked. "You've made your choices. Eduardo, Joseph, I believe that puts you with me. Let's see which boat has the highest level of competence."

Joseph and Eduardo turned on their friends. "Yeah, just you watch. We're going to be the picture of competence!"

Twenty minutes later, Felip rested his head in his hands. Joseph was trying to rescue the oar that Eduardo had dropped in the water while they argued over who was responsible.

"Boys, if you are unable to—"

"No, Mr. Segura, we're gonna get us back to shore without help. We can totally do this."

Ten minutes later, they'd managed to get the oar back...and about five centimeters of water in the bottom of the boat. Felip's shoes were soaked. The walk back to the hotel would not be pleasant.

Tui rowed his boat swiftly to their location, and Eduardo and Joseph sat staring at him.

"He makes it look so easy," Eduardo said quietly enough that only they could hear him.

"It probably is if you can bench press a freaking car, bruh!"

"You boys need a hand?" he asked as he pulled alongside. Cecilia and Aaliyah were no longer on the boat.

"Where is Ce—Señora?" Felip asked, catching himself.

"Aaliyah needed to find los servicios. I dropped them off and told the boat guy that I'd make sure you guys were okay."

"Bro, we got this."

It took both boys rowing to get them back to shore. It became a race, which Tui obviously pretended was difficult for him so his friends could feel better about their efforts. When they were back on shore, Tui helped them get the water out of the boat while Felip attempted to wring some of the water out of his trainers. Thankfully, he had another pair back at Tomás's flat, but that was a few kilometers away by foot.

"Mr. Segura, we're sorry about your shoes." Eduardo appeared beside him. "First you gave up your shirt for me, and now your shoes are wrecked...you must be sorry you met us."

Felip put a hand on his shoulder. "Absolutely not. I've had a wonderful time with your group," he said, and, surprisingly, he meant every word. "You three remind me a lot of my brothers and the catastrophes they would get into when they were younger."

"I swear, we didn't mean to flood the boat," Joseph said.

"It's fine, Joseph. Now, let's go find the rest of our group. We might have time for helado antes de salir del parque." He had a feeling food would brighten their spirits. Besides, it would give him some time for his shoes to dry...

Never mind. It was hopeless.

The rest of the group was already in the queue at the heladería when they arrived—except for Cecilia and Aaliyah. He was concerned they hadn't made it back yet.

"So, what's the deal?"

Felip tuned into the boys' conversation.

"I don't know, man, I've always liked her, you know? And now we're here and she's, like, actually talking to me. She's hella cool."

"I do feel you, bro, and I think you should buy her an ice cream and be like, 'say baby, this ice cream isn't as sweet as you, but—'"

"No. Just no. I'm not taking dating advice from you, Eduardo. Last time I did, you told me to tell everyone Frances and I were going out and she slapped me in the face!"

"That was in sixth grade," Eduardo protested.

"Exactly! And I'm not doing it again."

"I remember that," Joseph marveled. "Your face turned hella red, dude."

"Thank you." Tui looked up to the sky as though for patience. "So what flavor should I get her?"

"Definitely that chocolate one. I'm getting one, too. Or two, maybe. I could definitely eat two. That rowing took a lot out of me."

"What rowing?" Eduardo said. "Joseph, you're the one who lost the oar."

"Shut up, *you* did."

"Gentlemen? What kind of ice cream do you think your profesora would like?" he asked as they approached the front of the line. Cecilia still hadn't arrived. It was time to worry. He'd been scanning the park the entire time they'd been in the queue. When the boys didn't speak, he turned to face them.

Their expressions were almost comical. Joseph apparently decided to be their spokesperson. "What are your intentions regarding our teacher?"

Felip fought the urge to laugh, as he could tell they were serious about their inquiry.

"Intentions? How do you mean?" *That's it, Felip. Play ignorant. They'll never pick up on that.*

"You've been spending a lot of time with her," Eduardo said, crossing his thin arms over his chest. "We want to make sure you're not just tryna get at her."

He frowned. Their expression was unfamiliar to him, but he understood the meaning.

"Your profesora is a very special lady, ¿verdad? I enjoy talking to her."

They looked at each other. Then Tui cleared his throat. "I've seen you stepping up, watching out for her. That's cool. We just wanted to be sure, you know?"

Sure of what?

"She's a very kind and generous, and it's clear she cares about all of you. I simply want to make sure she has an enjoyable trip to my country."

Tui looked at him and tilted his head. "It was messed up what her husband did."

Felip was taken aback. She'd told them what happened? "You know about her divorce?"

"Yeah, Grass Valley's a small town, yo," Joseph said. "My dad knows her ex, and for real, the guy is a total douche—um, dumbass."

"How—"

"He hella cheated on her. He, like, had a side chick in the city. My dad saw them together and told my mom. I wasn't supposed to know," Joseph said.

Felip figured not a lot got by these kids.

"She is lucky to have you all looking out for her." He appreciated that they were worried about their teacher. "She deserves to be treated like a queen."

"How come you were in California?" Eduardo asked. "You go there a lot?"

He chuckled. "Recently, yes, but not always."

They glanced at each other as though they'd been planning to have this conversation all along and had rehearsed it.

"That's too bad," Tui said. "You seem like a good guy, Mr. Segura."

And that was the problem. Regardless of how special she was, she lived in California and he lived on another continent. She'd made it clear how she felt about traveling businessmen...and wine.

The whole thing seemed hopeless, and yet, he was still invested. In the nearly seventy-two hours since they'd met, he'd grown so fond of her. He could still smell her faint perfume from their close proximity in the palace. The subtle hint of citrus had been a nice discovery. One of his favorite smells, other than the aromas at their winery, came from the orange groves on the outskirts of the vineyard. Walking among the trees, taking in their natural perfume...

"They're still not back yet and this ice cream is going to melt. Mr. Segura? Should we go look for them?"

Felip had the same thought. "You boys stay here. Let me see if I can find them."

He trotted away from the heladería toward the small cultural center, where he knew they had aseos. Once inside, he asked the usher if he'd seen a woman and a teenager. He was about to describe them when they rounded the corner.

"Felip. Is everything okay?"

His heart had been racing, and upon seeing her face, it finally began to slow to the normal quick pace it seemed to have around her. "I came to see that you were all right."

Aaliyah blushed and looked down at her shoes.

"We, uh," Cecilia glanced at Aaliyah and smiled, "we needed a minute, but we're fine. It took us a little while to find this place."

Aaliyah snorted and Cecilia shushed her.

"I take it there is a story to be told?"

"We agreed to never speak of it again."

Both women nodded and looked firm in their decision. It was all Felip could do to raise his hands and step back, admitting defeat.

"Molt bé. But your ice cream is melting, so you'd better hurry."

Cecilia smiled excitedly at Aaliyah. "Ice cream? Oh, I was hoping we'd have time to stop!"

It wasn't a medal-level performance, but he loved her reaction nonetheless. "The boys were hungry after their difficult rowing experience."

"It looked as though your boat had some issues. You didn't step in and save them?"

Felip held the door for them and they walked back out into the heat. "They are decent problem solvers. I wanted to give them a good lesson."

Cecilia nodded, but she wasn't making eye contact. "It's tough to step back and let them handle themselves sometimes, but these kids are pretty resourceful."

"Here, Mrs. Galván. Mr. Segura got you chocolate."

She turned and gave Felip a nod and smile. "Thank you. My favorite," she said as she accepted the ice cream from Tui. She opened the wrapper carefully and walked over to the garbage can to deposit it. She didn't return to their group.

Felip should have said something after their conversation. He didn't know *what*, but not saying anything had obviously been a mistake.

"This one's for you, Aaliyah," Tui said.

She took it from him and thanked him with a shy smile as she was joined by the other girls, who led her away to probably gossip. Tui watched her go with an unreadable expression.

Eduardo patted him on the shoulder. "Patience, young grasshopper. Once you give her chocolate, her heart is yours."

Felip wished it were that simple.

Once the rest of the group returned from the botanical gardens, they began the walk back to the hotel. It was only two kilometers, but his heel rubbed on his wet shoe with every step and he had a blister forming on the underside of his little toe. With as much traveling as he'd been doing, he hadn't been walking as often as he normally did.

When he was home in Barcelona, he walked everywhere, only driving to and from the winery. And once he was on the winery grounds, he walked constantly. He should have been enjoying the walk…but his feet were bothering him, Cecilia's story was bothering him, and he needed a break.

His phone buzzed. June.

"Hola," he said, his voice sounding tired and frustrated even to his ears. He stopped walking for a moment, moving out of the way to see if he could shift his wet sock and give his heel some relief.

"Felip? You didn't return my call earlier."

He sighed. "I'm sorry. I've got my hands full with this group and I—"

"It's fine," she said, uncharacteristically understanding. "I wanted to let you know that the documents are ready for the hotel deal. Can I scan them to your phone for your signature?"

"You sign them," he said, figuring now was as good a time as any to tell her about her promotion.

"What do you mean? I can't—"

"I gave you signatory status before I left this last time. I'm making you Chief Operations Officer. I planned to tell you when I returned."

June was silent on the other end. He called her name to be sure they hadn't been disconnected.

"I'm here."

She didn't speak further.

"What do you think? Congratulations?"

"Thank you," she said quietly. "Really, thank you, Felip. I appreciate your confidence in me."

"I have complete confidence in you. And I know I've been a pain lately, I just need…"

"What do you need, Felip? *I'm* the one who's sorry. I've been pushing you lately on these deals, and—"

"But that's what I need you for. I need to know Cava Segura is running smoothly in your capable hands when I am away. I need…I don't know. I'm in a very strange place."

"You're a little young for a midlife crisis."

"Are you actually being funny right now?"

"Shut up," she said, this time truly laughing.

"I don't know what's wrong with me. Maybe I need…"

"A date?"

What? "Why would you say—"

"Come on, Felip. I know it's been a while since you've been serious about anyone…"

She trailed off, and Felip had the sense she was about to drop another bomb. They knew each other that well, it was very possible.

"What is it?"

He felt a hand on his arm and turned to see Cecilia.

"Are you okay?" she asked quietly. She pointed to the rest of the group up ahead, following Gabrielle and the Santiagos. The other group had split off to return to their hotel and would be meeting them for dinner later tonight.

He nodded and gestured with a finger that he'd be a moment. She stepped a few paces away to give him privacy. Felip couldn't tear his eyes away from her retreating figure.

"Your mother came by yesterday and we had lunch. She told me Francesca is getting remarried."

Felip stood straighter, and he felt the familiar tension in his neck whenever her name was mentioned. "She is, huh? That's…well, that's good."

June sighed. "It is good. But I know you. I know you feel—"

"I'm glad for her and that's all that matters. Look, I'm about to lose my tour group—"

June barked out a laugh. "Already? I bet Tomás it would be the second day. I guess he wins."

Felip smiled and something loosened in his chest. "I'd better be going. You're in charge."

"Whatever. I already knew that."

They hung up, and Felip took in a deep breath.

Francesca had moved on. He'd known she was seeing someone. They'd met over lunch to sign papers regarding the sale of their home in Barcelona eight months ago, before the troubles began at the California operation, and she'd mentioned it. It had been a blow knowing that someone else was able to make her happy like he couldn't, but then he'd realized he wouldn't have changed anything at the time. He'd known in his heart that the end of their marriage was the right thing for both of them, but that feeling of failure plagued him.

Say the planets aligned for him and Cecilia? Say there wasn't a whole world between them. Would he make the same mistakes? Would he leave behind yet another unhappy woman? Her husband had cheated on her, something he would never do, but he'd betrayed his own wife in other ways. She'd had expectations of him and he'd put the winery first. Claimed he'd needed to work so much for his family's sake. What if he'd been hiding behind his work so he didn't have to invest more into their marriage? What if he'd been present more and she'd still left?

That was the bottom line. At some point, he'd figured out that she was in the marriage for reasons other than companionship, and no matter how hard he worked, how much he gave of himself, it wouldn't have been enough.

Could he handle it if he gave himself to another woman and failed again?

He saw her walking a block ahead of him, slowly, as though she were giving him a chance to catch up, perhaps a chance to apologize. He wanted to take it.

No more failures, especially when it came to the heart. Whatever happened with Cecilia, he wasn't going to let her believe what she'd shared hadn't mattered to him.

CHAPTER FIFTEEN

5:15 p.m. Madrid Local Time – Plaza de la Provincia

They arrived at the hotel close to five o'clock and the kids were given two hours to shop in the local area, as long as they stayed in groups of three. They would be meeting for dinner at seven. Cecilia was tired, but she didn't want to take a nap. She was restless, and though she wished she could have some alone time, she knew better than to go wandering off by herself. She tagged along behind a group of kids as they visited shops looking at the clothes and remarking on the price differences.

Cecilia noticed they had some cute pants in one of the stores that were lightweight and would be very comfortable in this heat.

"Mrs. Galván, those would look so cute on you," Kristin said. "I think I'm going to buy one of these dresses to wear to the flamenco show tomorrow night. What do you think?" Kristin held up a dress made of similar material as the pants she was holding. It was a gorgeous gray-blue color.

"I think that would look lovely."

"I might get a dress, too," Janelle said. "I wonder what the guys will wear. I heard Mr. Segura telling them to be sure to dress nice. Do they even, like, know how to wear anything other than tennis shoes?"

The girls giggled and Aaliyah spoke up. "I've seen Tui dressed nice when he's been to church. He wears slacks and dress shoes and everything."

"And don't forget, Eduardo wears a suit every time he addresses the school as student body president," Cecilia added.

"I suppose I could buy a dress," Cecilia said. "I brought nice pants with me to wear to the show, but a nice dress would be…nice."

The girls fawned all over her, trying to find the perfect color.

"I think she should wear red," Janelle said.

"No, I think black is more sophisticated," Kristin said.

"Here, try this one," Aaliyah said with a grin. "I think Mr. Segura would like you in this one for sure."

Cecilia's smile dropped. "I'm not dressing for anyone but myself," she said to the girls, but inside, she was wondering. Would it be worth it to make the effort? She had absolutely no idea what to think after the way he'd reacted to her story about Greg. He'd been called away, again, by Gabrielle, and then they hadn't had a moment alone since. She'd waited for him on the walk back to the hotel to try to get a sense of what he was feeling. He'd seemed rather disturbed by something while he was on the phone.

And then she realized she was being silly. So what if he hadn't reacted to her tale? Maybe that was the response she needed to have. He may not have thought it was a big deal.

But no…if she were being honest with herself, he'd seemed angry when she'd told him Greg had cheated on her. He'd told her she deserved better, but then he hadn't spoken to her again. It was ridiculous to even be thinking of his reaction, or lack thereof, but she'd be fooling herself if she thought she didn't care. She wanted to know where she stood with him.

She wanted him to think about her.

She felt brave suddenly. Who cared about Anna, Claire and Babette? Or the former Mrs. Segura? Cecilia was an attractive woman, and she was worthy of the attention of a good man. She also needed to set a positive example for these girls who were watching her curiously as she stared at herself in the mirror.

"Hold my bag, would you please, Kristin?"

She slid the black dress over her head and adjusted it to lay smoothly, well, as smoothly as possible over her sporty dress. The neckline was a little lower than she normally felt comfortable with but it actually looked quite classy.

"Oh, you have to wear that! It's so pretty."

The sleeveless dress had an empire waist and a flowy skirt with different pieces of similar black material sewed together. The hem came to the tops of her knees in the front and hung a little lower in the back. It was casual enough to wear during the day, but with the nice black strappy sandals she'd brought, it would be dressy enough. She went to the counter and paid for the dress and the pants, because she wanted to be cooler tomorrow. The temperature had really sapped her energy. She also hadn't had enough water to drink.

"What do you say I treat you girls to some water over at that café?"

They all paid for their purchases and sat at an outdoor table in the shade. A server came out and Aaliyah ordered four bottles of water for them.

"That dress is perfect, Mrs. Galván. He's sure to love it."

"Now why would I care what he thinks of my new super-hot dress?"

They giggled, and Janelle said, "Because I heard the boys talking to him about you."

"They did not!" Oh, she was going to take a ruler to them...figuratively speaking, of course.

"They did. They were trying to be all protective, it was hella funny. But Mr. Segura, he said nice things about you. Don't you think he's amazing?" Janelle got a dreamy look on her face and Cecilia tried not to laugh. "He's, like, so handsome. He was hecking nice to them, too, when they flooded the boat and got him all wet."

"They did?" Cecilia hadn't paid attention. She knew they'd had some trouble out on the water, but she'd been too busy trying to encourage Aaliyah and Tui to have an actual conversation with each other using more than one-word answers. Felip's boat was on the opposite side of the lake by that point.

"Yeah," Janelle said, "and he didn't even get mad. Eduardo lost the oar—"

"I thought it was Joseph?"

"Anyway, Tui had to help them and then they had to dump a bunch of water out when they got back to shore. It was hella funny."

"He *has* taken all of this pretty well," Cecilia admitted.

"He's so funny, and he's so hot," Janelle continued. "Like, the men here, they're so beautiful."

"Heck yeah. I'm coming here for college," Kristin said.

The conversation turned, thankfully, toward the girls and their plans for after high school, which for Aaliyah and Janelle would be next year. Kristin was going into her junior year, so she had time. Cecilia thought back to her rush through college so she could hurry up and start teaching and get married to Greg. Boy, had she been foolish.

"The one piece of advice I would give all of you is to do what you want. Don't be in a hurry. Obviously you can't live with your parents forever. I mean, you *could*. Look at me, I just moved back in with my mom. But you get what I mean, right? You don't have to know what you want to be when you grow up. I still don't."

They all laughed, but Aaliyah tilted her head. "Do you regret becoming a teacher?"

"Never," Cecilia said with conviction. "That's the one decision I've never regretted. Not that I regret much, I've learned from everything that's happened in my life. But I was in such a hurry to grow up, I don't think I gave myself enough time to experience all that life had to offer in my twenties."

"Is that part of why you got divorced?"

Aaliyah looked like she was afraid she'd asked something she shouldn't have. Cecilia hadn't mentioned a whole lot to her students about it, but people talked. She took a long drink on her water and exhaled.

"Probably. We both wanted to be in different places. We tried to compromise, but then I wasn't willing to sacrifice my job for him, and he didn't want to wait anymore."

"That's so hard, when geography keeps you apart." Janelle said. "My sister and her boyfriend tried to stay together in college, but she wanted to go away to the East Coast and he went to Sac State, so they ended up breaking up."

"You can't argue with geography," Cecilia said and sighed. The girls seemed to get what she was saying. They all picked up their bottles and sipped quietly until they finished. Cecilia could tell they were all tired. "You guys want to head back and absolutely *not* take a nap?"

"Absolutely not," Kristin said, a mock serious expression on her face.

At seven o'clock on the dot, Cecilia made it down to the lobby—grateful that her siesta hadn't completely ruined her hair—and found some of the kids missing. Gabrielle had cornered Felip and they were deep in discussion. He'd changed clothes and was dressed in a light-colored pair of khakis and a button-down shirt rolled at the sleeve. The girls were right. He really was ludicrously hot.

Cecilia had put in a little extra effort. She added the slightest bit of makeup and wore another of her sundresses. She'd told herself it was for the heat, but in truth, she'd noticed his eyes wandering her legs the night before. So much for not dressing for him.

He glanced her way and did a double take. He excused himself from Gabrielle and headed her way with a serious expression on his face. "Will you walk with me?"

Cecilia looked at his outstretched hand and hesitated for a moment before taking it.

He led her outside and down the street from the hotel. She had to nearly trot in her sandals to keep up with him. He didn't let go of her hand, a fact she was very aware of.

"I told Gabrielle how to get to the restaurant and told her we would meet them there. I need to speak to you."

"Am I in trouble? Did something happen?"

He stopped and turned towards her. "No. Why would you think that?"

She laughed nervously. "I don't know. Because you're so serious right now."

He looked around them and pulled her into a little alleyway, crowding her against the wall. She could get away from him if she wanted. Which she didn't. She shifted her weight and her thigh brushed his knee as he moved closer.

"Is this better?" Felip took her other hand in his, doing that thing where he rubbed his thumb over her knuckles.

"Depends. If I'm in trouble, I suppose it's better not to be scolded in the middle of the street." Her heart was pounding now. Was he leaning closer? He was definitely staring at her lips. She didn't exactly feel intimidated, but she was a little thrown by this change in his demeanor. She kicked her chin up a bit, and his eyelids did that thing where they sort of fluttered closed and then his gaze smoldered. Yeah, he was definitely smoldering.

"Nothing has happened, no. But you *are* in trouble," he said, leaning so close she felt his breath against her hair.

He brought a hand up slowly and caressed her jaw with his thumb. People continued to pass by a few feet away, but her full attention was on the movement of his thumb and the way his eyes scanned her face as though he were unsure.

She opened her mouth to speak, to ask his intent, and he took her movement as an invitation.

His kiss was...all-encompassing. He kissed with his whole body. He wrapped his hand around the back of her neck, bringing her crashing against him. He embraced her with his other arm, pressing their chests together, and his thigh slipped between hers. He sort of undulated as though they were dancing without moving their feet. His chest would brush hers, he'd pull tighter with his hands, and then his thigh connected with her...

Ohhhhh. The pressure had her body answering his call over and over. Chest, grip, thigh. Chest, grip, thigh. He sucked at her lips, nibbled on them, licked at them, begging to be let in, and when Cecilia gasped, he went for it.

The first brush of their tongues sent her into a frenzy. She moaned against him, reached up and tangled her fingers in his wild hair, following the 1...2...3 of their dance. She began to see spots from lack of oxygen and let her head fall against the wall, wordlessly inviting him to move his attention from her lips to the tender flesh of her throat. She felt his tongue, and then his teeth...and the friction down below, which was *doing* things to her. Long-forgotten things. Her womb awakened and clenched. She was like a desperate woman lost in the desert, begging for a sip, just a taste of...

"Felip, if you give me a hickey, I'm going to kill you."

His laughter against her jaw sent jolts of desire straight to that thirsty woman and before she completely embarrassed herself, she placed her hands against his chest and applied enough pressure to give him pause.

"Cecilia," he breathed against her skin.

Laughter came from the sidewalk, and Felip moved his body to block her from the view of onlookers.

"I did not give you a love bite. Your fair skin, however, has the loveliest shade of pink to it." He brushed his thumb across her lips and kissed her once more, gently this time, but it had the same effect.

"I'm not sure how this means I'm in trouble," Cecelia said. "But whatever I did to deserve this, I'm doing it again."

Felip's laugh was contagious, and soon they were both clutching each other and gasping for air.

"I've been dying to do that," Felip said against her hair.

"Well, it's probably a good idea you didn't do it sooner. It might have been awkward, say, in the middle of the palace or—"

"On the bus. Right, you are correct. I apologize if I've acted impulsively."

"Don't apologize for being impulsive...but Felip? Can I ask you a question?"

He stepped back a little, allowing her to finally take a deep breath.

"Anything, cariño," he said, brushing her hair back from her face.

Cariño. She liked that too much. She liked *him* too much. His touch warmed her to her toes. He had such a soft, sleepy smile. His full lips, so perfectly formed they seemed unreal, had just been kissing her silly. She wished for a moment she was completely alone with him, the two of them touching and dancing in silence, the only sounds evoked from their pleasure.

But then what? And that's why she had to ask him.

"What are we doing?" She pressed her hand against his chest, on the skin showing between the two sides of his shirt. His heart beat as rapidly as hers.

"What we both want?" He stood a little straighter. "Is that so wrong?"

She shook her head and pressed her cheek to his chest. If she heard his heartbeat, maybe she could believe what he was saying.

"No. Not wrong. Foolish, maybe?"

"Why foolish? Are we not adults? I enjoy your company, Cecilia. A lot. I've had more fun with you in this short time than I've... Well, I've *never* had this much fun with a woman. You make me laugh."

Cecilia snorted. "That's me. A laugh a minute."

"You are fun, and caring, and strong. And I like you." This was the first time she'd really sensed a vulnerability to him, and she didn't know what to do with it.

"I like you, too, Felip. But what happens when..."

"When the tour is over?" he asked, as though he'd sensed what she was afraid of.

"Yeah. When the tour is over, and I have to go home. I know some people are all about the vacation fling, having a passionate affair with a stranger and then going back to their lives."

He wiggled is eyebrows at what she'd said and then pulled his face together in mock seriousness. "Go on, por favor, Cecilia."

Lord, the way he says my name...

"I'm not that person," she said. "I like routines. I do my job, I see my friends, I go home and read a book and I go to bed. I'm not very exciting, I don't know what to *do* with excitement. Yes, I like to have fun. I'm having a wonderful time."

"Then continue having a wonderful time. Let me show you my country. Let us get to know each other. When it is time for you to return home, then we'll talk about what we are doing. Vale?" He placed a hand over his heart and inhaled, the gesture accentuating his strong cheekbones and the stark hollows of his cheeks that gave him such a serious look...until he smiled. That crooked tooth continued to fascinate Cecilia, as did everything about him. His eyes, those lips, and when she walked behind him, that view—

"Cariño? Are you with me? You are having that look again that makes me think you want to be in trouble once more."

"Oh, I'm in trouble," she muttered. "Go on."

"Play with me, Cecilia. Let me show you how a woman like you deserves to be treated."

She'd really like to see him try. It would be nice to be wooed, especially by a man so handsome, so different than anyone she'd ever met before. Maybe she could relax and have fun. Not *too* much fun. Not dark alley kisses that threatened to wake her slumbering libido, not that kind of fun. No. But a few laughs, a few heated glances. And then she'd go home with some nice memories. It sounded great...

"We should probably get to dinner." She tried a smile, but she wondered if he realized that his impulsivity had rocked her world and had her completely disoriented, something she couldn't be. She had kids to take care of. She had to be a good example for them, especially the girls. After their questions at lunch, if things went south with Felip, all eyes would be on them. She was reminded of her words to Aaliyah.

"Here, step into the light." He pulled her toward the street once more and turned her to face the waning sunlight. "I want to be sure I didn't leave any marks."

She smacked his arm. "You better not have! What would I say to the kids?"

He brought a hand to his chin and stroked his scruff. "That is a good point. I suppose we could tell them that on our walk, a robber ran out of a store, crashed into you, left a…what did you call it? A hickey? And then he ran off." He shrugged all innocent-like and she rolled her eyes. "It could happen."

"And I think you'd better watch out. I heard my boys were asking you about me. I bet they could take you."

He chuckled and linked their fingers together. "You're probably right. I haven't had to fight for a long time. Not since my brothers and I were under one roof. Alonso, my brother before Tomás, he was the only one who could best me. I had to be on my guard at all times."

Cecilia could picture Felip and his mini-mes tussling with each other.

"I never understood that sibling stuff. I don't have any brothers or sisters."

"No? That must have been lonely."

She shrugged. "I had my mom and my grandparents. We had a good time."

"Do you think that is why, perhaps, you became a teacher?"

"I do," she said. "I love teaching. You're definitely never alone. It keeps you young, you know? Teaching Life Skills prepares them for the things they'll face in their lives and teaching them my language gives them another perspective. We live in a small town, so some of these kids don't have a lot of experience with people who are different."

"Do they see you as different?"

Cecilia thought about that for a minute. "Not so much as I some-times *feel* I'm different. To them, I'm just Mrs. Galván, another adult put on this Earth to make their lives miserable."

"Not hardly," Felip said, tugging at her fingers. "They respect you. That takes work."

"It's not work if you love what you do," she said, feeling every word of it. "Not that I don't get tired or frustrated from time to time, but I love it." She bumped him with her shoulder. "Do you love what you do? I mean, I know you love the wine…"

"I love wine, that is true. I love that I get to represent my family's history and that we are good at what we do." She noticed his smile slip a little, and he paused as though he was thinking of the right words to say.

"But?"

He sighed. "It's a lot. I have been working at the winery since I was barely a teenager, and I took over as CEO for my father when he had a heart attack ten years ago. I was newly married, I was ready to step up...I wanted to make my father proud. Now?" He rolled his neck around on his shoulders. "I'm...tired." He chuckled humorlessly. "I feel...resentful? Sometimes? I'm thirty-nine years old and what do I have?"

"A successful business? A brother who obviously loves you enough to stick you with a bunch of teenagers...ooooo. Yeah. Maybe not that one."

He wrapped his arm around her shoulders and laughed heartily. "Or perhaps he knew better than I knew myself what I needed to relax."

"Yeah? This is your idea of relaxing? Maybe you should get your head examined."

He kissed the top of her head. "It is time for me to keep my hands to myself. The restaurant is up ahead."

He let go, and Cecilia immediately wished he hadn't.

CHAPTER SIXTEEN

7:15 p.m. Madrid Local Time – Near Mercado de San Miguel

Felip let go of Cecilia and reality slapped him in the face.

He'd kissed her. No, not just kissed her. He'd backed her up against an alley wall like she was some casual hook-up and not the woman he'd come to respect so much. How could he have been so reckless?

How could he *not*? He had to know. Did she possess as much fire as he'd thought? Did she taste as sweet?

He'd gotten his answer, and God help him, but he wanted more.

She'd responded to him like a flower to the sunlight. Her passion bloomed for him, and he'd barely been able to resist lifting her skirt and taking things much further. If they were alone—which most likely they'd never be—he would love to make this woman sing.

Her words of caution and her uncertainty about getting involved were ridiculous. He *was* involved, and before the tour was over, he was determined to make her his. He would convince her that his country was so spectacular, she wouldn't want to leave...or leave *him*. He needed to begin planting the seeds, stealthily of course, or she'd balk.

Being by her side was so much brighter than he'd experienced in a long time, and he didn't want that light to ever go out. This time, he would not fail.

They entered the restaurant and the students were chatting loudly. Gabrielle gave them a knowing smile, and Cecilia made a frustrated sound.

"Lord, I'm never going to hear the end of this."

"Glad you two made it before the food. Felip? Can you please check with the staff and ask if there are any nut products used in the food? I checked our sheets and we don't have any food allergies, but the other school, they have a nut allergy."

"Sí. Just one moment."

He walked over to the bar and asked for the manager, who he'd met once before. The man recognized him as Tomás's brother and quickly confirmed that there were no nut products used in the paella, but that there could be nuts in some of the dessert offerings.

"Muy bien, gracias."

When he returned, Cecilia was sitting with the kids and listening to Bill and Tony share a story of the last time they'd been to Spain with Zoey and Mr. Barragan, who was the second Spanish teacher. When he retired, Gabrielle took his place.

"Mr. Barragan was hilarious," Tony said. "He got us lost every time we went out on our own with him. Zoey would always give him a hard time about it. 'You speak Spanish! How can you get lost?'"

Cecilia and Aaliyah suddenly broke out laughing.

"What's so funny?" Bill asked them.

Aaliyah looked to Cecilia for permission, and Cecilia nodded, then dropped her head in her hands. "Go ahead."

"Mrs. Galván and I got lost in the park. We asked three different people where the bathrooms were and we walked everywhere!"

Cecilia lifted her head and she was very red in the face. Felip thought she looked even more radiant, surrounded by her students, telling stories.

"The first guy spoke so fast, even Aaliyah couldn't understand him. So we found a lady leading a group of little kids and she pointed in the opposite direction. We followed her instructions and ended up at a building that was locked up tight. Then we asked one more person and that one pointed in the same direction as the first guy. Miraculously, this time, it was like the building magically appeared. I swear it wasn't there the first time! Anyway, we had to beg this guy to let us in. I had to do the pee-pee dance in front of him so he'd let us in. That was our adventure."

The group laughed with them and Cecilia rolled her eyes at Aaliyah. Then she caught Felip's gaze and her smile shifted, enough for him to tell that she hadn't wanted him to hear the story, but was willing to be embarrassed in front of the kids, letting them know that even teachers made mistakes.

"Ah, so you're the new Mr. Barragan! ¡Salud!" Tony toasted her and the rest did the same. Felip watched from the bar, where he was half listening to Gabrielle.

"So tomorrow we spend the day in Toledo," she said. "Is everything set? And tomorrow night we have the flamenco show? I hope the students enjoy it."

"Sí. I will talk to Tomás tonight and make sure I have all of the details. He's keeping me on a need-to-know basis."

"We'll be fine as long as you tell us where to be and when. Toledo was one of my favorite places when I lived here for a summer. I could swing it if we didn't have a guide, but it's great when the students hear from the locals."

"You lived here?"

"I did. After I graduated from college, before I started my fifth year student teaching. I'd already spent a semester here in an intensive Spanish program, and I knew I wanted to come back. I love it here. I looked for jobs here after I had my credential and was looking into moving here permanently, but then Zoey and I had to take care of our grandparents, so I stayed. Someday I'll be back."

Gabrielle tossed her hair and laughed. Felip realized she was definitely not vapid, she was actually quite intelligent and took her job as tour leader very seriously.

"That would be wonderful. There is a great need for English teachers here, especial ones who are bilingual. I'm sure Tomás could put you in touch with the right people."

Gabrielle smiled at him, and Felip braced himself for a come-on. "Your brother is hot. Is he single?"

Felip chuckled in relief. Good, she'd moved on. "Usually he is. It is sometimes difficult to find a true partner when you are traveling all the time."

Gabrielle sighed. "I would love to travel more. Teaching is perfect because I have the summer off. After the tour is over, I'm taking the kids to the airport in Barcelona and then I'm working my way south. I was disappointed that we weren't going to Granada on this trip, so I'm planning to stay and visit there, then make my way on the Camino de Santiago."

Felip perked up at her words. "You are not accompanying the students home?"

She shook her head. "There only needs to be one of us. Cecilia will be flying home with them. It's part of the reason we needed another teacher on the trip. That, and we'd already paid for another teacher chaperone. It's safer that way."

Felip's heart sank. She would *have* to leave at the end of the tour. In his mind, he'd been plotting ways he could entice her to stay on with him in Barcelona. He had to return to work before June's head exploded, but hoped he and Cecilia could do more traveling together.

It dawned on him that he didn't see an alternative to her staying. He wanted her in his life. Of course, there would still be the details to work out if she stayed long term, but those were simply details. Felip wanted more time with her, period. A lot could happen in the next nine days, though. She could decide she hated him. He could...

No. He already knew all he needed to know. He wasn't infatuated with her. She was exactly the kind of woman he pictured himself settling down with, for good this time, and having children with... What would his mother think?

"Felip, you're really going to have to do a better job of paying attention if you plan to keep this tour guide gig."

"What? I'm so sorry, Gabrielle," he said, placing his hand on hers on the bar. He was being an absolute ass. "I am preoccupied."

"I know. With her," she said, glancing at Cecilia. Felip's gaze followed hers and landed on Cecilia, who was looking at them with an eyebrow raised. It was only the briefest moment, and then she went back to talking with the students animatedly. Had he imagined a look of discontent? He realized he'd touched Gabrielle, and with them speaking in Spanish it might have looked different... He yanked his hand back quickly, and Gabrielle laughed and tossed her hair once more.

"I was saying that you have quite a challenge ahead if you plan to pursue Cecilia. After the way her husband did her wrong, she's not going to trust anyone easily again."

"How would you suggest I proceed then? Because I certainly intend to not only pursue her, but to win her affections."

Gabrielle gasped and pressed her hand to her chest. "God, that sounds so romantic. Although, she might view that as chauvinistic. She's quite the feminist, our Cecilia. In my opinion, that's a big part of why she and her husband didn't work out. She wasn't willing to move to be with him, which, hello, if a man was willing to support me, I'd be all over that."

Felip laughed, but he did not find that trait attractive. He'd had a wife who was willing to let him support her, but it often felt like she wanted his money more than she wanted him, and that had hurt. He'd love to have a wife who wanted to have children, but if she wanted to work, he would support that too.

"I wish you luck in finding that husband," he said. He saw the servers coming forward with the platters of paella and he took that as his opportunity to mingle with the others.

"This is so good, Mr. Segura," Joseph said as Felip rejoined the group. "Do you guys, like, eat this all the time?"

Felip chuckled. The two thin boys were shoveling the food in as fast as they could. He imagined with all of the walking they'd been doing, they were probably famished.

"We do tend to eat it a lot. Mi abuelita made it the best, though."

"It's so good," Joseph repeated—and then he coughed. And coughed again, covering his mouth to keep from spitting out the food.

"Dude, you okay? You choking?" Tui asked, jumping out of his seat to check on his friend.

"Nah," Joseph said, shaking his head. "My throat's like hella scratchy though."

"Oh my God, Joseph," Eduardo said with his mouth full. "Your lips are swelling! What's wrong with you? Mrs. Galván!"

She looked over from where she was chatting with Bill and Tony and immediately lost her smile. She kicked her chair back, leaving it to fall on the floor as she rushed over.

"Joseph? Can you talk?"

She held his face in her hands and his eyes bugged out. "My mouth is...what's..."

"Was there seafood in this paella, Felip?"

"There is a good chance. I can ask, but that looks—"

"Like an allergic reaction. Here..." She dug around in her small purse and brought out a bottle of pink pills. "Tui, get him some water. Here, Joseph, swallow these."

Joseph took the pills and gulped down the water, spilling nearly as much as he drank. His eyes were huge.

"Does anyone have an EpiPen?" she asked.

Mrs. Santiago jumped up. "I do. Jorge is allergic to bees. Here."

Cecilia calmly took the device from Mrs. Santiago and removed the cap. "Joseph, I need you to be still."

"Are you gonna stab me?" He squealed and tried to slide away. He was still coughing, but he seemed more affected by the impending needle stick than the swelling.

"Quit messing around and let her stab you, dude. You might die."

"Not funny, Eduardo," Cecilia said calmly. "Joseph, I need you to take a deep breath and trust me. You're barely going to feel this, I promise."

"Yeah, man. It won't be as bad as that time when you fell doing bleacher runs in PE, remember that?" Tui asked. He'd placed his hands on Joseph's shoulders from behind, calmly applying pressure and causing Joseph to look up to answer him.

"I remember that!" Eduardo shouted, glancing at Cecilia and nodding. "You, like, were two steps from the top and you slipped and rolled all the way down. How you didn't break your—"

"Ahhhhhh!" Joseph screamed and then sat back. "Oh. That didn't even hurt."

Cecilia had used the boys' distraction as her opportunity and brought the pen down firmly on Joseph's thigh. "Now sit here and sip some water, and let's see if this works."

Cecilia looked around until she spotted Felip, who was totally in awe of her. "Felip, can you call whatever emergency number you have? We might need an ambulance if this doesn't work."

Joseph appeared to calm down and the red splotches he'd started to get on his neck and face faded right in front of their eyes.

"I already called," Gabrielle said. "They said they'd send an ambulance or we could bring him to the nearest urgent care."

"I have to go to the hospital?" Joseph shrieked.

"Dude! You could have died! How did you not know you were allergic to shellfish?"

He shrugged. "I don't know. I've never eaten it before. It always seemed so squishy," he answered, his eyelids drooping. "Mrs. Galván? I'm really tired. Is that normal?"

"Yes, honey. Your body is fighting anaphylactic shock. You're going to be exhausted."

He nodded and leaned his head against Tui. "You do make a good pillow," he said, his eyes drifting closed.

"Joseph?"

"Hmm? I'm sleepy, I'm not dead."

Cecilia sat back on her heels and exhaled. "Can someone help me up?"

Felip rushed to her side and took her hand.

"Are you okay?" he asked as she stood beside him.

"Yeah, I bruised my knee when I dove over here. I'm fine. Can we take him to an urgent care? I want him to see a doctor."

Felip nodded. "Let's go."

Felip called Tomás to give him the information and he agreed to meet them at the clinic.

"Have Gabrielle walk the students back. I'll text you all the information you need."

Cecilia insisted on going with Joseph, so Felip loaded Joseph in the backseat and Cecilia slid in beside him. Felip rode up front and spoke to the driver.

"Is he all right?" Felip asked her once they were on their way.

Cecilia stroked Joseph's hair as he lay across her lap. "I think so. It was a close call, but I think he just needs sleep."

Felip smiled at her. "Are *you* all right?"

She laughed as though her body were expelling all of the stress she'd just experienced. "All in a day's work. It's always something with these kids," she said.

"And yet you handled it so calmly."

"It's not my first rodeo. I once had the secretary call me out of class and ask me to look over a student who had a swollen finger. We don't have nurses at our school sites, and I'm trained in advanced first aid. I got there, and the kid's finger was indeed swollen, about three times the normal size. He said he thought something bit him and that he'd never given himself a shot with his EpiPen. His mom showed up and said she'd never done it either, that it freaked her out. She gave me permission and I gave him the shot. Then he tells me, 'It's been like this since last night.'" She rolled her eyes. "I told his mother to take him to the doctor and she was grateful I'd stepped in. I knew what to do with the device because my grandfather had severe allergies to stings from bees. Of course, the idiot continued to tend bees for years."

"Was that what eventually led to his demise?"

She snorted. "Nope. He had a stroke. He was almost ninety, though, so he lived a full life."

Felip relaxed. "Then it seems like he knew best."

They arrived at the closest clinic and Felip spoke to the woman in charge. He provided all of the information Tomás sent him about Joseph in Spanish, and she told him they should take a seat at door number 13. He chuckled to himself as he returned to Cecilia and a very sleepy Joseph.

"Here we go," he said, pulling the young man up and supporting him as they walked down the hall past several benches until they found door 13.

"It is our lucky number, profesora."

They sat and Joseph immediately lay his head in her lap again. Cecilia smiled at him and played with his hair as one would a small child. Joseph was taller than her by a few inches, but as he slept, he looked much younger than sixteen years old.

"Right. Lucky thirteen."

Thankfully they were seen in less than thirty minutes. In a place such as this, one could wait hours to be seen. The doctor said it appeared the injection and pills Cecilia had given him had done the trick and they didn't think he needed to be hospitalized. He told Felip in Spanish that Joseph should be watched for twenty-four hours and if his condition worsened, he'd need to be taken to a hospital. The doctor gave Cecilia more medication and signed some paperwork and that was that. Felip called them another cab and they waited for it to arrive.

Back at the hotel, Felip carried Joseph up to his room, with Cecilia and Tomás following. He was tall, but he was thin and it was not a struggle for him.

"I will stay with him," Felip said, figuring it would be more proper than a woman sharing a room with a young man.

"Are you certain? Tomás asked in their native Catalán. "I've already asked so much of you, my brother."

"It's the least I can do."

Cecilia tried to argue with him, but he wouldn't budge. "You need your rest. Tomás and I will stay with him tonight and then we will decide what to do about tomorrow. I don't think he will be ready to walk around Toledo in this heat."

"I can stay with him tomorrow," Cecilia said. "They'll need their guide tomorrow. Gabrielle will need you."

She turned to leave them at the door, and Felip reached for her hand.

"Cecilia? What is the matter?"

She pulled her hand away and frowned. "Nothing. I'm tired. Please call me if there are any changes with Joseph. I'm going to let his mother know what happened. Good night."

She turned around and walked swiftly towards the other end of the hall. Had she misunderstood his conversation with Gabrielle? Was there something else the matter?

Then she halted. He saw her take a deep breath, and she turned around to face him once more.

"Thank you for helping take care of Joseph. I wouldn't have been able to deal with the doctor by myself. I appreciate it."

She didn't smile. Either she was worried about the young man or she was upset. He wanted to confront her, but the situation made that impossible.

"It was my pleasure. Anytime."

She nodded and turned to walk back to her bedroom, slightly limping.

Her knee. He hadn't seen to her injury.

"Cecilia!" He called to her, but she didn't turn around. Perhaps she didn't hear him? He cursed under his breath and returned to Joseph's room, where Tomás was putting the student to bed.

"I'll be right back."

Tomás waved him away with a laugh and Felip rushed down the hall. He realized he didn't know her room number. He climbed down the stairs, taking them two at a time, and approached the front desk. He asked them for a bag of ice and which room she was in. The clerk frowned, until he explained he was with the tour and showed his ID, the one that identified him as a guide—the one Tomás had insisted he get despite assurances that he'd never need it. The clerk returned with a baggie filled with ice from the bar in the back of the lobby, and Felip ran up the stairs to room twelve. He knocked on the door, but there was no answer. He knocked again a little harder.

The door next to hers opened and out spilled Kristen, Janelle and Aaliyah with their eyes wide.

"She said to text her if we needed her," Aaliyah said. "She takes her hearing aids out when she goes to bed."

"Can you please give me the number?" he asked, taking his phone out of his pocket. One of the girls took it from him, which caught him off guard, and she punched the numbers into his phone.

He thanked the girls and they backed into the room, still giggling.

Cecilia, it is Felip. I was worried about your knee. I brought you some ice, can you open the door?

The wait felt like an eternity. Several of the students walked by as he stood lurking outside her door like a mad man, pulling at his hair until it stood out from his head. June frequently gave him a hard time for doing the same thing while working under stress.

After ten minutes, he wondered if she'd gone to sleep. He hated not knowing if she was in pain and felt terrible that he hadn't insisted that she get looked at by the doctor as well.

After fifteen minutes, he was torn between getting the manager to check on her or leaving her alone. Her text finally came.

I was in the shower. I'm fine. Thank you for taking care of Joseph tonight.

As always, she put the students before herself.

. . .

I still have this ice. Would you like it for your knee?

He was beginning to think he should use it on his wounded pride. Everything had been wonderful between them just a few short hours ago, and now he was stuck standing outside her door, not knowing what he'd done to upset her and receiving curt answers. He was about to return to the boy's room and accept defeat when his phone buzzed again.

Are you still outside?

He answered right away that he was, and her door opened a crack. Steam from the shower and a sweet fragrance likely from her shampoo wafted towards him. Cecilia stuck her hand out and made grabbing motions with her fingers.

"Cecilia, are you all right?" he asked.

"I'm fine," she said, her voice muffled behind the door. "Thank you for the ice."

He hesitated before placing the bag in her hand, and he didn't let go. She tugged on it, but he kept his hold. He needed to see her face. He stepped closer to the door. "Cariño, can I see you?"

"I just showered. I'm a mess. I'm going to go to bed."

He looked around to see if there were any witnesses, and he didn't see anyone, but he heard giggling behind the door next to hers as though the girls were eavesdropping.

"I need to know," he whispered. "Are we all right?"

Cecilia leaned out. "Thank you."

Her hair was wet, her eyes were wide, and she was beyond lovely... He had so much he wanted to say, but where to begin?

"My hand is freezing, Felip."

He let go, reluctantly. "I'll see you tomorrow." He returned to the room he'd checked into this morning when he took over as guide. He changed into sweatpants and a t-shirt before heading back down to Joseph's room. They'd agreed to get another room for Tui and Eduardo, so Tomás and Felip could take turns staying with the young man overnight. The other boys were packing up what they needed for bed before moving to their room.

"He's going to be fine, right, Mr. Segura?" Eduardo asked.

"He will be fine by tomorrow afternoon, I predict. He took a lot of medicine tonight and needs to sleep it off. By the time you get back from Toledo, he will be ready to rejoin the activities."

Felip's phone buzzed.

I couldn't talk because we had company listening in. I'll be fine, Felip.

That wasn't exactly an answer to his question.

I wish you were coming tomorrow. Toledo is a beautiful city.

Her answer had him ready to throw his phone across the room.

I'm sure it is. Please watch out for my kids.

"Hermano, I'm going to go back to my flat and take care of a few things. I'll be back so you can get some sleep."

"I'll be fine," he said, although he wasn't fine.

"Are you sure? If you keep pounding on that phone, you will break it."

Felip cursed, and Tomás laughed. He spoke in Catalán to Felip.

"Your little teacher has you frustrated already?"

"Yes, something happened tonight. I think."

Tomás looked at the boys, and they immediately picked up their things and said their good nights. Joseph was asleep on the bed, snoring softly.

"You realize she is in a very difficult position, Felip? She can't have an affair while she's working like this. Not to mention, if you screw up, brother, it will hurt my company."

"Our company, Tomás. I know that, I am not stupid. But earlier, she...it seemed like she would give us a chance, you know, to see what could happen after the tour was over, and then...I don't know."

Tomás patted him on the shoulder and switched to English. "You have spent too much time around these kids. Have some patience. Let the old Segura charm win her over. Emphasis on the old, old man."

Felip responded by throwing a half-assed punch, which Tomás expertly ducked.

Of course I will watch out for the kids, but Cecilia, have I done something to offend you?

Felip thought perhaps she'd put her phone away as it took nearly fifteen minutes for her to answer.

Felip, you are a generous and wonderful man, but this is a terrible idea.

"What?"

Joseph stirred at Felip's outburst, and he felt awful waking the poor kid. He'd have to keep himself together.

. . .

Is it wrong that I wish to show you the beauty of my country? That I want to feed you tapas y pintxos en el País Vasco? That I want to walk on the beach with you en Barcelona? Is it terrible that I want to do all of these things with you, Cecilia?

"Please don't let this be it," he whispered.

No. Because I think it would be wonderful to experience all of it with you.

So why was this a terrible idea, he wondered? Where do they go from here? Her next text hurt his heart.

But I am leaving soon, and then we'll be back to our lives.

It doesn't have to be that way, he wanted to send back. When two people connect as they had, there had to be a way. He had the feeling that if he pushed her too hard tonight, he'd undo the progress they'd made this afternoon.

This is a conversation best had face to face. I will let you get some rest. Hasta mañana, cariño.

He forced himself to put his phone away and sighed. He slid down the wall and sat in a dejected pose on the floor. His thoughts were torn between recalling their stolen moment this afternoon and the look on her face when she'd left him in the hallway tonight.

He let his eyes drift closed, remembering how she'd felt in his arms, against his body. With one kiss, he'd experienced the kind of bliss he'd only ever wished for, the kind of passion that would feed his soul. He wasn't ready to give up that possibility.

CHAPTER SEVENTEEN

3 :00 p.m. Madrid Local Time – Hostal Persal

By the next afternoon, Cecilia was ready to climb the walls. It could have been because Joseph had been literally climbing the walls for the past two hours.   \

"Mrs. Galván, when are they going to be back?"

"Soon, I suppose. Now come sit back down and watch the rest of *Taken* 3 or 4...which one is this? I feel like we've watched ten of them today."

"It's only the third one. Seriously, though, how many times is this dude going to lose people? If he's such a badass, how do the villains keep getting one past him? If I was him, I'd have locked my wife and kid up and built a fortress around them."

"Joseph. Despite the fact that we're in a really old country right now, we don't live in the medieval times. A husband can't just lock up his wife and daughter. They have laws about that sort of thing in most parts of the world."

He chuckled and stood on the bed so he could look out the

window, which was very high up on the wall. "I feel like I'm locked up. We're on the second floor, how come this window is so tiny?"

"I don't know, Joseph. I don't have a degree in Spanish architecture." She tried to keep the impatience out of her voice, but she was going a bit stir crazy. And *stupid, stupid, stupid*, she missed that irritatingly beautiful man and his damn crooked tooth.

"I'm sorry you had to stay with me today and miss Toledo," he said, sitting back down on his bed. They'd remained in his room with the door open and Cecilia sat in the chair by the door, so as not to seem improper. She turned to look at him and saw the guilt in his expression.

"No, sweetie, it's not your fault. These things happen. I'm just glad I was with you and you weren't alone."

"Yeah, that was pretty scary. I've had friends with food allergies and I used to tease my cousin when we were little for not being able to have peanut butter. What a jerk, huh?"

Cecilia chuckled. "Then perhaps this is some pretty vicious karma for you." She looked down at her phone for the millionth time, hoping for a text from him, something. He hadn't attempted to contact her since last night, and she couldn't blame him.

Just how did he expect her to feel? The prospect of having another long-distance relationship, especially with someone as beautiful and charming as Felip, had her feeling completely hopeless. No matter how hard he'd try to make it work, she was sure she'd drive him away with her jealousy and feelings of inadequacy.

Face it, Cecilia. Are you really in a position to give your heart away again?

But if that was the case, she was screwed, because part of her heart already belonged to Felip, and the distance would probably only tug at that missing piece after she left Spain.

Frickin' ankle-banging, crooked-toothed, magic-abbed Casanova. She was done for.

"Hey, I think I hear them," Joseph said as he leaped over her crossed legs and rushed out the door. From the shouts down below, she guessed he was right.

She stood from the chair and stretched her aching back. She'd chosen to wear a long maxi skirt today to hide the awesome black and blue mark on her knee. She looked like she'd taken a pipe to the knee a la some mafia hit, and it didn't feel a whole lot better than it looked.

"Hey, Mrs. Galván? They're all going to get ice cream, can I go?"

She sighed. Their lunch had consisted of fruit and bread from the convenience store. Joseph had been hungry all day and stuck with her boring and cranky self. He deserved to have fun.

"Just avoid the coconut shrimp crème, or like, the lobster sundae, got it?"

He laughed. "You got it. No more shellfish, I promise."

She shook her head. "Go ahead and lock up, I'm going to go back to my room and clean up."

He thanked her again for staying with him and then was out the door and down the stairs in about three steps. She heard Gabrielle scold him and then saw her coming up the stairs.

"Hey, Cece, you guys do okay today?"

"I didn't strangle him, so I think that's a win."

Gabrielle made a sympathetic face. "I'm sorry. You guys missed a great time. The boys bought him a sword at the factory as a surprise."

Cecilia's eyes bugged out. "A sword? Like a real swashbuckling, rapier kind of thing?"

Gabrielle laughed. "It's not sharpened. He can't do too much damage with it."

"Huh. You'd be surprised the damage those boys can do. I'm pretty sure it was Joseph who had to be taken to the office for getting a magnet stuck in his nose in freshman biology."

Gabrielle frowned and looked down the stairs. "Right. Maybe we should hold on to it until he goes home?"

Cecilia laughed. "You aren't going to get ice cream?"

"I was coming to get you," she said. "You look like you could use some fresh air."

"Thank you," Cecilia groaned. "I've had about as much eau de Axe Body Spray as I can stand."

They left the hotel and found the kids down about a block with the Santiagos, devouring various-sized ice cream cones. Cecilia ordered a chocolate one and fought the urge to moan as the velvety sweetness hit her tongue. "This is delicious," she said finally.

She noticed Felip hadn't been at the hotel, nor was he with the group here. She didn't want to be super obvious, but Gabrielle must have noticed the desperate glances.

"Felip and Tomás went over to the restaurant where we're eating tonight to be sure everything's set up and we have no more food allergy issues. Don't worry," she laughed. "He moped around all day, too."

Cecilia hated that she looked so transparent. "I didn't mope."

Gabrielle snorted. "You keep telling yourself that."

Janelle and Kristin approached her with conspiratorial looks on their faces.

"Can we talk to you for a minute?" Janelle asked.

"Sure, girls."

They led Cecilia a little ways away from the rest of the group.

"So, I didn't know if we should say anything," Kristin said. "But Eduardo is out of money."

She frowned. "What do you mean, out of money? It's only the third day!"

"Well, today in Toledo, he bought a bunch of presents for his family. I don't know, but I think it all cost more than he thought it was going to, and he felt weird saying something and now he's not sure he has enough money to eat for the rest of the trip."

Oh Lord, she thought. This could get expensive.

"Alright. Let me talk to him."

They walked back over and she found Eduardo standing with the boys, watching them eat massive scoops of ice cream. It was a depressing sight.

"Hey, Eduardo? I wanted to order some of those muffins in that shop, can you come with me and help me with Spanish?"

"Sure, Mrs. Galván."

Once they were inside the shop, she turned to him. "Okay, tell me straight. You spent all of your money?"

His eyes got really big and then he looked at the floor. "I promised my mom and sisters I'd buy them something, and then I saw something for my grandmother, and I didn't remember about the exchange rate and thought I wasn't spending that much and then I realized I'd only left about fifty euros back in the room."

She patted his arm. "I think it's wonderful that you wanted to treat your family members, but honey, they'd want you to eat, you know? Do you have a card you can use to withdraw some more money?"

He nodded, kicking the edge of the step with his foot. "Yeah, but it'll be cutting into my college savings. My mom's gonna be pissed. And I don't have a job lined up when I get back."

Cecilia knew for a fact that Eduardo was going to need every penny he could get. His single mother supported him and his four sisters on her salary from working in the school district office. It didn't pay a ton. She thought of a possible solution.

"I might have a job for you," she said, tapping her finger against her lips. "It's not going to be fun, but it's work."

His eyes lit up and he finally smiled. "I'll do anything. I'm not afraid to work, Mrs. Galván."

"I know you're not, sweetie. You know how I had to move right before we left?"

The kids knew about her predicament because they'd seen the For Sale sign up on her quaint little home she'd lived in mostly alone for the past two years. She knew they'd find out sooner or later, so she'd told them she was getting divorced and moving back in with her mother, who many of them knew from town. They'd asked a bunch of questions, ones she wasn't really ready to talk about with students, but they'd all said they felt bad, that they loved her house.

She'd loved it, too. It had a big porch with a swing and a hammock and during the summer evenings, she'd often sit out there, wrapped in mosquito netting, reading a book with a book light. It was an older Craftsman-style home, and she and Greg had done a lot of the work to fix it up themselves, which had made her proud. But pride hadn't saved her marriage, not that she'd wanted to save it in the end, but still...

"Yeah, I heard. I'm sorry. That must suck."

There hadn't been the funds to hire movers. A few teacher friends had come over to help her for a few hours, but she'd spent days packing and had no desire to unpack it ever again.

"Well, I could use some help sorting through things. Some will be unpacked, but a lot will be donated. My mom also has a lot of...let's say 'family heirlooms' that need to be sorted and disposed of as well. Not that my mom's a hoarder by aaaaaany stretch of the imagination."

"No, ma'am. You've never seen my grandmother's house. Her house should be on an episode of that show."

"I can't pay you more than minimum wage—"

"It's fine, Mrs. G. I'd do it for free."

"I know, and I appreciate that. Let's talk about it when we're headed home."

Eduardo frowned. "So you're going to just leave when the tour's over?"

It was Cecilia's turn to frown. "What do you mean? Of course! Someone's gotta make sure all of you crazy kids make it back."

He shrugged and looked around. "I don't know. I thought maybe you would stay here, you know..."

"No, I don't know," she said, confused now.

"I thought you and Mr. Segura—"

"Whoa. Whoa whoa whoa. The only me and Mr. Segura is that we're your chaperones on this trip. I only just met him."

"I might have overheard him and his brother talking last night before we left the room. They were speaking Catalán, but I understood some of it—"

"How do you know Catalán?"

"I watched some YouTube videos before we left. And my tour book had a section on phrases. I thought it would be cool, you know, to see how different it was from Spanish. I mean, the Spanish here is hella different than my family speaks..."

"It's not nice to eavesdrop, Eduardo, even if you're trying to learn."

"I know. I think he said something about 'little teacher' and Tomás was kind of teasing him about texting so rough with his phone, and then he was really frustrated."

Damn. She hadn't meant to upset him last night. She was wrung out after walking all day, and then the nightmare with Joseph, which had scared her to death, and then banging her knee, which hurt like hell. But he had to have known she couldn't have talked to him about anything last night? Not only was she not in a place to have that discussion, but she didn't want the kids picking up on anything, although she should have known better.

Eduardo was smiling at her and chuckling. "I'm sorry, Mrs. G, but the dude is sprung."

"Sprung? Not hardly."

"No, for real. He's into you. What would be so wrong—"

"Just...let's stop right there," she said, holding up a hand. "Look, Mr. Segura is a very nice man—"

"A nice, *loaded* man," Eduardo said, then he noticed her teacher look and held up his hands. "I know, I'm sorry. It's none of my business. It's just, you deserve to be happy, Mrs. G."

"I *am* happy, Eduardo, and contrary to popular belief, it's possible to be happy without a significant other." She sighed. "Especially one who lives on another continent," she muttered. She shook her head. "Look, let's join the others. You guys have some time until we have to be cleaned up and ready for dinner. Just...no more presents, okay?" She laughed and elbowed him. "I'll give you some money when you need it, on the down low, right?"

"Mrs. G, no one really says that anymore."

"Oh. Right. Anyway, no one has to know about it, okay? And when we get home, we'll work out something."

"Thank you, Mrs. Galván. You're the best." He hugged her and she patted him on the back before they split apart. She didn't usually hug the kids, but this group was different. They weren't simply her students, they'd bonded on this adventure, and she felt close to them, like they were her own kids or something. Maybe more like nieces and nephews. She didn't want to think about being old enough to be their mother. She could deal with being the cool aunt.

"Now let's buy some muffins so no one knows we were conspiring in here."

He laughed and took the euros from her, buying a half dozen of the big, squishy chocolate chip muffins that had been in the window tempting her every time they'd walked by since arriving here.

Kids. She and Greg had put off talking about a family while he got his business going, and as she passed thirty, she assumed they probably wouldn't have them. She'd always said her students were enough, but sometimes she thought she'd been fooling herself to avoid the pain of disappointment. Now that they were divorced, she needed to decide if having children was something she wanted to pursue, and what that would mean for her life. Her mother had long ago given up asking her about grandbabies—

As if some cross-continental biological clock alarm had sounded, her phone buzzed. Mom.

How's the scenery? Any new developments?

She couldn't help but laugh at her mom's nosiness. Eduardo joined the boys, who were doing some sort of parkour over the benches while the girls watched them and laughed. She pushed the button for the voice text option since she was out of earshot of the kids.

"Spain is quite lovely. Period. We had a child nearly go into anaphylactic shock. Period. They have great muffins here. Period."

That ought to get her mom fuming. Sure enough, seconds later came her angry retort.

You sure as hell know I'm not asking about baked goods unless there's cupcaking involved.

Her mom signed off with a series of inappropriate emojis involving vegetables and body parts.

"You are such a perv. Period. Don't you have something to art? Question mark."

You and I both know we come by perving genetically. Your grandparents raised us both right. Now stop stalling and tell me about the conquistador.

"Oh my God, comma, Mom. Period. There has been no conquering. Period." Well, she wasn't exactly being truthful. "Okay. Period. Maybe some alley plundering, comma, but that can't happen again. Period."

No, as much as she wished it—

You let him plunder your alley? I knew I raised you right! Hope no children were harmed in the process.

More emojis. Cecilia placed a hand over her forehead. Her mom needed her own love life if she was using all the classic romance novel lingo to describe sex, and she told her so.

How do you know I haven't been doing some pillaging of my own? Freddy's back for the summer.

"Mom, please don't use the eggplant and Freddy's name in the same sentence, comma, or I'm not coming back from Spain. Period."

Good. Maybe you should stay awhile. Especially if he's good at plundering. Oh, and Freddy says hi.

. . .

Oh ick. It was early morning in California, so if Freddy was saying hi, that meant he was having conjugal visits with her mother. And if he was back for the summer, they'd be two doors down from her, pillaging or plundering or whatever the hell they did behind closed doors.

Freddy was actually a very nice man who her mother had been seeing off and on for years. He was a retired college professor who spent his time traveling the American west and writing historical novels set during the Gold Rush era. He also dabbled in painting and had taken classes from her mom years ago. Their connection seemed to thrive despite periods of absence. They seemed to be happy shacking up together when the opportunity presented itself.

Cecilia admired that about her mom, that she was independent enough to not need a man around, but to enjoy his company when she had it. She wanted to be like that. She was pretty good at the being alone part. It was the being away part she didn't want to deal with again. Her mom and Freddy had no wedding vows keeping them monogamous, they must have had an understanding of some sort. Was that who she was destined to end up with? A sometimes-around guy? Could she see herself in that situation with someone like Felip?

No. A man like Felip permeated a woman's space and consciousness until she needed his presence like oxygen and missed it immensely when it wasn't there. Like now. It felt strange to be wandering around with the students without him making an observation, asking a question, or laughing at their antics. Which was odd. It had only been a couple of days! Weird, right? Right?

Gabrielle shooed the kids back towards the hotel and Cecilia stirred from her thoughts in time to follow them back.

"Time to get dressed in your nice clothes, amigos. And be prepared for lots of pictures."

A few groans were heard as the kids climbed the stairs of their hotel. Cecilia and Gabrielle separated to change, and afterward, Cecilia got brave. She knocked on Gabrielle's door.

"Hey! Did you need somethi— Wow! Look at that dress! It's gorgeous on you."

She made Cecilia spin around and whistled loudly, which brought the girls piling out of their doorway and into the hall.

"You look so pretty, Mrs. G!"

"Thank you," she said, her cheeks feeling warm. "Gabrielle, I was wondering if I could borrow your curling iron? I thought maybe I'd try to do those ringlet thingies."

"Oh, Mrs. G. Why don't you let me do it," Aaliyah offered. "No offense, but I saw how you were with the flat iron the first day. I don't want you to hurt yourself or end up like that chick in the hair curling tutorial video."

"What girl?" she asked. "And hey, I know how to fix my hair! I'd just woken up from a coma, okay? Cut me some slack."

"This girl," Kristin said, shoving her phone in Cecilia's face.

"What? What's wrong with... Oh...honey...no, take it off...take it off! Oh God, you can't...and there it goes."

The girls laughed at her reaction to the viral video of a girl melting the side of her hair off while trying to film herself.

"Fine," Cecilia said. "I know better than that, but I'll let you do it. I know you have a gift."

And that was how Cecilia ended up in the girls' room while they giggled and fussed over her. She ended up with a full makeup job, which actually looked quite natural, and a head full of blonde ringlets that bounced when she walked. It shortened her just-above-shoulder-length hair to fall around her jaw and took several years off her age. If it weren't for the fine lines on her face thanks to years of perfecting her teacher look, she might have passed for a student herself. Well, maybe a college student...nearing the end of grad school.

Okay, it made her look slightly younger.

They made it to the lobby five minutes late. The others complained about their tardiness until they got a load of Cecilia.

The boys gasped quietly, and there was some elbowing going on, but it was the reaction from the men that nearly had Cecilia running back up to lock herself in her room.

Tomás and Felip had been having a heated argument in another language—she still couldn't always tell whether they were speaking

Catalán or Spanish because they were so damn fast—but whatever it was they were fighting about, they stopped the moment they saw her.

Tomás smiled broadly. Felip frowned deeply, his thick eyebrows nearly meeting in the middle at his consternation. Tomás bumped shoulders with him, but Felip didn't break his gaze from Cecilia.

Her knees wobbled a little as she joined them. Tomás turned to give Gabrielle instructions on the evening's activities. Felip crossed his arms over his chest and stared.

"Hi," she finally said, the verbal equivalent of snapping her fingers in front of his face.

"Ets tan bonic que em fa mal." He said all of that and then blinked.

"I have no idea what you said," she replied, laughing.

He shook his head as though attempting to see more clearly.

"You...I have so many things to say—"

She placed a hand on his forearm. "Don't say anything. Let's go to dinner."

His expression said he didn't want to be silenced, but then he looked around at the students and cleared his throat.

"All here, amigos?" Gabrielle asked the group.

The kids gathered around and Cecilia smiled. They all looked so adorable. Every one of them had done as asked and brought nice clothes for this evening. The girls wore dresses, the boys wore slacks and short-sleeved shirts. Joseph's traditional Filipino shirt looked dashing on him. Tui had pulled his hair back in a hair tie, making his features look dramatic. It also made him look like he was already in his twenties. Her babies were all growing up. Even Jorge, standing between his parents fidgeting with his shirt, looked fantastic, and she told him as much.

His mom gave him a look and he spoke.

"Thank you, Mrs. Galván."

Gabrielle asked the clerk at the desk to please take a picture of all of them and rushed about trying to gather everyone close together. Once they were in position, she ordered them to all shout "queso," to which the clerk rolled his eyes.

Felip moved in close behind Cecilia and she caught a whiff of whatever exotic Spanish fragrance he seemed to emit. It smelled like power, masculine charm, and exploding ovaries, if there were such a smell. He placed a hand at the small of her back and as she looked up at him, the clerk snapped the picture, the flash blinding everyone but her. She was blind to everything but Felip...and wasn't that something? To only have eyes for a man that she shouldn't want like this...

As the students began following Gabrielle and Tomás out the door, Felip held out his elbow to Cecilia. It was such an old-fashioned move, and despite everything in her feminist being cautioning her, she slipped her hand in the crook of his arm and allowed him to lead her out the door.

They were quiet as they walked. A few times the kids turned around to glance at them. Her scowl had them turning away immediately.

"One glance from you has them falling into line, just like that," he said with a laugh. When she didn't respond, he cleared his throat again. "It seems to have the same effect on me."

"Felip, I'm—"

"Cecilia—"

They both spoke at once and then laughed together at their anxiousness with each other. They acted as though they were on a first date.

"I'm sorry," she finally said. "I don't know why I was so off last night—"

"No need to apologize. It is I who should apologize. You are here in a precarious role, and I did not respect that. I tried to force you into—"

"You didn't force me into anything. Felip, I don't know how to do this, knowing that I'm leaving and we'll likely never see each other again."

He looked at her as though that was the most preposterous thing he'd ever heard. "How can you even think that, cariño? There is no way I will never see you again. I won't be able to stay away from you."

She sighed. "You say that now..."

He placed a hand over hers and squeezed. "I propose that we not worry about your impending departure. Can we please spend the next week enjoying ourselves? I promise," he said, tucking his hands behind his back, "I will not accost you again. We will simply get to know each other and have a wonderful time. No pressure. No worries. Can we at least try?"

She really was being foolish. She was adult enough to do as he asked. She just needed to channel her mother and have fun. Well, not that much fun.

Cecilia stopped walking and held out her hand to shake. "Alright, Segura. You've got a deal. Fun, no worries, no pressure. Deal."

He looked at her hand as though she was playing a trick on him, as though he expected her to have one of those hand buzzers and was lying in wait to zap him. He finally took her hand, but instead of shaking it, he bent down and kissed the back.

"You have a deal, profesora." He looked up and chuckled. "But we're about to lose our group," he said. "And for once, I'm not entirely sure where my brother is taking us. I haven't been to this restaurant before."

"Well, then let's hurry." She grabbed his hand and pulled him into a trot. "It's a good thing I wore sensible shoes."

CHAPTER EIGHTEEN

6:45 p.m. Madrid Local Time – Near Puerta del Sol

Felip sat with Bill and Tony over dinner and delighted in hearing the story of how they met on a tour such as this one. He watched Cecilia closely as she flitted about making sure the kids all had enough tapas to eat and enough water to drink, since "you all haven't been doing a good enough job staying hydrated." The black dress she wore had taken his sanity away when she came down the stairs, and paired with her subtle but transformative makeup and the intricate hairstyle that accentuated her lovely face and softened all of her features... All of his plans to keep his cool flew out the door. He could not resist her.

"Tony had just graduated college and I took the trip as my graduation present from my grandparents," Bill said.

"He was still so young," Tony said with a sigh. "Adorable, but young."

"Oh, okay then, old man," Bill said, shoving Tony's shoulder. "I tried to talk to him that entire trip, but he stayed away from me. He hung out with Gabrielle the whole time. They had been friends at Grass Valley High and he didn't have time for me."

"Shut up, that wasn't it at all. You weren't even eighteen yet, babe."

"Anyway," Bill said, giving him the hand. "After the trip, we didn't see or speak until two years later, when we both went on the Costa Rica tour."

"You'd grown up a lot," Tony said, and they shared a heated look before Bill launched back into the story.

"And we spent the whole time together, but, like, all we did was bicker."

"Because you always had to be right."

"Me?" Bill asked, pretending to be shocked. "Whatever. Then we came home and kept seeing each other and here we are. It's been two years and we're still inseparable."

"And still bickering all the time."

When Cecilia finally sat down, the men were at the tail end of their story.

"We saved up all of our money to make this trip happen," Bill said. "With me finishing grad school and Tony finishing undergrad, it was tough."

"We even moved back in with my grandfather when it didn't look like we were going to have enough."

The men were completely enamored with each other, and the way they fussed over each other reminded Felip of his parents. They seemed so young to have already adopted the ways of an old married couple, but then some people just had old souls, and when they met their soul's match, there was love.

"Felip? Are we meeting up with the other group tonight?"

Gabrielle had joined them and sat in the chair to his left. Cecilia sat across the table from him, with Bill and Tony sitting at the end of the table, their chairs pushed together.

"We are. And they will be taking the bus with us tomorrow to Segovia and on to Burgos. They had other events planned for Madrid and Barcelona, but they will be taking the road trip with us."

"Great," Gabrielle said. "I can't wait to break out the camera tomorrow!"

Bill and Tony groaned and then laughed at her shocked face.

"What? It's so fun!"

"She makes sure to catch everyone while they're sleeping and then posts the pictures in the group online photo album. She's caught everyone on every trip. No one is safe."

"And they're such awful pictures," Bill said, laughing. "She got one of us when we went to Costa Rica and you could see the wet spot on my shirt from where Tony drooled on me."

Felip grinned at Cecilia, but she was focused on the story.

"Whatever. You'd spilled on your shirt at lunch. That's totally what it was, not my drool. I don't drool when I sleep."

"No one is safe," she said with a wink. She stood and began rounding up the kids. "We walk from here to the flamenco club. This will definitely be one of the highlights of the trip."

Felip waited for everyone to leave the restaurant and made sure everything was set with the manager before joining the group outside. He thought about his plan for the evening, and hoped his idea would go over well, and not push his little teacher away. Her mood was much lighter tonight, and the few smiles she'd offered him over dinner had done a lot to wash away his worry. Now he needed to relax...not an easy thing for him. Once he decided he wanted something, he was like a dog after a bone until he had it. No matter how he'd tried to persuade Cecilia that he would be patient and casual about things, he intended to have her in his life. He didn't want to come on too strong, but that went against how he felt.

The club where they would see the flamenco was one he and Tomás had visited several times and they always put on a good show. The dancers were fabulous, but the singers were truly exceptional. Felip had enjoyed flamenco music since he was a child, listening to Paco de Lucía with his father. Music had been the thing that he and his father shared. With Alonso, it was their military experience, a time his father both hated and loved. With Tomás, his father shared his tales of the few opportunities he'd had to travel, which had given the young man a sense of adventure. Lastly, with Mateu, their father had already had his first health setback, so he encouraged Mateu to learn everything he could about the business because he feared he might not be around forever to teach him the things he'd need to know.

They each had a piece of their father, a set of memories uniquely tailored to their relationships with him. Having four sons meant that their father had needed to take extra steps to have those special connections.

When they arrived at the club, there was a flurry of activity as the waiters tried to get all of their party seated in an already full house. The tables were close together, and once the kids were seated, the only spots left were at high tables in the back of the room. Cecilia seemed to be a bit flustered. He approached her as she sent the Santiagos and Bill and Tony to the tables against the wall. The students were all shouting to each other over the din.

He touched her arm and she flinched.

"May I help?"

She blinked and turned away, leaning in close as the kids asked her questions. The lights dimmed and the patrons began to applaud. Felip took her by the arm and led her to an out-of-the-way corner where she'd have a good view.

"Can I get you a drink, profesora?"

She looked at him, confused, and shook her head.

"Are you all right?"

She shook her head again, as though she couldn't understand him, and finally pointed to her ears.

She couldn't hear.

He held up a finger and grabbed the first waiter, asking for a glass of water for her. The club was sultry already, and the bright stage lights would heat the room considerably in a short time. She accepted the glass and thanked the server. Before Felip could ask her anything else, the performers took the stage. He stood next to her stool and allowed himself to bask in her smile and excitement.

The women performing were not the most technically advanced dancers he'd ever seen, but they were incredibly passionate, beautifully costumed, and captivating to watch. The guitarists were equally zealous. They sang lyrics of losing love and staring death in the face in emotionally charged cries and pleas. When the solo male dancer came forward, his power swept the crowd into a frenzy. He dug his heels into the stage with rapid force and his emotions played across his intense face.

Felip watched Cecilia's reactions throughout the performance and hoped his plan would keep that smile upon her lips.

The dancers finished and the crowd showered them with applause and shouts of adoration. Tomás caught Felip's attention, and he left Cecilia's side to join his brother.

"Muchas gracias," the lead singer said. "We have a special group here today and we thought we would entertain them with some English songs tonight."

The dancers remained in their seats along the back of the stage while the guitarists launched into "La Cintura," by Barcelona singer Álvaro Soler, a song that had recently found international success. The kids all started cheering and some of the other patrons stood at their seats and started to dance. From his spot across the bar, Felip saw Cecilia moving along to the music and watching the students with affection.

He hoped she continued smiling when he took his place on the stage.

CHAPTER NINETEEN

9:16 p.m. Madrid Local Time – Flamenco

Cecilia had struggled a bit when they'd first arrived at the club. The background noise of conversations and the bar staff slinging drinks made it difficult to hear anything. She'd tried to see to the kids but eventually gave up and left Gabrielle to tend to them. It was so frustrating to not be able to communicate. It was too loud for her to hear, and Felip didn't know sign language so she couldn't thank him for getting her water and a seat. She'd hoped he'd understood her reaction, but then she'd become completely engrossed in the performance.

The women were breathtakingly beautiful, and the male dancer was the model of the quintessential Spanish man. Fierce, masculine, graceful, and passionate. And with Felip pressed against her side, her senses had been totally overwhelmed. When the show was over and the musicians began to play modern music, Cecilia had been delighted to see her kids jump up and start dancing together. Even Jorge danced with Kristin and Janelle.

She was so focused on her kids that she hadn't noticed when Felip left her side. When he appeared onstage, she nearly toppled off of her stool.

"Our friend, señor Felip Segura, has a special song he would like to play for you."

Felip shook hands with the men onstage and kissed the cheeks of the women before sitting down and taking a guitar from one of the men. The dancers all began to stomp and clap, creating a familiar rhythm—and then one of the singers called her name.

They were singing her song.

All of the students turned to look at her with wide eyes before Gabrielle encouraged them to join in.

Felip played the guitar like a natural. His hair fell into his eyes a little and he smiled that ridiculous smile with that crooked tooth she'd come to adore. His hands, the way they caressed the fret board of the guitar, were mesmerizing.

He caught her eye from across the room...and she realized he'd done this for her. This was his way of reaching out to her, to win her over.

How could she resist him? How could she keep him out of her heart?

It was too late for any of that.

After her song was over, everyone clapped and the musicians launched into another song she vaguely recognized from some school function. Felip left the stage, but he was caught up in the rush of people leaving the bar. The students made their way towards the exit, so she followed them, keeping her eyes open for Felip. She was nearly to the door when an arm caught her about the waist.

She turned on the man, startled, and then when she realized it was Felip, all hesitation was gone. She threw her arms around his neck, but she couldn't speak. She held him tightly and felt his body melt into hers. He pressed a kiss against her cheek, then spoke near her ear.

"Did you like your song, cariño?"

"How could I not? But you realize I'm never going to hear the end of this, don't you?"

He chuckled and then pulled back. "It was worth it. You look so lovely tonight."

She fought the urge to roll her eyes or make some smart-assed remark. He deserved better. "Thank you. You play wonderfully. When did you learn?"

"I will tell you on the walk back."

He took her hand and led her outside to her waiting students, who all teased her and cheered Felip on.

"Yeah, laugh it up now, kids, but you know me. I'll get you back."

The laughter ceased. The kids fidgeted. She smiled and they relaxed. For the moment.

"Check for amigos," Gabrielle said. The kids half-assed looking around while they chatted with each other, and they started to walk away when Tui shouted.

"Aaliyah's not here!"

Cecilia went to his side. "Do you remember seeing her come out?"

He shook his head. "She was right next to me in the bar, but I don't remember seeing her out here."

"Let me go look inside," Felip said, and he squeezed Cecilia's arm to reassure her as he walked away.

"I swear, Mrs. Galván—"

"Tui, she's fine. I'm sure. She couldn't have gotten far."

After a few agonizing minutes, Felip came out of the bar with his arm wrapped around a very frightened Aaliyah. Cecilia and Tui both ran over to check on her. Cecilia's heart dropped when she saw the poor girl had been crying.

"She'd gone into the restroom while we stepped outside."

Aaliyah went into her arms and Cecilia felt her trembling. She could kick herself for losing track of one of the kids, especially this one.

"I'm okay," Aaliyah said. "I'm sorry. I panicked for a minute and then Mr. Segura found me. I'm okay."

Cecilia held her at arm's length and found her smiling. Such progress. Cecilia gave her arms a gentle squeeze. "I'm so sorry. I should have checked for you before we left."

"No, it's okay, Mrs. Galván. I told Kristin and Janelle where I was going."

Her friends approached, their expressions guilt-ridden. "We're sorry, Aaliyah. I needed to get outside, it was so hot. We weren't going to leave without you. We just didn't hear Ms. Reyes call for amigos."

"Everyone is here? We can go?" Felip took charge of the situation and got their group moving and the attention off of Aaliyah. Cecilia enjoyed seeing him in this role. He was calm and collected, a man of action who didn't need to be a jerk to get things done. She bet he was a firm and fair boss to his employees at the winery.

"Mrs. Galván? Is Aaliyah okay?"

Tui had been hovering during the incident but he hadn't said a word.

"She is. I'm glad you noticed she wasn't here."

He nodded and chewed on a fingernail.

Cecilia sighed. "You should tell her how you feel, Tui. No more of this lurking routine. I know you guys have talked a lot on this trip. What would it hurt?"

"Yeah, but you said we'd be in the fishbowl."

She *had* said that. Amazing how a couple of days could change your mind.

"Maybe the fishbowl ain't half bad," she said, walking away with a wink. And she mostly believed it. There was always the possibility things could go horribly wrong, but that was true in life anytime anywhere. She was going to enjoy her time with the kids, and Felip. She was going to live in the moment and—

"Was it too much? The song?"

Startled, Cecilia spun around and crashed into a laughing Felip.

"You are dangerous, you know that?" She leaned into his side and accepted the arm he wrapped around her shoulders. They were at the back of the group, and she was pleased to see Tui had made his way to Aaliyah's side and the two were walking apart from the others. She wondered if he'd take her advice.

"Mmm, it's more fun that way. But I mean it, was it too much?"

She shook her head. "I thought it was sweet. However, the kids have already commented that 'old people music is weird.'"

He threw his head back and laughed, squeezing her even closer. "The song is much older than both of us, so we shouldn't feel offended."

"You were going to tell me about playing guitar," she reminded him.

"Sí, claro. I was a young boy, I do not remember how old, but my father played. I wanted to have special time with him, and since I was too small to be of much use to him in other ways, I thought if we could play together, we'd always have that. He agreed, and he began to teach me. It is quite a stereotypical Spanish thing to do, play guitar and sing."

"You sing, too?"

He shrugged. "Sometimes."

"Sometimes," she repeated. "I'd like to hear you," she said, feeling brave. They were nearing the hotel, and she could see the kids entering the building ahead of her.

"I'm happy to sing for you, cariño." He pulled her closer and kissed the top of her hair. She couldn't help how much she loved being this close to him, could she? Was it so wrong that she felt a bit like a princess, even though she didn't believe in fairy tales?

Cecilia felt her phone buzzing in the pocket of her dress. She stopped walking to pull it out. Greg. *Awesome.*

"Do you need to answer that?"

"No."

"No?"

She exhaled and hit the accept button. "You know I'm in Spain, Greg."

"Uh, Cecilia? Is that you?"

"Who else would be answering my phone?"

Felip's dramatic eyebrows raised and his eyes widened. She gave him the sign for ex-husband, but he probably didn't know what that meant.

"I'm sorry. Is this a good time?"

Cecilia smiled and wished she could say, "Yeah, I'm walking down a dark street in Madrid, one of the most beautiful places in the world, with a gorgeous man who just serenaded me in front of a whole roomful of people. No, it's not a good time," but years of practice attempting to be a good communicator kept her from shoving that in his face.

"What do you want?"

Felip gestured that he could walk away from her if she needed privacy, and she shook her head. She grabbed the front of his shirt so he would completely understand that she wanted him near. He looked down at her hand and chuckled, removing it from his shirt and pressing a kiss to her palm.

"Well, we got an offer on the house."

The news startled Cecilia. She moved out of the middle of the side-walk, dragging Felip with her. "That was fast," she answered him finally.

"It's ten thousand over our asking price. I think it's a good one."

They'd been unsure how quickly their house would sell. She'd done so much to fix it up over the years that the realtor had been pleasantly surprised by its condition and felt they could sell it as-is. But Grass Valley wasn't exactly a booming real estate market, part of the reason Greg had left in the first place.

"What does Nicki say?" Their realtor was an old friend of theirs from high school. It had been a bit awkward working with her since they were now a divorced couple, and everyone had assumed she and Greg would stay together forever.

"She thinks it's good. She said we might could get more, but seeing as we're in a hurry—"

"You mean *you're* in a hurry. You and Carol."

Felip leaned closer, and she assumed he could hear both sides of the conversation since she wasn't using the Bluetooth function on her hearing aide. She didn't much care if he heard.

"Well, yeah, honey. We talked about this. Carol and I need to find a place as soon as possible."

"And, *honey*, that isn't really my problem. You could always move back in with your parents. That's what I did."

Felip covered his mouth to smother a laugh. Cecilia winked at him. It was so nice to be free of Greg after two years of feeling like everything was her fault. She truly didn't wish him any ill will, but his pushiness about this house business had bugged the shit out of her, especially because she knew it had more to do with Carol than with him.

She heard Greg exhale on the other end. "Cecilia, I've waited a long time to make this move permanent. I'm ready to get on with my life."

His words chipped away at her buoyant mood but couldn't demolish it. Having Felip beside her reminded her that she deserved better, and her brief stint with a therapist when they'd first agreed to get divorced had convinced her that she had every right to do what was best for her. She had gone just to make sure she wasn't crazy for not feeling guilty or sad. It had been very much like dinner with a close girlfriend, and since her therapist happened to also know ASL, she'd been able to express herself in a way that had made those brief sessions a huge affirmation.

"Greg, you did move on with your life, and that's fine. We've been over this. I'm not trying to hold you back. I had no choice about taking this trip, you know that. The paperwork will need to wait until I get back so I can look at everything."

"I know," Greg said, sounding defeated. "I'm sorry, honey. I didn't mean to interfere with you having a good time. You deserve to have a good trip. Has it been good?"

Cecilia's cheeks hurt, she smiled so wide. She gazed up into Felip's handsome face and wished they were alone somewhere so they could kiss each other silly again. Feeling brave, she slid her hand around his back and pressed up against him, his smile matching hers in intensity.

"I'm having a wonderful time." She ran the fingers of her other hand through the sliver of chest hair visible where his shirt was unbuttoned. "Spain is quite beautiful." She smiled up at Felip, loving his lusty expression. His eyelids fluttered and he bent down to brush his lips against her forehead.

He suddenly turned his head toward the hotel, and she looked to see Gabrielle gesturing for them to come inside.

"I'll see what she wants," he said. "You take your time. I'll be right back."

He kissed her hair before trotting up the street. Cecilia watched him run with appreciation. He moved like a soccer player, as though running was effortless. She'd never understood that ability. She felt like a total clod when she tried to run.

"Are you still there? Who was that?"

"Hmm? Oh that? That was Felip."

"Felip? Cecilia...?"

"He's our tour guide, sort of."

"Sort of? You sound funny. Are you alright?"

"I'm great, actually. Sorry. Just distracted. We were at a flamenco show. It was amazing! The dancers, the singers... The club was really cool, too, and—"

"A club? Didn't the noise bother you?"

"It did, a little, until they started performing. I couldn't tear my eyes away. They were so passionate, so full of emotion when they danced."

Greg laughed, and she asked what was so funny.

"Nothing, you just sound so, I don't know... Different. Happy. I haven't heard you sound like this in a long time."

"I haven't *felt* like this in a long time." She watched Gabrielle and Felip having a conversation outside the doors of the hotel and wasn't even perturbed at the number of hair flicks Gabrielle made. They had no effect on Felip, and he likely didn't notice them because he kept looking in her direction.

"Cecilia...I'm—"

"Greg, if you think the offer is a good one, I'm okay with it. I don't want to hold you back."

He exhaled into the phone, sounding quite relieved. "Thank you, Cecilia. That means a lot. I'm sorry—"

"It's fine. You and Carol go start your life." *Maybe I'm about to do the same.*

"Thank you. I'll have Nicki contact you by email for the official signature stuff if she needs it before you get back."

"Sure. When I get back. I'm not signing anything until I return." Felip returned and gave her a look to see if she was okay. She signed to him that she was fine, and he shook his head. He tried to mime something to her, and it looked so ridiculous she held up a finger to him.

"I gotta go, Greg. Take care."

He said something else but she was done with her past. Cecilia clicked the end button and slid the phone back into the pocket of her dress. She held out her hand and Felip took it, allowing her to pull him close.

"You're going to have to teach me sign language," he said, slipping his arms around her waist.

"Mmmm, you do fine without words."

She pushed up onto her toes, determined to take the lead this time, and the moment her lips touched his, he moaned softly and opened for her. His hands gripped her tightly, pulling her body flush with his, and the contact shut out the rest of the world. He whispered something against her lips she couldn't quite make out, but then he wrapped his arms around her and pulled her so tight she forgot to breathe. All that mattered was this man standing before her, his kiss a promise of more passion and fun to come, if she simply took his hand.

He was right, she was silly to think they wouldn't see each other. This wasn't the dark ages. There were planes and FaceTime and Skype...

Oh, Lord she was in trouble. She'd scold herself, but then she knew it was too late. She was already involved.

"While I would love to continue this current activity, Gabrielle needs to speak to you about tomorrow, and I think she needed some help getting the kids settled in for the night."

"She's such a cock-blocker—Oh! God, I can't believe I said that!"

Felip snorted and brought his hands up to her jaw. "I believe I know what that means, and you are correct, she is."

"I really do spend a lot of time around teenagers, I have no other excuse."

He kissed her once more, this one simple brushes of his lips over hers that had her completely boneless, so much so that she clung to him, desperate for more.

"Let me see you to the door and then I must go to Tomás's for a bit. I need clothes for the next leg of the trip. I hadn't planned on being here this long, but I'm so glad that I am."

He pulled back, and she fought the urge to pout like one of her sullen teens, following as he led her down the street towards their hotel.

"Is this tour keeping you from anything important?"

He shrugged. "It depends who you ask. Since I'm the boss, I say no. Pero, if you asked June, my partner since I gave her a promotion, she would say all kinds of horrible things about me right now for being gone."

"I hate for you to be in trouble," she said, squeezing his hand. "But I won't say I'm sorry you're here."

They'd reached the front doors and the waiting Gabrielle. Behind her, the boys were roughhousing and shouting in the backroom where they'd had their breakfasts.

"Took you long enough. Do you see what I've been dealing with?"

"I'm sorry, that was Greg on the phone." She realized in all that kissing haze that she hadn't explained the situation to Felip, either. "We got an offer on the house."

"Wow, that was fast," Gabrielle said, her eyes wide.

Felip only frowned. "You are selling your house?"

"Yes. In the divorce, Greg agreed to let me stay in the house for the school year. I thought I'd have a bit of time over the summer to move out. We had a lot of stuff for only being married for ten years," she said with a humorless laugh. "The next Mrs. Galván decided I needed to be out before I left for the trip, so we could put the house on the market sooner than planned. Greg needs his share of the equity to put a down payment on a new love nest for them."

"That is…he kicked you out of your home?" He stepped away and said something that sounded like it might be a juicy expletive. He rested his hands on his hips and frowned.

"It's fine. I'm staying at my mother's and there's plenty of room for me." Although if Mom and Freddy were going to be shacking up, Cecilia wouldn't be staying there long.

"When my wife asked for a divorce, she stayed in our home until she was ready to leave Barcelona. I never would have made her rush to move out. That is a coward's way."

"Yeah, well, it goes with the Greg territory, amIright?" Gabrielle said.

Cecilia tucked her hair behind her ear. "It's not my problem," she said as she signed the phrase.

"Is that how you sign?" Felip asked. He mimicked her movements and laughed. "That would have come in handy with my brothers. You're going to have to teach me some more."

She raised an eyebrow. "Very well. You teach me Catalán and I'll teach you ASL," she said.

"Not Spanish?" he said, smiling at Gabrielle.

Cecilia shrugged. "She can teach me Spanish."

"Anytime, chica. I've told you that for years."

"And it looks like it's time I learn," she said, smiling at Felip.

He leaned in and kissed her cheek. "Hasta mañana, cariño."

He waved to Gabrielle and left them outside the doors.

"Cariño? Girl, that man is in *looooove*," Gabrielle said, laughing.

"Yeah, well…" She had no comeback. She hoped what Gabrielle said was true, because try as she might to treat this as a vacation fling, she was hopelessly falling for Felip.

CHAPTER TWENTY

10:30 p.m. Tomás Segura's apartment, or Headquarters for Viaje España

Tomás was sitting in front of his "command center" staring at the monitors and white boards when Felip walked in. His younger brother looked deep in thought.

"Hermanito, you're going to have to help me out with clothes. I'm in my last clean pair of—What's wrong?"

Tomás sighed. "Just going over the next couple of days. Thank God you were here to help out. It seems I have another problem over the weekend and will likely have to take a tour group to the south myself. It would be so much better if I had an assistant."

"You need to hire an office manager. You're doing a fabulous job, but as the company has grown, so has the number of tasks and tours you are running at any given time. Time for some office space, eh?"

Tomás rubbed at his unshaven face. Felip recognized that stressed-out look. He'd been seeing it in the mirror for far too long. He stepped up behind his brother and rested his chin on his shoulder. "Perhaps you need something, or someone else, as well?"

Tomás lifted his shoulder to dislodge Felip's chin. "Not all of us can find our perfect little teacher." He chuckled, then frowned. "What are you doing here, anyway?"

"I told you. I need clothes. Or laundry service. The bus leaves in the morning, ¿verdad?"

"Sí. The washer is empty. Throw in your clothes. I'll bring them by in the morning."

Felip knew his brother was distracted, but he wasn't going to look a gift horse in the mouth. "Gracias, hermano. I should have enough to get me through the weekend, but throw an extra pair of jeans and a shirt in my bag for me, ¿vale?"

"Vale. Yes, I do this for you." Tomás turned to face him and placed his hands on Felip's shoulders. "You have saved my ass by taking this trip. I owe you."

Felip hugged his brother and then messed up his hair. "You *would* owe me, except this has worked out perfecto. Hermano, tengo el corazón contento. Estoy enamorado de ella." His heart had never felt so light. He adored Cecilia, and being with her made everything that much lighter, as though he'd been carrying excess weight for years.

"I am happy for you, my brother," Tomás said, and he smiled sadly. "Perhaps a bit envious as well."

Felip's smile fell a little. "How long has it been, eh? How long since you found someone who truly made you happy?"

Tomás took way too long to think of an answer.

"That's it. You have been in this apartment staring at your boards for way too long. When was the last time you went out on a tour?"

He shrugged. "You mean before Rosana fell on her ass?"

Felip chuckled. "How is she, by the way?"

"She is better. She thinks she will be able to join up with the tour on Sunday. I've already arranged for her to bus to Bilbao on Saturday night to meet up with you and take over."

"That is...wow, well that is good, I suppose. I'm glad she is feeling better."

"But you don't want to leave, is that true?"

Felip nodded and looked down at his shoes. "I feel as though I finally convinced Cecilia to give this a shot with me, and now I will be leaving. I know June needs me back, but there is a part of me that doesn't care anymore. Is that terrible?"

"It's not like you, that is for sure," Tomás said. "You never act like the foolish one. You leave that to Mateu and me."

Felip sighed. Reality would be here soon enough. "I suppose then I can get back to Barcelona in time to help her with the event on Sunday. But I want to ask you something. Is there room in Cecilia's tour for a little detour?"

"What did you have in mind?"

Felip was back in his hotel room an hour later with a new plan and a promise from Tomás that he would do whatever he could to arrange a wonderful surprise. That, and he would bring Felip's clean clothes by in the morning. Felip took a long time to settle his mind, but finally he dreamed of himself and Cecilia walking. Through city streets, along the beach, and even through the vineyards...they walked, talked, laughed and loved.

He woke with a smile on his face and a thrill that he would be spending the day at her side. And he was going to sit next to Cecilia on the bus. They had language lessons to share.

Tomás was downstairs with Gabrielle working out the bill with the front desk when Felip arrived. The kids were already packed and eating breakfast. He spotted Cecilia sitting with Bill and Tony, and she laughed loudly at something they said.

"Buenos días," Tomás said as he handed Felip his duffel. "Do not let word get out that I run a laundry service. I'll have all of my guides asking for it."

"No problem. My lips are sealed."

"Does he have all the information he needs for the next leg?" Gabrielle tossed her hair over her shoulder as she spoke to Tomás. If Felip wasn't mistaken, Tomás was a little taken by her. His usually confident tone was missing as he attempted to reassure her.

"Sí. I've emailed him the itinerary. He knows what to do and where to meet your local guides. Cristina en Segovia y José en Burgos. He has all of the information for the hotel in Burgos for tonight, and for tomorrow in Bilbao as well."

She nodded, gave him an appraising look, then spun on her heel, causing her long hair to fly like a runway model's, hitting Tomás in the shoulder.

"She is something, isn't she?" Felip laughed, but Tomás watched her walk away with a frown on his face.

"Something. That is one way to put it."

Felip didn't quite know what to think of his brother's reaction to the attractive young teacher, but he also didn't have time to dwell on it. Gabrielle called for them to check for amigos and announced it was time to catch the bus. They had a long trek today. And he planned to spend it sitting with his profesora.

"Good morning." Cecilia had the loveliest smile on her face this morning. He wanted to take her in his arms, dip her, and kiss her senseless.

"Bon dia. Did you sleep well?"

She shrugged. "After dealing with an upset stomach, more blisters, and the boys, who for some insane reason thought they had become flamenco dancers and were stomping up and down the hallway...yeah, I slept well after that."

"I love that they are so enthusiastic. You always hear that American teenagers are too cool for everything, that all they want to do is play with their phones. I haven't seen most of your students using their devices since we were on the plane. Only to take pictures."

They walked together at the back of the group. He took her suitcase handle from her and moved it to his other side to keep her from taking it back.

"Felip, are we going to have a fight? I purposely packed that bag so it wasn't too heavy for me. We carry our own bags, isn't that the rule?"

He shrugged. "How should I know? I'm just a temporary tour guide. I haven't received the proper training."

He winked at her and she rolled her eyes.

"I'm serious. I can do for myself."

He stopped walking and handed it back to her. "I did not mean to offend."

She exhaled and shook her head. "I know you didn't, and I appreciate the gesture, but it's important to me that I do for myself, both as a woman and as a differently abled person."

"Differently abled? Do you mean your hearing?"

She walked forward. "Yes. I try not to make a big deal about it, but yes, I pull my own weight. My mother raised me that way."

He shifted his duffel over his other shoulder so he could walk closer to her. "*My* mother raised me that you are always to be a gentleman. You hold doors, you hold chairs, and you carry the load for your lady. It seems we have conflicting rules about interaction."

She didn't speak for the rest of the block. When they turned the corner, she said, "I don't think they're conflicting, necessarily. Doors and chairs are fine and much appreciated. If something isn't, I will tell you. If you try to respect my wishes, and I try to respect your desire to be a gentleman, we can overcome any conflicting rules."

He placed a hand at the small of her back. "See how easy that was?"

"Ooo, someone is cheeky this morning," she said in a voice only he could hear. "You better behave on the bus. It's going to be a long ride."

"What happens if I don't behave?" he asked as they waited to put their bags in the cargo area of the bus. The group from Rio Grande High School arrived to accompany them on the next leg of the tour. He'd have to check in with their chaperones to coordinate. Tomás assured him that their Spanish teacher and lead chaperone, Arturo Valencia, would be easy to work with, and Felip was glad, as that meant more of his attention could be given to Cecilia and her kids.

"If you don't behave," she said, "I'll make you sit with the boys. Or better yet, you'll be riding with Gabrielle again."

He brought his hand to his heart and feigned hurt. "You wound me with your lack of faith."

She smirked as she entered the bus in front of him, and he had to catch himself from missing the step as he watched her climb. Her short dress hit the backs of her thighs and swished with the movement of her hips.

Dios mío.

He gestured for her to sit in the row behind Gabrielle. Tony and Bill slid in across from her, and Tui and Aaliyah sat behind. He greeted the bus driver, an older man named José he hadn't met before. He explained that he was a substitute tour guide and the man nodded without smiling.

The students seemed particularly rambunctious this morning. The noise level was much louder than it had been. He raised his voice, but they didn't stop talking. He grabbed for the microphone and clicked it on.

"Buenos días, estudiantes. Bon dia. Today we have a long drive, eh? But we stop in Segovia for a nice tour and then we go to Burgos. Everyone say hello to José, our driver."

The kids shouted "hola, José," and went back to chattering. He thought again how difficult it must be to be a teacher. There was no time like the present to give the kids a little lesson, he supposed.

"Let's have a trivia game, shall we? Let's see how much you all know about España. First, can anyone tell me how many languages are spoken in España?"

The kids looked at each other and a hand came up in the back of the bus from the other school.

"¿Sí?"

"Two."

"Two? Vale. What are the two you know?"

The girl looked around and seemed to be sorry she'd raised her hand. "Um, Spanish?"

Everyone chuckled.

"And Catalonian?"

"Ah, bon. Catalán. Sí. Can anyone tell me the name we use to describe the language you call Spanish?" He couldn't look at Cecilia. It amazed him how strange it felt to be wearing another hat with these kids. The last time he'd talked to a group of kids would have been a tour of the winery...maybe? He couldn't recall. But this was a little bit fun.

"Castillian?" another student asked.

"Sí, bon. Castellano. Very good. But there are two other languages spoken in España. Does anyone else know?"

Blank stares greeted him.

"I give you a hint. One of the other languages is spoken in the region we will be arriving in esta noche."

Gabrielle sat up and turned around in her seat. "Any of you in my class better know the answer to this question."

Felip chuckled at her teacher look. It wasn't quite as effective as Cecilia's but then, Gabrielle needed a few more years, perhaps, before she would command the students' respect.

Jorge raised his hand.

"Sí, señor Santiago, ¿qúe idioma hablan en el País Vasco?"

"Basque. And the other language is Galician. Basque, or Euskera, is the language of the Basque people and it's a language isolate, which means it doesn't share any connections with other languages. It's the oldest language spoken in Spain. Galician is spoken by people in the northwestern part of Spain and in Portugal."

Felip had forgotten how much this young man knew.

"Gracias, Jorge. Muy bien. I have a handout—"

"Do people in the Basque country speak English?"

"You will find a lot of people know some English, and—"

"Do people in other parts of Spain understand Basque?"

"Not really. It is a difficult language to learn, as it does not have a common base with Spanish and—"

"Do you know any Euskara?"

Felip sucked in a breath and wanted to say *let me finish my sentence.* But then Cecilia placed her hand over his on the headrest of the seat he was leaning on. He turned to look at her, and she signed something to him that he took to mean he was doing fine, but he had no way of knowing.

"I know a few phrases. My family does some business in País Vasco, so I know the basic greetings—"

"Can you speak some?"

Felip inhaled and let out a long breath. "I do have a handout, let me pass this to you and you can practice with me."

Felip dug into his messenger bag and pulled out the papers Tomás had given him. He passed some back on each side of the bus. He read through the sheet with the kids, pronouncing the Basque words as best he knew how, and they all tried with him. It was a good feeling to be sharing with the kids.

"Now, who wants to learn Catalán? It is the most beautiful language in all of España!"

There were some chuckles and then Jorge raised his hand again. Felip braced himself for what was coming next.

"Is it true that during the Franco years, only Spanish or Castellano was allowed?"

"Sí. There was an effort by his government to assimilate all of the different people in the country. My parents learned Catalán at home, but in school it was all Castellano. Now students learn both in school in Catalonia, and there have been efforts by the local autonomous governments to preserve the languages of España. Can anyone tell me how many autonomous regions there are in España? Other than Jorge?"

Everyone laughed as Jorge slowly lowered his hand.

"It is good you know about the country you've come to visit, Jorge. You've really done your research, but let us not allow your classmates to be slackers, vale?"

Jorge nodded, and Felip hoped he hadn't hurt the boy's feelings. His father leaned in and said something to him and Jorge nodded again. He pulled out a tour book of Spain and started reading diligently.

"Really? No one knows how many? Aw, that is bad, estudiantes."

"Seventeen, plus two autonomous cities."

Everyone turned to spot a small young girl in the back of the bus looking quite proud of herself for knowing the answers. Jorge practically climbed over the back of his seat to see his competition.

"She is correct. Señorita, ¿cómo se llama?"

"Donna," she answered.

"Gracias, Donna. Now, it is a good idea for you all to get some rest before we get to Segovia. We will be doing a lot of walking and it is quite warm. Be sure to bring some water with you when we reach the city."

Felip switched off the microphone and placed it back in the holder by the door. He turned and flopped into the seat next to Cecilia.

"And you do this every day?"

She giggled and tapped his arm.

He turned to face her, and she began to sign with enthusiasm. After what must have been a full minute, she stopped and smiled.

"I have no idea what you just said, but it was beautiful."

She pushed at his arm and wrinkled her nose. She began to sign again, but this time, she spoke at the same time.

"Now you know how I feel listening to everyone speak Spanish here. It's beautiful, but I have no idea what they're saying. And yes, I do this every day during the school year, five periods a day. I teach three classes of ASL and two classes of Life Skills. I see well over one hundred and fifty students each day, and I know all of them by name. But other than that, my world is small. I know nothing about Spain except what I learned in history a long time ago, and I know even less about wine. So this is where we meet in the middle."

"Indeed it is."

They spent the next hour of the bus ride learning from each other. Felip gave her Catalán, she gave him signs to learn. The kids joined in, and it was a wonderful time full of laughs. Before they knew it, they'd arrived at the entrance to old Segovia.

"Anyone can tell me what this large stone structure is?" Felip asked before they left the bus.

"It's a Roman aqueduct. I read that it was built in the first century and they hardly used any mortar. They fitted the stones together tightly. It's over ninety feet tall and runs for miles."

"You are correct, señor Santiago," he said to Jorge, once again impressed by his ability to retain even the most detailed bits of knowledge. "Here we meet Cristina, our guide, and she is phenomenal. Be prepared to learn, because she is as full of facts as our friend señor Santiago. You will learn more today than a year's worth in your schoolbooks. Vamos, estudiantes."

Once the students were all off the bus, he introduced them to Cristina, then watched them all gather around to hear her more closely. He hadn't considered her thick accent until now, and he thought some of the kids might not be able to understand her. She set off with them at a fresh clip, and Felip brought up the rear. Cecilia had remained close to Cristina, nearly glued to her every word.

By the time they'd reached Plaza Medina del Campo, the students were panting and starting to lose focus. Felip recalled, however, that this next part of her tour would grab their attention.

"Sit, sit, sit, estudiantes. Now we have a history lesson. You have all heard of the rulers who united the kingdoms of Spain? Can someone please tell me their names?"

The students remained silent, even Jorge, who may have been trying to let others answer this time.

"Ferdinand and Isabella," Bill answered.

"Excellent. Now, I am needing your help, señor. This way I show you how Spain was united. Señor, you are King Ferdinand, and you, señorita, you are his queen, Isabella."

She took Aaliyah by the hand and brought her and Bill together in the middle of their group. Everyone laughed, especially Tony.

"Bueno. Now, the marriage of Ferdinand and Isabella was meant to unite the kingdoms of España. Tell me the names of the kingdoms."

The kids shouted out Castille, Leon, Aragon, Granada, Catalonia, and Navarre. Felip was distracted as Cecilia wandered over to a shop nearby, apparently to buy water. She handed one to Tui and to Eduardo and Joseph, who all seemed to be wilting in the heat.

"Ferdinand and Isabella, they had seven children, but only five survived to adulthood." Cristina then grabbed several people out of the group to be the offspring of the famous rulers. Janelle, Kristin,

Cecilia, and a young lady from the other school were the daughters, and Eduardo was chosen to be the lone son.

Cristina then told the stories of what happened to each of the children, who they married, which political alliances were developed, then she told the story of Juana la Loca, using Cecilia as the actress for this role.

"Juana was a very bright child and at the tender age of seventeen, she was married to Philip of Flanders, creating an alliance with the Habsburgs that would give Spain more power to ward off the threat of the French." Cristina pulled Tony into the play. "Juana was madly in love with her husband, and it is said that Philip the Handsome had many affairs."

The crowd booed him.

"Juana was eventually declared insane by her father and Philip. She had six children with Philip before her husband and her father had her imprisoned, where she remained for the rest of her life."

Cecilia gave them all ugly looks, and everyone laughed. She used two fingers to point from her eyes to each member of their group, as though she were going to make them pay for this. Felip chuckled at her performance.

"But then, Juana la Loca's son Carlos Quinto, or Carlos Primero de España y Quinto de Alemania—you call him Charles the Fifth—became the Holy Roman Emperor." Cristina pulled Jorge into the fray and everyone clapped, as it seemed fitting that Jorge become a powerful emperor with all of his knowledge. "And he kept Juana confined for the rest of her life."

Cecilia dropped her head in mock defeat and the crowd gave a sympathetic *awwww*.

Cristina talked a bit more and then the students were reenergized enough to finish their walk to the castle. Felip tried to catch up to Cecilia, but he was thwarted at every turn by student questions, cars squeezing by them on the narrow streets, or requests for him to take pictures of the students. By the time they reached the castle, he was ready for a break. He came across Cecilia standing in the shade of a large tree, staring thoughtfully at the castle.

"Perdóname, Juana," he said, bowing to her. She smiled and rolled her eyes.

"Of course, she had to make me the crazy one. What a fascinating story, though! I remember Ferdinand and Isabella for sending Columbus—thanks a lot for that fiasco, by the way—and I remembered them being responsible for the Inquisition." She glanced around to be sure no one was listening, then leaned close to Felip. "I know about the Inquisition because of Monty Python and Mel Brooks, but don't tell the kids."

Felip chuckled. "Monty Python? You mean the Comfy Chair?"

"The Comfy Chair!" she said with much exclamation. "You know Monty Python?"

"Noooooobody expects the Spanish Inquisition!"

She held up a hand to high five him and he slapped it gently, grabbing it in the process and giving it a gentle squeeze before letting go.

"Nice work, Segura," she said. She turned to glance back at the castle. "I don't get it, though. A woman as intelligent and powerful as Juana, and she still got screwed. See? There's no such thing as the knight in shining armor to save you. No. They'll have you imprisoned for threatening their power. Freakin' men." She glanced over her shoulder at him. "No offense."

He held up his hands. "None taken. It was pretty terrible what happened to Juana."

Cecilia sighed loudly. "This place looks like something out of a fairy tale, and yet the stories Cristina told us prove that being a princess was no fairy tale."

Felip had to agree. "It is true, life for las infantas was not easy. But I don't know if I'd say there is *no* such thing as a fairy tale."

"Everyone thought my marriage was a fairy tale. High school sweethearts, destined to be together, all that crap. Well, I waited in my ivory tower for my prince and he chose to find a fair maiden in every port. So much for that fairy tale."

Felip wanted to embrace her, but they were in the middle of the group and the kids were all around them. "I don't believe in fairy tales either. In a fairy tale, they fall in love and it is happy ever after. That is not necessarily the truth."

Cecilia turned to gaze up at him. "No, it isn't, is it?"

"No. The fairy tales don't show that there is work to be done, that the other person might not accept you for who you are, and you might not be able to make them happy despite whatever you do."

"Is that what happened with your wife?"

Felip wondered what she would think if he told her. Would she feel he was to blame? Would she see him like her ex-husband?

"I think perhaps we both had different expectations. I thought she knew I cared for her, and I thought she cared for me, and that would be enough. It wasn't."

"Do you wish that things were different?"

He paused to think about her question. "Now? No. I believe things worked out how they were meant. But then? Sí. It is no good feeling like a failure in the most important job of your life."

"When you put it that way, I guess I can see it. I got a lot of shit from Greg and his family and even some of our friends. They felt that I should have moved with him. But why did what I want not matter? Why did I have to give up the job I loved, with the people I loved, for *him*? I'd already sacrificed time and money so that he and his friends could build their company. When we got married, there was no talk of moving to the city. I never... It doesn't matter. Whether he wants to blame me and say I ended our marriage by refusing to leave, I know it's not true. I stayed true to myself, and I wasn't the one who cheated."

Felip couldn't resist touching her in that moment. He pressed a hand to her lower back, and she leaned in the slightest bit before turning to smile at him.

"Sorry, I didn't mean to get all morose on you. Are we going to be able to tour the castle?"

Felip shook his head. "No, I am afraid there is another event going on here. We will have to be satisfied taking pictures from the outside. Would you like to take a closer look?"

They walked closer to the ravine surrounding the castle. Cristina gave the students a little more history of the castle.

"The story is that Walt Disney and his people chose the Alcázar de Segovia as the model for Sleeping Beauty's Castle." There were murmurs of surprise and quiet discussion. "And do you see, above the bars of what was then a jail, there is a portion of the castle wall that juts out? And below, you see a hole? Can anyone tell me what this is?"

It was quiet for only a few beats when Jorge said. "Is that where the garderobes were?"

"Muy bien. Sí, those were garderobes for the royal families."

"What's a garderobe?" Kristin asked.

"An early form of aseos. The waste would drop through the hole—"

"Ew! Are you kidding me right now?" Eduardo exclaimed.

"That's nasty! They just dumped they business down the side of the house?" Joseph asked.

"And there were people in the cells right below?" Aaliyah asked. "Ohmygod, that's so gross!"

Cecilia and Felip chuckled as the kids carried on about the sanitation standards of the Middle Ages.

"Everyone poops, guys," Cecilia finally said. "Even in fairy tales."

Felip fell a little bit more in love with her at that very moment. She could make the basest of situations humorous. She could find the light in every situation. They were a good match. And he wanted her with a passion fairy tales could only dream of.

CHAPTER TWENTY-ONE

1:36 p.m. Segovia Local Time – Plaza Mayor, Segovia

Cecilia loved the quaint little town of Segovia. The site the city was founded on was a perfect place upon a hill, making for the most spectacular views. On the walk to the castle, she'd noticed several shops selling the most adorable artwork. She tried to keep track of which ones she wanted to stop in later, when she wasn't watching Felip interact with her students.

My heart, she thought. She was losing it to him little by little. Every time he teased one of the boys, or was charming with one of the guides, or looking after the girls, concerned about their safety. He'd shuffle them all onto the narrow sidewalks and doorways to keep them safe from the crazy drivers. He bought water for them on the way to the castle. He was everywhere, and was quickly becoming everything.

Why? Why was she falling for this man? She knew better than to let him worm his adorable-ass way into her heart. And yet she was helpless. She could say what she wanted about fairy tales not being real, yet here she was in a beautiful country surrounded by all of this history, and this incredible man kept surprising her at every turn. Her head was spinning.

After they visited the grounds of the castle, they split up for lunch and shopping for a bit. Felip agreed to take the boys on a little more sightseeing and to find food, and Cecilia took the girls with her to have lunch and shop. The Santiagos and Bill and Tony wanted to see the cathedral, as did many members of the other school, and they were all to meet up at the city gates under the aqueduct in two hours.

By the time she and the girls arrived, the boys were laughing hysterically with Felip by the bus. They all stopped laughing when the girls walked up, and Cecilia knew they were up to something.

"I don't even want to know," she said as she approached. "Whatever you guys are up to, you give it up right now."

The innocent looks on their faces were ridiculous.

"I want to thank all of you for coming to my city, and I hope you will always remember the history I taught you. Be sure to follow your leader, Carlos Quinto." Cristina held up Jorge's hand in triumph and everyone clapped.

Felip kissed her cheeks and handed her a wad of cash. Cecilia had no idea how much, because she still hadn't memorized the paper colors of the euros. The girls had laughed at her when she couldn't figure out how much to give the server at lunch.

They loaded onto the bus and Cecilia was grateful to be off her feet. Felip waited until everyone was on to tell them they would be riding the bus for a little over two hours, and that they should take their time to rest because once they arrived in Burgos, they would be touring one of the most important cathedrals in all of Spain. He reminded the ladies that it's required they cover their shoulders inside the cathedral, and that there would be other rules they'd all have to follow.

Once he finished, she could tell he was tired. He sat down heavily beside her and sighed.

Gabrielle turned around before Cecilia could say anything. "Felip, are we going to the hotel first when we get to Burgos?"

"Sí. We check in and then we walk to the cathedral."

She looked between Cecilia and Felip, gave a knowing grin, and then turned back around with a flick of her hair.

Felip gave Cecilia a lazy smile and rested his head against the back of his seat.

"You should rest," she said, patting him on the leg. "You were wonderful today."

Felip didn't speak for a long time, though he looked as though he had something very important to say. She wanted to ask him, but then Tui needed some tissue and Eduardo was hungry, and pretty soon she'd closed her eyes...

Two hours later, the bus began making some tight turns and frequent stops and starts. Cecilia opened her eyes and gasped.

Her face was smushed into Felip's shoulder, her body turned to face him. Luckily he, too, was asleep. His head was tipped back, his Adam's apple prominently protruding from his gorgeous neck. His lips were parted slightly and a tiny whistle sounded as he breathed in and out. Her gaze drifted over those high cheekbones and his long, perfect nose. In sleep, his brow was relaxed, and his full lips, so kissable, pursed out... Why did he have to be so damned beautiful?

"Oh my God, this is perfect." Gabrielle leaned over the seat with her phone and she took a picture of him. "Yes! That's great. I'm texting this one to Tomás. I've gotten everyone else in our group. Take a look." She handed her phone to Cecilia. "Flip through these. Wait 'til you see Tui, and then Tony and Bill."

Cecilia chuckled at the pictures. Gabrielle had gone row by row, catching everyone sleeping. Tui's head had dropped forward, his chin on his chest, and she'd somehow managed the get the phone under his face to see his features lax and his hair wilding out from his head. Joseph cuddled a sweatshirt like a child might cuddle a stuffed animal. Kristin and Janelle both had their mouths wide open with their heads back against the headrests.

"Oh," Cecilia breathed. This one was of her, snuggled up to Felip's side. It was taken through the gap in the seat, as though Gabrielle had tried to be sneaky. She looked ridiculous...but him? He gazed down at her with such a loving expression, her breath caught in her chest. The next photo showed him brushing her hair back from her face. And in the next, he pressed a kiss to the top of her head, his eyes closed. He looked so serene, so relaxed.

The final shot was both of them as they slept, him with his head back, her smushed against his shoulder.

Gabrielle smiled at her. "Told you they were good."

Cecilia raised an eyebrow and then texted each of them to herself, shushing Gabrielle when she started to laugh.

The bus pulled to a stop and Felip stirred next to her.

"Hey, Sleeping Beauty," she said quietly. "We're here."

He sat up, blinking a few times. He scrubbed his hands over his face, gave her a smile and then hopped into the aisle.

"Ladies and gentlemen, we have arrived to Burgos. This is our hotel for the night. We have a short time for you to go inside, drop off your things, and then meet back down here by four o'clock. We will meet our guide, José, take a nice walk, see a beautiful cathedral, and then dinner will be here at the hotel tonight. ¿Tenéis preguntas? ¿No? Vale. We go."

Felip left the bus, and Cecilia looked around to make sure they had all of their things. She noticed Felip's phone had fallen onto their seat. As she picked it up, a text came through. It was in either Spanish or Catalán, she couldn't tell. She felt guilty looking at it, even if she couldn't understand, so she hurried off the bus, bringing the phone with her. Felip was overseeing the unloading of the bags, and the entire group seemed to be between her location and his. Then he trotted up the steps to the hotel lobby. She called out to him, but he must not have heard her over the excited kids' voices.

Cecilia stepped around various suitcases and bags to get to the steps of the hotel. Inside, Felip was involved in a fast-paced discussion with the clerk that Cecilia had no hope of following. Instead, she stood and observed his behavior. He didn't even look rumpled after taking a nap. His hair was a little wilder than usual, the top standing on end, but it still looked stylish. He seemed wide awake, and she remembered him saying he enjoyed siestas, but it seemed criminal that anyone could be that put together after spending hours on a bus.

Just as she approached, he reached for his phone in his back pocket and came away empty-handed. He was patting his pockets frantically when Cecilia walked up and handed it to him.

His smile of thanks melted her right down to her toes. Most of the time he was simply a handsome, charming man who was pleasant to look at, but sometimes, the way he looked at her, she wanted to hop in his arms, wrap her legs around his narrow waist, and have him carry her away.

That thought had her wishing, again, that she wasn't so damned responsible. What would it be like to spend a night with him? She still thought of their kiss on the street in Madrid often, so often it was becoming like a favorite movie she'd watch over and over, replaying her favorite parts in her mind.

"Mrs. Galván? Did he say we had time to change? I'm so gross from sitting on the bus," Janelle said.

Cecilia tore her gaze away from Felip to attend to her girls. "It's three forty-five now. I think you only have about fifteen minutes. You should hurry."

The girls trudged up the stairs, obviously a little hungover from their bus naps. Cecilia waited for her key patiently while Felip handed them out to all of the others. When they were all gone, he turned to her and smiled.

"Do I get a key, Mr. Segura?" she asked with her hand out.

His smile slipped. "I didn't give one to you?"

She shook her head. "Nope."

He turned back to the clerk, and she watched as they spoke to each other before the man shook his head. Felip seemed to question him, but the man continued to shake his head. He walked away, and Felip slammed his palm down on the counter.

"Is something wrong?"

He turned to face her, the frown on his face so severe it was comical. "Somehow there are not enough rooms for all of us."

Cecilia shrugged. "Then we improvise. I can bunk with someone. I'm sure there's an extra bed in one of the rooms?"

He rested his hands on his hips. "Perhaps we can talk at dinner and rearrange some of our group. I am so sorry, Cecilia. I wanted you to be able to have a private room so you could rest."

She chuckled. "I can rest anywhere. Remember? I take the hearing aids out and I'm dead to the world."

He gave her a half smile, but she could tell he was still flustered.

"Can I put my things in your room for now?"

His eyes flared. "Do you need to, um, freshen up?"

"I'd like to, yes. Is that a problem?"

"No! No, ah, let me unlock the door for you."

He was acting really strange, and Cecilia couldn't figure out why for the life of her. He started to pick up her suitcase and then stepped back, muttering an apology.

She followed him up two flights of stairs and down to the end of the hallway. He opened the door and held it for her. The rooms in Spain had all been minimalist and efficient, and this one was no different. There were two twin beds and a small chair in this room. The bathroom, which she could see from the doorway, was tiny.

She set her suitcase and backpack on the floor inside the door and turned to face Felip. He'd moved outside, hovering in the doorway.

"Are you alright?"

He sure was acting funny. She moved closer to him as he leaned in to speak.

"I can't be alone with you in this room," he said in a voice just above a whisper.

"Why?" she asked, sort of playing dumb, but absolutely thrilled to see him so flustered.

"Cecilia, there is no way I can be alone with you in a room with a bed right now. Not that I would *do* anything objectionable. It's only that the *thoughts* I would have...would not be appropriate."

She pressed her lips together to keep from laughing. She leaned against the doorjamb and tilted her head to the side. "What kind of thoughts?" she asked.

He stared at her in disbelief, and then he checked the hallway again. He braced himself with his hands on the doorjamb and leaned in closer. "You teach sex ed. What do you think a man thinks of in a situation like this?"

Cecilia licked her lips. "Sleep habits? Proper hygiene? I have no idea. What kind of thoughts *does* a man have in this situation?"

"The kind of thoughts a man has when the woman he burns for is within reach, and yet she is not. Propriety declares that he should remain out of the way of temptation."

"Temptation?" she asked, only this time, she wasn't laughing. His declaration had her feeling rather heated as well.

"Sí. Cecilia—"

"Mrs. Galván? Can I use your charger again? I swear, I'll remember to borrow one from the guys tonight." Tui looked between them as though he realized he'd interrupted something. "I can come back—"

"No, it's fine. Mr. Segura was nice enough to let me store my things in his room. We seem to be short a room in this hotel."

"Oh, for real? We have four beds in our room! We have an extra one you—oh, well, *someone* can room with us."

"Thank you, Tui. We'll discuss it at dinner. I may have to room with Ms. Reyes tonight." She reached into her bag and handed Tui her extra portable charger. "Make sure you either plug it in tonight or you give it back to me, got it?"

"Yes, Mrs. Galván."

"See you downstairs."

Tui looked between them again and then returned to his room three doors down.

"Cecilia, I am very sorry. I will speak to Tomás and—"

"It's fine. I'm pretty flexible."

One corner of his delectable mouth turned up, and she wondered why they weren't kissing.

"Is it wrong for me to wish...never mind. I do not want to offend you. I will wait downstairs—"

"Felip." Cecilia grabbed for his shoulder. Just one touch and she was back in that alley in Madrid, wishing his kisses would never end. "What were you going to say?"

He cleared his throat. "Is it wrong for me to wish we were spending the night together?" He placed his hand over hers and brought it to his lips. "I know it is forward for me to ask—"

"It's not wrong. I'd like that, too."

His answering smile had her grinning.

"I mean, I've already slept *on* you twice, right? We're practically an old married couple by now."

Felip leaned in to kiss her cheek and spoke close to her ear. "The night I imagine we would have would not be like that of an old married couple." He took a step back and eventually the space between them required their hands to separate. "Go ahead and take your time. I'll be in the bar downstairs."

She watched him walk away and didn't remember to breathe until he was down the stairs and out of sight. Cecilia closed the door and leaned against it, her chest heaving with a deep breath.

Cecilia hadn't had sex since one of Greg's visits over the summer… during the time he was having his affairs. Their trip to London turned into the fight that ended their marriage. When she found out he'd been sleeping with someone else, she lost her shit. She immediately went to get tested, despite the fact he assured her he'd been careful, and was relieved she'd been negative for any STIs. After all the years spent teaching Life Skills, she knew better than most what the consequences of unprotected sex could be.

She'd only ever slept with Greg.

Felip wanted to spend the night with her.

She began to have all kinds of lust-filled thoughts involving Felip and spent the entire time she took to change clothes and clean up thinking of the following:

The kids wouldn't have to know.

They were adults.

It's not like she could get pregnant. Her IUD was good for another three years.

They probably had condoms in the hotel somewhere.

"What are you even thinking, Cecilia Grace? How could you face the kids if they knew?"

She stared hard at herself in the mirror of the tiny bathroom and frowned. She'd lost weight, even more than she had before the trip. Probably all the walking and the heat. She'd been checking her steps on her iPhone and she was averaging twelve- to fourteen-thousand steps a day so far.

This was not the face of a woman who had sex with a man she met on vacation. No.

No?

"Forget it. You'll have to take care of yourself."

She walked back into the bedroom and sighed. Who was she kidding? She wouldn't even know what to do with a man as beautiful as Felip in her bed.

As she changed into light linen pants and a sleeveless blouse for the evening walk, she chuckled as she thought about the respectful way he'd spoken to her. It was kind of adorable, and it had completely taken her by surprise. She had a pretty good idea how men were built, and after that kiss in the alley, if he'd wanted more, his wants had likely expanded to include sex. But he'd been worried she would be offended? What a silly man. She was not only flattered by how he'd acted, but the fact that he'd been so concerned about her feelings...

Silly, silly man. Couldn't he tell how much she wanted him, too?

She went downstairs to find Felip speaking with the boys, and when she approached, they all stopped talking, again, as though she'd interrupted.

"I don't know if I like this combination," she said, pointing to the four of them with the key. When she got to Felip, he took it from her and excused himself.

"I'll just be a few moments."

Felip took off nearly at a run up the stairs and down the hall.

Cecilia turned on the boys with narrowed eyes. "What are you up to?"

Eduardo, Joseph and Tui all did their best to look innocent. "Nothing," they all said at once.

"I so don't believe you."

They stared at each other, the boys fidgeting.

"It's nothing bad," Joseph finally said.

"Yeah," Eduardo said. "It's not bad at all."

Cecilia turned on Tui with her eyebrows raised.

"Aw, come on, Mrs. Galván. You can't. I swear, if it was bad I would tell you, okay? I swear?"

"I know where you sleep," she said, eyeing them suspiciously before heading over to Gabrielle.

"Hey, I heard about the room situation," Gabrielle said. "Darn, guess you'll have to stay with him." She tossed her hair and laughed.

"Right. And do the walk of shame in the morning. And lose my job. Anyway, you have an extra bed?"

"I do," she said. "You want to bring your stuff over now or when we get back?"

Cecilia rested a finger to her lips and looked up at the ceiling. "Seeing as Felip went back up there to change, I probably should wait. I wouldn't want to disturb him."

Gabrielle rolled her eyes. "Disturb him. Come on. He *wants* to be disturbed by you. He *needs* to be disturbed by you. Did I not show you the pictures?"

Cecilia knew her face and neck were beet red. "Stop it. There's no way. I couldn't."

"I know. But I'd sure fantasize about it a whole helluva lot."

"I'm sure I will," Cecilia said wistfully.

Felip was back in ten minutes, and Cecilia realized she'd forgotten a wrap for the cathedral. "May I borrow your key once more?"

"Of course." He dug in his pocket for the key and pulled it out.

"Oh, and I'm going to stay with Gabrielle tonight. I'll move my things when we get back."

He sighed dramatically as he handed her the key. "Pity. One can dream."

"You're so much trouble," she said as she reached for the key.

He didn't let go. She tugged on it. He held tight.

"Aren't we going to be late, Mr. Tour Guide?"

He shrugged. "The cathedral has been there for over five hundred years. I think it will still be standing when we arrive."

She started to protest once more and he let go, chuckling at her flustered expression.

"Can you blame me for wanting to keep you close?"

She looked around, grateful the kids weren't nearby. "Not when I want to be close."

Cecilia turned for the stairs, key in hand. She needed a moment to cool down. Why he was so intent on throwing her off-kilter—

"Cecilia."

He startled her so badly, she stumbled on the steps.

"Now you're trying to kill me? Why not throw me in front of a team of rabid mopeders!"

He chuckled, then she felt his hand at her lower back as they reached his room. She unlocked the door, and he pushed her inside and closed it behind them.

"Just one kiss, cariño."

"What happened to avoiding temptation?" she asked breathlessly as he approached her.

"That was so five minutes ago," he said, doing his best impression of the kids. "Now I am a man standing before the woman he adores, wishing for a kiss."

Cecilia let go of all the concerns holding her back. She threw her arms around his neck and then they were kissing, and it was even hotter than the alley. His hands were everywhere, and all she could think of was how incredible they would feel on her bare skin...a moment before he slid one up under her blouse, caressing her stomach.

"Felip, I'm going to be a mess when we go back down there. You can't kiss me like this and expect I won't be affected."

His lips left her neck, and he chuckled. "I see what you mean. Vale. I put kisses where it does not show on your tender skin."

Felip dropped to his knees and lifted her shirt a few inches. He gazed up at her as he nuzzled the skin of her belly, kissing, nibbling with his lips, his tongue darting out to taste her. He pulled down the elastic waistband of her pants a fraction and licked the skin there.

Cecilia's knees gave out, and Felip caught her weight, his hands gripping her hips and holding her in place until he was damn good and ready to stop.

"Felip." Cecilia's voice came out on a moan. "You don't play fair."

"I'm willing to let you play back," he said, using his teeth this time on her side, where her hipbone protruded. He stood, caressing her ass as he reached his full height. "I cannot resist you," he whispered. "You taste divine. How I long to take my time with you."

Cecilia was just shy of not caring whether everyone would know what they were up to, but then Felip's phone buzzed, reminding them that people were waiting. He stood to read it.

"It is Gabrielle. They are heading out. She told us to catch up with them." He smiled down at her, and the mischief in his eyes spurred her on.

"Well, we can't keep them waiting." She unbuttoned the front of his shirt slowly. "They're expecting us in church." Two more buttons. "We really should go."

Cecilia ran a fingernail down his pec, grazing his nipple lightly and making him moan. She followed the path of her finger with her lips and slid her hands down his torso to his waistband, letting her fingertips graze the skin below. Goose bumps spread across his skin, and he shivered.

"I'll be sure to give confession for being late." Felip mumbled something in another language—she couldn't tell the difference right now—and he brought his hands up to cup her face.

"Cariño, I wish we had more time together. I wish to show you how good you make me feel, how wonderful you are." He forced her to look at him. "Say you want this too."

She pushed up on her toes and pressed a kiss to his lips. "I do, Felip. I want you, too. But—"

He pressed a finger to her lips. "I know. It is not the time. I'll do my best to be patient, but there will be moments like these when I must remind you what we have to look forward to. How good it will be when we are together. Piel con piel, sólo tú y yo, toda la noche."

She gazed up into his golden soulful eyes and felt desire deep within her, where no one had ever affected her. She brushed her lips gently across his, delighting in the friction from his stubble. "I want to feel that all over me," she whispered. "I want—"

Felip picked her up easily and put her back against the wall. She laughed in surprise, wrapped her legs around him, and then melted as he positioned himself to show her how much he wanted her. He rolled his hips against her, and she let her head fall back, too boneless to resist. He kissed her chest over her shirt, taking care not to redden her skin any more than he already had. When he pulled at her nipples through the fabric with both his teeth and his fingertips, she cried out, wondering once more if it would really be so bad if they had less clothes on. The heat and pressure against her core had her writhing against him, desperate for contact.

"Of all the times to not be wearing a skirt."

Felip chuckled and stopped his movement. Her words seemed to remind him that he'd taken things to another level, one she desperately wanted to explore.

"I apologize, Cecilia," he said, letting go of her hips and allowing her legs to drop to the floor. "This is not at all how I would want to make love to you the first time."

Cecilia tried to get her breathing under control. "You're probably right. I'm sure they could hear everything out in the hallway."

He smiled, but he seemed frustrated. "You deserve better."

Cecilia raised her eyebrows. "Felip, you make me feel...desirable. And I like it. I like how you make me feel."

"Good."

They stood pressed against each other for several moments, attempting to catch their breath.

"Felip, do you go to church regularly?"

"This is an interesting time to be discussing religion, Cecilia. I'm pretty sure the church frowns upon ravishing women in hotel rooms."

She barked out a laugh against the bare skin of his chest. She could snuggle up here all day, and all night, so pretty much all the time.

"I know, I'm sorry. You mentioned confession so I was curious."

Felip sighed and pulled her closer, inhaling the scent of her hair. "Ah, sí, I did. I go with my parents at least once a month when I'm home. There's something comforting in the rituals, la comunidad, and the spirit. I wouldn't say I am a devout Catholic by any means, but I pray, I celebrate, I wonder... Do you?"

"I, uh, was raised Wiccan, actually. My grandparents were practitioners and my mother still practices. I guess I'm what you'd call agnostic. I'm still searching for answers."

"Really? That is...I've never met anyone who is Wiccan before. Does that mean you do spells or something like that?"

She shook her head, intrigued that he'd asked about spells. "No. We celebrate the traditional pagan holidays and mother grows herbs to make her own remedies for basic ailments. There was more to it when my mother was young, but my grandparents split with their coven and then they passed away. We basically celebrate nature and her gifts. It's pretty simple, actually. Do no harm, live your best life in harmony with the Earth, and so on and so on."

"That sounds nice. Sometimes I wish the church didn't have such a history of violence and discrimination, but I tend to look to the root belief that someone is looking out for me and there are those I can look to for guidance."

"It's too bad it wasn't that simple, huh?"

"Mmmm."

He nuzzled her hair and she remained curled against his bare chest, brushing her lips against his skin. "We really should go, shouldn't we?"

"Cecilia, I fear I've grown rather fond of holding you."

She chuckled. "That's terrible. I'm sorry."

"You should be."

"I know! It's a horrible affliction."

"Is there a cure known to man?" he asked seriously.

She snorted. "Apparently marrying me."

He stilled his gentle caresses. "Cariño," he said, his tone disappointed. "I hope you don't believe that."

She shrugged and stepped away from him. "It's all I have to compare to." She walked to the bathroom to see how much of a mess she was. "I know in my rational mind that it's not true, but in my more vulnerable moments, I wonder. Like, I wonder why I'm even telling you this."

Felip appeared in the mirror behind her, leaning against the doorjamb.

"When my wife left me, I felt like a terrible failure. I should have been able to make it work, I should have been able to make my wife happy."

Cecilia ran cold water on a washcloth and held it to her neck, which was flushed from Felip's kisses. He tried to apologize but she shushed him.

"Why do you think she wasn't happy with you? I have a hard time imagining how that could happen, but then, I just met you."

Felip smiled, but his gaze dropped to the floor and he began buttoning his shirt. "She complained I worked too much. She wanted to spend less time with my family and do more traveling and shopping. When I couldn't go with her, she'd go alone or with friends. She never quite fit with my family, our sense of humor and playfulness seemed to annoy her. I understand her new fiancé is German. Perhaps he will be able to make her happy more than I could."

"How do you feel about her getting remarried?"

"One door closes and another opens."

Cecilia turned to face him. "How do you mean?"

"It is the end of that chapter of my life. When we divorced, I had no choice but to move forward, and I wanted that. I want that still. I suppose I still felt responsible for her happiness, even though she left me."

"What is she like?" Cecilia asked, even though she knew she probably shouldn't.

"Sophisticated, serious, stubborn. She was much sought after in

Barcelona. She belonged to a social circle I never would have been connected to without her."

"What did your family think of her?"

He snorted. "That she thought she was too good for us. That she put on airs. My mother said that I would be miserable if I married her."

"And was she right? About the last part?"

"No. Not really. I think I was not very aware? I thought we were fine, for the most part. But then, that was the problem. I didn't think anything was wrong, meaning I wasn't paying close enough attention to the signs."

"Ah. Me too. With the signs. I knew we weren't happy, but I never thought he would cheat on me. Especially not with as much vigor." Cecilia turned around and shook her head at her reflection. "I suppose we all think it won't happen to us, that our relationship is too strong, and therefore we put on blinders."

"I suppose you are right."

Felip's voice sounded less confident than usual. His wife leaving him was obviously a huge blow. He seemed like the kind of man who succeeded at everything. She hoped that he'd healed from his loss.

"I think this is as put together as I'm going to look."

Felip lifted his gaze and smiled. "Perfecto. A hint of a satisfied glow remains. Qué linda, cariño."

Cecilia pulled her wrap out of her bag and placed the sky-blue fabric around her shoulders. "Will this do, señor?"

Felip appraised her with a smile. "You look lovely. Now, can we go? I cannot believe you'd make me late to church."

She elbowed him as she walked past, loving that his sense of humor remained after their heavy conversation.

"You sure you want to bring a pagan to church? Do they have rules about that?"

He ushered her out the door and locked it behind them, slipping the key in his pocket. "Sí, claro. Convert, convert, convert!"

Little did he know that while she'd probably never convert in her religious beliefs, she would likely be converted from believing all traveling businessmen were bad news.

This man was breaking down so many of her previously held beliefs that she felt helpless to stop it. He was quickly becoming someone she wanted to share more of her life with, and that was the problem. Their time was ticking away...

CHAPTER TWENTY-TWO

4:49 p.m. Burgos Local Time – Calle Madrid, Puente de Santa Maria

Felip would never tire of walking the city streets with this incredible woman by his side. Although he was getting a bit frustrated with their lack of alone time.

He'd acted impulsively again, by following her to the room a second time, and once he'd closed that door, he'd been overtaken by lust. It took every last ounce of the lessons of respect beaten into him by his mother for him to not divest Cecilia of her clothing and worship her until she understood the depths of his feelings.

But then, she never ceased to surprise him. She'd practically leapt into his arms. Her hungry kisses were nearly his undoing. And her touch on his naked skin? He'd nearly lost control when her lips pressed against his chest. She fit so perfectly against him, her muscular thighs gripped him so tightly, it would have been so easy...

Felip had dreams of seducing her properly. Someplace private, someplace luxurious, someplace they'd have all the time in the world to explore this magic happening between them. He'd already begun making plans.

He'd convince her to come back to Spain. He'd surprise her with a ticket somehow and bring her back within days of her landing in California. She'd obviously need time to get her affairs in order with the sale of her house, of course, but he'd bring her back and then they'd go…anywhere. He'd take her south, to the breathtaking Alhambra in Granada, or if she wanted more excitement, they could go to Ibiza. Hell, he'd be content to bring her back to his flat and not leave for days. He would cook for her, take care of her…

He had to convince her. He knew she was falling in love with his country, and hoped she was falling for him just as hard. He needed to strategize…the perfect time, the perfect way.

It was early evening in Burgos when they emerged from the hotel, and Felip could tell Cecilia was happy to have her wrap as there was a slight chill in the air. After days of intense heat, this trip north would provide a welcome relief for them all. Tomorrow they would go to Bilbao, and then…

He didn't want to think of leaving the group. Not just Cecilia, but the kids as well. He really enjoyed having them around. The boys had been incredibly helpful so far, teaching him all he needed to know to formulate his plan. There were a few more things he had to work out once he returned to Barcelona…

"Are we nearly there?" Cecilia asked, and he realized she'd been talking and he missed the last bit of what she'd said.

"Sí. I apologize, I am afraid I was preoccupied there for a moment."

"I was curious how far to the cathedral— Oh!"

They emerged from one of the covered walkways that led into the city center and Cecilia caught her first view of the Gothic wonder that was Catedral de Santa María. She stood gazing in wonder at the magnificent stone structure with a hand clutched to her chest.

"It is so beautiful," she breathed. "Are we going inside?"

Felip chuckled and took her hand. The group must have already been inside, as he didn't see their guide, José. As they approached the main doors, Cecilia craned her neck to take in all of the detail on the towers.

"Ooh look! Gargoyles!"

He spotted their group inside the main entrance listening to a jovial older man Felip had met once before. He'd gone with Tomás to interview local guides, choosing only the best to represent his company. Those trips had been a bonding experience for the two of them after living apart for years due to military service, higher education, and Tomás's travels.

Cecilia left his side and went nearer the front so she could hear better. José was telling them about El Cid, the Christian military leader who'd remained undefeated by both the Moors and Christian kings who had come up against him. He was legendary for his ability to best men in both battle and intellect. He was brought here after his death to be buried, as he'd been born nearby. Cecilia listened carefully to the guide, watching his facial expressions and craning her neck to catch every last word. As they moved between each of the fifteen chapels within the grand cruciform design of the cathedral, Felip watched Cecilia become enraptured with the smallest details.

The church bells, controlled by the figure known as Papamoscas, held her attention and when they began to ring, she gasped and stared up at the strange figure. It must have been a little loud even for her because she covered her ears and stepped back. She turned to find Felip watching her, and she grinned happily. This was the Cecilia he wanted to preserve in his mind when they were apart, which he hoped would not be for long.

José gave the group a few moments to take in the rest of the cathedral and Felip used the opportunity to kneel in one of the pews and have a moment of reflection. He crossed himself and bowed his head in prayer, thinking of all the blessings in his life: his parents and their ongoing support; his brothers, especially Tomás, who had enabled him to meet the most incredible woman... All thoughts seemed to turn to her, but he knew in his heart it was because something momentous was happening. He'd said to her one door closes and another opens.

Stepping through this door promised to be full of challenges, but also full of love.

Love.

He loved Cecilia, and he wasn't afraid of it. He knew it was audacious, to fall in love with an American woman who was only in his country for twelve days, but he also believed things happened for a reason, otherwise how else could one explain all of the circumstances which had brought them together?

Felip crossed himself once more and stood, taking in the ornate carvings on the altar before him. He knew there were many historically significant pieces of religious art in this cathedral and that it was a place of importance, but for Felip, Burgos would now be the place he gave thanks for the woman who had turned his world upside down. The place where that new door opened wide and a bright glow of sunshine came into his life.

The group split up for a short time to explore the shops along the river. Cecilia and Gabrielle walked with Janelle and Kristin and they seemed intent on spending some of their euros on souvenirs. Cecilia smiled at Felip and pointed to let him know where she was going and he waved to her, touched that she'd made the gesture and had thought of him. Felip found himself walking with Bill and Tony, who had many questions for him.

"How expensive is it to live in Spain, and which city gives you the most bang for your buck?"

"Barcelona."

"Which city would you say is the most LGBTQ-friendly?"

"Barcelona."

Where do you think is the friendliest to ex pats who—"

"Barcelona."

They laughed in exasperation at him. "Come on," Bill said. "You're biased."

"Es la verdad," Felip said. "I am biased in that I love my city the most, but there are so many wonderful places to live in España. Did you like Madrid?"

"We did! So much shopping, so much good food," Tony said, sighing happily. "When we came before I really liked Seville and Granada—"

"Granada is beautiful as well. If you want to be near the south, it is a perfect place."

"I've heard good things about Bilbao," Bill said. "What do you think of the Basque Country?"

"They have great food, they have the Guggenheim...you'll see for yourselves tomorrow."

"That's right," Tony said. "Maybe we should price apartments in all of the cities we like, and see—"

"We're going to need jobs, too, you know," Bill added, rolling his eyes. "It's not like we'll be independently wealthy when we get here. It's going to take every penny we make over the next year to save up."

"If we don't do it now, babe, I'm afraid we never will. We'll get older and stuck in our ways and we won't want to try anything new."

"I know you're not talking about me," Bill said. "I'm the king of new experiences."

"Oh, give me a break," Tony said. "You're one of the most predictable people I've ever met!"

"How can you say that? You were surprised when I threw you that party for your twenty-first birthday!"

"You did manage to pull that off," Tony admitted. "You got me so drunk, I barely remember, but it was a good night."

"It was a *very* good night," Bill said, and Tony pushed him away. Felip laughed at their banter.

"When did you know you were in love?" Felip asked, a little high on his own realization, and then he thought perhaps he'd overstepped his bounds.

Bill and Tony turned to face each other, sizing the other up to see who would go first.

"It had to be—"

"It was definitely—"

"Costa Rica—"

"San Francisco."

They looked at each other again and started laughing.

"I knew before we left Costa Rica that I was in love with you." Bill said.

"But we didn't tell each other until we went to San Francisco for our first date at home."

"But I knew," Bill said. "I knew after a few days. I can remember exactly when I knew."

"When?" Tony asked. "I can't believe you—"

"The night we got lost."

"No way," Tony said. "You were so mad! I thought for sure you were going to be done with me after that night."

"How can you say that? I was worried. You were scared, and I was pissed at myself that I couldn't read the stupid map and our phones were dead so we had no GPS."

"You are terrible at reading maps," Tony said with a laugh.

"I know. But I thought if I got us back to the hotel, you would forgive me for getting us lost—"

"It wasn't your fault. I was the one who wanted to find that bookstore."

"I wanted to get you back safely because I couldn't stand to see you upset. And that's when I knew. If we made it out of there alive, I was going to tell you."

Tony's eyes bugged out. "But you didn't tell me—"

"I chickened out. I waited until you told me."

They stood there smiling at each other, and Felip's eyes got a little misty. "And how long have you been together now?"

"Three years," Bill said. "We've wanted to move to Spain ever since we came here with Ms. Reyes and her sister two years ago. We went to Costa Rica with them, then Spain, and then last year we had to sit out because we were saving up for an apartment together, and now we're back. And I don't want to leave."

"It'll happen, babe. Don't worry." Tony put an arm around Bill's neck and kissed the top of his head. "But right now, I need food."

Felip looked at his phone. "We're going to be eating dinner in about an hour and a half."

Tony shook his head. "Too long. I've been hungry since we got off the bus."

Felip took in Tony's slender frame and figured he probably needed the food. Then his stomach growled. "I think it's contagious. Vamos. Let's find some food and we won't say anything when we get back to the hotel."

By the time they found an heladería and panadería, Felip was ravenous. He ordered three chocolate muffins and coffee and then turned to grab a table.

"You just ordered three muffins?"

"Sí."

"And you said we're about to have dinner?"

Felip shrugged. "I'll be hungry when we get to the hotel. Trust me, this is a small snack."

Bill shook his head. "How you Spaniards manage to stay thin is beyond me."

Tony elbowed him. "Maybe it'll work on us when we move here. Don't question it."

Felip watched as they did their best to order in Spanish. Bill was more fluent than Tony, which seemed odd since Tony was of Latin descent, but then, he knew not all Latin Americans spoke Spanish.

They grabbed a table and dug into their snacks. Bill and Tony opted for helado, which also sounded good to Felip. After a few minutes, Tui and Aaliyah came in, and Felip watched them interact with the woman at the register. Tui let Aaliyah order in flawless Spanish and he paid for both of them before noticing they weren't alone.

"Oh, hey. We, uh—"

"Tui was hungry," Aaliyah said, her cheeks red.

"You're welcome to sit with us," Tony said, grinning at the young couple.

"We're going to walk, I think," Aaliyah said. "But thank you."

They left and another group of kids came in from the other school. One of them approached the counter and ordered with only a little difficulty. The others came up after her and when the woman spoke to them in Spanish, they seemed to panic before leaving the restaurant. Felip felt bad, like perhaps he should have helped. He waved the first girl over to the table.

"Do your friends need help?"

She shrugged and had a taste of her helado. "If they're hungry enough, they'll make it work." Tony and Bill cracked up at Felip's stunned expression.

She walked out the door and shouted down the street, "You guys are hella stupid!"

Felip and the others laughed, and then Bill and Tony glanced at each other.

"We heard about your plan for Barcelona," Bill said with a grin.

Felip frowned. Who had told? "Gabrielle?"

Tony laughed. "Don't worry, she only told us. I can't wait to see your winery."

Felip breathed a little easier. "And you think Cecilia will like it?"

Bill shrugged. "I don't know, I don't think she's a big fan of drinking, at least that's what Gabrielle says—"

"But the winery is so much more than just the wine. It's a place that brings my family all together."

Tony sucked in a breath. "You're going to have her meet the family?"

"Sí. Claro. She means a lot to me. They will love her."

"That's pretty heavy, man," Bill said. "You don't think that's too much pressure?"

Felip frowned. "It is how we are built en España. Family is very important. We are very close."

"And she's already nervous about getting involved. Just...take it easy. Don't be so...Spanish."

Felip barked out a laugh at Tony's proclamation. "Soc de Catalunya," he replied, pretending to be offended by Bill's statement. Then he smiled and nodded. "I will take it under advisement."

They cleaned up their table and left to meet the rest of the group at the bridge. They found Cecilia sitting with Mrs. Santiago on a bench, giggling.

"You enjoy the shopping?" he asked as he approached.

Cecilia pulled him down to sit next to her. "Watch."

Felip watched as a family with a small boy approached the water fountain. There was a foot pedal on the ground, and the little boy was trying to figure out how to drink water and step on the pedal at the same time. His father lifted him, but he wanted to do it himself. The father put him down and the boy stomped on the pedal, making water shoot out of the top, and he laughed and laughed. Then he yelled to his father to hold him up to get a drink, and the father did so, splashing him in the face with the water.

Cecilia did not hide her joy at watching. When the family left, she waved to the little boy and he waved back to her with a smile.

"At least this one isn't making ugly faces at you."

She grinned at him but didn't say a word. The fondness in the way she'd watched the child, and the fun she had with the little girl on the plane... Did she want to be a mother? Felip loved children and always counted on being a father, a good one like his own. He thought he'd missed his chance. Maybe not?

But if he asked about children, was that putting too much pressure on her? His conversation with Bill and Tony had him questioning his actions. He knew how he felt about her and what he wanted, so it seemed only natural, but perhaps there were cultural concerns to take into account.

"Are you ready to go?"

Cecilia stood before him with her hand out. He took it and let her lead him over to the bridge, where the others were waiting. He noticed Tui and Aaliyah standing away from the group, her hands in his, and he smiled. Seemed the young man had finally let her know how he felt.

The walk back to the hotel was short and their dinner was served almost immediately upon their arrival. Felip made sure everyone was taken care of and then he checked in with Cecilia and Gabrielle, who sat at a table together. He had to inform them his time with the tour was coming to an end.

"Ladies, my brother has informed me that Rosana will be returning tomorrow night. She will be meeting us in Bilbao."

Cecilia's smile fell. "Does that mean you're leaving?"

"Sí. Pero, I will be sure to connect with you in Barcelona. How can I let you visit my city without showing you the best places?"

Gabrielle looked between them. "Excuse me one minute. I need to go check on the Santiagos."

Felip knew she was leaving to give them time alone. He sat with Cecilia. "I'm sorry. I didn't want to even think about it until I had to."

Cecilia tucked her hair behind her ear. "Of course. Tomás is very lucky you could step in."

She tried to give him a smile but he recognized in her the same fear that worried him.

"So we have tomorrow," she said, trying to be cheerful.

"Sí. And tomorrow night, I have a special surprise for the group. I need to check a few details when we arrive to our hotel, but I think you will like this surprise. It will be right up your alley."

"Another alley?" she said, giving him an exaggerated wink.

"Oh...well," he said, taking her hand on the table. "I'm sure we can arrange that as well. It's all part of your tour experience."

She'd been taking a drink of water and nearly spit it out. "Oh, really? You provide this experience to all of your tourists?"

Felip rolled his eyes. He should have known by now that she would get him somehow. "Remember, this is my first tour. You'll have to tell me if it's an effective strategy."

She smiled, then she looked down and began moving spaghetti around on her plate. "Depends on what outcome you desired." She pulled her hand back from him.

"Cecilia, you know what I desire."

She put her fork down and took a deep breath. When she looked up, Felip's heart nearly broke at the sight of her brave smile. "Then let's make the most of our last day."

CHAPTER TWENTY-THREE

:30 p.m. Outside the Guggenheim Museum, Bilbao, País Vasco

The day they'd spent in Bilbao was one of Cecilia's best days ever. They were almost busy enough that she didn't think about the fact Felip was leaving. Almost.

They'd climbed onto the bus after a hearty breakfast around nine in the morning. Everyone had been pleased to be able to sleep in a bit. The drive to Bilbao was almost two hours and Cecilia had basked in the warmth of the sun coming through the window of the bus, and the warmth of Felip sitting beside her and holding her hand. She'd given up trying to maintain professional decorum for the day. If this was the last day she'd have with him, she intended to enjoy it.

The city was different from the others in many ways, but their guide explained that much had been done to resurrect this once industrial-heavy town. Jean-Paul informed them that Bilbao went into a steep decline when Spain joined the European Union and it wasn't until a delegation of city officials met with a group of city planners from Pennsylvania that they'd begun to develop a strategic plan to get

Bilbao back on her feet. Cecilia found it fascinating to hear about this connection to America. He shared that now tourism and conventions had become the basis of their city's economy, and major environmental improvements had been implemented to save the river from pollution. Cecilia was impressed before they even stepped off the bus.

She and Felip managed to have a private lunch together in a steakhouse, complete with footsies under the table. Felip finally got her to taste his beloved cava, and she had to admit it was delicious. He fed her steak, she fed him prawns, and it was the most silly and romantic meal she'd ever eaten. Afterwards, they'd walked up and down the narrow streets, admiring the decorations for the PRIDE festival, which they learned would be later that afternoon. Felip showed her what pintxos were—small, open sandwiches piled high with meats, cheeses, and all kinds of treats held together with toothpicks—and she even tasted some he'd handpicked for her. By the time they met up with the group to climb back on the bus, she was so full she thought she might burst.

The bus took them to the Guggenheim, and she was blown away. It had been a long time since she'd been to anything other than local historical museums. She lost her mind when they found the Andy Warhol. The kids didn't quite understand why she was so excited, so she got to be the docent for a short time, explaining why he was important to American Modern Art and also telling them a little bit about Marilyn Monroe, who they only knew as that "blonde actress chick whose dress blows up." Living in a small town meant kids weren't exposed to art and culture and she made a point to try to expand their horizons whenever she could.

After the museum, they walked to the river and watched several party boats float by full of folks celebrating the LGBTQ community. So much love and happiness, it warmed Cecilia's heart. Felip wrapped her in his arms and they waved to the boats together. Bill and Tony stood next to them taking selfies, so of course Cecilia and Felip had to join in, seeing who could be goofier.

"My face hurts from smiling," she said, tucking her face into his shoulder. "I love this place. I love this day."

And I love you.

There was so much she wanted to say, but she'd sworn to herself that she would keep it together and not add any negativity to their last day. She would not lose her shit and cry. She would not burden him with confessions of her feelings, no matter if she thought perhaps he might feel the same.

Felip held her tighter and pressed his lips to her temple. "You have no idea how happy that makes me."

The rest of their group and Rio Grande High joined them on the steps outside the Guggenheim and a passerby took a group photo for them. Cecilia would remember this day for the rest of her life.

As the sun began to set, they took the bus back to their hotel for dinner. This hotel was much fancier than their past hotels, and Cecilia looked forward to taking a nice long bath in the large tub at some point...if there was time. Felip said there was still a surprise for them this night, so there was no time for relaxing now. She made her way to the bright white hotel dining room, which was massive and vibrating with adolescent energy. Not only were their kids and Rio Grande's students there, but at least four other large groups of teenagers. The kids all checked each other out, the other groups giving Tui a wide berth. He'd never use his size to intimidate anyone, but that didn't mean he didn't intimidate other kids.

Cecilia had followed instructions to change into pants and carried a light sweater with her. She moved through the buffet and found a seat at the table with Gabrielle, Bill and Tony, the Santiagos, Rosana and Felip. His smile when he saw her approach was nothing short of dazzling. He stood and pulled out the chair next to him, which was incredibly sweet, but the others watched with expressions that screamed *awwwww*.

"Rosana and Mr. and Mrs. Santiago have offered to stay behind with any of the kids who don't want to make the trek," Gabrielle said as she sat down.

"Merci, gracias. We'll likely be back late, well after midnight, I would imagine."

"Woo! A real bunch of party animals." Cecilia hadn't been out past midnight in years, maybe a decade. She didn't need Felip to know that, however. He was probably used to being out late, if what she'd seen of Madrid was any example. It had taken her a bit to get used to the Spanish way of staying out late every night, but tonight was going to be even more of a stretch for her.

Felip squeezed her leg under the table and she blushed. She wished there was a way for them to…but then it was impossible. Their affair would end tonight. Felip would go back to his home and his job and Cecilia would attempt to be cheerful and teacher-y for a few more days, before she went home and tried to navigate a life alone after finding the most incredible man she'd ever met.

That crushing thought sucked the air from her lungs and the sting of tears pricked at her eyes.

When they'd finished eating, Felip led her and the other adults to the tables where the students sat.

"Tonight, estudiantes, you will have the opportunity to take part in a celebration with the people of Bilbao. Tonight begins the Festival of San Juan, or St. John en inglés. La noche de San Juan is the night we celebrate the beginning of summer, or the solstice." He gave Cecilia's hand a squeeze and kept talking. "This night, Catholic and pagan rituals come together as bonfires are lit to chase away the evil spirits and water is used to cleanse and purify. It is celebrated a little bit different in other parts of España, but tonight we celebrate in País Vasco."

The kids all chattered excitedly, deciding whether they wanted to go. It didn't take long for all of them to agree.

"Molt bé. You will need sturdy shoes and perhaps a light jacket, as it could be cooler where we are going."

Chairs slid back in unison and all seven of the kids jumped up and rushed out of the dining room, almost taking out a server in their excitement.

"Bonfires? Pagan rituals? Is this what you meant was right up my alley?" Cecilia asked him. "Because before this trip, up my alley would have been a night in with a mystery and some hot cocoa."

He threw his head back as he laughed. "I love that you are living life like a true Spaniard while you are here. Do you have everything you need?"

"I hope so," she said, anxious to see what this was all about. She was a little apprehensive. A bunch of folks hanging out around a bonfire did not sound like her idea of a good time, nor did it sound safe, but it was exciting to think she'd get to experience something so unique.

The kids were all back in a record ten minutes and they started what would end up being a nearly two-mile walk, all up hill and stairs, until they reached a spot that overlooked the city. Cecilia walked at the rear with Gabrielle as Felip led the group. The kids all crowded around him asking questions, and Cecilia fell harder for him, it seemed, every step they took. Even Jorge, who could be a challenge for the most patient person, engaged Felip in conversation in which they both seemed engrossed.

"You okay?" Gabrielle asked.

Cecilia sighed. "Right now, yeah. And I'll continue to be until we get home, and I sleep for about forty-eight hours straight. Then it's going to really suck." Her eyes flooded with tears and she took a deep breath to keep them at bay. "I'm trying to live in the now," she said in a hippie-ish voice, and Gabrielle snorted.

"You two will find a way, I have faith."

Bill and Tony fell back to walk with them. "This is going to be crazy! I wish Zoey was here with us."

"I know," Gabrielle said. "I talked to her earlier today and she said to say hello to everyone. She's feeling much better. She's going to start the next phase of her physical therapy this week."

"I'm so sorry she didn't get to come," Cecilia said.

The other three looked at her, and Bill was the first one to speak. "It seems totally obvious that you were meant to be here."

"Yeah," Tony chimed in. "This all happened for a reason. First Zoey, then Rosana. I've never seen Fate work so hard to get two people together. You can't ignore that."

"That's actually really messed up, Tony. You're saying Zoey had to break her pelvis and Rosana had to nearly fracture her tailbone so I could meet Felip? I don't know how I feel about that."

"It doesn't matter," Gabrielle said. "You're here, he's here, you need to make the most of this opportunity."

"Yeah, otherwise that's like letting their pain be all for nothing," Tony said, all dramatic. "You owe it to them to make their pain mean something."

"Oh my God, you guys. Do you hear yourselves?"

"Listen, when it's time to head back, let us take the kids. You and Felip should take some time alone," Gabrielle said, elbowing her. "It's your last night."

"Well—" Bill started to say, but Tony shushed him.

"You guys walk behind us, like you have been, and once we get back to the hotel, go spend some time together. You can sleep on the bus tomorrow."

Cecilia chuckled. "I'm going to be up way past my bedtime."

Felip had halted the students at the top of the stairs and was waiting for them. "Vale. We will meet back here at twelve-thirty. How does that sound? Be sure to stay together, do not go anywhere alone, vale?"

The kids all gave their agreement. After everyone entered the park-like area, within moments, the kids all took each other's hands and disappeared into the huge crowd. The group of adults hung back a little, closer to the spot they had cordoned off for the fire. Behind some metal barriers was a pile about six feet tall of scrap wood and other materials. Cecilia was pleased to see a crew of firefighters standing next to their hose in preparation, in case the fire grew out of control. *Safety first.*

At the far end of the hillside there was a stage and a DJ playing some really cool music, which grew louder and louder. Soon she saw people running through the crowd with strange masks and head-dresses on, wielding pitchforks.

Felip turned to them with a frown. "I brought paper and pens and I forgot to give them to the kids. It is customary to write something you want to be done with on the paper, and you can throw it into the fire. Would any of you like some?"

The others all took a piece of paper and shared the two pens he'd brought. He approached Cecilia with a grin. "Would you like to write something, profesora?"

Cecilia held out her hand, and he placed a small piece of paper there. Felip then took one himself and asked Bill to turn around so he could write on the paper. Gabrielle asked her to do the same.

"You know what you're going to write?" she asked Cecilia.

"I do."

Coming on this trip had been so far out of her comfort zone, and she'd had the time of her life. She wanted to be rid of her hesitation and fear. If being in Spain and spending time with Felip had taught her anything, it was that she needed embrace life and reach for the things that made her happy. Her job made her happy, her home made her happy, and Felip made her happy. The three things didn't go together, sadly, but tonight was about moving forward.

"Vale. Hold on to your papers a bit longer. They should be starting—"

Felip's voice was cut off when the music blared even louder from the sound system. He put his arm around Cecilia and she pressed in close, a little overwhelmed by the sound. But the music! It was intense and powerful. Suddenly the men in the funny masks began running in circles around the fire pile, shouting and shaking their pitchforks toward the sky.

Felip had explained that the villagers would light the fires to chase away evil spirits, and she thought the masks themselves made the actors seem frightening. As the music began to build and build, fireworks erupted from actors' headpieces and pitchforks, shooting into the night sky. The crowd all cheered and everything seemed to get louder, until Cecilia had to cover her ears.

"Are you alright?" Felip asked, and she nodded, anxious to see what would happen next. She wished she could sign to him so she wouldn't have to shout. She wished she had time to teach him.

"I'm great. What is this music?"

He listened for a moment. "Basque metal. I don't know the artist."

"I love this!" She pulled out her phone and swiped to her Shazam app. Luckily it picked up the music and she had her artist. *Boom.*

"I got it! I'll have to look for a record store tomorrow."

Felip shook his head. "Sounds like you will have an adventure for sure."

The bonfire came to life and soon the flames licked at the sky. Sparks flickered overhead like fireflies doing a mating dance. The music thundered from the speakers on the stage and the masked actors danced around the fire, shouting and gesturing at the crowd. Onlookers gazed upon the fire with wonder in their eyes.

A couple of pallets slid down the fire and a series of loud explosions were heard as fireworks hidden in the bonfire exploded. A rush of people backed away from the barriers, nearly knocking Cecilia and the others over. Felip ushered them quickly up the side of the next level of the hill as the fire fighters shouted to each other, but the fire didn't spread and soon the crowd began dancing. Some folks approached the barriers and handed their papers to the masked actors, who tossed them into the fire. Sparks spewed up towards the heavens with each new sheet of paper.

Felip collected their papers and carried them to the barrier, where he handed them over. He hurried back and stood at Cecilia's side, his hand on her lower back.

Tony shrieked, and they all turned to look.

"What is it?" Bill asked.

"I just got an email from my boss. I got the promotion! That means we—"

"We'll have enough money to move! Oh babe!"

The lovers kissed and embraced with joy. Cecilia was thrilled for them, and a bit envious. To be their age and able to pick up and start over someplace, have a whole new life.

Their age? You're only thirty-five. It's not like you can't start over.

Felip shook hands with Bill and Tony and then turned to Cecilia.

"Walk with me."

She smiled at him, then turned to ask Gabrielle if they were okay. She shooed them away.

Felip walked her through the crowd of at least five hundred people to the far side of the cliff. A band took the stage and played music that sounded like Celtic drinking songs. When they got to a spot a little way from the crowd but still able to see the stage, she pulled on Felip's hand and pushed up on her tiptoes to speak in his ear. "This sounds like pirate music, like Irish folk music."

"The Basques and the Celtic people are related by DNA. There are some similarities."

She nodded and turned to watch the band. She could see Tui's puffy hair above the crowd so she felt the kids were most likely safe, although this large of a crowd had her feeling anxious. They were in a foreign country, anything could happen.

"Are you alright?" he asked, cupping her jaw.

"Yeah," she said. "Just a little worried about the kids."

He looked around, and she assumed he found the kids by the smile on his face. "I think they'll be fine, especially if they stay with Tui."

"You're right. It's hard not to be a mother hen, you know?"

He smiled at her and ran a thumb over her lips. "And I love that about you. You are wonderful with the children. You would make an excellent mother."

Cecilia wasn't quite sure how to take that. "I suppose. And if this trip is any indication, you'd make a pretty great teacher."

He laughed and pulled her into his arms. "I don't think I have near enough patience to do this every day. These kids make it easy. And I believe we are a good match. You and I make a great team."

"We do work pretty well together, don't we?"

And then there was a pregnant pause. Felip's expression grew serious, and he started to speak several times, until he crushed her against him and buried his face in her hair. Cecilia clung to him, tears once again threatening to spill, but she focused on breathing in Felip's scent, taking as much of it in as she could so that if the worst happened and she never saw him again, she'd never forget.

"It's time for us to see the students back to the hotel."

Her heart sank. Should she tell him? Should she confess her feelings? It was one of those now-or-never moments and she felt it slipping away.

"Felip?"

He pulled back. "There is so much I want to say to you, Cecilia, and not enough time." His eyes searched hers, and she saw within him what she thought might be a similar plight. To tell or not to tell? He shook his head and squeezed his eyes shut. "Just know, cariño, that when I leave you, I am leaving a piece of my heart with you. And I do not intend to leave it permanently. I want it back."

She laughed despite the fact she felt like she might fall apart at any second. "So it's like a lease? Or a loan? Do we need a contract? Is there a fee, or, like, a balloon payment at the end of the term?"

Felip barked out a laugh and lost his composure. The tension of the moment bled out of both of them until tears spilled down their cheeks, but they were from laughter. Cecilia loved that they would be parting on laughter, not sadness. It seemed fitting, given their experiences from the last few days.

"Mr. Segura! This place is off the hook! I'd heard Ibiza was the crazy place to party, but this was insane!"

All of the kids approached with their arms around each other, with Jorge in the middle. His hands were at his sides, and he was kind of looking around like he'd won the lottery.

"Mrs. Galván, wasn't that crazy?" Tui asked her.

"Indeed. Kids, you just witnessed firsthand the way the Catholic church and pagans have coexisted for centuries without admitting it."

"Yeah, because I was kinda thinkin' the whole masks-and-fire gig was not something I ever remember learning about in catechism," Joseph said.

"Yes, well, some beliefs were too powerful to deny, and the celebration of the solstice is important to many in España, especially anyone involved with agriculture, not to mention fear of evil spirits. I believe this fear extends to all religious groups."

Cecilia elbowed Felip. "See? You could take over a classroom anytime and hold your own."

He wrapped an arm around her shoulders and squeezed. "Let's begin the long walk back to your hotel and get you all to bed. Rosana will expect you to be awake and alert for your visit to San Sebastián tomorrow."

The students all looked at him, confused.

"Are you leaving, Mr. Segura?" Eduardo asked.

Cecilia sucked in a breath and forced a smile for the kids. At least that's what she told herself.

"Sí. Rosana is back, and I have an event I must see to at my winery tomorrow evening. I've been, how do you say, playing hooky? My partner is ready to have my head."

The kids looked at each other, and Cecilia wished they could start walking and forget the goodbye part, but she knew she needed to remind the kids.

"When we get back to the hotel, you can all say goodbye to Mr. Segura and thank him for being an excellent substitute tour guide."

They nodded and turned to walk back towards the gate where they were to meet.

"That went..."

"They think you're pretty cool," she said. She took his hand and tugged on it for him to follow her. Felip said something in Spanish and shook his head.

Once they collected Gabrielle and Bill and Tony, they began their trudge back. At least it was downhill. Cecilia's legs were wobbly after the long day. She and Felip held hands but didn't speak on the way back. The kids walked with them, asking him some more questions about the festival and about Barcelona, whether they would see him again.

"I have no doubt you will see me again."

CHAPTER TWENTY-FOUR

*1*:30 a.m. Bilbao Local Time – Hotel Bilbao

It was after one in the morning when they reached the hotel and the kids were beat. Felip shook hands with them all and told Gabrielle to let Rosana know that he'd be in touch with her. She gave him a chaste hug and looked between Felip and Cecilia before she left them at the doors to the lobby.

And then they were alone. And his heart was breaking, for even though he knew he would see her again, had made arrangements to be sure it would happen, he also knew this separation would be the first of many if they were to try to build any sort of relationship.

"Are you leaving in the morning? Or—"

"Sí. My flight leaves at six. I need to leave here in about," he looked at his phone, "three hours."

Cecilia, his lovely profesora, looked down at her feet and he could sense she was attempting to be brave. "You probably want to get some sleep," she said.

"That's not exactly the foremost thought in my mind. Not to mention, I gave Rosana my room."

Her eyes widened. "Oh. Oh...Felip, I—"

"I would not dream of accompanying you to your room, nor would I allow you to give up your bed for me. What I would like, if you wouldn't mind, is if you would...sit with me? For a little while. Let me hold you until we can no longer keep our eyes open. Then I will say good night to you, or good morning, I suppose."

She smiled, but tears welled in her eyes. "I would like that."

The lobby of the Hotel Bilbao went to great lengths to provide comfortable seating for guests who had reason to spend any amount of time in transition. They had their pick of low couches or modern-looking armchairs at this hour. Felip led Cecilia over to a couch by the window in the corner and they sat together. It took a moment of giggling before they settled with her legs over his lap and curled up to his chest. They shared a few laughs about things that had occurred on the trip and things the group had yet to experience. Eventually they were content to sit in silence. Felip stroked Cecilia's hair and she ran a fingernail over his chest and down his arm, giving him chills. She stilled, and he imagined she was asleep, but he wasn't through holding her. He never wanted to be through.

Had he made a mistake tonight? So many times at the bonfire it seemed as though she'd wanted to say something, and he'd wanted to tell her of his feelings, but ultimately he decided he didn't want to proclaim his love for her right before leaving. With her history, he didn't feel it was fair for him to tell her and then leave. But life was so precious, and what if...

Cecilia snuggled in closer and mumbled in her sleep. He bent to see if he could make out her words. It almost sounded as if she were singing.

"You're breaking my heart. I'm begging you please...don't go... please don't go..."

A sharp pain pierced his chest and he held her tighter. *The last thing I want to do on earth is to let you go, cariño. I can only hope my plan works and you will be back in my arms for good.*

Felip held her until it was time for his shuttle to pick him up. She stirred, and he kissed her head.

"Can you make it back to your room?"

She nodded. "I'll miss you," she mumbled and then tilted her head back for a kiss, her eyes suspiciously still closed.

Felip pressed a gentle kiss to her lips. "I will see you again before you have a chance to miss me."

He walked her to her room and helped her get the door open, as she was obviously still asleep. He'd never tire of her in this state. Cecilia asleep was at her most vulnerable, and he'd cherish the memories of even her drool, of which he had a small patch on his shirt even now. She stepped inside the door, turned and lifted her lips for him to kiss her. Her eyes were closed.

"Goodnight, cariño."

"Goodnight, stalker," she mumbled.

She turned, shuffled to the bed, and flopped down face first.

He could only laugh or he'd cry like a baby who'd lost his security blanket. He closed the door and then returned to the front desk, got his bag from the bellhop, and left more than a little piece of his heart behind.

The cab ride, the airport security, and the flight were a blur. Upon arrival at Barcelona-El Prat, a car waited for him to take him to the winery, where he would shower, dress, and put on a smile for his parents, June, and their invited guests. June had been relieved he would be attending the launch party for the new vintage. They'd all have to deal with half of Felip's attention. Between lack of sleep and a missing heart, he couldn't be expected to be his usual upbeat self.

"My son, what has happened to you?" his mother asked in Catalán as she opened the door to the main house.

"Mama, I beg of you that we have this conversation after I have caught the tiniest of siestas before the event."

"Of course, but you must eat first."

"I'm fine, I ate before I left Bilbao—"

"But that was hours ago."

He kissed her cheeks and moved past her. "Please, Mama. I can't think straight. Just a couple of hours and I'll be good as new. You can feed me then."

He climbed the stairs of the house he'd grown up in and moved on autopilot to the room he'd shared with Alonso as boys. He still kept a bed and clothes here for those occasions when their events ran late or if he simply didn't feel up to returning to his lonely flat in Barcelona. Most of the time it didn't bother him to be alone, but he had a feeling as he flopped into his bed fully clothed that he would mind it a lot more now.

Three hours later, and thirty minutes before they were due to start setting up, Felip joined his mother in the kitchen, where she'd prepared several of his favorite dishes.

"You are not leaving this table until you resemble my son."

"Then I might not leave for quite some time."

She sat across from him. "Speak to me. What is troubling you?"

And the tale of his teacher from California spilled out in between bites of the delicious food. He told her everything he could remember, from the moment she'd acted so curiously in the airport to their last kiss in Bilbao, and by the end, the tears burned his eyes.

"I love her, and the whole situation seems impossible."

"Of course it does," his mother said. "She is an American. How can it work?"

Felip snorted. "Her being American has nothing to do with it."

"It does if you are to believe the news right now."

"Estigueu tranquils, Mama. Don't say that. That's not fair. I promise you she is not like that. You can see for yourself. I arranged for Tomás to have the bus driver bring them here Tuesday before they go to Park Güell and Arenas for lunch."

"You are bringing them here? Does she know?"

Felip shook his head. "I wanted to surprise her."

His mother crossed herself and said, "I hope you know what you are doing."

Her words did not inspire much confidence.

The event that afternoon was a showcase for some of their larger clients. The newest cava was poured, dinner was served, conversation was had, and though Felip was exhausted, he thought he and June had done a good job with their clients. His father came to say hello and shake hands. At sixty-two years old, his father had suffered some health setbacks, so Felip had been in charge for over a decade now. He'd wanted his father to relax and enjoy his retirement, but his whole life had been the vineyard forever. It was hard to let go.

"June? Can you drive me back to town?" he asked when they'd wrapped up for the night.

"I suppose. Maybe along the way you can explain your disappearing act."

He was definitely not looking forward to that conversation.

When she pressed, he told her that he'd met someone on the plane, someone special, and that he'd likely be occupied for some of this week as her group was going to be in town.

"Fine, but when she leaves, I better have your full attention. We have the next phase of the launch coming up and I want everything to go smoothly."

Felip sighed and looked out the window of her Mercedes into the darkness. She'd never have his full attention, not so long as he didn't have Cecilia in his life.

June dropped him off at La Bouqería so he could pick up some food. He was famished. Again.

"I'll see you tomorrow. We have a lot of catching up to do." June sped away before he had a chance to say thank you. Felip sighed. He realized he'd left his suitcase at Tomás's and who knew when he'd be getting it back?

He was completely out of sorts by the time he picked up some fruit, meat, cheese and bread to take up to his apartment, which was only a block or so away on the corner of Carrer de Santa Anna and Las Ramblas.

He climbed the steps to his apartment and was hit with a foul smell. Perhaps Alonso hadn't come by in a few days? He'd agreed to watch over the place while Felip was in California. By the smell that hit him in the face when he opened the refrigerator, it had been well over a week.

Felip cleaned out the offending items and took them down to the garbage. When he returned, he changed out of his fancy clothes, reminding himself to bring another suit out to the winery and take this one to the cleaners, then he sat down to eat.

And immediately his thoughts went to Cecilia. It was late, they were probably back from their day trip. He pulled out his phone and was grateful to the girls for adding Cecilia to his contacts.

Cariño. How was your day?

He went about cleaning up the apartment, as he'd left it a mess and there was dust everywhere. The phone pinged several minutes later and by the time he reached it, it had pinged four more times. That made him hurry his steps.

We went to the beach! I had seafood from the Bay of Biscay! And I went on an adventure, you would have been proud of me.

What followed was a series of pictures from San Sebastián, and Cecilia in a record shop.

I tried to find the music we heard last night at the festival and this guy didn't have it, but he gave me directions to another shop...IN SPANISH...AND I FOUND IT! All by myself! Well, Aaliyah and Tui helped. But that shop was closing for

lunch/siesta, whatever. How are you? Did you make it to your event?

Felip undressed and climbed into his bed. He smiled at his phone. She seemed to have a lot of energy after such a long day. She texted again before he had a chance to answer.

ROSANA TOOK US TO FRANCE! Did you know we were going? I EVEN GOT TO SEE A FRENCH POODLE. LIKE, A REAL FRENCH POODLE! We pull up to St. Jean blah blah (I don't know how to say it) and there was a poodle! Just hanging out! Sorry, it was pretty amazing.

Felip laughed to himself.

I'm so glad you had a wonderful time. I wish I could have been there to see a real French poodle with you.

He loved that she was sharing these experiences with him, but his heart hurt to not be by her side.

It would have been more fun with you.

That shouldn't make him feel better. He shouldn't be so happy to hear her say that.

I wish I was there. I will be seeing you soon, though.

. . .

He wasn't going to spoil the surprise, but he wanted to see how she'd react.

You will? When? Tomorrow? Do you know where we're staying in Barcelona?

He switched over to text Tomás and ask him. It took a few beats and when the answer came, he frowned. Why the hell were they staying way out in Castelldefels? That was twenty kilometers from him.

I know where you're staying. I don't know if I can get out there tomorrow. Your group is outside of town and you'll be getting in late. But I will be sure to see you as soon as I can. Are you resting? Am I keeping you up?

He didn't want to hang up. Even texting was a lifeline for him right now.

I'm taking a bath in my giant tub.

That text made him sit up.

At this very moment? Am I disturbing you?

Felip's heart pounded wildly his chest.

. . .

You're not disturbing me. I miss you, is that weird?

If you only knew how much that is not weird.

Not weird at all. I miss you, too. So much.

Her response made him chuckle.

Good.

Good?

Yeah. Good.

They went back and forth for a while and Felip kept thinking she was in the tub. She was naked. And he wished they were together. He wished for so many things.

You know what I wish?

It was as if she'd heard his thoughts despite the fact that they weren't speaking.

. . .

I know what I wish.

If he told her, it would be inappropriate, wouldn't it? Her next text made him chuckle.

Let's both tell. At the same time. Get ready...

Felip crafted his text and hit send as hers popped up.

I wish we would have had a night together.

Felip had said he wished they were together right now, in her tub, and he was grateful she'd had a similar line of thinking.

We will have a night together, cariño. We will have many more than one, if I have anything to say about it.

Felip's fantasies began to multiply out of control in his mind. When Cecilia returned to him, after she took the children home, he might not let her out of his sight, out of his bed...

I just don't see how that's possible.

Her words wounded him. He needed her to have faith this would work.

. . .

Do you trust me? Even a little?

If she didn't, how could he—

As much as I can. I need to get out of the tub. I'm pruning.

Felip let out a sigh that brought his mood down with it.

I should let you sleep. Please know, Cecilia, you are in my every thought. I would move heaven and earth to be with you right now. Please trust me.

Her answer didn't come for a long time, and he almost thought she'd gone to bed.

I'm trying to trust you. I want to see you. At least I know our travels tomorrow will bring me closer to you. But then what? It seems so unfair that Fate seems to have brought me a wonderful man, only to dangle him just out of my reach. Good night, Felip. Thank you for texting me.

He wanted to call her and hear her voice, but he figured she'd already taken her hearing aids out, and besides, what good would words do at this point? He needed to act. He needed to show her there was a way for them to be together.

It had to work.

CHAPTER TWENTY-FIVE

8:45 a.m. Bilbao Local Time – Hotel Bilbao

The next morning when they loaded the bus, Cecilia had mixed feelings about leaving Bilbao. In her mind, this was the place she'd been the closest to Felip, where their relationship could have moved to the next level, but instead stalled out as neither of them were brave enough to admit how they felt.

The kids had been hyper at breakfast, so while Cecilia was trying not to turn up her nose at what was becoming their predictable and boring breakfast fare, she had a hard time not being the teeniest bit short with the kids. When Eduardo threw a roll to Joseph from the buffet, she lost her cool a bit.

"Guys! Really? Come on!"

She hadn't had to scold a kid the entire time they'd been in Spain. The school they were traveling with apparently had several kids come back to the hotel wasted last night, but her kids had been perfect. Almost too perfect. But this morning, her patience was thin.

She knew it was apparent to all of them that she was moping, but she couldn't seem to shake it. Gabrielle tried to talk to her when she came downstairs, and she'd asked her, as respectfully as one can at seven in the morning, to please not speak to her until she'd had some caffeine. Gabrielle gave her space and a sympathetic pat on the shoulder.

Gabrielle shared with their group, and Rosana spoke to the other group, about their itinerary for the day. They would be stopping off in Pamplona for a quick walking tour, then they would board the bus for Zaragoza and see another important cathedral, and then they would make their way to their hotel outside of Barcelona that evening. They'd have dinner, and if any were brave enough, they could join Gabrielle and Rosana on a walk to the beach.

Cecilia didn't much care. She was merely going through the motions this morning.

Her chat with Felip the night before had started out a bit fun and exciting and she'd thought to herself, *hey, I might be able to handle this. If I can't see him all the time, at least we have phones.* But then talk got serious, and he'd started in about them having some sort of future, and she couldn't see it. It was as if the longer he was away from her, the more she began to question everything, to think their connection was her imagination, although never in her wildest thoughts did she ever think she could conjure up a man as beautiful, sensitive, and funny as Felip.

She checked out of her room with a heavy sigh and met the others downstairs, taking care not to look at "their" sofa in the lobby. She barely remembered him leaving. It felt like a bad dream, Felip kissing her goodbye.

They walked around the block to the bus and she gazed up the hillside where they'd experienced the festival. It had taken hundreds of stairs to get there, and yet, she'd been oblivious. Walking beside Felip took her mind off her body's exhaustion, and now that he was gone, she felt every mile she'd walked.

"Uh, Mrs. Galván?"

Her thoughts were interrupted by the sight of Tui's suitcase's demise. It had exploded all over the street just as he was loading it into the cargo area. Kind of a perfect metaphor for Cecilia's mood.

"It's fine, Tui. We'll get you a new one when we get to Barcelona. Maybe the driver has some duct tape?"

They all worked together to get his things wrangled and loaded onto the bus. The kids were dragging as well. The bus ride was quiet as many of the students fell asleep.

Cecilia dozed on and off as well, the seat next to her empty, and tried not to think about whether or not she would see him before they left. After today, they had three days left and then she would board another long series of flights, take another bus ride, this time to her mother's house, and she'd go on without Felip Segura.

Her tour mates were determined to cheer her up. Tui walked with her through the streets of Pamplona and kept up a running stream of commentary as to whether or not he had what it took to outrun a bull. Their group followed the path of the annual San Fermín festival, and Tui and the boys joked about videos they'd seen and how their moms would beat them if they ran with the bulls and made it back alive.

After the tour, they were given a mere forty-five minutes to shop and grab a snack before they got back on the bus. Eduardo accompanied her, as he was hungry and had completely run out of money. She had him order her more of the delicious chocolate chip muffins, these ones even better than the ones she'd eaten in Madrid, and she remarked that she was going to have to keep up her walking when she returned home or else the muffins would be staying with her long after their trip.

Joseph wanted to stop in a unique shop he'd spotted called Kukux-umusu, and Cecilia loved the silly designs. She purchased herself a new lunchbox with a Slash-like dude on it and a couple of t-shirts for her and her mother. She hadn't done much shopping and wanted to pick up a few things. She wanted more memories than those of a man destined to break her heart.

Cecilia and the boys hurried to meet up with the others and found them huddled around Bill and Tony, laughing hysterically.

"What do you think?" Bill hopped out of their group huddle

dressed in the white outfit of those participating in the running of the bulls, and Cecilia couldn't help but laugh. "See, Tony? I can be unpredictable."

"Being ridiculous does not make you unpredictable. I've seen you be ridiculous before," he said, but even Tony couldn't stop laughing at seeing Bill in the tight white pants and shirt with the red scarf around his neck and red sash around his waist.

"Are you in training?" Cecilia asked him. "Are you seriously going to make us watch this insanity next summer?"

"Yeah, well, he obviously didn't pay attention," Tony said, rolling his eyes. "The guide told us no flip-flops." And sure enough, Bill was sporting a pair of flip-flops to round out his look.

"Tui, just make sure when you come to run, you don't run with Bill."

Everyone cracked up, and it felt good to be smiling again. She normally wasn't one to pout or sulk. She hadn't had that response to her divorce, why should she let herself feel down about Felip? This thing between them wasn't over 'til the fat lady sang, and the orchestra wasn't even warming up yet, despite the fact that she was leaving soon.

Back on the bus, she listened as Rosana spoke a little about the cathedral they were going to see and how there was an actual relic in the place. Cecilia wasn't familiar with Catholic beliefs, and once more she found herself wishing Felip was here to explain it to her in his sexy voice with his adorable smile...

Zaragoza was incredibly beautiful...and hot. She bought rounds of water for the kids and even scouted out an air-conditioned restaurant to eat in after they toured the Cathedral-Basilica of Our Lady of the Pillar. It was different than the cathedral in Burgos, but just as beautiful. She planned to do more reading about the history of the Catholics in Spain, so she'd understand more of the significance of the things she was seeing. Joseph and Eduardo had been the most prepared for the discussions about the items in the churches. The girls, it seemed, didn't attend church except for Aaliyah sometimes; Tui was LDS, and the Santiagos were Jehovah's Witnesses.

The bus ride from Zaragoza was long, and Cecilia was exhausted and sweaty from the day's events. She figured she'd perk up enough after dinner to be able to go to the beach though. Dipping her toe in the Mediterranean would be monumental for her. She'd only been to the Pacific a handful of times, never the Atlantic, so to say she'd been in this ocean? A big step in leaving her simple Cecilia ways behind.

She peered out the window for the last twenty minutes of the ride to see what she could see of Barcelona, but it hardly resembled the big city she'd seen in pictures.

Hey. From where I sit, your city ain't got much going on.

She hoped she could get a rise out of him. She'd resisted texting him all day, and after last night's bummer of a conversation, she wouldn't be surprised if he didn't text back. She didn't know why, but it seemed she was always more vulnerable at night.

And where exactly do you sit?

She looked out the window but couldn't tell anything from the road signs. She asked Rosana what road they were on.

Highway C 32 near Castelldefels. I think we're getting off here.

She knew they were near the coast and the sun was setting, but she was so discombobulated being on a bus. She had to admit, the countryside they'd seen yesterday and today had been absolutely stunning. Rolling green hills, big stretches of nothing but trees and cliffs and ravines. It would have been so much more fun to be driving these roads in a car, maybe even a convertible.

Felip? Do you have a convertible? Do they even have those in Spain?

Not that it mattered, but she could dream.

I do not have a convertible, only a moonroof, but my brother Alonso does. You are nowhere near my beloved city of Barcelona, and you have passed the mountains where Cava Segura is. You cannot make judgements until you see the city proper tomorrow.

She felt better about that, actually. The bus was now off the highway and making its way through narrow suburban streets.

I am not sure why Tomás sent you way out to Castelldefels, except perhaps it is the hotel of our cousin, Fermín. He gets a better rate if you stay there. At least you are near the beach. Will you be going tonight?

So close, and still so far away.

Yes. I think it's important that I go with the students. Letting them loose near a large body of water? Are you kidding me? And I know for a fact Eduardo can't swim.

. . .

The bus driver seemed to be having some trouble getting them close enough to the hotel. After a few frightening turns, during which he nearly took out a telephone pole and several pedestrians, he finally stopped and told Rosana they'd have to walk, or at least that's what she told them. The man rattled on excitedly, and then she'd jumped up with a nervous smile and told them to pack up, take everything, they were moving out!

For the thousandth time today, I wish I was by your side. However, if I am to see you again soon, I must do what my partner asks of me. She's very upset that I was gone, and she's been making me suffer all day for it. I must go before she takes out the belt again.

Cecilia felt a twinge of jealousy and then let it slip away. If he was telling her about this woman, she must truly be a coworker and nothing for Cecilia to worry about, right?

Tell her to use the comfy chair. It's much more effective.

She put her phone away and picked up her bag from Pamplona and her backpack. The walk to the hotel was mere minutes and when they arrived, she was a tad disappointed. It was nice enough, but it was nowhere near as fancy as their hotel in Bilbao...and there was no tub, only a shower.

She went through the motions of dinner and the like before joining Rosana and the others for the walk to the sea. By the time they arrived, it was after nine-thirty and the sky was pitch black, with the exception of the bright moon. She was as excited as the kids to strip off her shoes and let the cool waters of the Mediterranean lap at her ankles. Some of the kids went all in, despite their clothes and being unable to see what was around them, which made her nervous as hell, but they managed to make it back to the hotel in one piece.

Cecilia checked her phone but there were no more messages from Felip. She wondered where he was going to pop up next.

She got her answer shortly after they boarded yet another bus the next morning.

"Today, we have a surprise for you," Rosana said. "We'll be taking a little detour this morning that you will hopefully enjoy and learn something from."

That was all she said. Cecilia was curious. She asked Gabrielle if she had any idea where they were going, and even she claimed ignorance. Bill and Tony were awfully quiet on the subject, so she had a feeling something was up.

The bus drove for about forty-five minutes, way up into the hills, before coming to a stop. Cecilia was on the right side of the bus, and it wasn't until everyone on the left began to *ooo* and *ahhh* that she got a peek at their destination.

Cava Segura.

They were at the winery.

Felip was behind this, she was sure of it. She shook her head, beyond being irritated about the wine at this point. She was stupid excited to see him and knew that even if she still hated wine when it was all over, she would be interested because this was Felip's baby, his love.

A man approached the bus and climbed aboard. He and Rosana exchanged words in Spanish and then she let him have the mic.

"Bon dia, estudiantes. I am Alonso Segura. My brother told me we would be having special guests today and has asked me to bring you all inside our family winery and vineyards. You'll be having a tour and a round of hors d'oeuvres, and our staff will take very good care of you. As I understand it, you will not be allowed to try the wine, but we have some wonderful selections of nonalcoholic beverages for you. Most importantly, you will get a look inside the process of making one of the most celebrated sparkling wines in all of España, and with the birth of Segura International, you will see how we are sharing our little piece of heaven with the rest of the world, including California. Vamos!"

The kids seemed a little confused as to why they were at a winery, but Cecilia knew that at least her students would be gracious and perhaps might learn something.

They exited the bus and squinted into the already bright sun.

"My brother will be here shortly. He was delayed getting out of the city by some sort of protests." They followed Alonso through the gates. "We will take half of you to tour the property first, and the other half, you will go inside the main building where you will meet my father, Ernesto Segura."

Rosana split the bus into two groups, leading half toward the jeeps. Alonso helped everyone find seats and then he drove the one in front. Gabrielle led Cecilia, their students, and a few of the others from Rio Grande into the main building. Once inside, the kids were overwhelmed by the sophisticated décor. The building was made from stone and had a rounded roof. It was rustic inside, with distressed wood floors, but everything else was first class all the way. Cecilia chuckled as Tui prompted the boys not to touch anything. The girls gazed around in wonder and murmured their appreciation. It was likely none of the kids had ever been in a place like this.

Jorge walked with his parents and stopped at every one of the framed pictures on the walls to read the plaques next to them.

"Hola," a voice called out from ahead. Everyone looked up to see a handsome older man, probably in his sixties, approaching them. "Welcome to Cava Segura. You must be the students from California. Molt bé. My sons Tomás and Felip have told me you are an intelligent group of children. It is my job to make you even smarter. Vine d'aquesta manera," he said and gestured for them to follow.

He led them into a showroom with a projector screen. Tall tables were pushed against the walls with ceramic vases holding small red flowers Cecilia didn't recognize. Votive candles burned within small glass containers as well. There were sconces on the walls with more candles, giving the place a feel that harkened back to the days before modern conveniences. Chairs had been set up facing the projector screen and he gestured for them all to take a seat. Cecilia made sure all of the students had a chair, and then she stood at the back near the arch that led into the main hallway. The man approached her with a warm smile.

"You must be Cecilia," he said. He took her hand and startled her by kissing both of her cheeks. "Welcome to my home," he said in a low voice. He practically beamed as he gave her hand one more squeeze.

"Thank you." Cecilia was startled by his greeting. The rest of the group turned around to gawk, and she gave a pointed look at her students and signed for them to turn around.

Mr. Segura launched into the history of wine making in Spain, the screen showing some historical photos and paintings, and told the kids about the phylloxera plague of the late 19th century. "Many wine-makers thought Spain would escape the devastation, and for some time, Spain was able to produce wine when other countries, including France, could not. This ended around the turn of the century, when Spain suffered many setbacks from then until the late twentieth century, after Franco died and Spain began to rebuild. My family managed to hold on to this land and make a small living, and in the nineteen-eighties, my brother and I were able to bring Cava Segura to the forefront of the Spanish sparkling wine industry. We have worked very hard and have dedicated our lives to this endeavor. My son Felip is in charge of the company today, and under his strategic plans, our wines have gone international."

Mr. Segura continued to talk, but Cecilia's attention was drawn out to the hallway and a large picture window. A sleek black Audi pulled into the lot, kicking up gravel. Felip, dressed in jeans and a blazer, climbed out of the driver's seat, his face a mask of frustration. He hurried around the car to get the door for a woman.

Dressed in a business suit and heels, the woman pulled a briefcase from the backseat and seemed to carry on a heated argument with Felip as they walked by. She was stunning, her reddish-brown hair pulled up in a professional-looking bun, and she walked as though she owned the place, but since Felip never mentioned any sisters, she assumed this wasn't a member of the family. She must be the partner he spoke of. June.

"Ah, here is my son now."

Felip's face lit up as he entered the room, the woman waiting towards the back.

"Hola, estudiantes. Welcome to our vineyard. I realize wine may not be the most exciting thing to see for some of you in Spain, but I wanted to share with you a bit of my home in Catalonia. Papa, thank you for covering for me." Felip hugged his father, then his eyes searched the room. When his gaze landed on Cecilia, a nervous smile graced his face, and Cecilia felt a little thrill. Until she caught the icy glare of the woman at the back of the room.

"If you would like to see a little bit more about how the wine is made, I'll be happy to lead you through the cellars." Felip led the group through the building and across a courtyard toward another large but narrow building with a similar design. The landscaping was simple but elegant, drawing Cecilia's eyes toward bunches of the same red flowers located in strategic places. They looked similar to geraniums, but she wasn't sure. She'd have to ask about them. They were quite lovely.

"Let's have a science lesson, shall we?" Felip asked. He'd stopped them outside the doors to the newer-looking building.

The kids looked at him curiously. Cecilia loved seeing him interact with them. It was kind of...well, dammit, it was sexy. She pictured herself like that girl in the front row of Dr. Jones's class in the *Indiana Jones* movie. If Felip was her teacher, she'd probably do worse than write "I love you" in eyeliner on her eyelids.

"First of all, how many of you know whether your parents or family members drink wine on a regular basis?"

All of the kids' hands went up, with the exception of the Santiagos' and Tui's.

"Excellent. Does anyone know the type of wine we make here and how it is different from other wines?"

Kristin raised her hand and Felip smiled at her. "You make cava? I think it's, like, sparkling wine?"

"Excellent, Kristin. Sí. My family developed our particular brand of cava about forty years ago. It requires a certain type of grape called Trepat, a black-skinned grape. Now, how is sparkling wine different than, say, a cabernet sauvignon or a chardonnay?"

"It's got bubbles?" Joseph asked.

"Sí. Bubbles. And how do the bubbles get in the wine? What is the magic ingredient that causes the bubbles?"

The group was quiet. The kids looked at each other and eventually everyone's gaze landed on Jorge.

"I didn't study wine before we came on this trip."

Everyone laughed. Then Bill, thankfully dressed in regular clothes today, raised his hand. It had been hard to take him seriously in his previous getup. "Yeast?"

"Yeast. Correct. The yeast is added to the wine and here is where the science comes in. What does yeast do when it comes in contact with sugar?"

"It eats it?" Janelle asked.

"It eats it! In the process, carbon dioxide is made, and this process is called...?"

"Fermentation!" Joseph shouted, and everyone laughed again.

"Fermentation, yes. Basically, the bubbles in cava are produced because of yeast farts."

The kids lost their minds laughing like they were back in middle school. Felip seemed proud of himself for this proclamation, and he gave a little bow before instructing the students to enter the cellar.

"It will be noticeably cooler inside and the temperature will drop as we go down to the lower levels." He gave a maniacal laugh, and Cecilia couldn't help herself, she laughed along with him. Here, on his own turf, he was completely confident. She could see why he was so good at his job.

As she approached him, he turned and grabbed her hand, pulling her in for a quick kiss. "Surprise?"

"Yes, this was a surprise. It must be nice to know the tour company owner."

"Mmm, and to be his silent partner. Now, I have another surprise for you when the tour is over, but first I have to do my job, so stop distracting me." He shook his head and trotted down the steps away from her. "Where was I? Oh, yes. Yeast farts."

Cecilia watched him stroll through the group of kids, who gazed around in wonder at the giant vats and asked him a million questions, which he fielded like a pro without losing a step. By the time he reached the other end of the room, she remembered how to move her feet.

The door opened behind her, and she turned to find the austere woman joining them.

"You must be Cecilia," she said in a decidedly American-accented voice.

"I am. And you are Felip's..."

"New Chief Operations Officer, June Fontaine. I've heard a lot about you."

They shook hands. Cecilia didn't quite know what to make of that statement. "Wow. Okay. I've heard you're unhappy with him," she said with a laugh, leaving out the part about her using a belt on him. Didn't want to be too weird the first conversation they had.

"I wouldn't say unhappy. Irritated? Frustrated? His trip to California, though necessary, has put a major hitch in our production here. There are decisions he needs to make and I need him here for that. Thank God he solved the issues there."

As June passed her to go down the steps, Cecilia felt a stab of uncertainty. Did that mean he wouldn't need to come to California anymore? Like, he was all set to be here in Spain permanently? And if that was the case, why on earth would he lead Cecilia to think he wanted to have a relationship?

"Are you coming?"

June was waiting at the bottom of the steps that Cecilia should have descended by then. "Yeah. Sorry. My, uh, eyes were adjusting to the dark." *Nice one. Could you sound any more like a complete moron?*

June led her to the rest of the group and kept up a steady stream of dialogue that further ate at Cecilia's resolve.

"I'm so glad that him and Mateu were able to sort out the mess there. What a disaster."

"Yeah, I bet," she said, wishing the woman would stop.

They reached the top of another level of steps. "These lead down to the second-level cellar. He's probably showing them the next batch that will go through the corking process."

Cecilia tried to smile but it felt as though it came out more like a grimace.

"Mmm. More yeast farts," she muttered.

When they caught up to the group, Felip was showing the kids how the bottles are turned every so often.

"Sometimes, depending on the type of cava we are producing at the time, a bit of sugar will be added back to the bottle. We call that a dosage. This way, we can control the sweetness of the wine. Are there any questions?"

"How do you freeze just the top of the bottle?"

"Ah! Right now we aren't at that part of the production, but I can show you the presentation we give to our wine tasters. Speaking of which, can you think of what other types of jobs there would be at a winery? You are from California, and there are vineyards very close to where you live. Perhaps someday you will find yourself working for a place such as this."

The kids called out things like picking the grapes, cleaning and turning the bottles.

"Sí. Those are all jobs here, but do you know we also have sales, marketing, and an enotourism specialist. Does anyone know what that person's job is?"

"To lead wine tours?" Aaliyah guessed.

"Yes! And today, that is me and my brother Alonso. I'm glad you were able to meet him. And my father. My father taught all of us everything about the business, and now we run the company. Alonso, Mateu in California, and me."

"But not Tomás," Gabrielle said.

Felip smiled and shook his head. "There has to be a black sheep in every family, right?"

Everyone chuckled at his joke, but he waved his hands. "I'm kidding, I'm kidding. Tomás wanted to go his own way and our parents were perfectly happy with his decision. Just as I'm sure none of you would want to be told what you are going to be when you grow up, and not be given a choice, verdad?"

The kids all nodded their agreement. Felip went on about other jobs at the winery, something about a nose person, but Cecilia's attention was caught by a family portrait hanging inside the entryway.

In the center of the photo stood Mr. Segura and a woman Cecilia assumed was Felip's mother. They stood very close to each other, and she could tell that Felip and his brothers got their smile from their mother. She recognized Tomás and the brother she met today, Alonso, standing to one side. Another young man stood next to them, which was probably Mateu, and then on the other side she saw Felip...with his arm around what must have been his wife, Francesca.

Unbelievable. This woman was as beautiful as Sofia Vergara, but without a smile. She stood nearly as tall as Felip, and while he seemed relaxed in the photo, she looked stiff and uncomfortable. Perhaps Cecilia was reading into things, but knowing the little she did, she could make an assumption.

"I keep telling them we need to take a new photo, but with Mateu never here and Tomás all over the place, we haven't been together in one place."

Cecilia turned to find her and Felip alone.

"I've missed you, cariño," he breathed, before sweeping her into his arms and kissing her as though it had been months rather than days. Some of her uncertainty faded under the force of his enthusiasm, but it didn't completely dissipate.

"Where did everyone go?"

"The groups will switch places. Alonso will take your group to see the vineyards, and June has agreed to give the other group the tour of the cellars. This way, I have you alone long enough to kiss you, then I have something very important to do."

He kissed her before she could get any words out. Just before she was lost to him, she pulled back. "What important thing do you have to do?"

He took her hands with a nervous grin. "I'd like to introduce you to my parents. I know you met my father already, and I'm sorry. I wanted to be the one to introduce you, but June and I were stuck in traffic getting back from the city."

"You drive together?"

Cecilia could have kicked herself. That was definitely not the most important part of his statement, but that's what her stupid mind was stuck on. June in her fancy clothes with those long legs reclining in the seat next to Felip, like some damn car commercial.

"Not usually, but she had a flat and called me to pick her up, and then we hit traffic because there was some sort of protest near my apartment. So crazy! Twice since you have been here there have been demonstrations."

Cecilia felt her cheeks flush. For some reason, she felt awkward with him. She didn't know if he felt it too, but she desperately wished they were still easy together.

"Come and meet my parents, Cecilia. Por favor."

"Sure. I'm feeling a little underdressed, but hey. It's just your parents, right?"

He bent down to kiss her again, and she wished that was all they had to worry about right now, only kissing. "You are perfect. Come."

He led her from the main building down the driveway to a large house. It wasn't as fancy as the winery buildings, but it was lovely nonetheless.

"Is this where you grew up?" she asked.

"I did. The grounds have changed a lot, but the house is the same."

She shook her head. "I can only imagine the trouble you four boys caused your poor mother."

"We were angels. How can you think otherwise?"

They climbed the steps and Cecilia's palms were sweaty. "Do they know about...me? I mean, did you tell them?"

"How important you are to me? Sí. I couldn't wait to tell them. I've been very excited for them to meet you."

He called out to them, and Cecilia had to remind her feet that they could drag all they wanted but they weren't getting out of this introduction.

They walked through a doorway and down a hall to a well-lit kitchen at the back of the house. Felip's father sat at the table with some papers and his mother came around the counter of the kitchen. Felip kissed cheeks with both of them while Cecilia wished unsuccessfully for the ground to swallow her up.

"Mama, Papa, this is Cecilia, the woman who has my heart."

His words jolted her. Did he feel so much for her?

Mrs. Segura approached Cecilia with an emotional smile and held out her arms for a hug. Cecilia smiled nervously at Felip and went into his mother's arms. They were about the same height—Mrs. Segura might have a been an inch or so taller—but in features, they were the exact opposite. The woman was slender and didn't look to be in her sixties, as Felip had told her. She had the same golden eyes as Felip and the smile, complete with a crooked tooth.

"Mucho gusto," his mother said, which Cecilia knew to mean something similar to "pleased to meet you."

Felip's father stood and held a hand out and Cecilia took it, even as Mrs. Segura still had a hand on her shoulder.

"Hello," Cecilia said, feeling increasingly nervous.

"Wonderful to meet you, dear. Our son speaks very highly of you."

"You have a wonderful son. Sons! At least the three I've met. I mean, I'm sure the fourth one is swell, too… Anyway, thank you. For having us. All the kids." She turned to Felip for rescue and just the sight of him made her breath a little easier. "I liked how you turned this into more of a career example than about the wine. Thank you for that."

He shrugged. "Who knows? Maybe one of them will come work for me someday."

Not a bad idea, she thought.

"I think it's wonderful that you are a teacher," Mr. Segura said.

"We need more talented people like you working with our children."

"Thank you," she said, thinking the way he'd phrased that was odd. "I told Felip he could easily be a teacher, he's so great with the kids."

His mother seemed to get even more choked up. She placed a hand on Felip's cheek and smiled.

"I know we can't stay long, Gabrielle said you had a limited time here, but I wanted you to at least meet my parents, and when you come back, we can spend more time."

When I come back?

"We will look forward to having you back soon," Mrs. Segura said. "Thank you for coming today, and for putting the smile back on my son's face."

Cecilia nodded, but she was about to explode like a giant question bomb the moment she had him alone. She did that thing where you clench your teeth together to keep smiling when really you have no clue what just happened.

"Yes, please hurry back. I need my son focused on the winery, and he won't be until he has his sweetheart with him."

Sweetheart? "It was wonderful to meet you both," she said, using her last bit of sweetness before she turned on Felip with that "I'm about to lose my shit" smile. He said goodbye to his parents and led her back out the door.

"Thank you, cariño. I knew it would mean a lot—"

"When I come back? What does that mean, Felip?"

His confident façade slipped and he grabbed her gently by the biceps. "I wanted to surprise you. I want to bring you back here. After you go home, take care of what you need to. I was hoping you'd come back to me."

"Come back to you?"

"For a longer visit. To spend more time with me, to see more of my country. And, you know, see if you might want to stay."

Cecilia's cheeks burned. "Felip! I have a life, you know. A career. That I love. Or have you not been paying attention to a word I've said over the past week?"

His eyes grew wide. "Cecilia, I know you love teaching. I thought—"

"You thought. Right. You assumed I would quit my job and come flying back to be at your beck and call. Unbelievable."

"No, Cecilia, that's not—"

"I thought you were different. I thought you heard me when I said that my ex-husband expected me to drop everything to be with him, and how I wasn't willing to do that. You know, I may be the one with the hearing loss, but it sure seems like no one listens to me when I speak."

Figuring she'd done enough damage, she pushed past him to go... somewhere. The bus? *Shit*. It wasn't here. Well, she'd go stand by the side of the road if she had to and wait for her kids. She wasn't about to stay here one more moment with a man who—

"Cecilia, please. Can't we talk about this? I wasn't going to ask you to quit your job. I would never. I thought if we had more time together—"

"That you could convince me. Well, you were wrong."

He stepped back finally, and the warmth left his face. "Sí. I thought I could convince you that I love you, but I guess that doesn't matter to you."

She felt his words like a blow to the chest. *Love?* He was going to use the l-word while trying to manipulate her?

"It would matter if there was respect along with it. Goodbye, Felip."

She turned to leave just as the jeeps were pulling up and a huge cloud of dust washed over her.

Excellent.

She kept walking, past her curious students, down the long drive that led to the main road. She'd stand out there until the damn bus came back. If it didn't, well, she'd walk back to Castelldefels if she had to, but she wasn't going to stand here one more minute and hear Felip's plans for her any longer.

The gravel crunching under her feet felt oddly satisfying and kept her mind off the hot tears running down her face.

CHAPTER TWENTY-SIX

6:27 p.m. Barcelona Local Time – St. Sadurni d'Anoia, Penedes, Outside of Barcelona

The rest of the horrible day flew by in a whirlwind of saying yes to June. Sí, June, we will start the production on time. Sí, June, the grapes will be ready on schedule. Sí, June, I will go to London next week to meet with the distributor. Sí, sí, sí.

When really, his heart screamed *no, no, no!*

How could he have been so wrong? He'd thought for sure Cecilia would understand and would want to spend more of her summer with him. If he could see her only on vacations from the school year, he'd make it work. For a while. Perhaps he could come up with a reason for him to go to California…

No, that was Mateu's place, and like Tomás needed Madrid to be his own, Mateu needed his autonomy in order to grow.

He wanted time…time to figure out if they could make something of what was starting to feel like the most perfect thing Felip had ever had in his life. He loved her so relentlessly, so recklessly, he was nearly ready to walk away from the family business if it meant having a life with her.

But she'd been the one to walk away. Away from his admission of love. *Ouch*. That hurt more than anything, that she hadn't trusted him enough, nor given him the benefit of the doubt that he would never attempt to manipulate her like her ex did. Couldn't she see that he was different?

By the end of the day he was ready to dive into bed with a whole box of cronuts and a bottle of cava and let himself go. He was more miserable than he'd felt in his adult life. He was bone tired and sick of it all, sick of trying to make everyone happy, when he just wanted one woman to love him.

"Hermano, what do you say you let June take your car back to the city and we go have some drinks. You look like you could use it."

Alonso didn't offer comfort often. Felip figured his brother closest in age must see the path Felip was headed down. Perhaps he wanted to save him from eating himself into oblivion.

"I won't be very good company," Felip warned.

Alonso shrugged and pulled out his keys. "When are you ever? Go on. Get your stuff, give her your keys, and let's go."

Felip did as he was told, even though he wanted to be left alone.

They piled into Alonso's ancient convertible and sped off toward the glittering lights of Barcelona. The two brothers were constant rivals and were often at each other's throats, but they would call a truce long enough to drink together. This must be one of those times.

They spoke very few words on the forty-minute drive to town. They were lucky to find parking near to Felip's apartment, which was one building over from Alonso's. When they pulled up, Alonso went to the trunk and pulled out two bottles of their vintage cava.

"Sampling the merchandise?" Only occasionally did they take one of their fully aged cavas to test out. The last time was shortly after Alonso completed his required military and signed on to spend another four years. Their mother hadn't spoken to either of them for days, angry at Alonso for being selfish and furious with Felip for not being able to talk his younger brother out of a suicide mission. But

Alonso liked the work he was doing and wanted to learn more. Felip didn't see anything wrong with that and had supported his decision.

"You have food up there?"

"Sí. I stopped off when I arrived yesterday. Why?"

"Because we're going to drink and eat and you're going to listen to me tell you all of the ways that you screwed up this situation with your little teacher."

Felip snorted. "You mean you've thought of more than I have? Then you better grab a third bottle from your stash. This is going to be a long night."

When his phone buzzed the next morning, the previous day all came back to him like a car crash. His parents' happy faces, Cecilia's look of sheer panic and rage, and him uttering the words that he never thought would be used against him again.

Alonso told me you would be in late. Take your time. I'll put the fires out. Again.

"What would I ever do without you, June?" he said out loud as he typed the words to her. He'd somehow ended up in bed undressed down to his boxers and he sat up to find himself covered in crumbs and crushed grapes. His head felt as though he'd put it under the tire of Alonso's car and had him back over it a few times, and he had a large purple bruise on his shin.

Cecilia. He'd noticed her bruise had faded when he'd seen her the day before. He'd tried to take in as much of her as he could after being apart for only two days, but she'd seemed off from the moment he saw her. Perhaps something else had been at play? Maybe he'd been wrong to set things up the way he had, maybe he'd put her under too much pressure, but he needed to rule out anything else.

His phone rang. June. So much for peace.

"Yes, June, I am in misery with a hangover, are you satisfied?"

She didn't answer right away. "Now why would I be happy with you being miserable? That just means more work for me. I got a call from Mateu this morning. He needs to speak to you. I thought you said you'd cleaned everything up?"

"I don't know. I did what I could, but there may still be issues. Why?"

She huffed out a breath. "I assumed you were done with California."

The events of the day before flashed before his eyes and stopped on one particular memory. June and Cecilia walking down the steps together. Cecilia's expression one of concern.

"You didn't happen to tell Cecilia anything about me not going back to California, did you, by any chance?"

"Yes. In fact, I told her I was glad you were back and wouldn't be going out there anymore to clean up after your brother. Why? Was that not accurate? Were you planning to go again? Because if so, Felip, you and I—"

"No. Now it is time for *you* to listen, June."

Felip sat up in bed and pulled at his hair. This might explain part of Cecilia's attitude, but Felip also needed to face the fact that his little teacher might not feel the same for him. Regardless, June's attitude wasn't going to help matters.

"I understand that we are running an incredibly busy operation. I understand that I am the CEO, and therefore in charge of the direction of the company. But I get the sense that you are unsatisfied. I know you and I have different expectations about work—but let me make one thing clear to you. My family business has *always* been about taking care of each other.

"I took over to help out my father because that is what was expected, and I love what I do. No one wants to see Cava Segura blossom more than I. However, as a result of my drive to push this company international and to start up the California operation, I ruined my marriage. I've learned from that experience. I need to take care of the people I love. My parents, my brothers, and now, Cecilia.

Your pattern of hounding me has got to stop. Part of the reason I gave you this promotion is so that we can work more side-by-side than horse-and-cart, ¿me entienden? June, you are a wonderful asset to Segura, and I care about you, but I need to start taking care with my life, as well as the company."

There was a long pause before June spoke. "Felip, I had no idea...I never meant... I was only pushing because that's how we've always worked together. You had the ideas, I got things done. That's why you hired me. If that's not going to work for you—"

"What about *your* ideas?"

"Excuse me?"

"What about the things *you* want to do with the company? This doesn't always have to be about me having ideas and you making things happen. What I would like to see is *you* taking some initiative, *you* letting me know what could be done, and then all of us making decisions together. I know I should have outlined my plans better before dropping this COO position in your lap, but that's what I'd intended. Given that, do you still want the job? Because things have got to change."

"Of course I do, and Felip, I'm sorry. I'm not built the same as you. I'm about the company and its success. That's who I've always been."

"And that's one of your admirable qualities and why I trust you with my family's business. But June, there has to be more than just the company. There is for me, and there should be for you. Cava Segura and all of its holdings are doing phenomenally well, thanks much in part to you, and now it's time for me to go where my heart desires."

"California?"

Felip sighed. "Maybe? I don't know. I have a lot to think about, and a mess to clean up, this one of my own making. June?"

"Yes, Felip?"

"You are a treasure. I cannot thank you enough for being my right hand these past eight years. I hope you see this promotion as a sign of my trust and gratitude."

"I do. And I don't want you to be unhappy." Felip heard her

breathing deeply on the other end of the phone. "If she makes you happy, don't let her go."

"Thank you," he said, smiling for real. "I'll figure something out."

They took care of a little more business and then hung up. Felip laughed at what a disaster he was and felt relieved they didn't do video calls very often.

As he was getting up to strip his bed and to shower, he noticed he had a voicemail from an unknown number.

"Hey, Mr. Segura? Um, it's me, Eduardo Ruiz? From the tour group? I'm sorry to bother you, sir, but you gave us your card and mentioned you might be able to get us into Camp Nou? I know it's short notice, but is it possible you might be able to do that before we leave? The guys and I, we'd really like to go. Anyway, thank you again. You can reach me at this number, or at the Hotel Olimpic in Castelldefels, where we're staying. Thanks... Hey shutup, bruh, I know what I'm doing! Oh, shoot, I hadn't hung up yet!"

Felip chuckled, thinking he may have understood Eduardo's attempt, but his damaged heart told him it was too little, too late. Sure, he could get the kids into Camp Nou. He had a business connection there who would be happy to get a great deal on some wine, but he would be doing it for the kids. He had to think of some other way to talk to Cecilia. Which wouldn't be today, since today they were headed out to Figueres to see the Dalí museum and would be gone all day. It would have to be tomorrow. He'd call Rosana to see how to arrange it. And then they would leave the next day, with his heart.

And it was his own damn fault.

CHAPTER TWENTY-SEVEN

8:16 a.m. Barcelona Local Time – Hotel Olimpic, Castelldefels

If Cecilia never rode another bus in her life, it would be too soon. The day after the disaster at the vineyard, she'd still been angry, but then she did that thing where her righteous indignation started to fade and she'd begun to wonder if perhaps she maybe, might have, overreacted. Not that she overreacted on a regular basis. Of course not. No way. But this time she'd felt completely broadsided.

How could she have gotten things so wrong? How could *he*?

She'd allowed herself to enjoy the Dalí museum and the crazy cooking class afterwards, dodging questions about Felip and making sure Joseph stayed away from the shellfish. She declined another late-night beach session, though, for some much-needed alone time with a side of ugly crying.

When they met Thursday morning in the hotel restaurant for their last full day in Spain, her mood was melancholy. Much of it was Felip-induced, but she was also profoundly sad to be leaving this incredible country she had come to love, and the camaraderie she'd found with her fellow travelers.

She'd discovered that Mrs. Santiago loved to read the same paranormal romance novels she did, and they'd made a pact to start a book club when they returned. Bill and Tony wanted to organize monthly gatherings at their place where everyone would take turns teaching something, whether it be Gabrielle teaching Latin dancing, Mr. Santiago teaching them to paint, or Zoey, when she felt better, leading them in creative writing exercises. Having that to look forward to made the impending end of the trip a little easier to handle. As long as she didn't think about Felip. Which was easier said than done.

"Tonight, ladies and gentlemen, we have a couple of options. Our compadres from Rio Grande will be leaving us, as their flights are tonight rather than tomorrow, so we will be saying goodbye to them. We have La Sagrada Familia this morning, and the choices this afternoon are a bicycle tour or walking the Gothic Quarter, shopping this afternoon, dinner together, and then we now have a new option for tonight. Rosana received a call that a tour's been lined up at Camp Nou, or we can go see a flamenco show. Everyone please tell Rosana your preferences before you leave breakfast."

"Yes! He got my call!" Eduardo and the boys were excited to see Camp Nou, and Cecilia was happy for them. She doubted she would see Felip again, doubted he would *want* to see her after the way she'd shouted at him. It was just as well. Leaving this way meant she wouldn't wonder what might have been.

Oh, who the hell do you think you're fooling?

She spent the thirty-minute bus ride into Barcelona mentally castigating herself and tried to pull herself together as she left the bus. She had one last day to enjoy this wonderful country and she needed to remember the kids were watching.

La Sagrada Familia proved to be the most breathtaking place they'd seen in all of Spain. The brilliance of Antoni Gaudí was everywhere, and she loved how he combined religion and nature. The bits of pagan lore that wormed their way into Catholicism could be a whole subject of study for her. Spain was full of examples and it spoke to her soul. Her grandparents would have really loved it.

After lunch, the choice of activities was simple for her. There was no way Cecilia would be riding a bike. Country roads at home, perhaps, but not congested city streets, no way, no how. She and the Santiagos instead chose to wander the Gothic Quarter, marveling at the architecture and the narrow streets. Jorge stopped to listen to two men playing guitar, completely fascinated by them. That gave Cecilia an idea.

"Jorge? Want to help me with your mad Google skills? Can you see if you can find us a music store?"

He got to work on his iPhone and soon had an address and a route planned out. They had plenty of time before they needed to meet up with the others for dinner, so the four of them set off in search of Basque metal.

They managed to find the place, Revolver Records, which was close to where they needed to meet for dinner. The shop was full of her favorites and a variety of world artists. She could have spent hours in there. Instead, she headed straight for the Basque section and whooped in delight when she found the artist they'd heard at the festival. Which was now bittersweet. How could she ever listen to that music without thinking of Felip? Without remembering how wonderful it had felt to be in his arms as if they were the last two people on the Earth? She sighed, thinking there would be a lot of memories of Spain inextricably tied to him.

"Cecilia? Are you about ready? Jorge is concerned we'll be late for dinner, which probably means he's hungry..."

"Sure, yes, sorry. Let me pay for these."

She took her CDs up to the front counter and spied a Record Store Day shirt hanging high up on the wall. She asked in her lame Spanish if the shirt was for sale and the man nodded. He retrieved it, and she was tickled. She'd likely spend the rest of her summer in t-shirts and this one would become a favorite, she was sure of that. She loved supporting independent music shops like this, as they reminded her of all the times she and her grandfather went in search of music to load into his jukeboxes. Seeing her old favorites like KISS, Led Zeppelin, and Elvis Costello on the walls of this quirky shop in Barcelona made her feel like the world was a little smaller than she'd once imagined.

They arrived at the restaurant near Las Ramblas before the rest of their group and Mrs. Santiago went inside to see if she could order for Jorge ahead of time. It was buffet style, so the man said it would be no problem. Cecilia knew that Jorge had a difficult time maintaining his balanced emotional state if he went too long without food, and he'd been dragging most of the afternoon. They all were, honestly, and Cecilia certainly knew she'd been close to losing her cool a few times on this trip. Besides her conversation with Felip yesterday.

She started to wonder once more if she'd been too hasty. What if he really—

Thankfully, she was saved from her inner struggle by the arrival of the rest of the group.

"That was the scariest thing I've ever done in my life." A very shaken Bill sat down. Tony asked if he was okay and said he'd grab waters.

"What happened?" Cecilia asked. She looked around him to be sure everyone was accounted for.

"We nearly died at least once per block, that's what," Tony said as he came back. "I'm all for being better for the environment, you know, but I'm never riding a bicycle again."

Tui and Aaliyah came over, and she sat next to Cecilia, looking distressed.

"Do you need anything?" Tui asked her quietly.

She shook her head and crossed her arms over her chest.

Tui looked to Cecilia for guidance, and she figured out there must be trouble in paradise. *Yeah, that's going around.*

"Tui, could you grab me a Diet Coke?"

"Sure, Mrs. Galván," he said. He hung his head while he walked away.

"Want to talk about it?"

Aaliyah watched him walk off with a frown. "First, he got upset because I wanted to ride my own bike, not go tandem, and then I told him I'm going with you to flamenco tonight. He was upset because he wanted us to go to Camp Nou together. I told him I'd much rather see dancing, and it was okay for him to go with his friends. Now he thinks I'm mad at him."

Cecilia patted her leg. "It's hard, you guys have been together non-stop. Just let him go hang out with the guys. He'll be fine when we go back to the hotel tonight."

Aaliyah smiled and then went to go sit with Janelle and Kristin, who were flanking Jorge.

"It's always like this at the end of the tour," Gabrielle said. "They're moody and tired and they want to go home, but they also don't."

"I know the feeling," Cecilia said.

Gabrielle tilted her head and gave Cecilia a sad smile. "You sure you don't want—"

"I'm fine. Or I will be. Let's go have a fantastic time tonight."

So that's what they did. They split by gender, with the exception of Kristin, who decided to go to the stadium. She'd been playing soccer since she was a tiny thing and seeing the home of the famous Fútbol Club Barcelona was a dream of hers. Rosana agreed to go with them, and they headed out together, the boys riled up, with the exception of Tui, who was sporting puppy dog eyes as they left. The rest of the women walked the short distance to the Palau de la Música from the restaurant as the sun was setting in the sky. The famous walkway was very crowded as they passed by, and Cecilia made sure to stick close to the girls so they didn't get separated.

"You know what I'm going to miss the most?" Cecilia said.

"What is it?" Janelle said.

"Ice cream, gelato, helado, whatever they call it. Have you ever seen such beautiful ice cream displays in all of your life? It's every-where! I swear, there's more ice cream than Starbucks, or any coffee for that matter! These Spaniards have their priorities straight."

Gabrielle laughed, and so did Mrs. Santiago, but Janelle and Aaliyah fell quiet.

"What's wrong?"

"Nothing. I thought you were going to say—"

"The shopping? The muffins? I know I ate a lot of muffins—"

"Mr. Segura."

"Girls—" Gabrielle began, but Cecilia stopped her.

"No, it's fine. I *will* miss him. He's a part of many of my memories of Spain."

"But aren't you sad?"

"I am," she said, her chin quivering. "Of course I am. But meeting someone like him is sort of like the icing on the cake when you live a good life, and I *do* live a good life. I'm perfectly happy with my job, with my house—okay, maybe not that one." The girls chuckled with her. "But seriously, I have great friends, I live in a great place. Sure, having a boyfriend can be wonderful, but I learned from my marriage ending that I'm fine on my own, and I will be. Does that mean I'll never try again? No. But it doesn't mean my life isn't worth so much the way it is. Remember that, girls. Love is truly wonderful, but you can have it in your life *without* a boyfriend or girlfriend."

Cecilia checked her internal bullshit meter and was pleased to find that she was telling the truth. Though she was hurting now, she'd been hurt before, and she knew she'd make it through.

Then Mrs. Santiago squeezed her shoulder, and she almost lost it.

The Palau de la Música Catalana was one of the most beautiful theaters Cecilia had ever seen in her life. Stained glass was set into the center of the ceiling and was used along the walls, letting in colorful light even at dusk. There were ornate carvings of roses and designs resembling peacock-feather eyes set into the ceiling, surrounding delicate chandeliers. Pillars of marble lined the walls and a large carving of a man standing under a tree separated sections of the balconies. There was even a giant pipe organ at one end that Cecilia imagined might even rattle the glass with its power.

But their attention was focused entirely on the performers as soon as the music started. Well, nearly all of them. Cecilia was thrilled to see a woman dressed in black at the side of the stage interpreting in sign language! She was mesmerized as the woman signed in between the songs, as the performers told stories and explained what the songs were about. She'd strained to hear them speak, but she realized she could understand some of the signs the woman made. She pointed her out to the others and they shared in her excitement.

The musical performance consisted of a trio of master guitarists paying tribute to the late, great Paco de Lucía, as two dancers told stories with their hands and bodies, mimicking the dance of lovers testing each other. These dancers seemed to perhaps have more technical training than the ones they'd seen in the club in Madrid, but their performance was equally as passionate. While the club performance they'd seen was raw and powerful, these two were graceful, cunning, and Cecilia was moved to tears by the end.

As the women left the theater together, they laughed and gushed over their favorite parts, trying to determine which performance was better and unable to decide. It was after ten o'clock, and they knew they had to meet the other group, but the ice cream was way too tempting across the street. They strolled back towards Las Ramblas with cones in their hands and smiles on their faces.

Once they approached their meeting spot, though, Cecilia realized they were in trouble.

A group of men pushed past them on the corner of Las Ramblas, knocking Cecilia into the side of the building, and a couple of police officers ran after them. Cecilia grabbed the girls and yanked them back into a recessed doorway as more police stormed by them. Another group of people carrying flags and chanting approached. Gabrielle shouted, but Cecilia didn't understand her.

Suddenly, Gabrielle made a break for it with Mrs. Santiago and Janelle in tow. Cecilia started forward, but the hole in the crowd closed behind Janelle, and she didn't see any way through. Cecilia held Aaliyah close to her and tried to calm the young woman.

They had apparently landed in the middle of a protest, and a violent one at that. She couldn't understand what they were saying, and with all the noise, her limited hearing was toast. Aaliyah's face was pale. She shouted something to Cecilia, but Cecilia couldn't make out her words.

Cecilia signed to her, praying she'd remember some of the signs she'd taught them. "I can't hear anything. Are you hurt?"

Aaliyah shook her head.

"Can you reach my phone?"

Aaliyah signed yes to her. *Good*. The girl wasn't so far gone that she didn't remember. "Text Ms. Reyes. Tell her we can't get across."

Cecilia felt her phone being pulled from the pocket on her dress and a moment later, Aaliyah stuck it in front of her face.

Stay where you are. Felip is coming to you.

Right in front of them, police dragged a particularly rowdy group of young men to the ground and began trying to subdue them. Cecilia pushed Aaliyah all the way back to the wall and used her body to shield the girl. They had some protection there in the doorway, but Cecilia didn't know for how long. There were so many people, she couldn't see spaces between the bodies.

Within moments, from out of the crowd sprang Felip, like some sort of Clark Kent, dragging Joseph and Eduardo, with Tui bringing up the rear. They dodged protestors who were moving towards Plaza de Catalunya and spoke to more police officers, who were now standing in front of Cecilia, blocking any protesters from getting by. They let Felip through with the boys, and Cecilia was in his arms in an instant.

He tried talking but Cecilia couldn't hear a thing. She pointed to her ears and shook her head. He nodded and pointed to his lips. She nodded back. He mouthed the words slowly.

Are you hurt?

She looked at her arm, which was scraped and bleeding but not bad, and shook her head. Tui, Eduardo and Joseph had put Aaliyah between them, blocking her from harm.

Are you ready to go?

She shrugged and gave a weak smile.

Felip looked both ways and then stepped forward, pulling her along with him. He spoke to the police officer, and the officer shook his head. Felip tried to argue with him, but he shook his head again and put a hand on Felip's chest, pushing him backwards. They were stuck, it seemed, on the opposite side of Las Ramblas from their group with no way of getting across the massive demonstration.

Felip moved them back to the doorway and frowned. He pulled Tui close and spoke in his ear. Tui turned to Cecilia and signed.

We can't go. We go this way. Felip's house.

She shrugged and nodded. What else were they supposed to do? She couldn't risk the kids getting hurt and they had to get off the street. She saw lights flashing from police cars and the number of protestors didn't seem to be lessening.

Felip led the way, keeping her behind him but close. They hurried along the building and turned down the first street they came to. Felip moved quickly, keeping Cecilia between him and the wall of the building for protection, as protestors were apparently using side streets to get around the police.

They turned down an even narrower street to their right, and Cecilia reached for Joseph's hand to make sure they were still all together. They were nearly jogging now. Cecilia tried hard to keep track of the kids, but she was completely turned around.

Felip suddenly stopped and used his keys to open the door to an apartment building. He ushered everyone inside and made sure the lobby door was locked behind them.

"Is everyone alright?"

"Dude, that was some crazy shit," Joseph said. He was holding Cecilia's hand, and he was trembling.

"Aaliyah?"

She was curled up in Tui's arms with her face pressed against his chest, and he looked fierce, as though he would do anything to protect her. She turned to face Cecilia and gave her a weak smile.

"My flat is on the fourth floor. Are you all able to take the stairs?"

They murmured agreement and followed him up the four flights until they reached a dimly lit hallway. The building was simple and clean, but the fixtures and paint seemed to be showing age. Felip stopped at the second door and opened it with his keys, holding the door open for the group.

"There is a toilet to your left, and to the right is a kitchen if you are hungry or thirsty."

The kids knocked into each other trying to get to the kitchen, and Tui told the boys to chill out and let Aaliyah go first.

"I think I'd like the bathroom," Cecilia said, and Felip pointed the way. She paused to stare at him, and he frowned.

"Cecilia?"

"I'm fine. I'm...I'm really glad to see you."

He gave a half smile and then went to check on the kids in the kitchen. Cecilia went into the bathroom and closed the door. The room smelled strongly of whatever combination of products Felip used to create his signature scent. She chuckled at that thought and realized she was probably having a stress response to the activities they'd just experienced. She had to fight her body to stop laughing, use the bathroom and wash her hands. She looked at herself in the mirror and shook her head. Her hair was wild, along with her eyes. She used Felip's brush to try to tame the insanity, then rejoined the group in the kitchen.

"Rosana texted that they're on their way back to the hotel. Jorge mapped out a way using public transportation. I told her that I'll have you all back at the hotel in the morning, early enough to take the bus to the airport. I am so sorry for all of this, Cecilia."

"At least everyone's safe. You're all okay?"

Aaliyah hadn't regained her color fully, but she had a smile on her face and seemed to have quit shaking.

"Boys, two of you can take my spare room, there is a freshly made bed in there. Cecilia, you and Aaliyah can have my room, and I have blankets for the sofa. Have something to eat and then get some rest. You will all be feeling the effects of this excitement, I am sure."

"Thank you, Mr. Segura," they all said.

"You're all very welcome. I'm sorry if you were frightened by the demonstration."

"Those cops were no joke," Tui said. "I noticed in Madrid that they're all hella strapped. Way more than cops back home. They all look like soldiers."

"Es la verdad. And they are very serious. There is no fooling around with the Policía Nacional, nor the Guardia Civil."

Felip pulled out a bunch of food from his refrigerator. "It's not much, but then I've only been back a day or so. Eat whatever you like. Let me know if you need anything. I'm going to call my brothers."

He stepped out of the kitchen and Cecilia made sure the kids were okay before following him into a dining area. Felip stood staring out the window with his phone in his hand. A frown marred his usually jovial face, causing him to look so severe. Shadows from the streetlights left deep hollows in his cheeks.

"Thank you, Felip. I don't know what I would have done—"

"I'm happy I found you safe with Aaliyah. I was so worried."

They gazed at each other across the room, and it only took a beat for Cecilia to go to him and let him hold her tightly. He swayed a bit with her and kissed the top of her head. Cecilia felt as though she could breathe again for the first time since she'd last seen him at the winery...

It seemed they both realized there was unfinished business between them at the same time. Felip let go, reluctantly, and stepped back. He ran a hand over his mouth and planted his hands on his hips.

"I'll show you to my room. You can rest there."

"The last thing I want to do right now is sleep." It was true. She trembled all over, and she couldn't say how much it had to do with what they'd witnessed, what had happened between them, or how awful it was to stand this close, yet have him be so far away.

His golden eyes showed signs he was struggling. The whites were bloodshot, and the skin appeared bruised underneath, as if he hadn't slept well. His body language spoke of his exhaustion, as though he might drop where he stood.

"I'll take one of the couches and you take your bed. I can't sleep, and I want to be awake in case one of the kids needs me."

"Cecilia, you've been through a terrible experience. You need to rest."

She tried to smile bravely. "It's fine. I can sleep on the plane tomorrow."

Those words broke her, and she didn't have the strength to fight the sob that broke free.

Felip's words in whatever the hell language he was speaking tonight sounded exasperated as he caught her weight and held her.

"Come and sit. Please."

She buried her face in his chest and felt like an absolute idiot as he walked her over to a couch in his living room. It fit into a window nook and was almost big enough for the two of them. She tried to do the whole silent crying thing, but she was so wrecked, her sobs came out in little choked sounds that unfortunately were loud enough to catch the attention of Tui.

"Mrs. Galván?" He stood before her, almost a man but not quite, looking as if he wanted to tear someone's head off for making his favorite teacher cry, God bless him.

"I'm okay, honey," she said, reaching out to take his hand.

Tui went down on a knee as she'd seen him do many times on the football field, and he held her hand.

"My body is trying to let go of the stress from tonight, that's all. Some people laugh, some people cry—"

"And some people drop bombs like Joseph in the kitchen, oh my Lord!" Eduardo entered the room holding his nose, followed by Aaliyah, who was giggling uncontrollably, and Joseph with his mouth full.

"Come on, it wasn't that bad! I can't help it. I get gas when I'm nervous."

Cecilia gestured toward Joseph with one hand. "See? Stress responses."

"I sweat like a pig," Aaliyah admitted.

The boys gasped, then they started laughing.

"But girls don't sweat," Eduardo said.

"Yeah, and they don't poop either," Joseph said. They all collapsed into fits of laughter, and it did a lot to calm the kids.

"I guess I get nosebleeds," Eduardo said. "Sorry, J-man. But that was like decomposing corpse ass in there."

Aaliyah was laughing silently now, so hard tears were streaming down her face.

Joseph and Eduardo sat on either side of Aaliyah on the larger matching couch that took up the wall directly in front of Cecilia. Tui looked back and forth and sat on the floor in front of Aaliyah, with his back to her. She placed a hand on his shoulder and he covered it with his. Cecilia was glad to see the two of them had mended whatever was wrong between them.

She glanced at Felip, who sat with his arm around the back of the couch behind her and one leg tucked underneath him. If only Cecilia could mend what was broken between she and this beautiful man.

"Tui? Can I braid your hair?"

Tui scooted closer to Aaliyah. "You can try. It's kind of untamable."

"I can do it. Braiding helps me relax."

"Go for it."

"That's great that you can do that," Cecilia said. "I could never learn how to braid my own hair, but I could braid others. Never French braids, though. That's above my paygrade."

"What do you do to relax, profesora?" Felip asked.

"Hmmm. Listen to music? Read a book?" She took a chance that her tears had stopped to look at him. "How about you?"

His lips twitched. "Play guitar."

"That's so cool that you know how to play, Mr. Segura," Eduardo said. "I've always wanted to learn."

Felip stood from the couch and picked up a weathered acoustic guitar from the corner. He sat on the arm of the couch and plucked at the strings before launching into a series of scales at dizzying speeds.

His fingers nimbly ran up and down the neck of the guitar, and the kids expressed their admiration.

"That's hecking cool," Joseph said. "Can you play us something like we heard the other night?"

"Sí."

And what came from his hands was music so pure and raw, Cecilia felt it in her chest. There was something so emotional about flamenco music, it was unlike anything else she'd ever heard. She felt it more than heard it, and that sensation meant more to her than she could express.

As a hard-of-hearing person, music was a luxury she couldn't always enjoy. If it was too loud, it often hurt, or she couldn't make out the individual sounds. If it was too quiet, she couldn't hear it at all. As Felip played, the sounds echoed off of the walls and soothed her soul. The expressions on his face made her feel so much for him. His hair flopped forward and danced about as he moved furiously, his fingers alternately flying across the strings and aggressively plucking. Cecilia hoped he would stop and prayed he'd continue during the entire length of the piece, and when he finished, she exhaled as though she'd been holding her breath.

"That was amazing," Tui said as they all clapped. Except Aaliyah. She tugged on Tui's hair.

"Don't move or I'll mess up."

He blushed and grinned. "Sorry."

Aaliyah had parted his hair into four sections, and she was just finishing the first section. She'd braided it neat and tight against his head.

"Here," she elbowed Eduardo, "hold this. I only have his one hair tie, so I'm going to use it on all four when they're done. Don't let go."

"Yes, ma'am."

Felip continued to play quietly. He watched the kids with a smile. "And what do you do to relax, Eduardo?"

"Okay, but you guys can't say anything, alright?"

"What?" Tui tried to turn to look at him, and Aaliyah gave him another tug.

"Mrs. Galván knows."

Cecilia frowned, trying to take her brain back to three years ago, when she had him as a freshman. "Oh! Wait, can I tell them?"

He shrugged and grinned. "I guess. Someday it might make me famous and then you all can say you knew me when."

"Not the pictures," Joseph said, as if he was trying to be quiet about it.

"What? No! God! What the hell is wrong with you, dude?"

"Hey, I'm not the one who takes shirtless selfies—"

"Guys—"

"He writes poetry," Aaliyah said.

Eduardo turned toward her and almost dropped Tui's braid. "How—"

"Don't you dare drop that! I know because you showed me once, a long time ago, remember? When we were in eighth grade and you were trying to get Julia to go out with you?"

"Oh, right. Well, I think I've gotten better since then."

"Yeah 'roses are red, violets are blue, you have a cute smile, please go to the dance with me' doesn't quite count as poetry," Joseph said.

"Good thing I never wrote any crap like that."

Cecilia laughed along with the kids and Felip, and she thought maybe they'd survive this night.

The group of them talked for a while longer. Eventually Joseph took over braid-holding duties so Felip could show Eduardo a few things on the guitar. When Aaliyah was finished, she curled up on the couch and Tui covered her with a blanket. He sat on the floor in front of her and they whispered to each other for a while before she fell asleep, with Tui running his fingers through her hair.

Joseph went to the kitchen, came back with more food, ate it, went to the bathroom and then never returned. Cecilia went to check on him, and he'd fallen asleep diagonally on the bed, fully clothed. She slid his shoes off and tossed them in the corner. She found a blanket folded on a shelf and placed it gently over him. He didn't move, he was that tired.

When she went back out to the living room, Aaliyah was out, Tui was out on the floor with a cushion from the couch as a pillow and another throw over his top half. Eduardo and Felip were talking quietly in the kitchen, and she wanted to let them have man talk. She needed a moment to collect herself anyway.

Her emotions were all over the place. She adored these kids and soon they would be going off to college. Having this time with them was more special to her than she ever imagined it would be, and more than they would ever know. She couldn't help but admit that she and Felip minded them very well together. He was so good with them. If it was possible to spontaneously ovulate just from being near a man with such a nurturing way about him, she probably had tonight.

She collapsed back on the couch and closed her eyes. Felip's scent was everywhere and being in his space was calming. Her eyes popped open then, realizing she hadn't even taken the time to look around.

The color scheme in this room was deep green and light gray. For a bachelor pad, the furniture looked as if it had been chosen by a picky decorator. He had paintings on the walls that looked original, silhouettes of flamenco dancers. There were two more guitars stashed in another corner of the room. A decent-sized TV took up most of one wall, and there was a collage frame that looked like several different-sized frames had been glued together, and it appeared to hold pictures of his family members over the years.

But other than that, it didn't look lived in. Not like the house at the winery, which was a place of love and family. It had been evident in the cozy feel, the smell of food cooking, and the photos on the walls.

"Mrs. Galván? Do you need anything? I'm going to go to sleep."

"Bless your heart, Eduardo. I'm fine. But you'll need to sleep in Felip's bed, I'm afraid. Joseph kind of took up the whole bed."

He frowned. "But you need to sleep."

"I'm fine, honey. I'd be too worried about you guys to sleep anyway. We'll see you in the morning."

Eduardo looked to Felip, who just shrugged as if to say, "The lady's crazy, what can I say?"

"Bona nit," Felip said. He watched Eduardo go and then wandered back over to Cecilia on the couch. "Rosana messaged that the rest of the group is settled and safe in Castelldefels."

"Oh, thank goodness. That Jorge is a whiz with a map, isn't he?"

Felip rested his hands on his hips and sighed. "You should have taken the bed," he said. He ran his hands through his hair and made it stand on end. It would look ridiculous if it weren't so damned sexy.

"You can take this couch if you want to sleep."

He shook his head. "I can't sleep. I don't want to sleep. What I want—"

"I'm sorry. For everything. For tonight, for how I acted yesterday."

"I only wished you would have let me explain myself."

"What more could you have said? You want me to leave my home, uproot my whole life."

"I wanted you to agree to spend more time with me, to see if what we are feeling could become more than just a tour of Spain."

"And then what?" Tears burned her eyes again, and she was too tired to fight them.

"And then? I am not sure…but I would do anything to be with you, if you felt as I do."

"I think there's the problem of an ocean and an entire continent to contend with."

"You joke when you talk about your feelings. Why do you do this?"

"Because! Maybe I can't deal with my feelings! Coping strategies don't have to make sense, do they?"

Felip crossed his ankles and sat down on the floor in front of her. He glanced at the kids, probably making sure that they were asleep.

"I do feel as you do, Felip," she whispered. "I don't know what to do with those feelings."

He leaned forward and took her hands in his. "Cariño, I would never ask you to give up your job. I love these kids as much as you do. You are a wonderful teacher. There are airplanes, video phone calls… we could make it work—"

"I don't know if I can go through that again," she whispered. She looked down and sucked in a breath. "I know you aren't like Greg. At least, I believe you wouldn't do what he did. But I don't want to be lonely anymore. I'm fine *being* alone. There is a difference. And you deserve more as well, Felip. You need someone to care for *you*, for once."

He squeezed her hands, and she could swear she saw tears welling in his eyes as well.

"Then if this is for real, our last night together, please let me hold you once more."

"Only if you don't mind my tears getting your shirt wet."

They both laughed in that way that sounded like a heart breaking. She moved so he could sit beside her on the small couch. He scooped her into his lap and held her against his chest. She curled her hands in his FC Barcelona shirt and wanted to scream at the injustice of it all. Then she laughed.

"Is this the same shirt you were wearing on the plane? The one I drooled on by accident?"

He looked down. "It very well could be. I have a couple, pero I believe Eduardo still has the other shirt I was traveling with, so yes. It is. It only seems fitting that you sleep on me once more."

They chuckled and snuggled closer together.

"Tell me what that demonstration was about."

Felip sighed. "We Catalonians are in a bit of a fight with the Spanish government. Last October we held a referendum and they said it was illegal and tried to stop it. Many people were hurt and they jailed many of our leaders."

"That's awful. I didn't know. What was the referendum for?"

"We were essentially voting to be allowed to vote on whether or not we wanted to become independent from Spain."

"So, what you're saying is, they wouldn't let you ask if you could ask?"

"Something like that. There are other factors involved, of course. It's been rather tense for a while. You probably noticed the flags hanging from the balconies around town? La Senyera, or the Catalonian flag, is red and gold stripes. The flags with the stars— whether red and gold, or blue and white with red and gold—are for

Catalonian independencia. I don't know what will happen, but I am not too worried. Things will work out as they are meant."

"You have such a positive outlook on life. Do you realize that?"

He shrugged. "I guess. I never really thought of it that way."

"You do," Cecilia said. She snuggled closer and sighed. *I wish it were enough.*

CHAPTER TWENTY-EIGHT

6:08 a.m. Barcelona Local Time – Felip's Flat

There wasn't a lot of room on the small couch, but they curled around each other and eventually fell asleep. Felip woke with a cramp but refused to move, instead choosing to memorize every bit of Cecilia's weight on him, the citrus scent of her skin, and the silken feel of her hair.

He had so many things he wanted to say, but they'd already been over their predicament. Cecilia wasn't willing to try a long-distance romance, and Felip was tied to Spain. A seemingly insurmountable conflict. The only thing left for them to say was goodbye. Alonso was coming soon to help him transport the kids and Cecilia back to their hotel. Tomás had said that they needed to leave the hotel by eleven in order to make their two-p.m. flight. He also told Felip to assure Cecilia that he'd contacted the parents of the students with Felip, to let them know everything was alright, especially since the protests may have made the news. They were all incredibly lucky things had not been worse.

He'd nearly panicked when he and the boys arrived at their meeting place near La Boquería to find chaos...and no Cecilia. He'd escorted them after their outing at Camp Nou so he could see the rest of the group and say good-bye. And of course to see Cecilia one last time. They'd waited for nearly twenty minutes with no sight of her group, then Gabrielle and the others made it across the mob. But no Cecilia or Aaliyah, the most fragile young lady in the group.

He wouldn't listen to Rosana, who said they should take the group as far away as they could from the melee, then she'd go back, looking for them. There was no way he was leaving Cecilia alone in the middle of a demonstration. When he started walking away, the boys grabbed him and said they were coming, too. They wouldn't listen to reason, not even when he'd said that their profesora would be furious that they'd gone searching for her—not to mention furious with *him* for allowing it—and he'd had to be content with dragging them across Las Ramblas. He'd been so relieved to catch sight of her blonde hair in a doorway, sheltered from the rowdy protestors only a meter or so away from her.

Then la policía wouldn't let them through, and the crowds were growing more hostile. The only solution he'd seen was to bring them back to his flat, which thankfully wasn't too far from where they were, and they could get there without returning to Las Ramblas. He'd been so proud of the boys, how they'd sheltered Aaliyah with their bodies to ensure her safety without being told to do so, and they hadn't left her side until they were inside Felip's home. Once he could breathe easily, his anger and sadness from the previous day had returned and he couldn't look at Cecilia without pain.

Felip's mind ran with possibilities. What if he accompanied her back to California? June would likely kill him, and his parents would be disappointed if he acted irresponsibly, not to mention he'd be leaving them in a lurch.

He could ask her once more to come back, he could offer to buy her ticket, or he could give her space and hope for the best. Or...he could accept that they were not meant to be.

He thought back to what she'd said about his positive outlook. He supposed it was true, but then where was that positivity now, while his heart was breaking? This time hurt even more than his marriage ending. He could accept that he'd been responsible for many of the issues between he and Francesca, but this time? Never had something so important been so out of his control.

A soft knock on his door made him stir. He heard keys and knew Alonso was here, meaning his time was up. He attempted to extricate himself from the couch, but Cecilia was sleeping so soundly that his movements only caused her to shift a little and then curl back up against his chest. She lay half on his chest and thigh and half on the couch, mostly on her stomach, with her knees tucked under his opposite thigh. When she moved, cool air hit his chest where her face had been, and he chuckled when he realized she'd been drooling. He might never wash this shirt again, and didn't that make him a fool?

Alonso came in quietly—one of his skills from his military service was stealth—but he wasn't prepared for the bodies strewn around Felip's house.

"You have a party and not invite me?" He looked around the place before his gaze rested on Cecilia, curled up beside him. His humor faded, and he gave Felip an understanding look.

At his voice, Tui sat up, rubbing his eyes. He started to touch his hair and then paused, gently fingering the braids instead. Felip heard a moan from the other room, indicating the other boys were coming to life. Cecilia, however, did not move.

"You have a problem there?" Alonso's question prompted Felip's eyes to sting, as he was once more reminded of his predicament. He had a problem, alright.

Cecilia sat up suddenly, a confused expression on her face. She gazed around the room and then turned quickly, her eyes wide.

"Hey, are you alright?"

She didn't answer him. She bent over, scrambling for her bag. She rummaged through it, and Felip realized as she tucked her hair over her ear that she'd removed her hearing aids at some point in the night, placing them in a small container in her bag. Once they were in, she turned and gave him a sad smile.

"Sorry. They were bugging me. Are you okay? I did it again, didn't I?" She looked down at the dark spot on his navy shirt. She laughed, but it was hollow.

Felip couldn't bring himself to laugh. He tried a smile and his hand came up to his chest, like an involuntary reflex to protect his heart.

Cecilia excused herself and went to use the bathroom and wake the boys. Felip watched her go and felt somewhat relieved that her step was a little heavier, although that made him a real jerk. He didn't want her to suffer, but it helped to know she was hurting, too.

Felip stood from the couch and stretched. His calf was sore from the cramp and his back ached, but he wouldn't have given up the chance to hold her for the world.

"¿Tienes café?"

Alonso's suggestion was a good one. He stumbled through the doorway to the kitchen and shook his head at the mess there. He really enjoyed the kids, but perhaps he hadn't taken into consideration what a group of teenagers could do to his home. It didn't matter. He was going to miss them, too.

He made cafés con leche for himself and Alonso and they discussed their transportation dilemma. Felip was the only one of them insured by the tour company. Alonso had kept his fingers out of Tomás's business. Being the closest in age of all of them, they'd frequently fought over the most trivial things, and Alonso preferred to keep to himself.

"I can only fit the students in my car. I think it's best I drive them." Especially since they'd been separated from their group and had stayed in his home, rather than the hotel. Not exactly company policy.

"Vale. I will drive Cecilia and leave for the vineyard from there."

"As will I."

Alonso's answering silence let Felip know he understood. Felip would be saying goodbye and then doing the only thing he knew how to do, the only thing he had any control over. Leading Cava Segura and Segura Internacional to new heights. He'd just be doing it with an empty smile for some time.

After everyone had used the restroom, the kids gathered in the kitchen and Felip made more café for those who wanted some.

"We should make it in time for breakfast," he assured them.

"Good thing," Eduardo said. "I'm starving."

"Yeah, man, and I wish I had more of those donut thingies before we left. I dropped my bag when we ran, dude. I'm so depressed."

"I know a place we can stop," Felip said with a chuckle. A young man after his own heart. Felip's high metabolism meant frequent meals. He was the same as Joseph as a teen. It was only after his time in the military that he understood the difference between hungry and necessity. Now he ate frequently because he could, but he didn't need it any longer.

"Thank you again, Mr. Segura," Aaliyah said. "For everything."

He bowed to her. "It was my pleasure, señorita." He looked at the others and took the opportunity to speak to them before Cecilia joined them. "Please take care of her," he said. He swallowed hard and nodded when the boys assured him they would. It seemed none of them knew what to say.

He heard Cecilia's voice in the other room, and he went to tell her she would be riding with Alonso. He couldn't help but laugh at the expression on her face.

"Mom. Exclamation point. I'm fine. Period. I know the news said there were arrests, comma, but we were safe. Period. I will be on the plane today. Period."

She pressed send, and Felip watched as she waited for a response. Her phone buzzed and she growled at the screen. She held it away from her and yelled, "Oh my God, Mother!"

"Is something the matter?" he asked, and she jumped as though he'd startled her.

"My mom. I swear. She's ready to call the embassy. I told her we're fine but she's freaking out." She used her finger to tap out a return text and then slid the phone into her pocket. Her dress was rumpled a bit, but she still looked as beautiful to him as she had the first time he'd seen her...and just as frustrated.

"Alonso is going to drive you. Since he's not insured with the tour company, I thought it best I drive the students."

"Oh." She wrapped her arms around herself and shivered. "That's probably a good idea."

"Are you cold?"

"No, no, I'm fine."

Alonso stuck his head in. "Are you ready, señora?"

She smiled at him. "Yes, thank you."

She seemed to steel herself as she approached Felip, but he couldn't make himself move. She pushed up on her toes and kissed his cheek. The contact made his skin tight and his heart contract.

She didn't speak. She stepped back and used her right hand to touch her chin, then pulled it away.

Felip remembered what the kids had taught him and took this last moment to tell her once more how he felt. He pressed his thumb to his sternum, crossed his fists over his chest, and then he placed his hand before his face and made a circle with his fingers before clenching them. Next, he pressed his fingertips together and to his temples, and followed that by bringing his hands in front of him with his palms facing each other. *I love the beautiful teacher.*

Her eyes flared, her lip quivered, and then she nodded and signed back to him something that he didn't understand. She turned to leave the room, running into Alonso as she did. Felip heard her tell the kids she would see them back at the hotel, then the door closed.

Alonso raised his eyebrows, spun his keys around on his finger and followed her out.

And then Felip exhaled, nearly doubling over. He braced his hands on his knees and closed his eyes for a moment.

That was it.

She was gone.

"Mr. Segura?"

He straightened as Tui entered the room. "¿Sí?"

Tui stared at him for a moment and gave him a look that said he could relate. "Uh, I'm sorry, but Eduardo's got another nosebleed."

· · ·

It was just as well that he'd accepted it was over before Cecilia left, as it was another forty-five minutes before he was able to leave with the kids. Eduardo's nosebleed took a while to stop and then he asked if he could clean up, and if he could borrow another of Felip's shirts.

"At this point, you should help yourself to my wardrobe, verdad?"

It was another fifteen-minute stop at the shop where he took them to get cronuts, then thirty minutes until they arrived at the hotel. The kids had just enough time to pack and clean up before they had to leave for the airport. Rosana told him Gabrielle and Cecilia had gone with the others to see the beach one last time.

"As she should."

"Are you going to be alright?" Rosana asked him in Spanish.

"Eventually. Possibly. Don't ask me that for some time."

She nodded and patted his shoulder.

Eduardo tried to give him back his shirts, but Felip held up his hands. "You bled for them, you keep them."

The young man laughed, and before Felip knew what was happening, Eduardo hugged him.

"Thank you and I'm sorry," he said in Spanish, and Felip smiled.

"Merci," he answered in Catalán."

He pulled out his wallet and found one of Mateu's cards. "You boys need work this summer or perhaps after you graduate, call my brother. Tell him I sent you."

Eduardo held the card in both hands and thanked him. The shock on his face made Felip think perhaps the boy might indeed need the job.

"Say goodbye to the others," he said to Rosana before climbing back into his car, which smelled like cronuts and boys.

"Take care," she said.

Felip waved as he drove away to resume the life he'd led before he knew just how much one blonde teacher could turn his world upside down and fill it with love. He wondered if he would have been better off without ever knowing, but he cut off that thought, cursing at himself.

He turned on his music and asked his car to play her song. He saw Mateu's name pop up on his phone screen, but he was in no shape to care for his youngest brother at the moment. He opened the sunroof and sang at the top of his lungs. "You're breaking my heart. I'm down on my knees…"

CHAPTER TWENTY-NINE

*T*wo Weeks Later
3:39 p.m. Pacific Standard Time – Grass Valley, California

The endless number of boxes seemed to be dwindling with the help of Eduardo, Joseph and Tui, who had been stuck to her like glue for the past week. Eduardo had texted her the day after they'd returned home and asked when she was ready to start working, said he'd recruited helpers. She appreciated his enthusiasm, but she didn't even want to see herself, much less anyone else. She answered she'd let him know and turned off her phone, which had been buzzing off the bedside table. It took two days for her to get out of bed, then another day of crying on her mother's shoulder, and then a meeting to sign paperwork with Greg and Carol until she was back to her jolly old self. Sarcastic emphasis on the jolly.

She broke down the fifth box she'd emptied that day, most of its contents going in the donate pile along with an alarming amount of things she realized she didn't need any longer. Her mother and Freddy had gone to the hot springs for the weekend, giving her some much-needed time alone, and she'd cranked up her favorite jukebox her grandfather had painstakingly repaired. The Wurlitzer was loaded with a collection of 45s she'd kept in good condition over the years. She prayed the thing would last forever, as her grandfather promised, because there was virtually no one left who could repair these dinosaurs. She used it sparingly, but today, the first day she'd had by herself since before Spain, she wanted the company of her childhood best friend. Music.

The manual labor should have been enough to help her clear her mind and relax, but she should have known better. She'd been plagued with doubts since returning from Spain. Had she done the right thing? Could things have worked out long distance for a while? Several times she'd picked up her phone and opened his contact before pushing it away. She was even tempted to send him the pictures from the bus trip, but she didn't think they'd be well received. The one thing she *had* done was write a funny but gracious review online of Viaje España, including humorous bits about their substitute tour guide.

Then she wrote him a thank you card. She may not have been strong enough to tell him exactly how much she felt for him, nor had she been strong enough to consider returning to Spain, but she had to thank him for how very much he'd gone out of his way for her and the students.

And yet she was unsettled. Would it have killed her to go back to Spain? She didn't exactly have the funds for another European trip, unless she took some of the money from the sale... There *would* be money left after she and Greg finished the house business.

Oh Lord, the house business.

They'd met at Nikki's office to sign papers the Tuesday after she returned and she'd had to scrape up every ounce of energy to make herself look stunning...the beautiful "I had a wonderful vacation, thank you" way, not the "Jesus, Cecilia, you've really let yourself go" way.

She'd been thankful for her tan, and pleased that sleep had gotten rid of the dark circles under her eyes, but it literally hurt her to smile. Her eyes looked dull behind the extensive makeup she'd put on. She'd worn one of her nicest business-casual dresses, one of those wrap-in-the-front numbers that never seemed to sit right between her boobs, but showed off her shape nicely, except now it hung a little too loosely. She'd weighed herself and found she'd lost a total of twelve pounds since before the trip, which was a lot for her. Playing with five pounds was more her speed. She just didn't want to eat.

Correction, she didn't want to eat the choices in her mother's house.

She wanted a good steak. And prawns. And tapas. And bread. God, she never thought she'd want bread again after eating it with every meal, but she longed for that crusty goodness with the chewy insides.

She wanted helado. And to curl up on the couch and mope.

But no, she had to be an adult for a little while longer.

The meeting with the realtor had been a series of revelations:

Greg no longer appealed to Cecilia whatsoever.

Even after she'd filed for divorce, she'd still had some feelings for him. Their shared lives together since the tender age of sixteen had given her a fondness for him that had survived their divorce, but now it was barely there.

She was shocked at the Greg who'd shown up. His hair had receded. He was dressed like a fucking hipster in a plaid shirt that hugged his midsection like a girdle and was buttoned all the way to his neck. As if that wasn't bad enough, he'd taken to curling up the sides of his moustache and had grown a pointy beard.

Not all beards were bad. No, her grandfather had sported a fine, long, ZZ Top-version for years, and she'd loved it. But on Greg? Nope. It didn't work.

She'd met Carol for the first time. Who looked very much like her, right down to the hairstyle. But that's where the similarities ended.

Carol had a septum piercing.

Carol couldn't have been many days over twenty-one years old.

She was thin, her skin likely hadn't seen the sun in years, and she had giant blue eyes.

And tattoos. Lots of them. Including on her throat.

Cecilia had to admit she was adorable, but *so* not who she figured Greg would end up with.

Then she'd noticed the baby bump.

So that's the hurry.

"You could have told me," she'd said when Carol left the office to use the bathroom.

"She didn't feel comfortable telling anyone until she had her twenty-week ultrasound. She's had a couple of miscarriages in the past—"

"In the past? She's a child herself."

"She's twenty-six. Look, I'm sorry, Cece—"

"I'm not mad, Greg. I'm glad you're happy."

Nikki'd sat behind the desk looking mortified. She began going through the paperwork, pointing out the lines they needed to sign, and Cecilia found the whole process rather liberating. Once she found out what her share of the equity was, she planned to put it away, a little nest egg until she decided what she wanted to do. She couldn't stay at Mom's forever, but she had time. Now that she'd had such a terrific time traveling, she was even considering planning another trip next summer. Perhaps she'd even go with Zoey and Gabrielle. They were talking about Argentina next.

Or she could go where her heart remained.

"And that's all I need from you. As soon as everything's finished, I'll let you know."

They'd shook hands with Nikki, turned and looked at each other awkwardly, and then Greg had patted her shoulder.

"I really appreciate this, honey."

She'd waved a hand at him. "Good luck. I'll keep positive thoughts for the pregnancy."

Carol hadn't come back in, so Greg'd said goodbye and walked out, his too-tight sky-blue khakis making him look like he was clenching his ass cheeks. Maybe he'd thought Cecilia would throw something at his retreating back.

When the door closed behind him, Cecilia'd sighed, and Nikki'd burst out laughing.

"Wow. I guess Oakland really had an effect on him."

Cecilia had shaken her head. "He always did struggle with fashion. I dressed him better. Didn't I dress him better?"

Nikki came around the desk and hugged her then. "You did *everything* better. Now, you okay? You want to go have a shit-ton of margaritas?"

Cecilia'd given her a squeeze. "Nope. Thank you, though. I just want to go home and rest. I'm exhausted from the trip and I still have laundry to do, not to mention the entirety of my grandfather's old workshop is filled to the brim with junk from the house I need to go through. All I had time to do was throw it in boxes and move it to Mom's."

"Was Spain amazing? I've always heard it's like the best-kept secret in Europe."

Cecilia had felt like if she opened her mouth, the whole sordid tale would come tumbling out, like in the cartoons when the character's tongue comes rolling out and hits the floor. "It was great." She'd snapped her mouth shut and put on a weird little grin.

Nikki'd acted like she didn't pick up on Cecilia's struggle. "Well, you have the rest of the summer. Let me know when you're ready to start looking at something for yourself. With the amount you received, plus your alimony—"

"I didn't take alimony."

"What? Oh, Cecilia—"

"I just wanted to be done. He's going to reimburse me for his student loans that I paid for while he was working on getting the company up and running, but that's all I wanted."

"You're a better woman than I am."

She didn't feel like a better woman. She felt wrong.

Elvis Costello's "Pump It Up" ended and Queen's "Crazy Little Thing Called Love" came on. Cecilia used that as an opportunity to shake off her memory of Greg and the hipster pants. Hipster dad pants, actually. So odd to think of Greg being a father. She'd thought, once she'd gotten home from Nikki's office, that she might cry over it or feel all empty inside because she didn't give Greg children, blah

blah blah, but strangely, she felt relieved. She'd been saved from making a mistake by his infidelity. They weren't meant to have children together, she knew that now.

She still thought about kids, however. The trip had sure given her maternal heebie-jeebies. She was naturally a nurturer, it was part of what made her a good teacher, but she'd actually enjoyed all the Band-Aid deliveries, taking care of Joseph post-allergic reaction, and even her arrangement with Eduardo. Maybe she would do the motherhood gig eventually.

Cecilia was doing her best Freddie Mercury impression around the living room, using the grabber from the pantry as Freddie's famous half-microphone stand. She tossed it up, narrowly missing the top of the vaulted ceiling. As her eyes tracked it to catch it, she saw a shadow outside the front door.

Startled, she let the grabber drop.

The song ended, and she bent down to pick up the grabber thinking it would make a decent weapon. Or maybe she should grab one of her mother's statues from the shelf by the window. She heard the next record drop onto the turntable, which was barely audible over the heartbeat throbbing in her ears. Who could be at her door? The house was on the outskirts of town and no one came out here except delivery men—

The shadow knocked on the door the moment the familiar hand claps played over the speaker, and it startled her so badly she screamed. The shadow laughed outside the door.

No. Way.

She knew that laugh.

"Cecilia. You're breaking my heart," he shouted. "Will you please come to the door?"

"Ohmygod." She broke out into a frenzied attempt to do something with herself. She was dirty, sweaty, her ponytail was half in and half out of the hair tie, she was wearing an old white t-shirt tied up under her boobs, with no bra, and a pair of boxers—

"I'll keep singing if you don't open the door."

Her lip twitched.

She moved toward the door, but was too slow apparently, as he began belting out the lyrics.

"Making love to Cecilia—"

She pulled the door open and stood with a hand on her hip. "No one will hear you. We're at least a half mile from the next neighbors."

He exhaled, and that damn crooked-toothed smile of his lit up like Times Square at Christmas. "You doubt I can project my voice?"

She blew her bangs up out of her face. "I'd ask what you were doing here, but it's obvious you're delivering a singing telegram."

He frowned. "I'm actually here because I've decided it is crucial for me to continue learning American Sign Language." He pressed his lips together in an attempt to be serious, but it was useless. He couldn't stop smiling.

Cecilia gave an exaggerated sigh. "I get these requests all the time, you know. Strange men show up on my porch, disturb me from my work—"

"Are you planning to audition for a singing show?"

"Shhh! What I was about to say, before you so rudely interrupted, is that I don't simply take on any student. I have a stringent screening process."

She was putting on a brave front, but her skin was flushed, and it wasn't from the heat or her previous activities. She was scared to death to see him.

"Oh, well, I see. Is there an application—"

"Felip."

He sighed and nodded. "Vale. I tell you the truth. My brother called me the day you left. It seems he, too, has been having a bit of an existential crisis and he wanted to return home to España."

Cecilia's eyes flared. "Oh no. Is he alright?"

Felip frowned. "I am not sure, but I know some time back with my parents will put him on the right path." He cleared his throat and shifted his weight. "I could have sent Alonso or June, but to be perfectly honest, I'd already booked my flight to California, and I didn't want it to go to waste."

"Really? I mean...really. You'd already booked a flight, huh? To get these ASL lessons?"

He slid his hands in his pockets and rocked on his heels. His silliness faded and she saw a glimpse of the man she'd met in Spain, the one who was vibrant and full of life on the exterior, but there were cracks in the façade, and beneath was a man who had been pushing himself for a long time. A man who was looking for a home.

She opened the door a little wider and stepped forward to lean against the doorframe. "Once again, it's Felip to the rescue."

"It seems that way. Pero, this time I was not reluctant to come."

Cecilia's heart rate had slowed from her earlier fright, but his words caused it to speed up. "So, you're here."

"I am," he said, his smile not quite as full of confidence as it was. "I wanted to discuss the possibility of a courtship with you."

She pressed a hand to her chest. "Courtship? Oh, my. This sounds suspiciously like a fairy tale, or some sort of medieval proposal. Pray tell, what do you have in mind, señor?"

Felip bowed like a true fairytale prince and held out his hand for hers. "I intend to spend the time I am in California with a beautiful teacher, so that we may see if we are compatible in a more natural setting than while thrown together on a tour, constantly surrounded by students and under scrutiny from others who have high expectations of our propriety."

Cecilia's voice was hoarse when she spoke. "Whoever this teacher is, she's a lucky woman." She cleared her throat. "Who should I tell her is calling for her?" She slid her hand into his, cringing a little when she thought about how sweaty she was.

Felip lowered his head and pressed his lips languorously to her knuckles. "The man who adores her."

Her breath caught, and she felt the familiar sting of tears. "But Felip, what's changed?"

He stood to his full height and took a step back, giving her space. "I cannot pass up the opportunity to give this match made in Spain a chance. I am here indefinitely, and I want to spend the time with you. Cecilia, we're either going to discover that we cannot stand to be in the same room for one more second, or we're going to fall deeper in love. If you tell me you do not feel for me as I feel for you, we will part as friends, and when I've cleaned up my brother's mess…again…I will return to Spain."

"And if…" She couldn't bring herself to say the words, because she already knew. She loved him. Absence had only made her heart grow fonder, just as the old folks always said. She knew spending more time in his presence would only make her love him more.

"And," he continued. "If you and I fall deeper in love, then there is only one thing for us to do."

He stepped closer, cautiously at first, his eyes drinking in her lack of clothes.

"What will we do?"

Felip slid his hand slowly around her waist to her lower back, his fingertips pressing insistently into her until she gave in and allowed him to pull her flush against him.

"We will live happily ever after, wherever the teacher desires to be." He brushed his lips against hers, and she almost surrendered.

"Felip, I can't ask that…"

"Cecilia! When are there ever guarantees in life? When *isn't* there a time in life when it becomes necessary for someone to compromise to have what he wants? How many more signs have to point to this being meant to happen for you to give us more than a Spanish tour?"

She heard the frustration in his voice and had to admit he was right.

"I'm so glad to see you. So glad you're here." Cecilia pressed her hands against his chest, sliding them up to his neck. "I suppose the fact that my mother and her Casanova are away for the weekend might be one of those signs." She smiled up at him in invitation…and man, did he take it.

If she thought their first kiss in the Madrid alley was all-consuming, this one burned as hot as the bonfire at the Festival of San Juan.

Cecilia grabbed the front of his shirt and pulled him into the living room and then reached behind her to shut the door. Felip stumbled over the step down into the sunken living room. If it weren't for

Cecilia being attached to him like a barnacle, they would have gone down together, but she managed to get them over to the giant sectional before they fell, with her on top of him.

"Cariño." The way he breathed her name fanned the flames of her desire for him. He placed his hands on the sides of her face and held her still. He spoke in Spanish barely above a whisper as she straddled him. He presented his neck, which Cecilia had missed terribly. He allowed her to trace his Adam's apple with her tongue and lips, but when she started to unbutton his shirt, he stopped her.

"Cecilia, I did not mean to come in here and begin ravishing you—"

"Why not?" She sat up and frowned. "What's wrong with ravishing?"

He pushed up onto his elbows. "Nothing is wrong...I...I made reservations. I wanted to take you to dinner and I wanted to pamper you. I wanted to say all of the things to you that I couldn't say before we said goodbye—"

"That sounds great, Felip, really, but I think we're going to need to do all that later."

She bent to kiss him and he groaned, sitting up farther and wrapping his arms around her.

"Cecilia—"

"Felip. Please. There's a lot of pent-up angst right here," she said, gesturing to herself with one hand while the other went for his buttons. "I can't even concentrate on words. You told me on the plane you never had trouble with sex, so—"

"I never—"

"Silencio," she breathed, and she kissed him so deeply, he finally surrendered. She finished his buttons and slid the shirt off of his shoulders, touching him everywhere, kissing every delicious inch of his exposed skin. When he started to untie the knot on the front of her t-shirt, she stopped to warn him.

"I really, *really* should shower."

He shook his head and kissed her once more. "There is no time. I need you, cariño."

Felip deftly untied her shirt and slid his hands under to discover her bare breasts. He moaned as though he'd tasted one of his favorite pintxos. The calluses on his fingertips gently scratched over her highly sensitive nipples, and she gasped. She pulled the shirt over her head and he moaned again at the sight before him. Cecilia watched as he licked his full lips, his eyelids fluttering as he inhaled.

"Tan perfecta. Jo necessito, cariño. T'estimo."

"You have so much to teach me," she said with a laugh.

"Then what are we waiting for?"

There was a flurry of activity as they yanked at each other's buttons and zippers. There was some wrestling before she stood on the couch to remove her shorts. Once she was bared to him, Felip took over. He guided her to sit on the back of the sofa, giving him access to teach her what it meant to be worshiped, what it meant to be turned inside out in the best possible way. She made his hair stand on end and decided the way he looked up at her from between her thighs was Felip at his most beautiful.

He held her close as her body tensed and shuddered. She may have been the sex ed teacher, but Felip seemed to know exactly what she needed, wanted desperately, but didn't know how to ask for. They lay intertwined, attempting to catch their breath.

"I told you you'd make a great teacher," she said, and he chuckled.

"Pero, I am unprepared for the next phase of your lesson. Lo siento."

She pushed up and frowned. "Unprepared?"

"Sí. I told you I had made other plans to seduce you."

She rolled her eyes and sat up, taking down what was left of her hair in the scrunchy. "Unprepared." There was no way she wanted to stop here, but years of teaching her students the dangers of unprotected sex wouldn't go away, no matter how much she loved this man.

She turned to face him, finally ready to say what she should have said in Bilbao. "Love. I love you. I love you, and I'm so glad you came for me."

The frown line between his eyebrows deepened and he brought their linked fingers to his lips to kiss. "In this fairy tale, the prince will always come for his beloved. He's determined to show her how hard he is willing to work to deserve her love."

God, that's so romantic. Cecilia couldn't help that the part of her forever tainted by the time she spent around teenagers emerged. She burst out laughing.

"What is so funny?"

"You've worked *hard* but you haven't *come* yet," she said, then she fell over laughing at her own dumb joke. She supposed it was best that he knew exactly what a fairy tale with her would be like.

"Your mind is delightfully naughty, my love. I still have work to do."

"Not without the proper protection, Mr. Princey Pants."

He laughed and shook his head, pulling her down to lie with him.

"I suppose I will have to take leave of you to procure the proper protection," he said, chuckling himself now. "But after working *hard*, it will take me a moment to recover."

She pinched his side and he laughed, but then she had an idea. "Mom."

"Perdón? Your mother?"

"Yes! I bought her a giant box of condoms for Christmas because she told me Freddy was coming. Could they possibly have some left?"

"Tengo muchas preguntas, profesora. When you say giant, how many are we talking about, and how young is your mother and her suitor if they are to be using that many?"

Cecilia stood from the couch and groaned. "They're like newly-weds every time he comes to visit," she said. "Come on." She reached for his hand and pulled him off the couch. "Let's go see."

"I don't know how I feel about this," he said, but then he fell quiet as they climbed the stairs with her in front. She heard him muttering something in Catalan and figured she had his full attention. It was invigorating to have a man as droolworthy as Felip admire her mid-thirties divorcée body. He'd been good for her ego from the get-go. But he was so much more than that.

They turned right at the top of the stairs and she led him to her mother's room. At the doorway, he tugged at her hand.

"I think I should wait here," he said, looking around nervously.

"What's the matter?" she asked as she walked towards the bathroom, only slightly self-conscious that she was naked in front of him. The way he looked at her gave her confidence that surprised her.

"Nothing. This is strangely reminiscent of my teen years, sneaking around behind my parents' back."

"For condoms?" she asked. She opened the medicine cabinet and cursed. No dice. Where would they be? There had to be sixty condoms in that box when she'd bought it in December and the expiration date had been at least two years out. She'd made sure. She turned and looked in the cabinet behind the door.

"Bingo!" She pulled the box out and showed him. "Were you sneaking these from your parents?"

He frowned and made a disgusted look. "No way would I have ever wanted to find condoms in my parents' bedroom."

Cecilia shrugged. "When you meet my mom, you'll understand. She's really young for her age." She opened the box and gasped. "Are you freaking kidding me?"

"What's the matter? Is it empty?"

She looked at Felip and laughed when she saw his expression.

"Don't worry, it's not empty, but Jesus! He's only been here two weeks!"

Felip's mouth opened and closed a few times and then he shook his head.

Cecilia approached him with a strand of condoms and wrapped her arms behind his neck. "Shall we take this elsewhere?"

"Sí," he said, kissing her hungrily. "I would very much like to make love to you in a bed, Cecilia. Allow me to do something proper for my love."

Cecilia loved his idea of proper.

CHAPTER THIRTY

4:19 p.m. Pacific Standard Time – Grass Valley, California

All of Felip's good intentions left him the moment she opened the door. He'd nearly fallen to his knees in relief when she'd greeted him with a smile, that she'd opened the door at all. The previous week had been pure torture, knowing he was in the same time zone with her, the same state, and yet he'd waited until he felt in control of his emotions to go to her.

That control shattered when she kissed him. She didn't hold back, she let him feel the full power of her passion, and it was even more than he'd imagined. If he'd thought he was lost to her in Spain, it was nothing compared to touching her, seeing her body bared to him, tasting her with all the time in the world for him to explore.

And now as they lie together, in a bed for the first time, his heart so full of emotion, he feared he might be dreaming.

Cecilia smiled at him invitingly, the jokes finally out of her system, and he was grateful she did not seem afraid or hesitant to express her feelings. She'd said she loved him, confirming what he knew but what he'd been afraid he'd never hear spill from her lips. He hadn't realized how much he needed to hear her say those words.

"Felip?"

"Hmm?"

"How do you say I want to make love in Catalán?"

"Vull fer l'amor. Or en Castellano, quiero hacer el amor."

"I don't think I'll ever be able to make those words sound as beautiful as you do," she said, brushing his hair out of his face.

Felip covered her with his body, once again marveling at how well they fit together, and he nuzzled her neck. "How would you sign it?"

Cecilia made two fists, touched them together, one on top of the other, and then she crossed them and moved them rhythmically towards her chest. He found her language incredibly sensual, every movement drawing his gaze and taking his breath away. He could watch her forever. He intended to.

"Is that what you want, cariño?"

She held up her fist and moved it up and down while she nodded. "I want you, Felip."

And Felip intended to give her whatever she wanted for the rest of their lives, starting right now.

He forced himself to forget the condoms came from her mother's room as he rolled on the first of several they would use that weekend. Sliding inside this remarkable woman was truly the feeling of coming home that he'd been missing in his life. The Fates certainly knew what they were doing when they placed them together, as everything they did, every move they made, was in sync. Their bodies moved in a lovers' dance orchestrated by Felip's slow movements. He loved the burn, the slow build of pleasure as he desperately sought that place deep inside his woman where he longed to be, with both his body and soul. As their passion burned hotter and hotter, Cecilia writhed beneath him, her pale skin flushed the lovely pink color he adored.

"T'estimo, Cecilia," he breathed against her cheek, his movements more urgent now. Images flashed in his mind of all they'd been through to get to this moment, including the searing-hot kiss in the Madrid alley, the taste of her in the Burgos hotel room, the feel of her tears when they'd said goodbye in Barcelona...it all seemed so long ago, and yet each memory was so vivid. His heart swelled, accepting the piece he'd left with Cecelia would always be with her, as would the rest of him. There was no holding back now. He'd known there would be no distance between them for long. He was right where he'd longed to be, and this time he would have his damn fairy tale, no matter how hard he had to work to make it come true.

"Are you here with me?" Cecilia asked, a curious smile on her face.

"You have no idea how much I am here with you," he said, increasing his pace until it was impossible for either of them to speak.

Their passion was at a critical point, and he needed to be closer to her. He lifted her hips onto his thighs and wrapped his hands over her shoulders, pulling her as tight as possible against him, thrusting insistently, her cries spurring him on.

"Felip, let go, my love. Let me catch you."

One look in her blue eyes, and he let himself find his peak and fall...

"Cariño," he moaned as his body became hers, his soul hers, his heart...hers.

Throughout the rest of that night and all the next day they did many of the things he'd longed to do. They fed each other, they made love all over her home, they showered together, they soaked in the hot tub, and they even danced naked in front of her grandfather's jukebox.

"So you can set it to play all of the songs?"

"Yep. That's what I was doing yesterday when my prince arrived."

The smile he'd put on her face hadn't faded, not even when they spoke seriously of the challenges they would face as they attempted to deal with the reality of two people from different countries who fell in love. She'd been optimistic, and that was what Felip had hoped for more than anything.

"Your prince is grateful that you opened your kingdom to him."

She snorted. "Yeah, well, he's pretty good at plundering. I don't think my kingdom had a chance."

Felip pressed a kiss against the top of her head and laughed.

"A prince must do everything in his power to win the hand of his princess."

Cecilia placed her hand in his and squeezed. "It's yours," she whispered.

He held their linked hands against his chest and leaned in to kiss her. As things got heated once more, she stumbled and fell against the jukebox they'd been admiring. The record playing skipped, and he pulled back.

"I'm so sorry," he said. "I would feel terrible if I damaged this priceless treasure."

The record ended and they listened closely to hear the next one drop. When the signature hand claps began, Felip threw his head back and laughed.

"Your song, cariño!"

She rolled her eyes. "Okay, I get it. I get it, Fate! You win!"

That was music to Felip's ears. He began singing along with Simon and Garfunkel and they swayed together. When it was over, Cecilia raised an eyebrow.

"You think you would still love me if my name was Lucille?"

He paused, rubbing his chin until she poked him in the ribs. "I'm thinking. I would love you, but I would be concerned about our odds."

"The four hungry children?"

"Mmm, sí, and the lousy crops."

"I'm not leaving," she whispered as she kissed him once more.

"Good. And I'll make sure our children don't go hungry."

She burst out laughing. "Children? Geez! I don't remember the part of the fairy tale where I get sick and fat and stretch marks."

"I will love you regardless, despite, in spite of, because of, all of those things. I will love you through all that Fate has in store for us."

Cecilia's smile was tinged with tears for a moment before she laughed.

"Okay, I love you, too, but my mom and Freddie will be back soon, and that's not exactly the end to the fairy tale I'd like to see."

"I suppose then you will have to help me track down my clothes. I can't recall where I left them all."

They spent a half hour finding Felip's clothes, straightening the house where they'd left evidence of their activities in several places. Back in the living room, they debated on ordering in, cooking something from the freezer, or going out to eat. They settled on going out for a pizza, and Felip waited on the porch while Cecilia left a note and locked up the house.

She turned to face him with a frown and for a moment, Felip felt panic clawing at his chest.

"What is it?" he asked.

"Are you really here? Are you really staying?"

"Sí. Mateu needs some time off and then he will go to work with June. Let her take the belt to someone else for a change."

"And you're sure? I hate for you to be away from your family."

Felip took her hands in his, concerned about her apprehension. "I do hope to return eventually, that is, if you are willing to accompany me for visits?"

"I want that, as long as I have you to talk to me on the plane."

Felip nearly groaned in relief. "Whenever you are ready, I would love to take you for a proper visit."

She tugged on his hand and led him toward the steps. The setting sun caught her hair and she absolutely glowed before him. He'd never seen a sunset so beautiful in his life.

"I guess it's a good thing I get lots of vacation time."

"I suppose it is."

He kissed her once more on the bottom step before they walked to the car, just as an old truck came toward them down the long driveway. Felip had been surprised at how rural the area was where Cecilia lived. Her home was about an hour's drive from the winery they'd leased near Roseville and two hours from the vineyard they'd contracted for grapes. He'd been staying in the apartment on the winery grounds but figured he would make a more permanent decision once he and Cecilia had mended things.

"There's still time to make a break for it," she said before the truck pulled to a halt. "This is not likely to be without some embarrassment."

Felip grinned. "I'm ready."

Cecilia's eyes widened. "You're not ready. No one is ready."

Cecilia's mother climbed down from the cab of the large, antique Ford truck and flung her long hair back behind her shoulders. Felip saw immediately the resemblance, including the stern expression Cecilia usually reserved for her students.

Her mother began signing furiously, and Cecilia groaned.

"Oh my God." Cecilia signed back with as much intensity, and Felip didn't know whether to back off or step in and offer a distraction.

After her mother responded, Cecilia finally sighed. "Felip, this is my mother, Roberta Simon." She signed to her mother, and her mother stuck out a hand, but her gaze was anything but inviting.

Felip took her hand and shook, smiling widely. "I am honored to meet you."

"I don't know about that," Cecilia said. "She just asked me if we used all of her condoms and said we'd better replace them before Freddie gets back from town."

Felip felt his smile slip—and then Roberta laughed hysterically. She signed something to Cecilia, kissed her on the cheek, then walked past them into the house.

I really need to learn to sign.

"She said she picked up more in town, not to worry, and that you're even sexier than I told her you were."

Felip swallowed hard. "Um—"

"Come on," she said. "You want to drive or…"

"Sure," he said, but then he pulled out the keys. "Actually, why don't you take the wheel, show me around my new home."

"Home? Hey, where are you living, anyway?"

"I hadn't really planned that far ahead."

She grinned again. "You're really here."

"I am here, with you. Where I belong. Now please feed me, I'm famished."

She shook her head. "And they lived happily ever after."

THE END...

ACKNOWLEDGMENTS

So many people helped shape this story into the book you've just read. Here are a few folks who were instrumental:

Kilby Blades and Eva Moore thank you so much for all of your wine-y knowledge. For anyone who has seen my Wine and Metal tastings with Eva Moore, you'll know I'm famous for not being a fan of wine. However, I do love cava and sparkling wine and sangria is awesome. These two lovely women were not only there to hold my hand through the process, but they cheered me on and believed in this book when I wasn't sure whether it would see the light of day.

Marielle Browne, my accountability partner. I miss our chats and work sessions. You were instrumental in giving me the support I needed to get this book done.

Rebecca Hunter and Theresa Rogers, I'm so grateful for all of your support as Ro branches off to Rochelle and for advising me on making the right career moves. I appreciate you both more than you know.

Thank you to Laura Bailo for reading and offering suggestions as a native Spaniard. You offered some great feedback that made my Catalonian vintner more authentic and I loved catching up with you.

Thank you to Phyllis for loaning me your daughter Allison to proofread the finished project. It gave me peace of mind, and that's huge.

Thank you to Angela James for your support and for creating such a fantastic community in From Written to Recommended.

To Avery Flynn, thank you for your brand coaching and for introducing me to Rachel, who I can't wait to get started with!

Thank you to Grey's Promotions for your assistance in spreading the word far and wide.

To my Roadies and long-time readers, thank you so much for your continuing support. Thanks for following R.L. to Rochelle and I hope you'll stay with me on these new adventures!

SBC for life! Shannon, Anne, Rebecca, Amy, Kilby, Alex, Elizabeth, Jackie, and Adrienne, I can't even express how much your support has meant through this last year. Here's to Tuesday night solving the world's problems sessions!

Stay Tuned for more from Rochelle Merrill...

ABOUT THE AUTHOR

Fun, Fresh Fiction with Feeling

If R.L. Merrill is your local hard rock/metal radio station, Rochelle is her Adult Contemporary alter ego. Spinning feel-good stories to make you laugh and swoon, Ro writes romance for grown-ups who use their words (mostly) and take care of business. She's a mom and wife who's on hiatus from a career in education while she explores the new terrain of mid-life adventures. You can catch her walking and gardening in her neighborhood by the Bay, spoiling her rescue pets, and dreaming of attending concerts and theaters again someday. Stay Tuned for more hits coming your way...

OTHER BOOKS BY R.L. MERRILL

You can find links to all of the books on BookBub:

https://www.bookbub.com/profile/r-l-merrill or my website www.
rlmerrillauthor.com

M/F Contemporary Romance

Haunted Series:

Haunted

Fated

Bated

Jaded – (Coming Soon)

Hollywood Rock 'n' Romance Trilogy:

Teacher

Teacher: Act Two

Teacher: The Final Act

Rock 'N' Romance Series:

The Rock Season

Road Trip

You Fell First (Formerly "Mud and Honey" in the Down and Dirty Anthology)

The Heart Knows (Re-Release Winter 2o22)

M/F Paranormal Romance Series

Minded Series: (Paranormal Spinoff of Haunted Series)

Minded

Blossomed

Father F'in' Christmas

A Peculiar Prom Night

Magic and Mayhem Universe: (Funny Paranormal Romance in the universe created by Robyn Peterman)

Shifted

Ghoul Me Once

Gator Me Twice

Fang Me Three Times

Fangtastic Four (October 2021)

Gifted Series: (Supernatural Suspense)

Healer

Connection (Fall 2021)

M/F Horror

(FREE on www.rlmerrillauthor.com)

Friday, October 13, 1978

Friday, October 13, 1967

M/F Horror Anthology Stories

The Fourth Man (The Banes of Lake's Crossing) (Historical Horror Romance)

A Piece of Him (Gone With The Dead) (Horror)

Breaking Bread—Dark Divinations from HorrorAddicts.net Press (Horror)

LGBTQ Romance

Pinups and Puppies (Originally in Love Is All Vol. 2)

I Want, More – Bolder Breed Studios #1 (Originally in Love Is All Vol. 3)

Love and Pride - Bolder Breed Studios #2 (Love Is All Vol. 4)

Let Me Stand Next To Your Fire (Coming Soon)

Forces of Nature Series: (Gay Contemporary Romance)

Hurricane Reese

Typhoon Toby

Earthquake Ethan (Coming Soon)

Summer of Hush Series: (Gay Contemporary Romance)

Summer of Hush

Brains and Brawn

Book Three (Coming Soon)

LGBTQ Horror

The Redemption of Nathaniel Bane

A Kept Woman (Coming Soon)

Strange Things Happen Every Day (Coming Soon)

LGBTQ Anthology Stories

Thanksgiving Day Parade From Hell (Worst Holiday Ever) (Gay Contemporary Romance

Valentine's Day From Hell (Worst Valentine's Day Ever) (Gay Contemporary Romance)

Salty and Sweet (Summer Fair) (Lesbian Contemporary Romance)

Exchange (Renewal) (Science Fiction)

Tap-Tap-Tap (Impact) (Horror)

Human Sacrifice (Innovation) (Horror)

Joy Is A Phone Call Away (A More Perfect Union) (Lesbian Contemporary Romance)

The House Must Fall (Haunts and Hellions from HorrorAddicts.net Press) (Horror)

LGBTQ Holiday Romance

A Peace Offering

Love and Pride - Bolder Breed Studios #2 (Love Is All Vol. 4) (Solo Re-Release
Fall 2021)

Made in the USA
Middletown, DE
21 September 2021